Have Ye No Homes To Go To?

NEVILLE THOMPSON

POOLBEG

*This book is dedicated to my Publicist in Ireland,
Margaret Daly. Not only is she brilliant at her job, but
she's also one of the nicest people I've ever met and
someone I'm proud to call a friend.*

Published 1999 by
Poolbeg Press Ltd
123 Baldoyle Industrial Estate
Dublin 13, Ireland

© Neville Thompson 1999

The moral right of the author has been asserted.

The Arts Council
An Chomhairle Ealaíon

A catalogue record for this book is available from the British Library.

ISBN 1 85371 950 1

Cover design by Splash
Set by Poolbeg Group Services Ltd in Times 10.5/14
Printed by The Guernsey Press Ltd,
Vale, Guernsey, Channel Islands.

Acknowledgements

A big thanks to everyone who not only bought my previous books but then went out and spread the word. Thanks for all your support and for the feedback I get from your correspondence.

My books have now started doing the rounds in the UK and I would like to thank everyone who turned out for the readings and signings in London.

Thanks to our sales reps on both sides of the water for their belief in my books. And to the bookshops for giving me so much support.

Thanks to the hard work of agents Edwards and Fuglewicz. You can now read *Jackie Loves Johnser OK?* in French, German and Polish too!

To my own family and Jean's, who have once again supported me in everything. They came to readings, launches and just about everything else in between. Thank you for making the events so special.

A special word of thanks to Lucy, Mick and their gang. If I told you all they do for me you wouldn't believe it. Thanks to all our friends and family members for travelling from every corner of this country and from the UK to get to the launch in Toners last October. You always make my launches so special. And, on the subject of launches, a big thanks to Toners for giving us a great night, to Philip MacDermott for launching me so well and all the Poolbeg crowd for showing their support.

A big word of thanks to all the local radio stations who once again gave me so much air time.

A special thanks to Grace Brennan of Shannonside, the best interviewer bar none. Brendan Cronin for getting me my first nationwide radio interview in the shape of the superb *Murray and Mackey Show* on Today FM.

The local and national newspapers deserve credit for the exposure they continually give my work.

Also, a big thanks to all at the *Late Late Show* for helping to ease the nerves. To Brigid Ruane for never losing faith, and to Mr

Gay Byrne for being a great host and a gentleman, in the way he treated the family backstage.

I owe *Open House* a huge amount of gratitude. Not alone did they help me lose nearly nine pounds on their three-day diet . . . not alone did they let me plug my favourite book on their show . . . but, they also gave me the use of a computer when mine had gone down and there was a real chance that the manuscript was lost. And, on top of all that, they were the inspiration behind the title of this book. Both Trevor Friday and I thank you.

And so to this book. As I say, due to a faulty computer I nearly lost the entire manuscript. So once again, a big thanks to *Open House*, the Irish Writers' Centre and most of all Mick Rooney (computer wiz) for saving the day.

Also, a special thanks goes to Jean who worked tirelessly to get the computer up and running.

A big thanks to Poolbeg for all the encouragement, especially Paula Campbell who has the thankless job of promoting my work.

To that sadistic pair of instructors at Litton Lane Fitness Centre, Garath and Sandra, thanks for getting the body in shape.

I'd like to thank a very supportive Ulster Bank in Castlepollard. In particular Breeda Finnegan, she is what all bank managers should be.

A writer's road is never straight nor even, but Breeda's understanding has lessened a very bumpy ride. Also, Leader in Westmeath. Their grant aided me last year while I was still writing this novel, thank you.

Thanks to John and Sandy of Mobile Windscreens, (Limerick Branch) for once again getting me out of a jam.

Finally, and most importantly, thanks to Jean, my wife. The song featured in the book, sung by the character John Michael, "Sunshine in the Morning" was written for Jean in 1996.

Once again she's been there for me. While I'm busy being all arty Jean goes out and earns a crust to keep the wolf from my door.

Well Jean, just in case I don't tell you often enough, you're very much appreciated.

ARE YE GOIN FOR A PINT LADS?

THE BOYS

Chapter One

– Davey –

Davey Brady checked his look in the mirror, combed his hair to one side with his hand, brushed his sports jacket down, then ordered a drink –

"The usual please, Paddy, *mor shay the hull*."

"Who died and made you Peig Sayers?"

"Ah, you know yourself, I always like the bit of Irish, yeh know, *cupla fuckall* and all that." Davey looked round as he said it, looking for a smile from the other three drinkers at the bar, but there was no reaction. He spotted John Michael up at the stage plugging in the amp. "I hope you have a union card for that. We don't want a picket on the door tonight."

John Michael didn't look around or acknowledge him.

"Jasus," Davey sighed, "you lot are a right bunch of laughter. I'll have to sit down, I've such a stitch in me side listening to yehs."

He took his pint and sat in the velvet corner-unit that was his usual seat. He was early but he liked to get here before her and get a few pints down, a bit of Dutch courage to get the tongue moving and the aul "sweet nothings" flowing. He searched in his pocket and pulled out a small jewellery box.

He opened it and looked at the eternity ring inside. He was sure she'd like it, but still, it was a big decision to be making after only three months. Tonight would be the night. Three months, imagine! Who'd have thought that first night that they'd still be together now?

– Joe –

"Thanks be to Jasus," Joe Dolan whispered, as he saw Davey Brady take his pint and sit down. He was afraid Davey would have started his usual slagging. He definitely seemed in form for it, what with his gobshite pronunciations of Irish. And Joe felt that if he'd started tonight he might, just might, have hit him. If he'd as much as mentioned Joe Dolan the singer, even begun humming *"Dom de Dom"*, he was likely to have a black eye. Because tonight he had other things on his mind and today was a day he, Joe Dolan, never wanted to have to go through again. He rubbed his face as though washing it, let his hands run around the back of his neck and massaged his shoulders. It gave little relief but even if a herd of elephants ran up and down his back, he doubted if he'd feel any better. *Guilt, guilt* and more *guilt* – that's all his life was, that's all it ever had been.

– John Michael –

John Michael had the amp set up and was just about to head back and finish his pint, when he saw Davey Brady walk into the bar. That's when he disconnected all the wires and started fiddling around the back of the amp again. Even when Davey tried to bring him in on the conversation, he couldn't bring himself to look him in the eye. Not after all that had passed. It wasn't as though he felt guilty or anything, he would confront him but not now. Not yet.

– Simmo –

Paul "Simmo" Simpson sat looking at everything through the bar mirror. They were a weird shower of fuckers that's for sure, but still, Paddy Mac served the best pint of the black stuff this side of the Liffey and you never got any hassle while drinking.

Besides, today had been one of those days when everything had gone right. You know, one of those perfect days when all the plotting and planning of the last while all fell into place. And now tonight, at the end of that perfect day, Paddy Mac had just served up the perfect pint and Simmo knew that at the end of the glass when he'd drunk the dregs, there'd be four little white rings left as a sign of the pint's perfection. Simmo raised the glass and toasted the air, then he muttered –

"Cheers, Simmo. You never lost it son, did yeh?"

THE GIRLS

Chapter Two

– Amanda –

Amanda Roberts had the stereo on full blast and as she applied the finishing touches to her face she sang along –

"And I . . . I . . . I . . . will always love you-oh-oh, will always love you."

"Jesus Christ, Amanda," Celine shouted as she came into the sitting room, "will you turn that fucking racket down."

She walked over to the stereo and switched it down herself.

Amanda kept fixing her makeup and teased Celine –

"You're a right granny all the same."

"I am not, it's just the fucking noise of it was going through my brain and you crowing along with it didn't help."

"Crowing? I'll have you know I've been told I have a lovely voice."

"Who in their right mind told you that?"

"Davey did."

"Was that before or after he got his hole?"

"Meoow," laughed Amanda, "Are we a little jealous?"

"Jealous? Of Davey Brady? That'll be the day. No thanks. I'd prefer to get me own man and not leftovers, thank you very much."

6

With that she exited from the room. As she left, Amanda made a face in the mirror at her but Celine didn't notice.

Still Celine, the last of the virgin soldiers, could say what she liked, it wasn't going to spoil Amanda's night. She was really looking forward to the talent night final and on top of that, Davey had left a mysterious message on her answering machine saying he had a surprise. Amanda loved surprises. Surprises and danger were the spice of life and since meeting Davey she hadn't been short of either.

– Tracy –

"Well, fuck yeh Davey!" Tracy Brady shouted. She had been sitting here waiting for him to go shopping for the last hour and a half. It was nearly half seven now and he still hadn't rung. A simple phonecall, that's all it took, just to say –

"Howya, I'm running late,"

– or –

"Sorry, something's come up and I can't make it,"

– but no, not Davey.

He thought the whole world had to revolve around him and him alone.

Well, tonight he was wrong. Tonight Tracy was going to put him straight about a thing or two.

– Debbie –

Debbie Collins had never felt this way before. As she lay soaking in the bath, nothing mattered – not Simmo, not Peter, nothing.

NEVILLE THOMPSON

– Mary –

Mary hadn't bittten her nails in years, not since her mum had bought that poison and put it on them all those years ago. Everyone commented on them. They tended to be the first thing people noticed about her, except fellas of course; they always saw her chest, then her nails. She had the longest, hardest, best-kept nails she knew. She took care of them like they were little babies – her very own babies. But tonight, she sat looking at the minutes passing on the clock and biting them, one by one, down to the bone. She looked at the clock again; she had to go. Whatever his news, it didn't sound good. Still, there was no point in sitting here destroying her nails. She may as well go and face the music.

PART ONE

DEBBIE'S DILEMMA

Chapter Three

Debbie Collins lay back in her bath and thought –

"How have things gone so bad? What have I done that was so bad, that's got me in such a state? It must have been really bad because, as things stood, it just couldn't get any worse."

She strained her mind back, thinking about her life and trying to figure it out.

"If I knew, if I was able to say, well, I killed six million Jews, or, I was the one that gave AIDS to the world, then at least I'd feel this was pay-back time."

But nothing like that stood out. She swallowed another pill, gulped back her last mouthful of whiskey and her mind raced back to the first memory . . .

It was pissing rain and I was crying, wanting to go out. Mammy had had enough of me whingeing and grabbed me by the scruff of my neck –

"Righ', you want teh go out, do yeh? Righ' then . . . " With her free hand she opened the front door and, swinging me like a rubbish bag, threw me straight into a large puddle that sat nestled between road and path. "There . . . now I hope you're happy."

I sat in the puddle, the rain beating down soaking what parts of me were still dry. I shivered, picked myself up and walked to Thomonds'. I could just about manage to reach their doorbell. I must have grown a bit because I couldn't remember ever being able to reach it before. Thomonds' bell had a happy jingle to it. I wanted to press it again but just as I stretched up on my tippy toes, Mrs Thomond answered the door.

"Hello, Mrs Thomond, is Jenny coming out to play?"

Mrs Thomond looked very sad –

"Yeh poor thing, come in, come in, ye'll catch yer death."

She ushered me into their sitting-room. I loved the Thomonds' sitting-room. The fire was always on and it always had loads of coal on it. Sometimes even a log and a few briquettes. Our fire was rarely lit, unless there was a load of rubbish to be burned or some bags of coal had fallen off the back of a lorry. But even then we were only allowed to use half a bucket a day. Thomonds' house was like a little furnace and there in the middle of the furnace sat Jenny with her massive dolls and their posh clothes and doll's house. I ran and sat beside her, giving her a big hug. Jenny was my bestest friend in the whole wide world.

"Is your mother not in, Debbie?" asked Mrs Thomond.

"Ah, she is, yeah, but she thought Jenny could do with some company," I laughed heartily. "Sure, as Mammy says, isn't there an army of the O'Maras and only one Thomond."

"Quite, is your mammy still taking her . . . medicine?"

"She is, yeah, she was half way through a bottle of it this morning while I was on me way out."

Mrs Thomond sighed –

"Well, we'd best get you out of those things before you get pneumonia."

She came back to the room with the most beautiful dress I'd ever seen in me life and I put it on and danced around the room –

"Look, Jenny, I'm a ballerina."

Mrs Thomond arrived back in the room with two bowls of soup and a whole loaf of piping hot home-made bread –

"Now I don't want a single slice left behind."

Sure you couldn't let the woman down now, could you? And besides, it was only when I started eating that I remembered how long it had been since I had eaten. The box of cornflakes had been empty for two days and we'd eaten the last of the beans for supper yesterday evening. Just as well I was hungry 'cause Jenny had the appetite of a bird. I waited till Jenny went to the toilet and I wrapped up three slices of brown bread into the napkin, and hid them down the underwear Mrs Thomond had given me. I'd bring it back for Liam, Sean and Conor. Sile was too young to be eating brown bread and the twins were bottle-fed.

There was only one bad thing about visiting the Thomonds' and that was the time went too fast. You were only in and you were eating, then you played with the dolls and it was time for orange and cakes. And it wasn't that diluted stuff. No sir, it was the real thing – Mr Savage Smyth himself – and cakes from the Kylemore bakery no less. Ye'd only have the cakes eaten and just time for one last change of the dolls' dresses, when lo and behold Mrs Thomond would be standing there –

"Now, Debbie, I think it's time you were heading home, sure your mother will be wondering where you've got to."

"She will in her barny. She'll be happy to be rid of us little blackguards." I'd laugh and Mrs Thomond would laugh too, but there'd be no getting away from the knowledge that I had to go.

Going home was the only time I ever took my time. I'd count the cracks in the footpath, I'd walk to the zebra crossing and I wouldn't even mind if the trucks didn't stop when I put my foot out. Mrs Thomond said I could keep the clothes –

"Not at all, Mrs Thomond, me mother will have them washed, dried and ironed first thing in the morning."

"No, I insist, they're old really and they look so lovely on you."

"Well, if you're sure."

Eventually I was home. The house was deadly quiet. I walked into the kitchen. It was dark, so I went to turn on the light but it wasn't working. I found my way to the sitting-room; as I opened the door, from the shadow of a dim light something grabbed my leg –

"Debbie, you're back."

"Liam, what's up, where's Mammy?"

He started to cry. I looked to where the light was and seen Conor, Sean and Sile all huddled around a candle.

"Sssh, Liam, it's all right."

He started talking in a rush, like he always did when he was nervous –

"Ma went out this morning and she hasn't come back and we don't know where she's gone and we're all starving and there's nothing to eat and the man from the ESB came and he cut the light off and now it's dark and Conor is afraid and . . . "

"OK, OK," I hugged him, "Mammy will be home soon, she will, honest."

An hour later Mammy wasn't home, neither was she home after two or three hours for that matter. We sat up and made figures of animals in the shadows of the candle. I made a rabbit, Liam made a dog and Conor made something that no one could figure out but, he was convinced was a bear. We played until the candle went out, then we went to bed. The twins woke crying for their bottles and to be changed. I made a bottle but it was cold and they wouldn't take it. I took their nappies off them, but I had nothing to put back on their bums so I just left them naked. I gave the boys the bread and forced the babies to drink the cold bottle. Sile started crying for food but we'd nothing for her. I felt guilty now that I hadn't taken some cakes from Thomonds'. There had been three left on the plate.

We all got into the same double bed. It was uncomfortable but at least it was warm. We could hear the stereo from next door and I sang along with The Bay City Rollers as they sang "Bye Bye Baby", with Rod Stewart as he went "Sailing" and The Carpenters' "Only Yesterday". I sang until they were all gone asleep. I was just about to fall off myself when Liam jumped up –

"Debbie!"

"What! What is it?"

"Today was your birthday."

And he was right, it had been. I'd completely forgotten.

He kissed me –

"Happy Fifth Birthday, Debbie." Then he leaned back down between the others and was asleep before his head hit the soiled pillow.

I pulled the blanket up over us all and we slept.

Chapter Four

By the age of ten I was an adult. I had to be up first in the morning to make sure we all got something to eat before we went to school. Usually it was porridge. Porridge was one of the few things we always had. Whenever Mammy sent me for the shopping I'd buy bags of it. We preferred toast or cornflakes, but at least if we had no milk or if we had no bread, I could still make porridge.

Mammy still took her "medicine", except now I knew it wasn't *medicine* but gin. Not just gin, sometimes vodka would be on special in H Williams and she'd drink that. I hated the drink, I hated the fact that she spent every penny that came into the house on drink. But above all I hated the vodka. When Mammy drank vodka she was cruel; with gin she just got plastered but with vodka she reminisced about the old times.

I'd just got the twins off to school with Sean one morning when she came down the stairs. She said nothing as she brushed by me and headed for her cupboard. She took out her bottle of tablets –

"Fuck!" she screamed as she realised that it was empty. "Be a pet Debbie, and go down to the Van for me."

"Mammy, I'll be late as it is."

"Well, another few minutes won't make any difference, will it?"

She took up her purse and as she opened it said, "Get us some tablets and twenty Benson and Hedges." She searched her purse, then her bag and then her coat. "I could've sworn I had a tenner last night. Just tell Colin to put it on me tab. Good girl."

"Colin said he can't give us any more credit until he sees you."

"Jesus fucking Christ, what's wrong with him? He knows fucking well enough that he'll get his poxy money as soon as I get me dole."

"He said you said that the last time and the time before."

"OK, Christ, give it a rest will yeh, you sound like me fucking mother."

The noise of her own voice seemed to split her head, she held it and sat down –

"Make us a cuppa. Your mother's not feeling the best."

"There's no teabags."

"Ah Jasus, you could have left a tea bag."

"Mammy, we haven't had a tea bag in the house since last week."

She sighed –

"I can't take this, I'm going back to bed."

"Mammy, you know you've to get your dole today."

"Yeah, I know."

"And you've to pay the electricity today or they'll cut us off again."

"Eh?"

"But Ma, they said . . . "

"I thought you had to go to school?"

She climbed the stairs and as I closed the door behind me I could here her fall heavily on the bed.

As soon as school was over I ran home. The other girls were all going back to Claire Boylan's house to play on the swing her parents had bought her for her birthday but I couldn't go. Firstly, I wasn't able to afford to buy her a present and secondly, I knew I had to get home and get the money off Mammy to do the shopping before she headed off to the pub. Mammy would be well home from the dole office by now. Her appointment was at eleven, so she'd have got the 77 bus from the village at quarter past ten. Even allowing for delays in the dole 'cause Mammy said they were the "dossiest shower", she'd be well home.

As I rounded the corner the ESB man was coming out of our house.

"No, Mister, you can't cut us off, me Mammy paid the bill, honest she did."

The man looked guilty –

"I'm sorry, love, there's nothing I can do about it."

"But she paid it, she did."

"Listen kid, I'm just doing me job. When your mother comes home get her to call the office and they can sort it out. Me, I have to cut off the numbers on me list, it's me job."

I walked into the kitchen, laid my head on the sink and cried. I didn't even hear Liam come in –

"Debbie, are yeh OK?"

I wiped me eyes –

"Yes, fine."

"But you're crying?"

"It's only a bit of dust in my eye, I'll be grand."

That night we sat around the candle and made monsters in the shadows. I took out the camper stove I'd bought for emergencies and cooked porridge. They were all in bed and asleep when I heard her coming down the road. She was singing Patsy Cline's "Crazy". She fidgeted at the keyhole without success. She giggled and a male voice beside her laughed too, then started banging the door –

"This is the police! Open the fucking door!"

They laughed.

"You're an awful man, Michael Maguire."

"It's Sergeant Maguire to you." They laughed again and he banged the door harder.

"Ssssh, you'll wake up me neighbours," Ma giggled.

"Fuck yer neighbours."

He took a few steps back out into the garden as I opened the door.

"Do you hear me? Michael Maguire says fuck the lot of yeh."

As Ma fell in the door laughing I turned on her –

"Mammy, where have you been?"

"Why? Did I miss somethin'?"

He was beside us now.

"They cut off the electricity."

He hiccuped –

"Well, sure you don't need it this hour of the night."

She giggled and nudged him –

"Shurrup you, it's not funny." She tried to look sincere as she turned to me. "I know, love, but it wasn't my fault. You tell 'er, Michael, sure it wasn't my fault?"

He stumbled closer to me and I could get the stink of his breath –

"It wasn't her fault."

"See it was the dole . . . "

He repeated the end of her conversation –

" . . . the dole."

"There was a mix-up . . . "

" . . . a mix-up."

"Something about back money . . . "

" . . . back money."

"I was there until after five . . . "

19

" . . . after five."

"I missed all the buses and then I met Michael and he left me home."

"Mammy, it's a quarter to one."

He staggered –

"Jasus, she's very good the way she's able teh tell the time."

I glared at him.

"Oh Jasus the look on her. I need the jacks."

Ma pointed to the stairs –

"It's the first door at the top."

He turned to her and winked –

"Are yeh comin' up?"

She nodded –

"I'm right behind yeh."

He staggered up the stairs, on occasion looking as though he was about to come down on us. She turned to me, pulling my ponytail –

"What's your game, madam? Making a fucking spectacle of me in front of Michael. Michael was good enough teh give me a lift, God knows what could have happened teh me if I'd stayed on the streets. You hear terrible things but you, you couldn't care less, you just start whingeing into me face . . . you have no idea the day I've had. While you were in school, sittin' on your arse with your sambos and milk, I was going without a bite, not a single scrap crossed me lips, trying to get money off those cunts in the dole. Money I wouldn't mind we're entitled teh, and in the end I had teh leave without a penny."

She could see the look of shock on my face.

"That's righ' . . . first thing in the morning I've teh go back and go through the whole thing again."

She looked at me, watching for tell-tale signs of sympathy in my eyes –

"You don't believe me, do you?"

And I didn't, but I couldn't bring myself to say it. I couldn't bring myself to say that my mother was a low-down drunk, a woman who put her bottle before her kids every time.

He was standing at the top of the stairs in his vest and faded Y-fronts –

"Are you comin' up here or not?"

"In a minute."

"Well hurry it up, for fuck sake."

She stared at me –

"I'm waiting for an answer."

I looked down at my feet –

"Of course I believe you."

"And are we sorry we made a fuss?"

I nodded.

"I'm sorry, I didn't quite catch that."

"I'm sorry, Mammy."

"That's a good girl. Now, give Mammy a big kiss and get yourself teh bed."

I lay in the bed and listened to the gentle rocking of her headboard against the wall. There had been nights when it had knocked harder than that against the wall, nights when her noises and her friend's moans had kept me awake all night but tonight I drifted asleep.

Chapter Five

I left school. I hadn't much choice. Things hadn't got any better. I was fifteen and Mammy was drinking more then she ever had in her life. Every night there was a new friend. They were getting older and uglier. But then again, the years were taking their toll on Mammy too. She'd been good-looking, I could remember that. I could remember the wolf whistles as we walked by the building sites. I could remember the best-looking fellas coming out of our house. I remembered the rows about women's husbands and who did she think she was. But not anymore, she hadn't had a proper hairdo in years. Every now and then, especially if she'd been drinking vodka, she'd take a scissors to it. Her clothes were all tarty. Once upon a time she could get away with it but lately her belly meant she had to keep the top button of her skirt open.

Men started calling during the day, with forty cigarettes or a bottle. There'd be very little conversation between them. They didn't hide the fact of what they were there for. If the conversation took too long they'd say –

"Listen, can we go upstairs. I'm only on me lunch hour."

They'd disappear and from above we'd hear the creaking of the bed.

Once or twice the boys went to answer the door –

"Is your mother there?"

And the boys would call her.

"Can I help you?" She'd say, coming into the hallway.

They'd smile that smile, the one that said not bad for a packet of cigarettes –

"Johnny Reilly said you might need some fags."

And before she'd answered they'd be closing the door and heading for the stairs.

I had to get a job so we could have some of the comforts that everyone else on the street took for granted. I started work packing shelves in H Williams. The money wasn't great but at least it was more than we had. I saved every penny I could. I made sure we always had food, that the electricity was paid and that we got a television. It was by the week, but at least we had one. Mister Marlow let us run a wire off his pipe telly on the understanding that we'd take it out if we affected his picture or if the pipe telly company came around. The first weekend we had it Dennis Taylor sunk the final ball against Steve Davis to win the world championship eighteen to seventeen. I'd never liked snooker, none of us had, but the excitement was unbelievable, especially when Steve Davis missed his shot and left it on for Taylor. The roars in the house when his shot went in, you'd swear we were related to him ourselves.

I got hooked on *Eastenders*; others said it wasn't as exciting as *Coronation Street* but I hadn't ever seen soaps before, so I enjoyed it. I had a crush on Dirty Den, though my real crush was on Andrew Ridgeley out of Wham. All the other girls thought George Michael was a ride but there was just something cheeky about Andrew that I thought was great. We bought a tape recorder, I bought their cassette "I'm Your Man", and drove the boys mad.

Liam had grown up a good kid. He worked at the car-wash

on Saturdays and gave me every penny he made. We saved it for special things like the cassette player and we were busy saving to get a washing machine. Imagine not having to wash everything by hand and not having to get the boys to run the clothes through the mangle. I couldn't use it, I just hadn't got the strength.

Conor was wild. We'd already had the police to our door about him and I knew he was drinking. Sean was a bit slow, his reading wasn't as good as it should have been and he squinted a lot. I'd an idea that it was his eyes and I'd promised myself that as soon as we had the washing machine bought, the next purchase would be a pair of glasses. Sile was so quiet that some days you wouldn't know she was there. The twins were a handful, always fighting with each other and anyone who came in contact with them.

Mammy was always short on money, but no matter how much she moaned we never gave her any. Our stash had to be carefully hidden. I knew she'd turned my room upside down looking for it but it wasn't there. I kept it in a little metal box that we hid under the grate in the fire. Even when we lit the fire it never burnt and we all knew that Mammy never cleaned out the grate.

If it wasn't for the others being so young I'd have left as soon as I got a job. I hated the woman. I know she was my mother and all that but I hated her. I hated the way I could never have any friends back to our house. You could never trust what you'd find and sometimes she did things just to embarrass you. Liam brought his mates from the car-wash back home one evening, so they could all watch *Match of the Day* together. She'd been drinking all day and was getting ready to go out. She waltzed into the sitting-room with just bra and knickers on. Liam nearly died, his mates thought it was great gas but he never invited them back again.

I became the greatest liar on two feet. It was second nature to me. I didn't even have to think about a lie, it just came straight out.

"My father, he was a sailor but he fell overboard."

My father, from what mammy told me, was a drunk just like her. He didn't want any kids. I was told I was just a mistake. They were stupid and young and didn't take precautions. Sean had been the result of a miscalculation on her part and when he heard she was pregnant with Conor he didn't even wait to find out what it was. She couldn't remember who the father of Sile was and the twins' dad was "that bastard" who had told her he was leaving his wife for her.

"My mother is in England looking after our Granda, they don't expect him to make it through."

"Sorry, I'm late, but there was an accident in the village and I had to give mouth-to-mouth to a man who was trapped in his car."

It didn't matter what it was, I lied about it.

I didn't like tuna but I couldn't just say, "I don't like tuna."

I had to say, "I'm allergic to it; if I ate tuna I'd have to get to a hospital within the hour or I'd die."

Chapter Six

Five things happened that made me move out. One was that I was now eighteen and that meant that the youngest in our family were the twins. We could all cook and look after ourselves.

Secondly, Mammy was getting more and more unbearable. She never left the house during the day. Her friends were getting wackier. Of late she had become a bit of a punch-bag. There was a group of older men who were using the place every night and sometimes she went upstairs with two men. They fought and when it came to punching they thought nothing of lashing out at her. She'd had a few black eyes and two of her teeth were missing. Her nose was slightly off-centre and there was a small but deep cut over her eye.

I'd also met someone. His name was Peter, he worked in the wine section of the shop. I had a lot of attention from all the lads. My mammy had given me only one thing in her life and that was her looks. I had a great figure and I swore to myself that I was going to use it to get out of this hell-hole I was calling a life. I liked Peter, he was funny. He was never going to be the man I would spend the rest of my life with but he was OK for the time being. We started dating. We'd go to the pub but I wouldn't drink. He thought I was mad. In the disco bars he'd sit drinking and I'd get up on the dance-floor and dance my heart out to all the Stock, Aiken and Waterman tunes that were playing. We had tried going to the pictures but he wanted to go to see the likes of *Die Hard* and *The Last Temptation of Christ*. There was no way I was going to go to a film with loads of violence or loads of sex, and he said he wasn't going to watch *Rain Man* 'cause it was about a spa. I tried to explain to him what it was about but there was no talking to him. It was the same with food; I always wanted to try out a Chinese meal but he said there was no way he was eating anything those "slanty-eyed bastards" cooked, 'cause he'd seen *Deer Hunter* and he knew what they put in your food. He couldn't see why we couldn't just get fish and chips and go back to my place. So in the end the easy option was to stay in the pub.

I'd only ever let him walk me to the end of our road. So before we got there we always took a walk under the bridge. The bridge kept us hidden from everyone and there we kissed. Peter always wanted more than I was prepared to give. He wanted me to touch his "thing". The thought of it! God Almighty, that was what he peed with! And he wanted to touch me *there* too. God, I wouldn't even put me own hand near *there* without a tissue. Peter couldn't understand it, he said everyone did it and I knew from talking to the other girls that they all *did*. And more besides.

Most nights we ended up rowing, him storming off and for half the next day we'd ignore each other at work.

Everything happened at once. Mammy hadn't been out in a few nights. She was moody, banging things around the place and hitting the twins for the slightest thing. Peter had got himself a room in a house with his friends and he wanted me to go back with him so we could have a bit of "quality time together".

Liam and I had finally saved enough money to get our washing machine and I was going to go in the next day on my lunch-time and pay for it.

I went and met Peter and just to keep the peace I said I might, just *might*, stay overnight the next weekend. We headed under the bridge and as we kissed he pulled my hand down to his trousers –

"No, Peter, I told you I'm not touching it."

He was kissing my neck and mumbling into my ear –

"Just rub it through me trousers."

And he started moving my hand up and down on the stiffness that was always there when we were under the bridge. So I did – I rubbed my hand up and down on it and as I did his breathing deepened and he bit my neck –

"Peter, that hurt!"

"Sorry," his voice was funny, hoarser, deeper than I'd ever heard it, *"don't stop."*

He nestled his head back against my neck and I kept rubbing. His moaning grew.

"Peter, shut up, someone will hear you."

"I don't care . . . rub faster." I did. "Faster, please faster . . . Oh yes! Oh Jesus! Oh God, don't stop! Oh *Debbie, Debbie, Debbie . . . Debbbbbbie."*

He pulled my hand away. My wrist was killing me –

"That was fucking brilliant."

I looked at my watch –

"I'd better get home."

We walked along, Peter's arm firmly around me and Peter telling me how much he enjoyed the night –

"But I'll have to leave these trousers in for the wash."

I looked down and saw the huge stain –

"Oh Jesus, will that come out?"

"Don't be worrying, I'll leave them into the cleaners' tomorrow."

"Well, don't leave them into the one in the village, because they know the two of us."

"So?"

"So, I don't want them seeing that stain and knowing what we were doing."

As we reached our corner I could hear music from our house. There were cars everywhere and every light in the house was on.

I started running –

"I have to go."

"Do you want me to come with you?"

"No, I'll see you tomorrow."

"See you, and hey . . . tonight was great."

I ran through our gate and up the pathway. I could feel the neighbours curtains flicker. In the garden one man was puking up on the grass while another was watering the next-door neighbour's flowers with his pee.

Inside there were bodies everywhere. I pushed by them, got to the stereo player and turned it down.

"Hey!" The object that had been dancing with his top off shouted, "I was listening teh tha'!"

"So was half of Tallaght!"

There was drink everywhere and in the corner, unconscious and a bottle of tequila in his hand, was Conor. I slapped his face hard until he came around –

"Conor, are you OK?"

He tried to focus on me –

"Ah Debbie, it's a fucking great party, fucking great."

I pushed my way into the hall and from upstairs I could hear me mammy. I pushed by the queue on the stairs ignoring the "Hello, gorgeous!" and the whistles. I got to the top of the stairs and I could see Mammy's door was open. She was in full view, face in the pillow and naked from the waist down. A very fat man with glasses and a bald head that had a wisp of hair across it stood, with trousers to his knees, behind her.

There were others watching the event and cheering every time his belly slapped against her backside.

"Go on, Joe, give it to her!"

Someone else shouted –

"Turn her over."

The fat man shouted back –

"Fuck off, she's an ugly bitch!"

They all laughed.

I pushed into our room. Liam was curled up on the bed with Sean, Sile and the twins. There was a man with my drawer open and he was looking at my undies. I grabbed them off him –

"Get fuckin' out!"

As soon as he was gone I went to the others. In the other room the fat man grunted like a pig and someone shouted that he was next.

"What happened?"

There were tears in Liam's eyes –

"She found the money."

My heart sank.

The next morning I took the twins and Sile to Nanny's. Nanny had stopped coming to visit but I knew she still cared. I asked her to keep the girls for a while and without asking questions she said she would. I felt guilty leaving the boys to fend for themselves, but I had to get out of there.

Peter looked shocked when I knocked on his door –

"Debbie, what's up?"

I started crying, sobbing like a child in his arms.

"Jesus, Debbie, what the fuck has happened?"

"Can I stay here, with you?"

He looked puzzled –

"Yeah . . . sure . . . but what's after happening?"

"Not now Peter . . . please . . . I'll tell you some other time, just not now."

Chapter Seven

After the initial novelty of having his "mot" living with him, Peter got bored. The lads in the house hated having a girl staying.

"After all," they'd say, "what if we wanted teh bring back some girls and party, what then?"

I hadn't the heart to tell them that the chances of them getting a girl to talk to them, and they slobbering their pints, was almost impossible. The chances of them then getting that girl to come back to their place wasn't even on the cards. They were the dirtiest fuckers I had ever known. They never picked up after themselves, they only ate breakfast cereals and take-aways –

"No point in filling the fridge with food. Sure where would the cans of beer go?"

And even then, the same bowl would be used for the cornflakes and the Chinese noodles without it so much as seeing the sink, never mind being washed. Stale smells came from every corner of the house. I gave up trying to clean the place because, every time you had it looking half decent they arrived home and within seconds the place was like a bomb had hit it again.

At first Peter couldn't get enough of me. Every night he'd come home he'd be mauling me and as soon as we were in the bed he was on top of me. It was like a contest to see how many rides he could get. I hated it. I hated having lost my virginity in a box room of a house with four fellas in it. I wanted it to be special. Not movies, roses, music and sun rising special, but special all the same. Fellas don't seem to realise that these things matter to a girl. It matters where the first time is. It matters who it's with and it matters who can be listening in the next room. I didn't want anything too glamorous. A simple bed and breakfast in Brittas would have done. We could have gone for a nice meal and stopped off in a pub for a few drinks, not too many, not falling down drunk or anything, just enough to get over the nerves, so that we would open up and talk. Then back to the bed and breakfast where he'd slowly undress me, kissing every bit of newly exposed flesh until I was naked and then he could take me.

But my introduction to the joys of full-blown sex was on the day I arrived at his door. There I was, crying my eyes out on his bed, too upset even to talk, and there he was, with his hand sneaking around to open me bra. I pushed him away and for a second he sat still but eventually he was back, clumsily trying to undo the clips. He couldn't even be bothered to spend the time to do that. Unsuccessful, he just pulled up the cups and started mauling me. Before I knew what was happening, he had me on my back on his bed, my top pulled up exposing my bare boobs. He buried his head in them as I cried.

"Shush Debbie, everything will be grand," his hands had my undies down around the ankle of one leg and off the other, "we don't need anyone but each other."

He fumbled down below, his hardness trying to enter but not quite succeeding. A finger probed, I cried, two fingers now prising open and suddenly a sharp pain as though he had cut through a layer of thin skin. I cried out. His movement was frantic and with every push he went deeper and hurt more. The bed creaked and the headboard banged against the wall which was full of pictures of Liverpool. Ian Rush looked down as Peter groaned and I cried.

Eventually he moaned loudly, his body jerked, and inside I felt a warm rush of liquid ooze through me.

He fell to one side and lit a cigarette –

"Jasus, that was *fucking* great."

And that was the way for the next few weeks. Every time I looked at him he was making eyes for the bedroom.

Sometimes I'd ignore him or even bluntly tell him *no*. That would send him into a sulk. We'd sit there with the other lads and he'd ignore me. Once he even put on a blue movie and they all laughed their heads off at the capers of the virgin from Switzerland. I got up and walked out. Ten minutes later he followed me to the bedroom and I gave in. I always gave in.

Then it was as though the novelty had worn off. As though his friends were more important than me. I sat in waiting for them all to come home and when they *did* they'd be drunk and laughing at stupid things. They'd stay up late and they didn't care what hour in the morning I had to go to work at. Whenever I complained, Peter would say I was a right "stick in the mud" and that if I wasn't happy living with them, I knew where the door was.

I hated the way he spoke to me, especially since I had confessed everything about my mammy to him. The night I told him he just sat there and didn't say a thing. But since then, any time I said anything he always threw it in my face –

"Ah, just 'cause yer aul one was a drunk doesn't mean I am."

Or when I wouldn't go to bed with him –

"Jesus Christ, it's not my fault your aul one was a good thing."

He always threw it in my face, it didn't matter who was there or where we were, he'd just blurt something out about her.

I was thinking of leaving him. He was a pig. I wouldn't be going back to Mammy, even though she was supposed to be going to AA. There were a couple of the girls thinking of getting an apartment and if they did I was going to share with them. Then I missed my period. I had always been like clockwork. Once a month I'd be like a demon, no one could say a word to me or I'd jump down their throat and sure enough, that night I'd wake with cramps and I'd have it. Peter always got a face on when I had my period. It meant he wasn't getting a ride for four days. You'd swear I'd done it on purpose or that it was a life-time of celibacy the way he went on. He'd sulk –

"Yeah, well yeh know when you get used to getting it all the time it's hard to do without it."

And I'd end up having to take his thing in me hand and play with it until he came. It didn't matter that all I felt like doing was to roll up in a ball, take some tablets and go to sleep.

At first I wasn't worried. It had been a bad month, we'd been rowing a lot and I put it down to all the upset. But it didn't come. Peter never noticed or, if he did, he never said anything. I suppose he was just happy that he hadn't to do without a ride. I waited until I'd missed my second period before I went to the doctor. I had to get a bus to one in Clondalkin, because there was no way I was going to one in Tallaght. You'd think no one had seen you and yet the next day it would be all over the shop.

I hated waiting-rooms. I'd gone to the bother of making an appointment, I had to get a taxi to be sure of making it on time, because the 76 bus couldn't be trusted. Yet when I got there I was still asked to wait. The waiting-room was a kip, with loads of women and their snotty-nosed kids. The kids were running around chasing each other and banging into everyone. I picked up a magazine and started reading my horoscope.

"You and your partner are in for a big surprise."

You could say that again. One of the kids bumped into me for the third time.

"Dolf, come *here*, don't be annoying that woman."

Of course, I was supposed to say that Dolf wasn't annoying me but he was, so the next time I saw Dolf heading for me I just stuck out my foot and Dolf went smack into the wall. He stood *bawling*, the mother was up and over with her cigarette still hanging out of her mouth. She started smacking his arse after every word –

"Didn't *(smack)* I *(smack)* tell *(smack)* you *(smack)* not *(smack)* to *(smack)* be *(smack)* running *(smack)*."

She dragged him screaming to her seat –

"Sit *(smack)* fuckin' *(smack)* still *(smack),* de' yeh *(smack)* fuckin' *(smack)* hear me *(smack)*?"

She looks over at me, pointing down at him –

"He's not well, I think it was tha' cod from the chipper, there's nothin stayin' down." Then she leans toward me and, bellowing her smoke out, whispers, "He can't tell if he's shit or not."

Lovely, I thought, and if he has, you've slapped it all into him.

Eventually the doctor brought me inside and before she even told me the result, I knew I was pregnant. I felt numb. I was three months short of my nineteenth birthday and I was pregnant. I was going to be another one of those unmarried mothers that were in the waiting-room. I was gonna end up just like them, with a snotty-nosed kid and a tracksuit. The doctor was making a whole load of noises about preparation and dates and partners and hospitals, but that's all it was – noise. I walked out, down the street and waited an hour for the 76. I paid my fare and ignored the busman's chat-up line.

When I got back home Peter was waiting –

"Where the fuck have you been? I was expecting you home hours ago."

I knew what the fuss was. It had been his day off and he was skint, so he'd spent the day in bed and now he was ready for a few pints down the pub, with the lads, courtesy of a sub from me.

"Peter, we need to talk."

"Yeah righ', can it wait 'til I come home? I'm late enough as it is."

"No, it can't wait 'til you come home. We need to talk now."

He sighed –

"Jesus Christ, Debbie, yeh know tonight is the pool competition. We're in with a chance of winning the league, but we all need to be there." He was ranting on and on. "You know the lads are depending on me, it's against those fuckers from Sherriff Street, the ones who beat us last time."

"I'm pregnant," I said in a low voice.

He didn't seem to cop what I'd said.

"Yeh know I like to get down there early and have a few bevvies before we get started . . . yeh know, to loosen up a bit."

I stood looking at him.

"OK, what's so important, that I can't go to the pool match? Don't tell me, yer aul one has gone back on the batter, righ'?"

"I'm pregnant."

He stared in silence, his mouth slightly ajar.

"Well, say something."

Still he stood without a word. I was losing my cool –

"Peter, say something."

"What do you want me teh say?"

"I don't know, say you're happy, say that's great, say you hate me, but say something."

He rubbed his hand down his face –

"I need time to think."

"Think? What's there to think about? We're having a baby, I'm carrying your baby, so tell me, Peter, what the fuck is there to think of?"

"I gotta go, can I have a lend of a fiver?"

"Peter!"

He shouted –

"Are yeh gonna give me a lend of a fiver or not?"

I pulled out my purse and threw it at him –

"There, have the fucking lot!"

It hit him and fell to the floor. He picked it up and took out a tenner –

"I'll take this just in case."

He was gone.

For a week Peter refused to talk about it. In work he avoided me, at home he either sat in silence watching the telly or went out with the lads. Then out of the blue he spoke –

"When's it due?"

"May."

"You'd better put your name down on the housing list."

"What?"

"The housing list, yeh don't want teh leave that till yeh have the . . . " He hesitated.

"The baby, it's a baby, *our* baby."

He went quiet. I got angry –

"What are you saying? Do you think this isn't your baby?"

Again he said nothing.

I got up and headed for the door.

"Debbie, where are yeh goin'?"

I said nothing, I grabbed my coat off the hanger and opened the front door. He was at my side, his arm blocking me. It was taking all my strength not to cry –

"Get outta my way, Peter."

"Debbie, what's wrong?"

"What's wrong? You're accusing me of having a baby for someone else and . . . "

He cut across me –

"I never said that."

"Only because you haven't got the guts to."

He looked hurt, the look that usually got me to feel sorry for him, but not tonight –

"Out of my way Peter, I'm having a hard enough time coming to terms with one baby, without having to deal with a second."

I pushed by him.

"Debbie!"

I ignored his call and headed down the pathway.

"Debbie!"

His voice was close.

"Debbie, please!"

He was right behind me. I stopped and stared at him.

"Debbie, I'm sorry."

"Is that it? Is that what you ran the length of the garden for? You should have saved your breath."

"No, Debbie, I mean it, I'm sorry. I've been a right brat, it's just . . . well, yeh kinda caught me flat-footed with this baby thing."

"I wasn't exactly expecting this either."

"I know, but it's different for yous."

I knew there was no point in arguing the point, this was the first time he'd ever apologised to me.

"Come on back inside," he had that puppy-dog look that made me turn to jelly. "Come on, it's freezing out here, come back in and I'll make you a nice cuppa."

Chapter Eight

Magellan was born the day of the FA cup final, so Peter was nowhere to be seen. He headed off to the pub early in the morning. It was tradition. He got up, got dressed in his Liverpool jersey and met his pals down the boozer. The day was spent watching the build up, and switching over to watch the horse-racing, the gee-gees as Peter liked to call them.

I could understand wanting to see the match, but not watching the fans get on their coaches or the players sitting on their arses in their hotel. Still, I didn't give out. Since our little talk, he'd been as good as gold. We'd even moved into our own flat and Peter had spent three nights painting it, without once going out to the pub. It was very small but it was *ours*. There was no one making a mess while you were out, no one in the room next door when you were doing *"it"*. Not that we were doing *"it"* that much anymore. I was too big and no matter what position we tried, I just wasn't comfortable.

Even that morning, he went and got me the paper, milk and a packet of wine-gums. He kept telling me about the match and its importance –

"This is the big one, this one's for the fans who died in the crush at Hillsborough. And after losing last year, we have to beat Everton."

I smiled at his explanations, and kissed him goodbye from the hall door.

"I'll be back as soon as the match is over."

He was gone. He'd only just left when the baby kicked, and Christ could she kick! I sat down but the pains got worse. I counted the time between the pains and got myself to the hospital on the bus. The nurse laughed when she saw me coming through the door –

"Don't tell me, your husband's a Liverpool fan, right?"

I was brought into a cubicle and she checked me over; without a word she was gone, and when she came back she had a doctor and another nurse with her –

"I think she's gone to sleep."

They smiled, the doctor felt around, then spoke –

"We need to get you to the operating theatre now."

It was all a haze, they weren't talking to me but about me. I couldn't understand a word that was said, all I knew was that they weren't smiling –

"What's wrong? . . . will someone tell me what's wrong?"

"Debbie, who's your next of kin?"

They were running along the corridor. Suddenly there was a suit shouting –

"There's no time for that. Debbie, listen, we're going to have to do a caesarean."

"But I wanted to have a natural birth."

He started spouting the reasons why that was no longer possible. I couldn't take it in, they were rushing me into the operating theatre and he was spouting those big words that only doctors and nurses and chemists understand.

All I remembered was bodies everywhere and a mask being put to my face and then nothing. I woke to the gentle rocking of the nurse –

"Debbie . . . Debbie, wake up . . . Debbie."

I started to come round. At first I couldn't remember, then it hit me where I was, I tried to rise, but I couldn't. My vision was slightly blurred but I recognised the doctor. I panicked –

"Where's my baby?"

He came to the side of my bed. This was bad. If it was good news he'd either tell me from the end of the bed or get one of the nurses to tell me.

"Debbie . . . "

"Where's my baby? What have you done to my baby?"

"Debbie, your baby turned in the womb. Ninety-nine times out of a hundred that's not a problem, but she got caught up and lost too much oxygen."

I screamed and the nurse grabbed my arms. The doctor continued –

"She didn't have a chance. We've kept her on a respiratory machine, so you can say goodbye."

That silenced me.

The nurses helped me into a wheelchair and brought me to her. She was so small, but she looked perfect, she looked as though she had just gone off for a sleep.

The priest was beside me –

"Debbie, do you want your precious baby baptised?"

This wasn't real, it couldn't be. It was all so rushed. I said *yes* and gave the name Magellan Mary. Magellan had just been in the news. It was the name of the shuttle America had sent to map Venus. I had joked about naming a girl that and Peter had said I would, over his dead body. But I thought it was a good name, after all Magellan was somewhere out there too. I hated Peter, he had missed all of our daughter's life.

I was wide awake when Peter arrived. I'd left a message on the table telling him that I was heading to the hospital. It was nearly two in the morning. I knew it was him by the singing –

"We Are The Champions Of The World" and "Ferry Cross The Mersey."

He was at reception and I could hear him talking shit –

"What a day, Liverpool winning the Cup and my Debbie having a baby. Tell us, where is she?"

And I knew the head nurse was trying to explain 'cause he was getting annoyed –

"What the fuck do you mean complications? Where's my fucking kid, I want teh see me mot and me kid, OK?"

The nurse spoke softly and he fell silent, I could hear him crying and then she must have asked him if he wanted to see me, 'cause he said –

"I can't face her."

Three days later, without a single visitor, I left the hospital. Peter had rung each day, but he never once spoke to me.

Chapter Nine

Things were never the same between us after that. We tried real hard but something in our relationship died that day. Peter had left a huge bouquet of flowers in the flat and he came home that night full of apologies and saying how much he loved me.

We married. It was a small reception with just immediate family. Mammy stayed away from the drink for the whole day, although at times she seemed to be suffering. The boys were men now. We'd all grown so quickly and I knew by the girls hanging out of them that it wouldn't be long before we had another wedding. Sile looked beautiful as my bridesmaid, she was so confident, so out-going and all the boys eyed her up. The only one who didn't come was Conor. Conor had got in with a bad crowd, started robbing cars and selling stolen goods and he'd ended up in jail. They were going to let him out for the wedding, but he got into a spot of bother in the prison and had been put in solitary confinement.

The wedding went off without any hiccups. The priest seemed happy that a couple who were living together anyway, were now finally getting hitched. We had the wedding reception in the Thomas Davis Club. Peter knew someone who knew someone who was a member. I slagged Peter about it –

"I thought you said that Gaelic was a game for muck savages?"

"It is, but sure they're the only ones who'd get a big enough grant to build a social club like this."

His sister, who I'd only met on two previous occasions, baked the cake. It was really lovely and we had a buffet that seemed to go down well with everyone there. Peter's brother took the pictures, he said he was in a photographic club but whatever happened the photos never came out. We couldn't afford a band so Peter's best mate Andy did a karaoke and disco. A few of the girls from H Williams came up after they'd finished work and after a few stiff G&T's, they dragged me up and we sang "Girls just wanna have fun" and "Sisters are doing it for themselves".

Our honeymoon was a night in the Green Isle. I loved the whole idea of swanning around as Mr and Mrs Collins and having a private suite with its own en suite bathroom, teasmaid and even a hairdryer. There was a phone for room service but Peter said it would cost an arm and a leg to get drinks brought up, so he went down for them. While he was gone I changed into some lingerie I'd bought from Dunnes Stores. It wasn't the real thing, it was 70 per cent polyester; but I switched off the big light and from the dimmer light of the lamp it still looked good. I lay on the bed and tried to position myself in a real sexy pose, like the film stars do, but I had to confess that posing sexily was very uncomfortable.

After half an hour I was getting worried, Peter wasn't back. I picked up the phone and dialled reception, but before it was answered I slammed it down. I felt stupid, what was I going to say –

"Excuse me, this is the newly-wed in room 204, you don't happen to have seen my husband, do you?"

I must have fallen asleep, because the next thing I remembered was Peter pawing at me.

"Hey, what's all this? Where did you get this gear from?"

He was pulling at my stockings –

"Careful Peter, you'll *rip* them."

His breath smelt very strongly of drink. I looked over his shoulder and spied the clock –

"Where have you been? It's nearly four o'clock."

He laughed, as he tried undoing his shirt –

"Yeh wouldn't believe it, I met Richie and Darren down in the bar." He saw the look on my face and mistook it for interest. "You know Richie and Darren, the wine reps from England."

"I know who you're talking about, but, Peter, it's our wedding night."

He looked peeved –

"For fuck sake, Debbie, don't start. They insisted on me having a drink with them, and you know the way it is, you get talking and suddenly you forget the time."

"And the fact that you have a wife waiting for you doesn't come into it, no?"

He got defensive –

"Sure you were asleep."

"Only 'cause you were gone so long."

"Jesus Christ, I can't believe the fuss you're making. I had a few lousy drinks and I get all this hassle. "

"I'm not *fucking* hassling you. If it means that much to yeh go back down to them."

He stood up, unsteady on his feet –

"Oh, ye'd fucking love that, wouldn't yeh?"

I looked at him like he'd two heads –

"Don't start."

"Yeah, ye'd love me teh go down so you could call up the night porter."

"Wha' the fuck are you going on about?"

"I seen yehs, making eyes at each other."

"You're mad."

"You batting your eyelids," he mockingly imitated me, "oh yes please, take our bag."

"I'm not listening to this, I'm going to sleep."

"And all this . . . this whore's gear . . . who's that for? You never dressed like that before, at least not for me."

"Peter, you're drunk, go teh sleep, we'll talk about this in the morning."

"Why? 'Cause you say so. I want to talk about it now. I want to know exactly what you were doing while I was downstairs?"

"Peter, go to bed."

He mimicked me again –

"Peter go to bed, Peter do this, Peter do that."

I sat up –

"Ah, do what you fucking like!" I pointed to the lingerie, "See this, this was all for *your* benefit, but typical you, yeh couldn't be bothered. Now I'm tired, it's late, so I'm going to sleep."

He grabbed my arms –

"Well come on then, if it's for me, let's have it."

"Peter, let me go."

He pushed his head into my boobs. He was biting –

"Oh the bitch likes this."

"Gerroff."

His hands let go of my arms and grabbed at me, one pulling at my boob, the other right into my crotch –

"Come on, Debbie, give me a little of what the porter got."

I hit him –

"Fuck off."

Without hesitation he slapped me back –

46

"Don't you ever hit me, de yeh hear?" He had me pinned down, holding my hands over my head with one hand, while the other ripped my undies off.

Without another word passing between us, he took me. I stared straight at him, watching his face distort in ecstasy and hating him as he did it.

I swore to myself that that was that. That tomorrow morning I'd get up and leave. But I didn't.

He was all apologies, it was the drink, he'd never do it again. We were good for each other, just one more chance . . . and I gave him one last chance and one last chance after that and one last chance after that and when the kids came along, he no longer asked for another chance, it was just accepted that he'd get it.

Chapter Ten

Peter didn't make it to the birth of any of our children. Nine months to the day almost, Catherine was born. She was a little *beaut* and I brought her home to an empty house, because Peter was still wetting her head.

We got a corpo flat. Peter got his wish. Less money needed to pay the rent meant more money to drink.

"But, Peter, we've an extra mouth to feed."

"Isn't that what you get your children's allowance for?"

We had nothing. A couple of sticks of furniture, a battered old telly, a double bed which his sister was throwing out and a cot I'd bought in a second-hand shop and repainted myself.

I breast-fed and even that Peter gave out about –

"It's disgusting, you with that hanging out and me trying to eat me dinner, you look like one of those monkeys yer man Attenborough is always showing on them documentaries."

By the time Peter junior came along I lost hope. I no longer even expected him to make an effort. I got myself into hospital and back out on my own. Ma visited, she said she was OK but I'd heard she was back on the drink and it showed.

I got very depressed. I was two weeks short of twenty-two, I'd two kids, a husband who slapped me around and . . . and that was it. There was nothing beyond that. And that's when it happened.

Peter came in early, and sober. I thought he must be broke –

"I wasn't expecting yeh in yet, I've nothing on."

He was agitated –

"Look at that."

He threw an envelope on the table. I picked it up and read it –

"What does it mean?"

"It means that from next week I'll be getting stopped an extra fiver in tax."

"How come? I thought with the extra child you'd be getting taxed less."

"I would be, except that thick bitch in the accounts made a fuck-up of it again. Well I told them they can go fuck themselves. I handed in me notice."

"You what?"

"I handed in me notice. I'm not slogging me guts out for that kinda money."

And that was that.

He just jacked in his job, sat on his arse, under my feet and collected the dole. His father and his brother told him about all he was entitled too. Our rent went down, we started eating real butter again, because we got vouchers for it and when a bill came in he just brought it off to the health board and it was paid.

And though it was crazy to say it, in a roundabout way, we were better off. I didn't have to worry about the ESB being cut off, I didn't have to worry about the threatening letter in the door, it was all sorted. And me and the kids were no worse off.

With Peter at home, I decided to get a little job, nothing much, just a few hours in the local shop. Things went well, I started saving a few bob. I decorated the sitting-room and bought a duvet. But then Peter started acting up. He'd come in from the pub and start on about me being flirty with the customers in the shop. I'd argue the point and say I had to be, it was all part of the job, but he said that someone had said I had a great body.

I don't know how he managed it, but he went from "great body" to "slut", to "slag" and "local bike" all within a split second.

The end result was a black eye and I couldn't go to work for a week. The shop were understanding, at first. But then Peter started popping his head around the door of the shop and shouting –

"I'm off, the kids are up there on their own."

And I'd have to leave the shop and go and mind them. Eventually they had to let me go. They were apologetic and told me if ever I got my private life sorted there was a job waiting for me.

I left it until the kids were old enough to go to school before I worked again, but I did go back to work. It's hard to explain, unless you've been a child in a one-parent family, but regardless of what kind of a bastard Peter was, he was still their father. Oh, he beat lumps out of me and at times I hated him more than I loved him. At times, as he lay in a drunken slumber and I lay covered in bruises, I thought of killing him. I'd look at the state of him, slumped in the chair, trousers half off and I thought it would be the easiest thing in the world to do. But I never did. You see, regardless of the fact that he was a piece of shit, he was the piece of shit that was my children's father. OK, so he didn't lend a hand to help raise them, and he drank and gambled the money for food, but to the kids he was still Dad. He was still there for them to show what they had done in school, he was still there sitting watching *The Simpsons* with them and he never hit me in front of them.

I'd hated my childhood and when I thought about it the only thing I could put our hard times down to was not having a father. I used to convince myself that if we had a father it would be different. I was determined that that would never happen to my kids. Still, I had to get work, if not for the money, for a bit of sanity. I needed to have something other than a husband whose only delights in the world were his pints, his bets and tormenting his wife. I had to get adult company, people who would talk to me as an equal, people who would value my opinion. I realised it would have to be somewhere there was little chance of meeting the opposite sex. I didn't want him getting a load of pints into him and convincing himself that someone found me attractive.

So, much to his delight, I got a job as a cleaner.

He laughed about that –

"Jasus, it'd be more in your line to get this place in order, before you start going out teh clean other people's shit."

But I did go.

Every morning I got up, got the kids to school and headed off to clean three houses in Ranelagh. They were rented out to trainee doctors, but despite the mess, they were cleaner than Peter. There were three of us who did it and it was great to have an aul chat and a laugh. Mainly it was just everyday things, like the children and what was on the telly the night before. We all followed the soaps and *Prime Suspect* and we loved listening to Gay Byrne on the radio. We used to listen to Gerry Ryan but all he was ever interested in was the size of his listeners' boobs, I swear to God, you'd be afraid to ring him if you hadn't got your best bra on. We had a great laugh the day that Lorena Bobbit went to court for cutting off her husband's penis.

"Oh, imagine!" says Martha, "God, I couldn't!" She shuddered at the thought, "I couldn't even touch my Philip's mickey."

"Sometimes," says Alice, "I think someone has cut off Timmy's already, because I never see it."

We all laughed. Alice gave her husband a terrible time.

I'd come home from my day exhausted, but in great form. I'd find myself humming a song I'd heard on the radio as I waited for the children from school. I never asked Peter to pick them up, I didn't want him ringing me at the last minute to tell me he couldn't.

I saved every penny I could. Peter cut back the money he gave me 'cause I was earning, but I was one step ahead of him and had told him I was getting a tenner less than what I was.

It was coming towards Christmas and I was expecting the kids to write the usual long list of things. But they surprised me –

"Mum, you know the way Santy always brings us loads of things?"

"Well, only if yous are very good."

"Yes, but just supposin' we are."

"OK." I was curious to know what was coming next. "Go on."

"Well, we were thinking, if he didn't mind, do you think he'd bring us one big present between us?"

I was afraid what this big present was; they'd been talking about a pony earlier in the day. But I had to ask –

"How big is this *big* present?"

They giggled.

"Well? This *big* present wouldn't have four legs and a tail would it?"

They couldn't stop giggling –

"No, Mum . . . it's a stereo system."

"A stereo system?"

"Yes, with a CD player and tape decks and a radio."

I felt sorry for them. They weren't greedy, all their friends must have had them –

"I don't think Santa would mind that."

They went to leave the kitchen but Peter junior stopped –

"Mum, do you think Santa would bring us a pony as well?"

They both went back into a fit of giggles.

"Get out of my sight, the two of you," I laughed, "or I'll tell Santa to leave you nothing."

I knew the prices off by heart by the time it came to buy it. I'd been around every store in Dublin, three times over. I could have got a cheap one, but the children were so good, I wanted them, for once, to have the best.

Finally the day came for collection; I brought Peter with me to help carry it. He knew I had been saving money and I knew by the state of the place every evening when I came in that he'd been searching for it. I hid it where I knew he'd never search – in the hoover.

He nearly died when he saw the price of the stereo system –

"You saved all that? I must be giving you too much."

When the assistant came out with it, there were too many boxes for the two of us to carry.

"No problem," says he, afraid to lose the sale, "we'll deliver."

I paid the deposit and made him promise that he'd deliver

today, as the kids were on a sleepover, and that would give me time to hide it.

We got home and Sile was waiting at the door. Her eyes were red.

"Sile, what is it?"

She fell into my arms –

"It's Ma, she's in hospital, they say it was an overdose."

"An overdose? An overdose of what?"

"They wouldn't say."

Peter cut in –

"You'd better get to the hospital."

We nodded, and started for the lift.

"Debbie, do you want me to wait and get the stereo off yer man? Or do you want me teh go with you?"

I hesitated. Trusting Peter with money was like putting your hand out to be slapped. It was as though he'd read my mind –

"I know you don't trust me, but they mightn't deliver again, not this close teh Christmas."

I handed him the money and left.

The doctor said Mammy had taken an overdose. He wasn't sure of what, but the mixture of the tablets and the drink had put her in a coma. Three hours after we got there she died. Conor was on his way from prison, but didn't make it in time.

We sat around, held her cold hand, talked to her and tried to remember our childhood with some happiness.

I got home and knocked on the door, but there was no answer. I opened the door into darkness. I turned on the light and saw a note on the floor. Peter must have had to go out, I thought. It was from the delivery man; he'd called and there'd been no answer.

I buried my mother with the kids by my side. It took a further two days before he came back.

He cried, he knew he was a bastard . . . he needed us . . . things would be different . . . don't do this, not this close to Christmas . . . and I took him back.

Simmo, the local moneylender, arrived at our flat, all smiles. The kids were in bed and he was sorry to hear about my recent bereavement –

"She was a lovely woman, your mother."

"She was a drunk." I walked to the table where he sat and placed my hands on it, "Listen, Simmo, cut out all your crap. The only reason I have you here is because of him." I pointed at Peter, without looking around. *"He, fucking prick that he is,* spent the Christmas money."

(I got a beating for that after Christmas, when we were back to normal.)

Simmo didn't seem affected by my outburst –

"It don't matter the reasons, love, don't matter that you don't like me. All that matters is that you need money and I have money."

He made me cringe, he looked through my clothes, I was naked in his eyes, peeled off everything, every trace of self-esteem and dignity. And he didn't have to hide his looking.

"So how much do you need?"

He asked my boobs but I answered –

"Four hundred and seventy five pounds."

"Will I make it a bit extra, it's a very costly time of the year?"

"Four hundred and seventy five pounds, please!"

Peter shot a look of anxiety –

"Debbie, make it an even six hundred."

I glared at him –

"NO."

So four hundred and seventy five pounds it was, at twenty pounds a week. And now, two years later, we were still paying.

The only good thing was that I knew Peter wasn't brave enough to leave Simmo without his money. Anyone else yes, but not Simmo.

PART TWO

SIMMO'S STORY

Chapter Eleven

You know, people have a bad view of the likes of me. As far as I was concerned I was a self-made man – you know, wheeling and dealing and the likes – but I didn't push people into meeting me. I didn't force people to take me money, and it wasn't my fault when they reneged on a payment. No, say what you like, I was an independent businessman and proud of it.

I'd have loved those Christian Brothers to see me now, especially Brother Iggy and his leather strap. Jasus, he was one fucking sadistic bastard. He'd leather yeh for nothin' and I mean *leather*. Your hands would be left with welts that didn't go away for days, and if you pulled away he really let you have it. Firstly, when you pulled away his strap would catch the top of your fingers right where there was hardly any skin or fat or muscle to protect yeh and the strap rapped straight across your bony fingers. *The pain*, I can still remember it. Then, because you pulled away, it meant he gave you an extra five smacks. It was always on the hand you didn't use for writing, so as you couldn't use it as an excuse to get off homework.

Of course, they couldn't do that today, they wouldn't get away with it. Sure you couldn't look sideways at a kid today or you'd have every do-gooder in the country on your back. Like

I know I wouldn't wish the likes of Iggy on anyone, but there is a happy medium. Still, I couldn't complain, sure wasn't it part of the reason why I was creaming it in the way I was? What did they call it? *Peer pressure*. A fancy little name for *keeping up with the Jones's*. Well, whatever name you put on it, long may it reign! Parents can't say no, if you *do* the powers that be have you believe that you have psychologically scarred the child for life. It was great! Little Johnny wants a new United jersey so little Johnny has to get a new United jersey. Fuck the cost, fuck the fact that United bring out a new jersey every time they buy a new player. And not just a new jersey, ah no! there were the shorts and the socks and the shinguards and little Johnny couldn't drink out of anything that didn't have United on the side of it and as for his bedroom: how could you expect him to sleep on anything other than a United pillow with matching sheets and duvet? And, not to be outdone, little Rosie had Barbie, but not just Barbie. Barbie had friends and any friend of Barbie's was a friend of Rosie's. Then Barbie had a boyfriend and the boyfriend had friends who had kids and houses and cars and outfits for everyday life and every occasion. Barbie loved to go riding, but she couldn't just make do with a horse, not at all! Barbie had to have the riding gear, the horse box, the Land Rover and the fucking jumps as well! And then Rosie had to look just like Barbie with her matching bag and jewellery and pens and watch and on and on. And there was no way that you could say no. Sure, didn't Mrs Brown's kids have them and the snotty cow two doors down. So if they were having them Little Johnny and Rosie were having them too! And while they were at it they needed a Playstation. Having a Playstation meant games and two consoles 'cause they couldn't use the same one, God forbid! Then there was the telly, no portable or black and white, *ah no*, it had to be big, coloured and with remote control, 'cause the poor little mites couldn't be expected to get up off their arses to turn it on or off.

Then there's the clothes. You couldn't buy them Dunnes runners, not a chance! It was Nike, Adidas and Kickers and it couldn't be an ordinary tracksuit *no, no, no* – it had to be tear-aways. The fact that they looked like gobshites in them didn't enter the equation. The fact that they were impracticable never raised its head. It didn't matter what they cost, they had to be got.

And that's where I come in.

Along with high fashion, high costs and high ideas there were other *highs* – *highs* that had quite a bearing on the whole situation. Things like high unemployment, high numbers of families on the bread line. High percentages of unmarried mothers and highrise blocks for them all to live in.

The Corpo was very good to me. The man who built the flats must've been related to a moneylender, 'cause he bundled the fucking lot of them under the same roof, thus saving on shoe leather and soakings. All I had to do was park the Beamer up, run the few short yards to the front door and *Hey Presto*, I was in. Paul *Simmo* Simpson's bank for the needy was open.

Roll Up Roll Up! Mr Simpson's Bank Has Once Again Opened For Business – Not The Most Competitive Rates, I Hear You Say – Well Maybe Not! But At Least Here You Can Get A Loan, Which Is MORE Than The Banks Will Ever Give You.

So Roll Up! All You Unmarried Mothers, You Dregs Of Society, You Fulltime Losers, You Long Term Unemployed. Roll Up Roll Up! No Legitimate (Or Illegitimate) *Request Refused.*

You know, people have a very bad opinion of moneylenders; we've received some bad press of late and that shower on *Primetime* and *Questions and Answers* are always having a go at us. But what do they know? As far as I'm concerned, I'm giving the community a valuable service. I'm what you might call a *necessary evil*. How many banks are going to take a chance with some geezer who hasn't worked an honest (or dishonest) day in his life, for fuck sake. A fella whose father and father's father hadn't worked a day in their lives. Who wouldn't know a P45 or a P60 if it came up and bit him on the arse. What bank is going to lend him money? How many building societies would think that an unmarried mother (or, as the politically correct would say, Lone Parent Low Income) was worth a loan?

You know, you get all these fancy little ads put on between Gerry *"the housewives' favourite"* Ryan and Larry *"is he still alive?"* Gogan. Like the one with the snooty girl and the husband who seems to have a firecracker up his arse. And she says to him –

"Darling, I really would love a conservatory to have our morning bagels and cream cheese in."

And he, of course, doesn't say, *"I'll give yeh a fucking conservatory all right!"* Not a chance! He ignites the cracker and in soprano tones replies, "Oh golly, what a whizz of an idea and while we're getting it done let's jet off to New York and buy bagels."

Then Miss High and Mighty says –

"But darling, how on earth can we pay for all this?"

And he replies just as his arse is alight with the banger –

"Why, dolls, we'll just go to the bank that likes to say, *Yeah, why not.*"

So while they jet off to New York a little voice comes in with those magical eight words: *Subject to Terms and Conditions and Lending Criteria.*

That all sounds fair enough. Those eight words seem

simple – I mean if Miss Bagel and Mr Banger-up-the-arse can get a conservatory and holiday, surely to Jasus the ordinary Joe Soap will have no trouble getting a few bob for Christmas? Well think again, 'cause all that *Lending Criteria* means is:

You prove to us that you don't need the money, that you have bags of dosh and a rich mother who's gonna snuff it any day and leave you the guts of her fortunes, and the loan is yours.

So who does the ordinary Joe Soap have? The credit union, oh yeah, great! the banking institution for the workers; the common man's Lloyds. Only one problem: you need to *save* to be able to get a loan. Save for twelve weeks and you can get twice what you put in. So we have a family on the scrap heap who start saving, say a *tenner* a week; that entitles you to about £240 of a loan and you have to agree to pay it back over a certain time and continue saving as well. Well £240 isn't exactly going much further than Johnny's new gear and a Barbie – so you're still in trouble. And if you ask for more they'll tell you *no*, 'cause they think you'll have trouble paying it back.

Now me, I'm a different kettle of fish.

I understand the pressures of keeping up with the Jones's.

At The Bank Of Simmo Things Are Different. A Friendly Representative (Me!) Calls To Your Door, Yes That's Right! YOUR DOOR. No More Long Queues.

The Utmost Privacy Is Assured. You Just Go About Your Daily Business, WE COME TO YOU.

There's No Prying As To What The Loan Is For – That's Your Business.

No Tricky Subjects Like Security Or Guarantors.

Our Policy Is A Simple One, WE KNOW WHERE YOU LIVE.

AND YOU ARE ATTACHED TO YOUR KNEECAPS, AREN'T YOU?

And What About Those Unexpected Emergencies That Crop Up From Time To Time?

That's Not A Problem, Simmo's Bank Are Only Too Happy To Help Its Loyal Customers Out With A Top Up Loan.

Now Wouldn't You Agree That A Service That Offers All This Is Worth That Bit More?

Wouldn't You Say Our Interest Rates Deserve To Be That Tad Higher?

Of Course You Do.

As We Say At Simmo's –

"Come For The Communion, Stay For Life."

And that's the way this business goes, I help generation after generation of the same family. I knew as sure as Mrs Hardup was borrowing for the few bits and bobs for her daughter's wedding (tell the bride I hope she has a lovely day and in case she goes into labour on the honeymoon wish her all the best with the babby) that her daughter would be borrowing to wet the baby's head.

Yet despite all this, despite my role in the community, people still moan. They start whingeing and saying the rates are too *high*, that it's *criminal,* that there ought to be laws to stop us. Still, where were all the do-gooders when the money was being handed out? Where were the do-gooders when no one wanted to give these people a loan? And then they go on about extortion!

Extortion is when the shops have fucking £100 runners and pretty-boy footballers to advertise them!

Extortion is mind games like –

Wear or Be Square.

What parent wants their kid to be *square*? And there's no point in telling these people that the runners in Dunnes are as good and only a fraction the price.

The kids won't wear fucking cheapo runners, so what's the point in buying them?

And who the fuck do these do-gooder politicians think they are anyway?

Why should a kid settle for second best just because he comes from a highrise block?

What made it all right for some toffee-nosed shite to have a pair of Nike Air Runners and not him?

As far as I'm concerned I'm a fucking national hero.

Me giving the folks a few bob means that little Johnny gets his fucking runners and doesn't have to rob them. I'm doing the guard's job and no one thanks me. I'd love to hear someone try to explain to little Johnny the unjustness of the sharing of wealth in the modern-day western world. The telly tells the little Johnnys of the world all they need to know.

Nike were it, Ronaldo wore Nike and so if Nike were good enough for a kid from some ghetto in the arsehole of Brazil, they were good enough for him.

Christmas had come and gone. It was mid-January and all the clothes had been worn, all the toys had been played with, all the beer drank, all the turkey ate. Everyone had either taken out a new loan or topped up on the old one. And, seeing how it was the season of good will, I hadn't bothered anyone over the festive period. I didn't bother telling them that I'd be adding interest for missed weeks because of it. What they didn't know wouldn't hurt them. Anyway, the holiday period was over, like it or not it was payback time.

Chapter Twelve

It was always early morning when I started my rounds. That was the best time to catch everyone in. Unmarried mothers were back from leaving the kids to school and busy tidying up the mess that had been left behind in the rush that morning. Married ones were either doing the same or, if they were the kind that worked scrubbing floors or packing shelves, their lazy fucking hubbies would still be in the bed. I hated those shits the worst. I mean, what man in his right mind would have his wife scraping other peoples' shit off toilets, while he had a breath in his body? It'd be different if the fella was an invalid or something, but these whores had fuck-all wrong with them. Other then a severe case of *"couldn't-give-a-bollox-itis"*.

And it was the same story at all of their flats. Take Peter Collins for instance.

I'd rap on the door, give it a good forty-five seconds, then rap again. On the second or third rap I'd hear the cough. A wheezy rasping cough, then a clearing of the throat. That was the sign that the dead had arisen. Now, the door needed one more really good thump, just to make sure that the dead didn't slip off back to sleep. Eventually, after two or three more coughs he'd croak –

"All right, I'm fucking coming."

You could hear his heavy sleepy footsteps across the floor. The door was always opened with the words –

"What the fuck do you want?"

Now in my book, that's the height of bad manners. I mean, they didn't know who was at the door and the words were out. With his eyes in the back of his head it'd take him a good ten seconds to realise it was me, *"good old Simmo"*.

He'd go to slam the door –

"She's not in."

Thanks be to Jasus for the man who created the hob-nail boot. Every week I had to stick my size elevens in at least ten doors. And nowadays aul Mr Hobnail wasn't just making boots. You could get a pair of runners or a nice pair of brogues and sure no one would be any the wiser of the true power of your foot. You know, a good hob-nail with the steel toe could break open a door, mortice lock or no mortice lock, with the minimum of effort. But still, gut reaction made them try to slam the door and there'd be me foot stopping them.

It got a bit boring, I mean what was the point?

They had to know that even if they got to close the door it didn't mean that I'd go away. No, all this little game did was scrape me shoes. The scruffy bastards mightn't mind looking like something the cat dragged home but I *did*. I had a certain standard to keep, and scruffy shoes weren't part of it.

So he'd say, she's not in and I'd put me foot in the door and gently push my way past him –

"I couldn't give a fuck if she's in or not. I couldn't give two tosses if she's fucked off and gone to Timbucktoo with the milkman. I couldn't care less if you'd gone after her . . . it's Thursday, it's nine thirty and I'm due £25. Now Peter, my man, I don't care who's here to give it to me. It can be the Mrs, it can be you, it can be that daughter of yours, it can be your poxy granny. I don't care . . . *I want me money . . . and I want it now!*"

At this point two things happened. One, I pulled open the drapes and let in some light (nine times out of ten I'd open the window too, to let in some fresh air) and two, he'd reach for his fags. I liked to try to bring the tension down.

There's no point in coming across as the big bad wolf –

"You know, Peter, you should really think of giving those up, that aul cough of yours isn't getting any better."

And that's when it happened.

They should do a survey on it. You got the world's biggest gobshite who couldn't put two words together on a normal day but, put a fag in his mouth, let him suck that nicotine deep into his lungs, let it go all the way to his veruca-ridden feet and when it came back up and out of his thick gob, lo and behold, he was a fully certified smart-arse.

"Who died and made you king?" or

"Jasus Simmo, if I knew yeh was a doctor I'd have paid you with me medical card."

Now there's me, trying to show some concern and meantime this fucker, who owes me big time, thinks he's BAMBER FUCKIN' GASCOIGNE. It wasn't on.

But still, experience had taught me to give them the benefit of the doubt –

"I'm only trying to be neighbourly."

He'd suck another lungful and reply –

"Yeah, well you're not a neighbour so don't fucking bother."

"OK, fine, give me me fuckin' money and I'll leave you to rot in this fuckin' hole."

He strolls across to the sofa, flops down on it, hits the TV remote and starts watching *Trisha*, shitting on about someone who has left her husband for a fella forty years her junior –

"I told yeh, she's not in."

"And I told you I don't care, I want me money."

"You'll have to see her."

"I'm seeing you."

He taps his ash on the floor and turns the volume up another two notches –

"Fuck all point in seeing me, I'm not earning."

"I don't give a fuck, you weren't working when I gave you the loan. In fact, you lazy cunt, you've never worked a day in your poxy life."

"Times are hard, listen . . . when I have it . . . you'll have it."

"That's not good enough."

"Well, Simmo, that's as good as it's gonna get."

I'm across the room and on him in a flash. I slap his face hard, first to the left, then to the right. His hair is long, dirty and standing up like Rod Stewart's does. I grab it and yank it back. My knee is in his stomach, the weight of my body behind it, I hear the air fly out of him and he gasps for a breath but can't get one.

"DON'T EVER get smart with me again, do you hear me? Don't think that you can make a fool out of me 'cause you can't. And don't think that you're tough 'cause you're not. You're nothing, Collins, do you hear? *Nothing*. You're just a thick bollox who scabs every penny he can from the welfare and sits on his arse all day, while his wife breaks her fucking back."

He wheezes and turns a funny colour. I release him, pushing my knee into him one more time as I do.

I wipe my hand in his shirt –

"Look at the fucking state of you, would yeh?"

I move away from him and for a moment I say nothing, I just look at him with contempt.

He sits up and lights another fag. His breathing is hard and his hands are shaking –

"Simmo, I ain't got your money I'm sorr . . . "

"DON'T . . . don't give me this SHITE."

I move back over him and raise a fist. He cowers. I grind my teeth, his eyes are watering. I look around –

"Jesus Christ, you must have something."

"I don't, Simmo. Honest to fuck, I wouldn't lie to yeh."

"Empty out your pockets."

I move away again, he pushes his backside off the sofa and plunges his hands deep into his pockets, first his front ones then his back ones. I pick up his jacket and empty the contents out. I look down at the table –

"Is that it?"

He nods.

"You mean to say, that's it?" I poke at the things in front of me. "A lighter, that you get five for a pound in Moore's Street, a paper snot-rag, a bookie's docket that's probably not worth a fuck, and what? Fifty-seven pence in change. For fuck sake, you couldn't even buy a litre of milk with that!"

I looked around me again. I walked to the wall-socket and disconnected the telly; at last *Trisha* shuts up.

Collins came over –

"Ah Jasus, Simmo, don't take the telly! We got it for the kids at Christmas."

"Well, tell them Santa's little helpers repossessed it."

"OK, OK, I'll get you your money."

"When?"

"Next week, I swear."

"With a fiver's interest and next week's payment too?"

He hesitated, I went to walk out –

"Yeah *righ', righ'*."

"An' how are you gonna manage that?"

"I'll think of something."

"OK and while you're thinking I'll keep your telly, but don't worry, I won't sell it until we talk next week."

Chapter Thirteen

Being a loan shark isn't all easy pickings. The likes of Peter Collins isn't a one-off, they crop up all over the place and they never learn. You see Peter, despite it all, will think he got one over on me. I knew his wife and there's no way Debbie hadn't left the money. Debbie hated having the debt, and she'd never have faulted on it. No, I knew Debbie had left the money before she went to work and he had skived it. He would have let me batter the shite out of him as long as I didn't find the few bob. I took the telly down to the car and put it in the boot, then I sat and waited. About twenty minutes later out popped Peter, cigarette in mouth, shoulders stooped against the wind and shuffling along, as though he was on a mission. I gave him a head start and followed.

His first port of call was the newsagent's, money changed hands and out he came with the *Sun* and twenty Carroll's. I'd say he's been buying the *Sun* since it came to Ireland. It was the classic paper for the pub, you know, tabloid, so you didn't have to spread it across the whole of the counter to read. It had a good soccer report, great racing and for the likes of Peter, a page three. I could just picture him opening up the page and showing it to the fella next to him –

"Hey wouldya?"

Wouldya? As if Sally from Swansea, aged eighteen, with

her pert little nipples, would look twice at Peter, thirty-six, jobless, from Dublin, or any of his mates. He was pathetic, he was lucky to have a wife, never mind an eighteen-year-old nympho. And from a photo Peter would be able to tell you everything –

"I'd say she loves it . . . I'd say she's a right goer in the scratcher."

Peter wouldn't know a right goer if she came up and lap-danced around his pint. Sure if any of them were being honest they'd admit that there hadn't been a decent-looking bird in the *Sun* since Linda Luscardi and Sam Fox hung up their size 38s.

Peter strolled out and, walking along the street, opened the paper on page three and smiled to himself. If his Missus was there he'd swear he only bought the paper 'cause of the horses. Next stop was the boozer on the corner; there were three other pubs closer to the flats but Peter always went to this one 'cause the bookies was next door. I looked in the window and saw him hand over a twenty-pound note.

"I fucking knew it!"

Pint in hand, Peter studied the form. I could imagine him knowing every jockey, every stable, every horse, who's hot, who's not and every course between here and Britain. I could imagine him being able to tell you every fact about every horse, who could and who couldn't ride it, what ground it liked, whether it liked right-hand or left-hand courses and at the end of it all he couldn't pick a winner.

He indicated to the barman for another pint and while waiting, he headed into the bookies, placed a tenner on something and then back to the bar. The publican knew what side his bread was buttered on. He had satellite telly so all the no-hopers like Peter would come in, guzzle pints, read their *Sun*s and rip their dockets up in unison. But wonders would never cease! Judging by Peter, *he'd actually won*. He sat on his chair like a jockey, holding his hands as though he had reins in them. His body rocked and though I'm no lip-reader I could make out what he was saying –

"Go on . . . go on boy . . . go on . . . hit him . . . hit the fucker . . . take the bleedin' rail . . . that's it . . . yesss go on . . . keep going . . . yes, YEH GOOD THING!"

His hands punched the air and he called another pint and collected his winnings.

I could have walked in, there and then. If I did I'd have had to break some bones. I couldn't let people think they could pull the wool over my eyes. But, I didn't. I knew at the end of the day he'd have lost every penny he had. People like Peter Collins were born losers, they never knew when to quit.

I pitied his Missus, she had it hard. But then again, she only had herself to blame. She'd married a loser, probably knew he was a loser before she married him and yet she thought she was gonna be the one to change him. She was going to be the first woman in history to make a leopard change his spots. Now whatever hope she'd had when he was chasing her, when he wasn't guaranteed that she'd be waiting at home for him, she had fuck all hope after she'd spouted two kids in the first two years of marriage. And hadn't that been his idea too? He knew the system, knew that the Corpo had to house them when they had kids, especially when the baby got a bad chest infection from the damp.

Their flat was a dump. A pokey two-bedroom existence on the fourth floor. He hadn't worked in years, if at all, and any extras they had she got. She scrimped and saved, went without, let the kids go without, even got the electricity cut off one time, yet he never got up off his arse, not once, to lend a hand. And not only that; if he knew she had a few bob he'd moan into her face until she gave him enough for a few pints.

That's how I got to do business with them. Peter's whole family lived in my area and every one of them had permanent loans out, everyone bar Peter. Debbie told me in no uncertain terms that she didn't want my type calling and I respected her for that. I'd see her heading off first thing in the morning and home last thing at night – but she didn't care. Seemingly she was buying the girls a whole electric package for Christmas: a top of the range stereo system. She was getting it in one of the big shops but she couldn't pay by the week, so she had to keep the money hidden in the flat. Peter nearly drove himself mad looking for it but he never did find it. They went out, picked the system and paid a deposit, with the rest payable on delivery.

When she got home her sister was sitting waiting with the news that her mother was after being taken into hospital with a heart attack. Peter told her to go and not to worry, that he'd wait for the delivery. She handed him the money and ran all the way to the hospital . . . even so she was too late. Later that night she arrived home with their kids and found a note from the delivery man to say they had called, but there was no reply. Peter stayed away for two days and had only come home after all the money was gone. She cursed him from a height, made him sleep on the sofa for a week, but in the end he wormed his way back in. I was called and asked for a loan; that was three years ago. Debbie worked hard to get it paid off but unbeknownst to her, Peter kept topping it up. And although I didn't like what he was doing, who was I to refuse business?

Chapter Fourteen

I couldn't let personal feelings get in the way of business. This had been something handed down from generation to generation in our family; I'd worked hard to get it back on the rails. Da had been a useless loanshark. When he died people owed thousands and had no intention of paying it back either. You see he'd grown up with most of the people he had loaned to and he never liked to put too much pressure on them. The whole business started with his father, my grandfather. I don't remember him meself; he died a year before I was born. In his early days Granda was a paperboy. In those days there were loads of kids selling newspapers up and down O'Connell Street for a penny a time. Granda used to run between trams and cars shouting outrageous headlines and sure the people would flock to buy the paper. It's hard to believe that in those days this would have been the only way for most people to get any news. Not everyone had a radio and tellies were unheard of. It's hard to imagine a time without *Sky News* never mind without *telly* – Christ, we're spoiled really!

That's where he met and chatted up me granny and it wasn't long before they were an item and granda needed to make a decent living. He started working for a scrapdealer as a picker on the dumps. A *picker* was as it sounded. He had to scrounge around the dumps picking out tins, bottles and brass and metal. It was a dangerous job, between the ground giving way and you ending knee high in other people's junk to cuts from the broken bottles and jagged cans. But the worst was the rats! They were everywhere and they shat and pissed on everything. Now that's disgusting in its own way but if you have a cut and fresh rat piss gets in it, you may as well start digging a hole in the cemetery, 'cause sure as hell you'd end up in it.

Granda moved from working on the dumps to being a tugger. Tuggers were usually women going round from door to door getting things off the rich women in the suburbs. But granda had a cheeky baby-face and the rich aul ones fell for his constant banter. They'd be out to their doors the minute they heard his basket car, with its cane base, wooden handles and its three wheels, on the cobble stone.

Granda, they say, could charm the birds from the trees and rumour had it that his boxcar could often be seen parked in the laneways around the back of the posh houses. Whatever the truth, he got the best of gear. No holes in the arse or soles out of the shoes. And with a new mouth to feed every time he so much as blinked at Granma, he realised that in order to make a decent living he would have to stop working for the scrapdealers and start dealing with the pawnbrokers in person.

There were up to seventy pawnshops in Dublin at the time and they'd lend you money on anything. The pawnbrokers were supposed to be Jews but they had a heart. They realised that people needed money to survive from day to day, so they'd take in anything on a Monday in the knowledge that the same item would be taken out again on Saturday. The pawn shop was nearly a meeting place; everyone would go and on a Monday the queues would be right down the street. There was no stigma to the pawn. It was kinda *the people's bank.* And people didn't mind having to pay the tuppence interest on the pound. It was a small price for food on the table and the knowledge that your item would be safe until you picked it up again. People would take their shoes off and hock them and there were stories of whole families who couldn't go outside because their clothes were in the hock. So granda got a good price for his suits on pawn, as much as a pound – and with the extra money he made he began to give loans to the people around the flats. Pretty soon he was making three times his money on the lending. If someone fell a bit behind he got them to bring suits in to the pawn for him, that way he could move twice as much gear without questions being asked.

But all good things come to an end. The Second World War hit and times got hard, even for all the rich biddies. Suddenly they were bringing their own things down to the pawnbroker. Grandad wasn't getting any younger, he had lost his effect on the women and his drinking, that in his youth had been a sign of his bravado, now was a source of embarrassment to the family. Me da and his brother Joe had taken over the lending and there wasn't any work for a drunk. He started backing cars into parking spaces and living on the generosity of the man behind the wheel.

He had to grovel with his cap tipped, his hand out and his *"Thank you very much, sir,"* and *"Three bags full, sir."*

But even parking cars became unionised in the early fifties and granda used to have to hide from the unionised men who now owned the pitch. When their backs were turned he'd come out of the shadows, with his cap, and a makeshift green ribbon round it, pretending to be official and back the cars in. Then he'd have to try and grab the money and run before being spotted . . . Straight to the nearest pub. More times as not he didn't make it and his face would be bruised and battered from the digging he'd receive.

Just a year before I was born he died. The police found him

battered to death in a gutter just off Stephen's Green. Joe went out and took revenge on one of the unionised parkers, slashing his face from one ear to the next. The man survived and Joe had to hot-foot it to England to avoid being locked up. Da found himself in total charge and for a while everything went well. For the most part people tried to pay their debts and once they made an effort, Da tended to lay off them. Ma would go mad saying that those whores he was lending to had more money than us. She was the one that made us move. She said if he was away from them, away from the flats he wouldn't treat them so friendly. Three kids later she got her way and we moved to Ballyfermot. It was 1957, I was four and I hated it.

Chapter Fifteen

People were great at making promises –

"No problem, 'course I'll pay you back . . . a tenner a week, sure that's no problem, honest . . . "

And for the first few weeks it wouldn't be a problem, then it became a bit of a burden; whatever the money had been used for was well and truly gone or had lost its appeal and suddenly the payments became like a tax, something that they resented having to pay back.

Da had a good set-up, what with all the flats . . . and during the school holidays he'd bring me on the runs. For Da, introducing me was just a bit of fun and I was treated like the son of a friend by his clients.

"This is Paul." He'd say.

They'd come over, toss me hair and say something like –

"Christ Jack, he's a good-lookin' kid, must be a good-lookin' milkman around your way, eh?"

And they'd all laugh and I'd get another ruffling of me hair and Da would get his few bob. Sometimes I'd get a penny, Da would look and say –

"Ah, you shouldn't."

And they'd say –

"Sure it's only a penny."

Then Da would say –

"He'll want this every fuckin' week, you know?"

And they'd all laugh and pat each others' shoulders and ruffle me hair again.

It used to really piss me off, them ruffling me hair and giving me a penny like I was some kind of child. I was thirteen years old, nearly a man, for fuck sake.

At first I was under strict instructions just to stand, watch and say nothing, but as the weeks went on Da would let me collect from the head patters.

The man would come to the door and seeing me he'd call to his wife –

"Hey Peggy, come quick, Jack Simpson has sent around one of his heavies."

The wife would come to the door, face flushed as if in a panic. But on seeing me she'd laugh –

"Oh well, Kevin, you'd better pay him, we don't want no trouble from the likes of him."

The man would put his hands up as though we were going to fight, then the money would be handed over, me head patted and as the door closed behind me, I could still hear their laughter.

But fuck them, someday they'd know not to mess with Simmo.

Still, for every one person that saw it as just another bill there were five who saw it as a burden. Da would stand there arguing. Sometimes he'd even get annoyed and grab the man by his lapels but more often as not, he let them con him into leaving without money for a week or two. Da hated me seeing this, he'd tell me to wait outside, but it was pointless. The walls were paper thin and once the shouting started I knew things weren't going well. He'd come out face all red, start scribbling in his notebook and I'd know.

I'd know the fuckers had got one over on him.

When the school holidays were over Da wanted me to go back to school but I didn't want to. Even when he said I couldn't join the family business I still didn't want to go. All my mates had jobs. We didn't see the point in school, none of us were actually what you'd call academic. We were never going to pass the civil service exams. Francis Fowler was barely two years older than us and he was getting two quid a week selling shoes. Even after paying his keep at home, he had enough for his own ten Woodbines and tickets to the Ambassador Friday, Saturday and the matinee on Sunday.

Me, I had to ask . . . no, beg, for the money to get out for one night –

"You're not going to the flicks again, are yeh?"

"Jasus, all them pictures, you'll go deaf with the noise of them cinemas."

"What do you think I am? Made out of money?"

It was stupid. I saw nothing and Fowler would be off watching *Alfie* and *A Man For All Seasons*. He'd rave on about Michael Caine being a brilliant actor and what a great director Lewis Gilbert was and meantime, I'd be lucky to see *Georgy Girl* with yer man Mason and one of the Redgraves (though I could never remember which one it was).

While Francis Fowler spent his time noticing things like actors, directors and who wrote the script, I spent me time trying to figure out if I had enough for popcorn and a coke as well as me bus fare back home, with one eye on the screen and the other on the back row.

All the older lads and their girlfriends were in the back row. They were cool, with their Beatle haircuts and their girlfriends with miniskirts. They shared their popcorn and their drinks and even their cigarettes. They chewed gum, carved their names on the back of seats in front of them and before the main event spent the time singing "Good Vibrations" by the Beach Boys and "Cherry Cherry" by Neil Diamond. And they wouldn't shut up until the aul one with her varicose veins who sold the ice creams up the front at the interval shone her torch right into their faces.

As soon as the lights went out they were all over each other. The hand that had earlier barely touched her shoulder would now be buried deep under the girlfriend's blouse and turning furiously as though trying to unscrew something. Their faces were joined at the mouth and a gentle sucking noise could be heard. As soon as they broke for air his head buried into her neck, like Bela Lugosi did in *Dracula*.

I could never make up me mind which I preferred more, watching the film or the back row. Sometimes you'd get a great view, especially if you were within watching distance of Sally Knowles. Sally must have gone to every film that ever was. Francis said he often saw her queuing for a matinee with one bloke and the evening show with someone else. She was at least seventeen and although she wasn't good-looking, all the older lads said she was a good thing. We didn't know what a good thing was, but I guessed it had something to do with letting them unscrew her, 'cause she was the only girl who let them unscrew with two hands, She also let them put their heads under her top and once when I looked around one fella had his hand up her skirt and was unscrewing that too.

The night I saw Francis Fowler in the back row with Sally was the night I decided that whether me Da wanted it or not I wasn't going back to school.

Chapter Sixteen

I got a job in the markets. At first it was OK, all I did was load and unload trailers, carts and vans all day. It was early September and the sun was splitting the sky so that meant that the girls were still going around flashing as much flesh as was decently possible. Every time you turned the radio on you heard "The Green Green Grass Of Home" but no Beatles. Seemingly John had said that they were more popular than Jesus Christ and the church had taken offence, so once they put their tuppence worth into the pot the radio stations stopped playing the Beatles.

I worked with an aul fella called Tiny Reilly. No one ever knew his real name but because he was the nearest thing anyone had ever seen to a giant it was only natural that he got the nickname "Tiny". Tiny could lift three bags of spuds all on his own and if you let on that you thought he was great, sure, he'd nearly clear the trucks single handedly. Tiny was a hero on the market. It had all happened years ago, long before I was on the go, but even now they talked about it.

It happened in the run-up to Christmas. The market was a-buzz with every type of person; people who wouldn't normally be there were around buying their Christmas veg and their fresh turkeys. The women would bring down their children who in turn would be very excited by the sight of all the hundreds of turkeys in the pens. The noise was unbearable, it was as though the turkeys knew it was a bad time for them. All year round they were fed and watered and let run riot around the farm, watching the trucks pull up to take the pigs, cattle and chickens away, never to come back again. But come Christmas the truck would pull up as usual, except this time they were the ones to be herded on. And from the moment that the back of the truck hit the farmer's yard until the women pointed them out, they never shut up. Of course, it's not as though they could think they were mistaken. The seller would ring the neck of the chosen turkey there and then, in the middle of the pen.

Once you got the turkey home it had to be plucked and hung up in the coldest room of the house. There were no freezers back then. I hated that, because in our house the turkey was hung in the bathroom, on a pipe, over the bath. Da use to put a small see-through bag over the turkey's head to catch the blood, but still it was a horrible sight to have looking at you as you tried to wash. And nine times out of ten, either on the way into or out of the bath, you'd touch against it and it would feel like a dead person's skin.

Still, at that time of year there was a real buzz to the market. The seller didn't want to be left with any turkeys so he'd spend the whole day calling out funny lines to the passers-by –

"Right ladies, pick your own turkey here today, then at least you'll know where your hand is going this Christmas."

Or

"Mrs, once I've plucked this turkey it'll look so good you won't know whether to eat it or marry it."

He had a line for the fellas too –

"Right, men, get one of my turkeys and at least you know you'll be stuffing something this year."

And every day, guaranteed, someone would try to grab a turkey and make a run for it. The poor turkeys would be just standing in bunches, crying at the top of their voices and watching the seller all the time. Then suddenly someone would lean across the wire of the pen and grab one by the neck. The turkey would scream, the villain would take to running with the seller in hot pursuit and the whole market would fill with feathers. They never got away with it. The turkey would slow them down too much and they'd have to drop it or risk getting caught. It all added to the atmosphere of the occasion.

So it was Christmas, the turkeys were frantic, the dealers were all trying to outshout each other. The man selling the Christmas trees was busy convincing everyone that his trees wouldn't lose a single needle and the carol singers sang everything from "Sleigh Bells Ring" to "The First Noël". Suddenly there was an unmerciful cry and everyone stopped doing what they were doing and turned to where the cry came from. One of the trucks had been backing out and the driver wasn't really concentrating 'cause he was in a fierce rush and in his haste he hit a horse, breaking its hind leg. The horse collapsed in agony as though it had been shot and the poor thing fell straight onto a pram and rolled on it in pain. The mother of the child screamed for her baby, the driver of the truck stood motionless as did the owner of the horse and just about everyone else. Everyone bar Tiny. Tiny was off-loading a truck nearby and he ran all the way to the scene, pushing through the crowds. When he came upon the scene he didn't lose a beat. He jumped on the horse and with one swift jerk of his body, broke its neck. The horse stopped moving and three other men ran to Tiny's aid as he pulled the lifeless lump off the pram. Suddenly from the wreckage the baby cried. The mother ran and pulled him out and they say there wasn't as much as a scrape on the child.

Tiny was a hero, the men tried to pick him up on their shoulders but they weren't strong enough. The woman kissed him and the turkey man gave him his choice of a turkey for nothing. That night Tiny had to get a lift home with all the freebies he got and even to this day he could get drunk for free on the retelling of the story.

I liked Tiny and he me. He taught me how to lift without hurting my back and how to stack a stall so even the most rotten of fruit looked fresh. And we had a good laugh together, we were a team. I'd look out for him when he snuck off for a quick pint and he'd cover for me when I wanted to go off early. But as a job it wasn't for me. It got me out of school but the winter was coming and, believe me, there's no fun in being knee-deep in ice-cold sludge, or in having a northerly wind blowing into your face all day.

The world was changing. It was 1966, England had won the World Cup, Alan Ball was sold for £100,000! Imagine, *One Hundred Grand!* He was good, but Jasus, he wasn't *that* fucking good. Blackpool must have seen Everton coming.

The Russians and the Americans were playing cat and mouse to the moon. The Russians landed *Luna 9* on the moon, then the US did likewise. Not to be outdone the States did the first link-up of a crew in space and then the reds crashed into Venus.

It was fierce exciting. They were reckoning within a year there'd be a man on the moon – imagine, a man walking on another planet, and here was me thinking a day out at Bray playing the slots was an adventure. I had to get a life.

Chapter Seventeen

Everyone had a girlfriend bar me. I'd look in the mirror and think –

Jasus, I'm not bad-looking.

I'd no scars – well, no major scars, just a little one from where I'd tried to shave my eyebrows off. Me nose was a bit crooked from too many fights but I thought it gave me a bit of character and, OK, so I had a few spots but no carabuncles. And anyway I'd seen girls in the back row with fella who had carabuncles. I was nearly fourteen, for God sake. I'd been working for the guts of a year and I'd even managed to grow a moustache like Errol Flynn the actor. Tiny had said it was like two long hairs coming out of a mole on me top lip but I thought it was cool.

I was in love with Cassandra Murphy. She was sixteen and gorgeous. She was all smiles when she came to the market and once, when I let a crate of tomatoes fall, she helped me pick them up. I couldn't get over her looks. Her eyes were like a Siamese cat's and her hair was so long it was like something out of a fairy-tale, you know, like the princess locked up in the tower. It was longer than her skirts and she had a lovely little pair of tits. Tiny had said they weren't even a handful but I would have loved to have been unscrewing them in the back row. It was hard to get to talk to Cassandra on a one-to-one basis. There was always one of the older lads flirting with her and anyway, even when I got the chance, I never knew what to say. I couldn't compete with fellas in suits, telling jokes and smelling of Old Spice. Not while I was in overalls and smelling of Brussel sprouts and potatoes.

So one morning as the rain belted against the window and me ma stood at the end of the stairs, shouting that me brekkie was going cold, I decided that enough was enough. I went down to the market and told me boss that I was jacking it in.

Tiny was upset –

"Simmo, me lad, what are you going to do with yourself?"

"Dunno Tiny, but I got to get out of here, it's doing me head in."

"What about me?"

I laughed –

"You'll be fine. You know, I bet you don't even need anyone to help you offload that truck behind you."

And as if to prove that he still had a lot to offer, he started lifting three bags off at a time and by the time I walked to the gate the truck was passing me empty. I turned around to wave goodbye to Tiny but he'd already started unloading the next truck.

Next stop was to McBernies where I purchased a suit off the peg. It was green velvet and I felt a bit stupid in it, but the man assured me it was the latest fashion in London. I got a shirt and tie and shoes before heading for the men's hairdresser's. Up to this I'd always gone to the barber, there never seemed any point in spending the money in the hairdresser's. The girl was a looker and as she ran her fingers through my hair her left tit rubbed ever so lightly against the back of my head. She smiled down at me suggesting what I should have done and all I could think of was the fact that if I turned around now her diddy would be in my mouth. I just nodded to everything she said. Once she got my consent her bust never even came near me again. An hour later I came out with a haircut not unlike Paul McCartney's and a week's wages out of pocket.

The last stop was the chemist where I bought a bottle of Old Spice. I walked home and let myself in, then headed straight for my bedroom and . . . my transformation. Having put the suit on, squeezed into me shoes, put some Brylcream into me moustache to make it look darker and doused meself in Old Spice, I knew it was time to face them downstairs.

I walked into the kitchen. Da was sitting in his customary seat at the top of the table. His head never looked up from his paper. Ma had her back to me and was busy searching through the bags of shopping she had just brought in –

"Ah Paul, I didn't know you were home. I'll get the dinner on as soon as I've unpacked these few things."

"It's all right, Ma, I'll just have a crisp sandwich."

I walked to the worktop and buttered the bread.

"So how was work today, son?" Ma asked.

"I didn't go."

Without looking up from his paper Da put in his tuppence –

"What do you mean you didn't go in? You won't keep a job long not going in."

"I don't care, I jacked it in."

"Oh, that's just great. That's real clever, isn't it? Tell me, Einstein, what are you going to do now?"

"Dunno, I'll get another job I suppose."

"Sure that's right, silly fucking me, sure I forgot they'll be queuing outside looking for ye." He looked up as he spoke, "And what in the name of Jasus are you like?"

The sarcasm in his voice made Ma look up. She looked stunned but regained her composure quickly –

"It's great to see you make an effort, is there a special occasion?"

Da cut across –

"A special occasion? More like a fucking bet."

"FRANK," she screamed, "leave the lad alone!"

Then she came over to me. "You look very . . . smart."

"Ah, would ye stop, he looks like a fucking walking talking bit of grass."

I tried to defend meself –

"This is all the fashion."

"Fashion! Where? The only place you could fucking go in that is a Paddy's Day Parade."

"The tailor sai . . . "

"Tailor? No fucking tailor made that – a drunken sailor, maybe, not a tailor." He shook his head and went back behind the paper. "You've been had boy, good and proper."

Ma shot a glare across at him but he didn't even notice –

"Come on son, let's go into the front room."

We walked out, me Da still sniggering, and went into the warmth of the sitting room –

"Don't be minding him, your father has no sense of fashion."

I just smiled at her.

She put her hand on my knee and continued –

"So? Tell me, why all the changes?"

I answered too quickly –

"No reason."

She gave me that mother's look, the look that let me know that she knew I was lying through my teeth.

"Come on, love, this is your mother, I know when something is bothering you."

That really cracked me up. She was right. She always knew when things were going wrong. Like the time years ago when I was sent for milk and bread. She told me to go to the second shop because even though they were another five minutes' walk away, their bread was fresher. Me, I wanted to go to the first shop for two reasons. Firstly, the bread was a penny cheaper, which meant I could get a penny's worth of sweets for myself, and secondly, we were just about to start a game of soccer and if I was late, the teams would be picked, and I'd have to wait for the first goal before I got on. So I ran all the way there, got the bottle of milk, the bread and a few blackjacks for meself. Purchases made, I legged it back home, calling to me mates not to start picking for a minute. I hit the front door running and Ma came out with a terrible face on her –

"What the hell are you doing?"

I was out of breath –

"Sorry, ma . . . it's just . . . " I pointed to the lads putting their jumpers down for goal posts, " . . . there's a match . . . "

Ma looked at me, then the pitch, then the bread and milk –

"You weren't long?"

"No, Ma. I ran all the way there and back." I went to run.

"Hold it there a minute, young man, open that mouth of yours."

"Maaa, the lads are waiting."

"Open it," she demanded.

"But, Maa, the match'll start."

"Paul Simpson, are you going to open your mouth or do I have to prise it open for you?"

Reluctantly, I opened wide and knew as I did that the blackness of my mouth would give my secret away.

"Where did you get money for blackjacks?"

I started to cry and she filled in the blanks for herself –

"Ye little shite, you didn't go to the right shop, did you?"

I was too busy tripping meself up with snots to answer.

"Well, you can take these back and go to the proper shop."

She rummaged through her purse and produced another penny,

"And I'll be taking that out of your pocket money at the weekend. Now go and come straight back, do you hear me?"

I turned still sniffling and started running. I could hear her shouting after me as I ran –

"And you can tell your friends that you won't be playing any football today 'cause when you come back, you're scrubbing the the hall, stairs and landing floors."

Ma was all *knowing* and all *conquering* then, and little had changed. I looked at her and knew that I had to tell her the truth before I'd be allowed to leave the room.

So I told her about me job and Cassandra and wanting something better from life. She sat and listened, at times I could see her face fill with hurt at the thought of her son being so upset but she said nothing. She just smiled and nodded where appropriate. Then, when I'd finally finished, she said that Cassandra would be a fool if she didn't go out with me. She reached into her purse, pulled out three crisp one-pound notes –

"Go and buy her the biggest box of chocolates you can find. Girls can't say no to chocolates."

Chapter Eighteen

I hugged Ma and for a moment she wouldn't let me go –

"Ma, the suit."

She let me loose and tried to laugh, to hide her tears –

"Would you look at me, what am I like? You go," she sniffled, "go on, knock her dead."

I bolted out the front door, jumped the front garden gate and ran to the corner shop. The woman behind the counter was suspicious of anyone without a pension book in their hand –

"Can I help you?"

I looked around –

"I'm looking for chocolates?"

"What type?"

"Dunno, what have you got?"

She frowned –

"Whatever's behind me."

"Well, could you take some down, so I can have a look at them?"

"I can't be taking them all down, point out which one you like and I'll get it for you."

I craned my neck and stood looking up at them.

She sighed impatiently –

"What's the occasion?"

"Huh?"

"Well, is it a birthday, an anniversary, what?"

I said nothing.

"Does she like dark or light chocolate?" She looked at my suit and sneered. "Assuming, of course, that it is for a girl."

I gave her a dirty look. What was she trying to suggest? That I was one of those queer boys?

"I dunno what she likes."

She sighed again –

"Well if it's any help, I personally love dark chocolate."

"OK, I'll take the biggest box of light chocolate you have."

I walked out and took the shortcut through the laneway. It wasn't really a shortcut but at least no one would see me with a box of chocolates. I got to the corner of Cassandra's road and I nearly backed away. If there had been anyone walking down the road I'd have turned on my heels and gone home. But there was no one around, so I took three deep breaths and walked up to her door. I rapped hard on the knocker but there was no answer. I knew she was in 'cause her push-bike was parked in the garden. I knocked harder and stood away from the door, fidgeting from foot to foot. On the third rap a shadow came to the upstairs curtain. Suddenly the window opened and a head peeped out –

"Whatever you're selling we aren't buying, so fuck off!"

I recognised the face. It was the *Suit and Old Spice Fella* that was always hanging around Cassandra. He must be a brother, I thought.

"I'm looking for Cassandra, is she in?"

He called over his shoulder –

"Cass, there's someone here wants to talk to yeh."

I heard her mumble but I couldn't make out what she said. He answered –

"I dunno, I never seen him before."

It took a few seconds for her to come to the window. She was wrapped in a white sheet. She looked down –

"What is it? Can I help you?"

"Cassandra! It's me! Simmo."

At first she looked puzzled, then her face turned to a smile, as she remembered –

"The fruit and veg boy, right?"

I nodded, but my heart sank.

"God, I hardly recognised you, you look . . . different."

I still shifted from one foot to the next –

"I got my hair cut," I brushed my hand through it, "And I got a suit too."

She laughed –

"So I noticed."

"And I got you these." I held out the chocolates.

"Ah God, that's sweet . . . eh . . . eh . . . "

"Simmo."

"Yes of course, Simmo."

For a moment I stood still with the chocolates outstretched. She stood motionless too. Then Old Spice came back up behind her and started kissing her shoulder –

"Listen Simmo, I'm a little busy at the moment."

He was pulling at the sheet and she giggled as she half-heartedly told him to stop. Then as he dragged her back from the window she called to me –

"Leave them down, I'll get them laterrrr . . . "

Her words trailed off into a long "gerroff, you pervert".

And for a moment I listened as her giggles stopped and I could hear her softly moan. I didn't want to be sweet, I wanted to be *Gerroff you pervert*, up there with her and not standing like a fool at the door.

Chapter Nineteen

Things were never the same after that day. I walked away real quick and when I was out of sight I fucked the box of chocolates on the ground and danced on them in a temper. I ran home, tears burning my eyes but not one fell. I ran upstairs, pulled off me clothes, not caring that the buttons on my shirt all burst open. I dragged on me Arsenal tracksuit. It wasn't a real one, Ma had got it for a quid 'cause they'd spelt Arsenal with two L's instead of one. Normally, I wouldn't even look at it but I didn't care what I wore or who saw me. I bundled the suit and the stupid tie and that fucking poncey shirt all together, ran back down the stairs, into the front room and threw them on the fire.

Da jumped out of his skin –

"Jesus Christ, what are yeh doing?"

He tried to grab the bundle out of the fire but in the few seconds that they were on they'd turned into an inferno.

"For fuck sake! What the fuck has got in teh yeh?"

He was jumping up and down like a madman because he'd burnt his fingers.

"Well, you said you didn't like it, you said I looked like a fucking – what was it? A fucking leprechaun!"

"I know I did, but I could've got a few bob for it all the same. There has to be some other gobshite who'd wear it."

I started hanging around more and more. Ma and Da kept asking me about work but I just shrugged my shoulders, said nothing and just kept on hanging around. It was a great year to be alive. The Beatles had brought out "Sgt Pepper's Lonely Hearts Club Band", the Monkeys were singing "Last Train To Clarkesville" and Procul Harem had a song called "Whiter Shade Of Pale" – none of us had a clue what the song was about but, it was great. By the mid-summer the "Summer Of Love" had even hit boring old Dublin. And what a summer! Everyday the sun split the sky. You could be guaranteed the minute you opened your eyes in the morning it was sunny. We never had to bring a raincoat "just in case it rained", 'cause it never did. We all started growing our hair and wearing beards. Some of us could get a real growth, others had goatees, it didn't matter. It didn't matter what colour it grew, what shape it grew or what you wore, everything was cool.

I hung around with Rasher Riley, Spike Connelly and Dammo Ryan.

Rasher got his name 'cause he'd worked as an apprentice in a butcher's; he jacked it in when he was told he had to do deliveries on one of those old black bikes that were relics from World War Two. Rasher said there was no way he was getting up on a fucking pensioner's push-bike. When the owner said if he didn't he'd be sacked Rasher held a cleaver to his neck and told him no one sacked the Rileys. And when Stuttery Arse apologised, Rasher quit.

Rasher was the coolest fucker in town. His hair grew quicker and longer and with kinky curls that always looked just ruffled enough. Never what you'd call messy, never that tight look that made you look like a Motown backing singer. When Rasher grew a beard, it grew in a week and it was the same dark colour of his hair. Not like the rest of us. We had red and brown and grey and blonde streaks coming through ours. He looked like Cat Stevens and anything that Rasher said always sounded cool, anything he ever did was cool and anything he ever wore looked cool. No one laughed when Rasher wore white jeans, no one called him a woofter when he got both his ears pierced, none of the girls complained of beard rash when Rasher kissed them. Anyone else would have to shave every five minutes to get a French kiss but Rasher could look like a black-bearded version of Santa Claus and still they'd let him tickle their tonsils.

Spike was fat, pimply, prematurely bald and the butt-end of all our jokes. He got his name from when as a kid he'd been walking on the spike fence around Stephen's Green and he fell straight on it. The poor fucker nearly lost his manhood but we all broke our bollox laughing. Spike had brains to burn, still what was the point in that when you were pig ugly? Brains were for when you were older or for when you were looking for a job and as none of us wanted work and we had no intention of ever getting older he was rightly fucked. Right now what was important was Girls, the Gang, Soccer, Films and Music, though not always in that order. But no matter what order you put them in, Spike was last. He was tone deaf, blind as fuck, he'd two left feet and a face that resembled the pictures they were showing us of the moon's surface. His only saving grace was that he was in the gang.

Dammo was short for Damien. He was small and stocky, but what a goer. Dammo didn't care what size the other fella was, he got stuck in and always won. He'd bite, kick, gouge your eyes out, anything that he needed in order to win. I always thanked the Lord that he was on our side, 'cause I'd have hated to have had to fight him. Dammo didn't really fit in with the "Summer of Love". He was only happy when he was fighting, but Summer of Love or not, there was always someone looking for a fight. You still had the mods and they thinking they were still it, but one snarl from the bould Dammo and they soon disappeared.

We had a stupid initiation ceremony for new members. I didn't know 'til after I joined that I was the only new member that the gang ever had. There were three things you had to do. First you had to rob cigarettes. That wasn't a problem. Mrs Ageey in the corner shop was a bit doddery. She should have been put out to grass years ago but thankfully for me, she was still there. She still lived with the opinion that everyone was very honest. All the other shops were well wise to us, but good old Mrs Ageey still hadn't copped on. She was a dirty aul bitch though. There was a pong the minute you opened the door. A smell of damp and old rags and fruit that was gone off. Her bananas were as black as the ace of spades and any worm with a bit of sense would have left the apples that took pride of place on her counter. Mrs Ageey had a beard. Not just two or three hairs sticking out of a mole, a full grey goatee. And she always wore the same black clothes and a shawl wrapped around her shoulders. She sat in her darkened shop, right beside the Calor Kosangas heater and the collection of fumes from her and that stale heat that comes from no ventilation along with the whiff of rotten fruit, was enough to knock you down. Yet we all went in, day after day, for one good reason: Dirty Ageey sold cigarettes, in ones, to the kids on their way to school, so regardless of the smell, she was always busy.

And she sold buttermilk. I was convinced it was just milk gone off but still she was the only shop you were guaranteed to get it in. I use to have to go for it every once in a while when Ma took a fancy and decided that she was going to become all domesticated. It was usually after watching yer woman Fanny Craddock on the telly. Jasus she was an awful-looking sight and the way she used to give out shite to her husband wasn't on. Sure the poor fucker would only be trying to get a sip of the sherry or wine and she'd snap the head off him. Da used to say you'd need something stronger than a drop of sherry to get up on her. It was the only time that I agreed with him.

Anyway, Dirty Ageeys was the place to go for the buttermilk and she had to go into the back store to get it for you. They said the back store was haunted. They said her son had hanged himself in there and that at night he still roamed the stores. Well, that might be, but it was never for the bananas anyway, 'cause they were more rotten than he'd have been. So when she went into the back to get the buttermilk I jumped the counter and grabbed two packets of ciggies before she came back. Then I was out that door and down the street.

The second part of the initiation was to get some drink. Again that wasn't that difficult. Da always had a few bottles of whiskey for visitors, so I just nicked one of the ones from the back of the press and left the bottles in the front intact.

The last thing I had to do was to meet up with the lads in the field around the back of the school. The field was overgrown and the grass had lost its battle with the weeds and the nettles. We had a little patch worn down and covered with cardboard so it would always be dry. They were all there, ready and waiting.

Rasher, who was sitting rolling a cigarette, spoke without looking up –

"Didn't think you were comin'."

Dammo cut in –

"And if you hadn't showed up I'd have got you and I'd have . . . "

"Well, I'm here, amn't I?"

"Did you bring the gear?"

I pulled the cigarettes from me pocket. Then I unzipped me jacket and held out the bottle.

Dammo made a grab for the bottle –

"Yeesss!"

He opened the cap and took a gulp, like it was a bottle of orange, then he coughed, spitting the mouthful out and holding his throat.

Rasher jumped up, rubbing his white jeans –

"You fuckin' eegit, be careful will yeh!"

Spike agreed –

"Yeah, Dammo."

Dammo was coughing and talking in a whisper –

"Sorry, right, but that's fuckin' white spirits, not alcohol."

Spike laughed –

"How could it be white spirits when it's brown in colour?"

"OK, Mr Fuckin' Professor, but it still tastes like shite."

We lit cigarettes and it was a joy to have your very own cigarette, one you didn't have to pass round. I hated getting the butts off Dammo, he hadn't a clue how to smoke and the tip was always wet when he'd had it. We passed around the whiskey, each of us taking a sip but no more. Eventually the taste got better, or else our taste buds got so damaged that we didn't know what was happening. It started affecting our talking, our speech slurred and we talked about the weirdest things on earth, things you'd never talk about in a month of Sundays at a normal time.

"Do yeh wank?" says Rasher looking up at the sky.

"Who?" says I.

"Any of yehs."

We all looked at each other.

Dammo took a real mouthful of whiskey before answering –

"I'm no fuckin' wanker, righ'?"

Spike agreed with him –

"Yeah, Rasher, fuck off."

I laughed.

Rasher laughed too –

"Well, Simmo, do you?"

"Mind your own business."

Dammo burst out laughing again –

"Ahhh, Simmo's a wanker."

"No I'm not. I never said tha'."

"But ye never said you didn't either."

"I do." Rasher said, his eyes never leaving the sky.

"Fuck off."

He sat up, took the bottle off Dammo, gulped back and continued –

"I do."

Dammo couldn't believe his ears –

"When?"

"All the time."

"Where?"

"In the jacks, in me bed, anywhere."

"Yeh do not."

"I'm telling you, I do."

"Well at what?"

"At the fuckin' dog, wha' do you think? Girls, of course."

"Wha' girls?"

"Any girls, girls on the road, on the telly, in the paper."

"That's a lot of girls, Rasher."

Rasher grabs hold of his mickey through his jeans –

"That's a lot of mickey, Dammo."

I laughed –

"You'll wanna be careful, Rasher, yeh'll run out of spunk if yeh keep on playing with yourself."

Dammo looked worried –

"Tha' can't happen, can it?"

"Sure what are you worried for, Dammo?" Rasher smiled, "I thought you didn't wank."

"I don't . . . well . . . not often."

We all cracked up, Spike started singing –

"Dammo is a wanker. Dammo is a wanker."

Dammo jumped on him –

"Shurrup righ'?"

Spike stopped. Dammo asked again –

"Ye can't run out, can yeh?"

"Fuck, yeah," says Rasher, "and yeh can go blind too."

Dammo's face was a picture, his eyes were flicking from one of us to another and back –

"Yeh can not, fuck off, you."

"Who said that?" Rasher replies holding his hands out as if he couldn't see.

In the end we all admitted that we wanked, which was a relief in a way as I had thought I was the only one who did. I turned to Rasher –

"Who's your favourite?"

"What do you mean?"

"Who's your favourite to wank to?"

"Depends. You know your woman in *Bonnie and Clyde*?"

"Faye Dunaway?"

"Yeah, her, or your woman in the Mama's and Papa's . . . "

I laughed –

"Who? Mama Cass?"

"No, not that fat fuck, the other one."

Spike joined in –

"I like Twiggy."

"Naw she's a dog. If you were riding her you'd be afraid she'd break," says Dammo making a face in disgust.

"Well don't worry, Dammo, I think Twiggy's not into you either." I said. I turned to Rasher again –

"And what girls on the street?"

"Not really girls, I like the older woman, more mature, knows what she wants."

"For fuck sake, Rasher, you're wanking to them, not riding

them. What difference does it make whether it's an aul one or a young one?"

"Big difference! I'm telling you."

We were all breaking our hearts laughing, tears were rolling down my face. He slugged the bottle and continued.

"I live in number six, righ'? So I couldn't wank to yer one in number eight, I don't know why, but I couldn't. And even though I think that young one round the corner on the Avenue is gorgeous I couldn't wank to her either, 'cause I hate that giggle of hers. But yeh know that one in the Close? The one who just moved in three weeks ago, she's married to yer man who works in the fire brigade. Now I could gladly wank to her all day."

Dammo answered casually –

"That's me Aunt Annie."

Rasher jumped up –

"Wha'?"

"Your woman, the one who moved in, who's married to the fireman. She's me ma's sister."

"Ah Jasus, Dammo, what did you have to say that for?"

"Well, she is."

"Fuck yeh, now I won't be able to wank about her anymore."

Spike and me were laughing, but Dammo was deadly serious as he answered –

"Ah no, it's all right, I wouldn't say she'd mind."

"It's not her I'm worried about, it's me. I couldn't wank to her anymore. Imagine, every time I did, I'd picture you."

That put an end to our conversation. It was time for the third part of my initiation. Rasher lit a cigarette and I pushed my two arms tightly together.

"This," he said "is the ultimate test of your loyalty. We'll count to twenty and you have to keep the cigarette between your arms. If you let it fall you can't be part of our gang, and if you're not with us you're against us . . . "

"Yeah," interrupts Dammo, snarling, "and you don't want to be against us, do you?"

Rasher dropped the cigarette between my arms. At first it was OK, but slowly my skin heated and as the ash grew longer, so did the pain. Rasher counted fast. Anyway, there was no way I was gonna falter but near the end it really hurt and when he said twenty I pulled my arms apart and grabbed the bottle, downing what was left, like a cowboy in a western who was about to get a bullet removed.

From that day on we ran together. We looked out for each other. Nothing could keep me away from them, or them from me. Ma and Da weren't happy, I wasn't bringing any money into the house but I didn't care; I knew that Da still had a good scam going with the money lending. I never asked for money, it was too much hassle. Ma would say to ask Da and Da would start on about when he was young and what he had to do to get a few bob and even though, nine times out of ten, he ended up giving me the money, it wasn't worth it. Besides, we had our own way of making money.

We had a crowbar. Dammo had spied it stuck in a pallet outside a factory and before anyone else claimed it he had it gone. At night we'd prise a telephone off the wall of the box and grab all the money. On a weekend that could be the guts of two or three quid. The trick was to prise it in such a way that you could fix it back without anyone realising it had been tampered with.

During the week there wasn't any point in robbing the phone boxes. No one ever used them, except maybe to ring the ambulance or the fire brigade, and that didn't cost anything anyway.

But one night things went wrong. It started off as usual. We watched the sky cloud over and the lights go out one by one in the houses. We sat on the hill of the Callyers. The Callyers was just a patch of waste ground but it was ideal for us. We could watch everyone and everything, we could see other gangs long before they saw us and by the time they spotted us, we'd have them ambushed. We could watch the squad cars and know that once they'd left, we'd have time to raid a phone box or two. We could also spy on the girls.

One night we spotted a group of three girls we'd never seen before, we chased down the hill, pushing and shoving each other.

"I don't like your one," I joked with Rasher.

"What do you mean my one? They're all mine."

We caught up with them and got chatting. It turned out they were from Inchicore and had been up visiting a girl from Ballyer who was in their school.

As there were three of them, it was understood that Spike was gonna be the odd man out, but Dammo had got a bit mouthy with one of the girls and instead of talking to him she blanked him completely and started talking to Spike. At first Spike didn't know what to do, after all, none of us had ever seen him with anyone before, but, as the conversation went on, the gap between one sentence and the next shortened for him and before the end of the night you couldn't shut him up. Dammo was being a right fucking eejit. We had an unwritten rule that if this kind of thing happened and there was an odd man out, the odd man out made himself scarce. But not Dammo, he kept butting in on everyone's conversations, saying stupid things, things fellas only said out of earshot like, "I'd say you ride" and "All Inchicore girls are good things".

The girls were getting really nervous around him and we were all gettin' pissed off. Rasher tried to change the subject –

"How about a few chips?"

We all walked to the chipper and between us all we had

enough for three singles and three cans of coke. Rasher handed a single and can to me and Dammo.

"What about me?" says Dammo.

"Later," says Rasher, turning to his girl and offering her chips.

"What de yeh mean 'Later'?"

Rasher walked back –

"Dammo, your being a fuckin' wanker here, yeh don't have a girl so yeh don't get chips and coke, OK?"

"So if I had a girl I'd get the chips?"

Rasher nodded.

"Righ' then," says Dammo, and he grabs Spike's girl by the arm, "I've got this one so give me the fucking chips."

She tries to push him off but he's too strong.

"Leave her alone," shouts Spike.

"Or wha'?"

Dammo pushes her away and moves toward Spike –

"C'mon Stud, wha' the fuck will yeh do?"

"Just fuck off."

Dammo starts roughing Spike's hair –

"Will you make me, yeh spineless little fuck?"

He starts pushing Spike. I can see the girls are nervous, so is Spike. I'd had enough –

"Give it fuckin' up, Dammo."

Dammo swung round and I could see that hate he got in his eyes when he was about to fight.

"You," he hissed through his teeth, "mind yer own fuckin' business."

I couldn't back down, the girls were watching for one, but I also knew that if I let Dammo win this he'd start treating me like another Spike.

"I'm making it my business."

He started waving his hands at me, encouraging me to have a go –

"Right, come on, you and me, here, now."

The girls all took to running, Rasher called to them –

"No girls, come on, everything's cool, the lads are only messing."

I wanted to look in their direction too, but I knew the minute I took my eye off Dammo he'd be on me like a light, so I stood staring him out.

He called me again –

"Well, come on Simmo, I've been waiting for this for a long time."

Rasher had turned back, he was fuming –

"What the fuck are you lot playing at?"

We stood staring at each other. My eyes never shifted as I spoke –

"Why don't you ask this lunatic what's wrong?"

"Dammo, what the fuck was wrong with you tonigh'?"

"Me? Fuck all wrong with me, it's you lot, you get a smell of pussy and you all forget your mates."

"Is this about the chips?"

Dammo laughed –

"The chips, yeah it's about the chips."

"For fuck sake, we hadn't enough money teh buy anymore fuckin' chips."

Dammo takes to runnin' to the telephone box –

"You needed money, did yeh?"

He has the crowbar out and starts pulling the box off the wall. At the roundabout we see a squad car.

"Jesus Christ, Dammo, the pigs."

But Dammo keeps wrecking the phone box.

The squad car spots us and quickens up.

Rasher shouts again –

"Dammo, give it up."

But Dammo ignores him.

Rasher runs to him and grabs his arm. It's like slow motion

as Dammo swings around and connects with the side of Rasher's head. Rasher's skull opens, there's blood everywhere, it's only then that we realise he's hit him with the crowbar.

For what seems like minutes we stand and watch. Suddenly the squad car is there.

Spike's voice brings me out of my trance –

"Run, Simmo, come on, we have to get out of here."

I ran faster than I ever ran in my life. Spike was yards behind and he was shouting –

"Simmo, hold up."

But I couldn't, I couldn't stop my legs running or the tears from streaming down my face. His voice faded, I knew he'd stopped running but I kept going, I ran the length of the fields across the dump, jumping rubbish heaps, avoiding the rats that had come for their midnight snacks. I fell but my momentum kept me moving on all fours until I was back on my feet, upright and running again. I was on the path, I could hear an ambulance in the background, siren blasting the peace of the night – Rasher's ambulance. Suddenly in front of me a couple, walking hand and hand. I ran through them –

"Hey, watch it mate . . . " I kept moving, not muttering a word. "Fucking prick."

I was home. I searched for my key, trying all my pockets before I found it. I let it fall, butter fingers. I scraped it around the brass Yale keyhole before finding its place and inserting it. I pushed hard and the door flew open, slamming against the hall wall.

"Is that you Paul?" Da's voice.

I said nothing, just hurried to the kitchen.

I opened the cold press and took out the milk, I shook it hard so the cream wouldn't be at the top of the bottle. Then I pressed down on the tinfoil top and took it off. For the first time I realised how out of breath I was. I took a mouthful and couldn't take it away from my lips, as I gulped I could feel milk escape my mouth and cascade down the side of my cheeks. I kept the bottle to my lips until there was nothing left. I slumped onto the nearest chair, held my head back, and breathed hard through my nostrils. Long hard breaths that filled my lungs the way the PE teacher had taught us, and when I couldn't take another inch of air, I exhaled hard until there was nothing left, not one morsel and then I started all over again.

"Jesus Christ, look at the state of you!"

Da's voice startled me. I could feel a cold shiver run the length of my spine and ruffle the hairs on the back of my neck. As the words registered I looked down at myself. He was right. I looked like something the cat dragged in. My top was stuck to me with sweat, steam was rising from me like a horse after the Grand National and my jeans were destroyed with the filth of the rubbish dump. I was cut and the blood was matted in with dirt and clay and clothing.

"Who did this to yeh?" He was over me. "Tell me son, I'll kill him, I'll fucking kill him!"

"Leave it, Da." I went to get up but I couldn't.

"We'd better get you to the hospital."

"No, Da, please, leave it."

"Leave it? You're in bits, you need stitches."

"I can't go teh hospital," I fell silent for a second. "There's been an accident . . . Rasher's . . . dead."

"Dead? What do you mean dead? Rasher can't be dead! Have you been taking that funny stuff?"

"Rasher's dead, Da, DEAD."

For the first time in his life my Da didn't shout at me. He pulled up a chair and sat feet away from me, listening. And for the first time in my life I talked to him, I told him everything, every little detail. I never looked up from my shoes until the last word was spoken. He looked at me in silence for what seemed like minutes but what could only have been seconds.

"You're in big shit, son. BIG SHIT." He stood and walked to the window. "First off, we need to get you out of them clothes, they have to be burnt, and you, you need to be cleaned up."

He cleared the sink of the couple of cups that were in it and started running water into it.

"Get out of them clothes."

He took the Zip firelighters out of the press and placed half the box in the grate of the fire. Normally he was giving out about the amount of the stuff we used. As I stripped, he threw the clothes on the fire, they were that damp that they were nearly put out the firelighters. He walked to the press under the sink and took out his tin of lighter fuel. He sprayed it over the clothes and they turned into an inferno. I stood in me Y-fronts.

"Come on, give me them too."

I hesitated.

"This is no time for modesty, give me the fucking things."

I got out of them and threw them on the fire.

"Right, get washed. I'll find you some clothes."

He came back with the Arsenal tracksuit and a pair of shoes, socks, Y-fronts and a T-shirt. The cuts didn't look too bad when they were cleaned up.

Da made a few phone calls and spoke in mumbles. Minutes later we were driving to Spike's house. The only conversation between us was my directions.

Da went in on his own. When the door opened, there seemed to be a lot of waving of hands and suddenly Da had Spike's Da on the ground and he was kicking lumps out of him. Spike's Ma was screaming, I was out of the car and over like a light.

"Give it up, you two, will ye?"

Da didn't stop kicking him.

"Da! For fuck sake, do you want the guards on us?"

That seemed to do the trick, he stopped kicking. The poor fucker struggled to his feet with the help of his wife.

Da spoke to him as if nothing had happened –

"Listen, all I want is for your son to keep his mouth shut."

The man composed himself –

"And I'm telling you, my son, has done nothing to keep shut about."

Da looked ready to get stuck in again, I had to do something –

"Is Spike here?"

They looked at me like I'd two heads –

"Michael, is Michael here?"

They looked at each other, then the man nodded to his wife and she went up the stairs. He started into the hallway –

"I suppose you'd best come in."

The kitchen was small but tidy. Da pulled out a packet of cigarettes and offered the man one.

"No thanks, we don't smoke in this house."

Da shrugged –

"Suit yerself."

Then lit up his own. I'd have loved a cigarette but I didn't think now was the right time to tell him I smoked.

Spike came into the room followed by his Ma. His eyes looked raw with redness and I knew he'd been crying. He was nervously fixing his glasses on his nose as he stood there.

His father spoke –

"Michael, where were you tonight?"

"Out."

"Out where?"

"Just out hanging around with me mates."

I knew he was trying to bluff his way out of this. None of our parents knew our mates, so he could say he was anywhere.

"Were you with this . . . " His father contemplated calling me a little fucker, but changed his mind, "this lad."

Spike answered too quickly –

"No."

Da remained seated but his voice was coarse and to the point –

"This ain't the time for your fucking lies, lad. You're up to your neck in shit so my advice is to start telling the truth and QUICK."

Spike started crying, I knew he would. His mother put her hand around his shoulder –

"It's all right, son, it's all right."

Da laughed –

"I'm glad you think it's OK, 'cause I think a murder charge is far from OK."

"I never done nothin'," cried Spike.

"Don't matter. Rasher's dead and you were there."

Da tapped his ash on the floor and proceeded to tell Spike's ma and da the whole story. By the time he'd ended they were speechless.

"So, I think you're going to have to get your son offside for a while."

They looked puzzled. Da sighed –

"Get him out of here. If the police ask him anything he's liable to spill the beans."

"But you heard him, he didn't do anything."

"And since when did it fuckin' matter what you did or didn't do? He was at the scene of the crime, he was part of the gang, he'll go down, it's as simple as that. So my advice is to get him offside until this thing blows over."

"But where can he go?"

"Jesus Christ, I don't know. You must have some fuckin' family down the bog."

Spike's mother started crying, his father looked defeated –

"There's an uncle in Meath . . . "

Da cut across him –

"That's perfect," he reached into his pocket and threw a twenty pound note onto the table. "That'll cover his travel expenses and keep for a few weeks."

We walked out, Da stubbing another fag on the ground. As

we left I looked at Spike and he at me and at that moment I knew something had changed forever.

We drove around 'til early morning but we didn't catch sight of Dammo. We'd been to his house and after a little of Da's persuasion we found out that he had been home but had packed some things and was gone again.

Da drove for home. As we turned our corner we saw the squad car at our driveway. Luckily they hadn't noticed us. Da turned the car and headed towards town –

"What now?"

He drove for a while without answering, then once again smoked half a cigarette before talking –

"We have to get you offside too. The guards are looking for someone to pin this one on. They've nothing to tie you to it but if they get you today they'll find something. You'll have to go to your Uncle Joe in England. I'll ring him."

We drove to a bank and Da came back with a large brown envelope. From there we headed to Dun Laoghaire. There was a boat in. Suddenly it sank in –

"Da, I haven't even said goodbye to Ma."

He couldn't look at me –

"I'll look after your mother, she'll be grand." Not turning, he pointed to the envelope. "Take that with you, there's a few bob in Irish and some English."

I looked inside it. There was at least five hundred quid going by the amount of fifties in it.

"Go on," he said. "That boat won't wait."

I got out. At that moment I wished we could have been more like the Waltons, with hugs and kisses and I-love-you's but I just stood awkwardly and he just puffed on the butt in his hand. He started the engine –

"I'll make sure Joe is waiting at the other end. Take it easy, Paul."

He drove away and I watched 'til he was out of sight.

Chapter Twenty

Uncle Joe picked me up off the boat and drove me to London. He hardly spoke a word all the way down, except –

"How's yer aul fella?" and after I said OK there was a half hour silence before he continued the conversation where he let off –

"And your ma?" and that was that, apart from cursing me from a height when we got a puncture.

"Fuck yeh," he said, looking at the shredded tyre, then he looked at me, "This is all your fucking fault, if it wasn't for you I wouldn't have been fucking driving the bollox out of her."

He started undoing the nuts but the ratchet slipped and caught his hand –

"Fuck it!" he screamed, jumping to his feet and kicking the wheel. He sucked the blood that was pouring from the cut.

"Fix the fucking thing, would yeh? Do something con-fucking-structive."

It was the first time I'd ever done it but eventually I managed to get the wheel off and the new one on.

The reception in his house wasn't any better. His wife grunted something about the hour of the night it was and that she didn't know where I was going to sleep. They'd two kids, a fella about me own age who didn't even look up from the telly and a daughter who looked a right tart with her caked-on make-up and her chewing gum that she insisted on blowing bubbles with all during dinner.

I slept for six months on their sofa, eating the shittiest meals I ever ate, and spent the days cleaning cars in Uncle Joe's kippy garage. I got three letters from me Ma, none of which ever mentioned Rasher. One day I just had enough. I'd been cleaning shitty cars all morning and the mechanic, if that's what you could call him, had spent the day calling me Paddy. I'd told him I was Paul or Simmo but he smirked his ugly face and said –

"Naw, as long as you're on English soil you'll be Paddy, just the same as he'll" (he pointed to the turban-headed young fella sweeping the floor) "always be Paki. OK?"

All his cronies laughed in unison.

"And if you want to get technical about it, it's Paki Bastard and Paddy Bastard!"

They all laughed again. He grabbed the little Paki lad by the shoulder –

"Ain't that right, Paki Bastard?"

"Yes, yes that's right, whatever you say, boss."

He pushed him away and kicked the neat pile of dust, oily rags and paper that the lad had swept up, scattering it all over the place again.

"I thought you were told to clean all that up?"

The lad started sweeping again –

"Sorry boss, I'll get it done this minute."

They went to walk away.

"I'm no bastard."

He turned slowly, calling to his mates –

"I don't think my hearing is what it used to be. I could have sworn I heard Paddy say something." He looked at me, his eyes full of hate. "What did you say, Paddy?"

"I ain't no Paddy and I ain't no fucking bastard, yeh fuckin' bastard."

Paki ran for cover.

The mechanic turned smiling to his friends. I knew what was coming. He talked to them –

"I think thick Paddy needs to be taught a lesson or . . . " before he finished the sentence he swung around, propelling the chain he held right at my face, "twooo . . . "

I ducked and was ten yards from him before he regained his composure. He shouted to his gang –

"Get the little fucker!"

But it was too late. I was gone. I ran to Uncle Joe's, packed my bag and was out of there before anyone even knew I'd been.

I still had most of the money Da had given me. I stayed two nights in a hotel. The manager was a bit dubious but once I'd paid up-front he agreed. I walked the streets and everything I saw was just so much bigger than Dublin. The shops were ten times the size, the streets twice as wide. The cars were newer, everyone seemed to be driving around in brand new cars and the girls were gamier. You knew by the look in their eyes that the streets of London might have been paved with gold but that there was a distinct lack of virgins around. I reached paradise, it was called Soho, but to me it was paradise. Girls stood on every corner offering their services. And they were goodlooking too and black. I'd never seen a black girl before, not 'til I hit London and now that I *had,* I couldn't get over how many of them there were. I couldn't help but stare either, I mean to say they look so fucking different. I could imagine the lads back home hearing that Simmo had got a bit of black. We'd often talked about girls and how they looked and we all agreed we'd love a black bird. Tommo Crosby said his brother had been to Barbados with the navy and he said black girls knew every trick in the book. My thoughts were disturbed by a voice –

"Hey man, are you gonna stand there winda shoppin' awl night or is you up for some business?"

I hadn't even noticed that I'd been staring at the one girl for so long, I went to apologise but she was over grabbing my hand and running it down the length of her body –

"Naw need to apologise babee, you feel Tilda, feel how much Tilda wants you."

I could feel my face go red and in me jeans I could feel a hard-on coming, "Jesus, of all the times for a hard-on!".

She ran her hand along my body and of course found me horn –

"Ohhh, seems Babee wants Tilda too."

I pushed her hand away, she laughed –

"That's OK, sweetheart, that's no reason to feel embarrassed, Tilda would love to get that sweet white pudding between her legs."

Freddie twinged. Jesus Christ, this was getting embarrassing. I'd called me prick *Freddie* one night with the lads. It was Rasher's fault, Rasher always started those stupid conversations. He'd asked had anyone got a name for their dick. We'd all told him to fuck off but he'd insisted –

"Ah come on, we name everything else, so why not our dicks. My Da calls the car *Maisie the Mini*, Ma calls her bike *Mike*, so we have to christen our dicks."

"OK," I said, "so go on, you name yours first."

He sat looking studerious, then answered –

"Padraig!"

"Padraig? Where the fuck did you get that from?"

"I thought I'd keep it Irish, so *Padraig the Prick*."

It was Spike's turn; he chose *Tommy the Todger*.

Dammo, after much coaxing, said *Jock the Cock*, and I picked *Freddie the Flute*.

So Freddie twitched away, eager to get out and get to tasks

with Tilda. I wondered had she got a name for her part. Like *Paula the Pussy* or *Nanny the Fanny* but I hadn't time to answer myself. Her hand was back on my jeans and caressing Freddie. Freddie was loving the attention –

"Soo Baabbee, do you want to have a good time?"

I couldn't answer, Freddie was as hard as I could ever remember him and with all the rubbing he was getting, I was sure it wouldn't be long before he was shooting his load into my jocks. I had to concentrate; I started counting numbers.

One . . . two . . . three . . . four . . . five . . . six . . . seven . . . eight . . . nine . . .

Her hand rubbed the inside of my leg –

"Oohhh, you must work out!"

ten . . . eleven . . . twelve . . .

"Babbee, we can make sweet music, yeah?"

I nodded.

Thirteen . . . fourteen . . .

Her hand reached for my pockets –

"You got some money for me, honey?"

I grabbed her hand. She smiled and her other hand moved like an octopus around and into my pocket. I stopped that too.

"Honey babe, you wouldn't deny Tilda a little pressie for being a good girl, would you?"

Freddie was willing to swear his life savings away –

"How much?"

Tilda pulled away from my grip and rubbed Freddie again, Freddie jumped with delight –

"Tilda really wants to see that, it feels so eager, so young. It's twenty pounds for half an hour and you can come as many times as you like."

"OK." I replied. Freddie was delighted, he dribbled with delight.

I opened my jacket and took out my wallet. Tilda's eyes

opened wide. I pulled the twenty out and handed it to her. She was eager to get her hands on the rest –

"Honey, we need a twenty pound deposit on the room too," she saw me hesitate, "unless you want to do it out here?"

I handed over the twenty.

She tucked both twenties into her bra.

"You know, Babbee, that jacket will be on the floor when we go into the room and anyone could come in and rob it."

"I'll take my chances."

Her hands were off me now, and her eyes were darting all around. Freddie was getting frustrated, he wanted to be out and at it. She pointed to a darkened doorway on the opposite side of the road –

"See over there?" I nodded. "You go over there and go in, wait at the end of the stairs for me, I'll be with you in two minutes."

I looked suspiciously at her.

"Don't worry, baabbee, Tilda ain't about to miss out on your young meat. It's just the place is crawling with po-lease and you don't want your scrawny white ass hauled up in court do you? You go over an' Tilda will be with you in a mo."

Reluctantly I left her, Freddie rushing me across the road and into the doorway. I waited ten minutes and watched as a series of fat men came guiltily down the stairs. Eventually I went out into the street and looked for Tilda but she was nowhere to be found. As I left Soho, a pretty Chinese girl called to me.

"Save it, love," I replied, "I'm not interested."

She moved back into the shadows, Freddie quivered in my jeans.

"And you can fuck off too," I said out loud. "You've cost me forty quid already tonight."

* * *

It's amazing how fast you grow up in London. I walked the length and breadth of the city looking for work. Finally I found a site run by a fella from Kildare. I worked as a labourer. The work was hard but it paid well and we were out in the sunshine having the crack most of the time. The winters weren't fun at all. If there was work you got pissed on and if there wasn't any work you ended up spending your money in the pub. When you ran out of money the pub let you run a tab. It was great at the time but later when you were paying half your wages across the counter for something that was well down the sewage system, it wasn't a laughing matter. I tried to stay out of the pub but there was nothing else to do. We all shared the same digs, so there'd be no one in, and it wasn't as though we were good housekeepers. Our beds were mattresses on the floor and we'd little or no furniture and only a radio that was as temperamental as the weather.

In 1972 things changed. Shit had been happening in the North for a while but still, despite British soldiers getting killed, it never carried over to the mainland and so the English were happy to have the "Paddy" doing all the grafting. In a strange way the troubles were a talking point. They'd say that they felt sorry for us when Bloody Sunday happened and they felt it was only right when the British Embassy burned down a few days later. But when the IRA bombed Aldershot, the tide changed.

We were spat at walking down the street, pubs refused to serve us. The digs, kip that it was, asked us to leave and the boss lost his contract. Christ almighty! They didn't care what your circumstances were; they didn't care if you were Catholic or Protestant, if you were a nationalist or not. You were a Paddy and that was enough. The police began to raid houses and clubs and God help you if you as much as said boo to them. Most of the lads went back home until it cooled off, but I didn't.

I'd just start going with Nancy. She was from Middlesex and although we had only known each other for six weeks I knew this was it. Nancy worked as a nurse. I met her at a dance in Kilburn. At home I'd have run a mile from a *céilí* but in Britain it seemed more practical and in fact, I used to long for the next one to come while walking out the door of the one that had just finished. And it was there that I saw Nancy, standing in the row of girls that always stood against the wall, waiting to be asked to dance. All us fellas used to stand along the bar, looking at the girls in the same way you'd look at cattle in a mart.

Podge the gaffer was fifty but he'd still eye them up and as they went by he'd shout –

"Heifer!" as if he was by the rails of the cattle sale in Kildare town.

The girls would look at him as though he had two heads but he had a load of pints in him and another in his hand so he didn't give a shite. To the gaffer a heifer was the biggest compliment he could pay a girl. He used to say a heifer had a great pair of hind legs and their main asset was the fact that they hadn't had a calf yet. Nancy was a great heifer.

I watched her from the comfort of the bar, our eyes meeting and holding for a few seconds until she'd look away, only to look back and find me still staring. I'd come a long way in London with the girls, a long way from my experience in Soho. I'd filled out, all that lugging of bricks and mixing of cement had hardened my body and I noticed that I often got a second glance from the girls in the factory across the road from where we were working.

* * *

It was one of them that I finally lost me virginity to. I met her in the local shop, I was getting myself a ham roll and she invited me to a party in her new flat. I arrived in my jeans and T-shirt to find everyone else in suits. They all sipped wine and I'd brought cans and when the sandwiches came around they were so small I had to keep a tray all to myself, just to get a few decent mouthfuls.

I could see a few of them sniggering at me, down their rimmed glasses. I was about to leave. I'd been standing on my own for over twenty minutes. I headed for the door but she was there –

"You can't go."

I looked around –

"This ain't quite my scene."

She smiled, looking out at them –

"Oh, they're good fun really, they just take a bit of getting used to, that's all."

"Maybe I don't want to get to know them."

She rubbed her leg up against my thigh –

"And what about me? Do you want to get used to me?"

"Maybe."

"Maybe? You don't sound too certain."

Her hand reached Freddie and she squeezed –

"But he is."

She pulled me into the nearest room. We kissed as we fell on the bed, she ripped at my clothes as I ripped at hers. She bit me, hard, right on the nipple but I was that mad to finally lose my virginity that I wouldn't have cared if she cut the nipple off. I was clumsy; I couldn't get the buttons on her top open, she, meanwhile, had my shirt off and was well on the way to having all the buttons on my Levi's and the buckle of my belt open. She yanked my jeans down, I got another button open, her hand pulled hard on Freddie. I'd no clean underwear so I'd decided to wear none, it seemed to turn her on.

I'd four buttons open. She stopped and pulled her blouse over her head, I buried my head in the breast fat that hung over her bra, she pulled mercilessly at Fred. I thought she might break the skin but Fred seemed to enjoy the sensation. Then much to both our surprises, I came. It happened in a flash. One minute I was busy trying to worm me tongue past her bra and onto a nipple, while she was busy chugging at Freddie. Next thing Freddie was standing in an arched position, the one that stiffens not just him but the rest of me body. The one that starts somewhere in the far recesses of my belly, runs through my balls at about three hundred miles an hour and shoots out of the purple little hat at the top at the same time as I say –

"Yes, Yes, YES."

Except this time I was saying –

"No, NO, NOOOO . . . "

As the fountain erupted. It shot everywhere, I bit hard on her saggy flesh and she, excited by it all, pulled harder as my spunk shot out. I didn't think it was ever going to stop, she was pulling like a woman possessed and just as I thought nothing else could happen, Freddie began to harden again. I took her hand away and lay her down. She helped me to help her out of the rest of her clothes. She lay before me, the layers of pink flesh in contrast to my bronzed labourer's body. She pulled me close and directed me into her wet openness. Inside I started moving deeper, helped by her heels that dug into my calves and dictated the pace of my movement. She was loud, instructing me every step of the way –

"Oh, yes . . . that's it . . . yes, like that . . . a little harder . . . Oh, yes, make me come . . . not so fast . . . take your time."

But once again Freddie was getting ready for another

offloading. He started dictating my strokes which suddenly had me jerking.

This time it was her turn to scream "No". But it didn't matter, for the second time I was coming and resigned to defeat, she pulled me tightly to her, eager to drain every drop.

I collapsed beside her, out of breath and totally fulfilled. She looked disgusted as she lit her cigarette. I asked what was wrong.

"What's wrong? What was that? What the fuck did you think you were doing? Running the hundred metres? I kinda had a marathon runner in mind."

I clumsily tried to apologise.

"Christ, don't make it any worse by apologising for coming. God almighty, anyone would think you were a virgin."

Suddenly it clicked with her. She was up on her elbow, her massive tits swayed toward me with the movement. She smiled –

"You are a virgin, aren't you?"

My silence gave her her answer. She laughed out loud –

"I don't fucking believe it."

I got annoyed –

"Yeah, go on, have your laugh."

I turned away from her and went to get out of the bed. She grabbed me –

"No, don't go, I wasn't laughing . . . "

"The fuck you weren't!"

"No, I don't mean I wasn't laughing. I mean . . . I'm happy . . . I can't believe that someone like you hasn't had a string of broken hearts behind him."

She pulled me into the darkness that was her cleavage and over the course of that weekend and, every evening for weeks afterwards, she taught me just about everything I had ever dreamt about . . . and quite a few things that the lads had never even contemplated.

Eventually Nancy came over, I watched her move across the room, she walked right up to where we were all standing –

"Are you going to ask me to dance or are you going to spend your whole night just looking at me?"

As we moved to the dance floor, Gaffer shouted –

"Heifer."

The rest of the night was spent dancing with Nancy and when the dance was over we headed to the local kebab shop and sat and talked until the sun rose. I walked her to her flat and outside she kissed me in a way I had never been kissed before. Within two weeks we'd moved in together and I spent every moment of my day thinking about her. We even talked about marrying. One of those crazy eloping weddings where we just went off and did it and didn't tell a soul about it until afterwards.

But the Aldershot bomb ruined everything. She stood by me despite all the abuse, despite me losing my job, despite the fact that her friends and family ignored her. No matter what, she was there for me, but it was *me, I* had to become independent again. *I* had to be the one paying in the restaurant, *I* had to be the one paying the rent and buying her flowers on a Friday like I had done every Friday since we'd met. My mood changed, I spent day after day watching stupid kids' programmes, answering job adverts, knowing once they heard my voice I didn't stand a chance. I walked the streets, going from site to site looking for work but there was none, at least not for the Paddies.

Then one day, as I walked from another site around Hyde Park, a car pulled up –

"Hey, Simmo."

I spun round and saw Dammo. I smiled instinctively, then I remembered back to Dublin and that night –

"What the fuck do you want?"

I went to walk on but he drove alongside me –

"Come on, Simmo, water under the bridge, yeah?"

Water under the bridge. He had killed our best mate and all he could call it was water under the bridge. I was at his car like a light, through his open window, me arms around his neck –

"Yeh little fuck, *yeh little fuck!*"

His hands were flapping but I had a hold of his windpipe and I was sucking the life out of him. Out of the corner of my eye I spotted a policeman looking in our direction. He stopped, studied our movements and started to walk our way. I released my grip. Dammo spluttered out and gasped for a breath.

"Is everything OK here, gents?"

Dammo still couldn't talk but he nodded in the bobby's direction. I answered –

"Everything's grand, nar a bother. He just swallowed the wrong way, yeh know yerself, a chicken-bone. They're deadly so they are."

He studied us.

"Are both of you Irish?"

"Yeah, that's right."

"What are you doing 'round this area?"

"Looking for a bit of work."

The policeman moved closer –

"Well, why don't you get back into your car and fuck off back to Ireland or whatever sewer you crawled out of. There's no jobs for your kind here!"

I said nothing more. I just got in and Dammo drove. The first corner we turned I shouted –

"Let me the fuck out of here."

Dammo pulled in, I opened the door –

"Jesus, Simmo, can't we talk?"

"Ain't nothin teh talk about."

I went to get out.

"I know of some work, good pay, no shit."

"I'm not interested."

"Suit yerself, I just thought you was desperate."

"Not that desperate."

I got out.

"For fuck sake, Simmo, do yeh think I *meant* to kill Rasher?"

I looked at him –

"I don't know whether you did or not, all I know is you did."

"Yeah, and I've had to live with that ever since, every fucking night I wake up in a cold sweat 'cause of it."

I leaned into the car –

"Answer me one thing, why the fuck did you run?"

"'Cause I was scared shitless."

I had never thought of that. It sounds funny but in all the time since that night, in all the different scenarios that I played out, not once had Dammo run because he was scared.

"You shouldn't have run."

He looked straight ahead again –

"Don't I know it, but I did. I lost me head. I panicked. I keep thinking I should have stood me ground, taken the heat off you and Spike. And maybe if I had, the police would've called the ambulance sooner and Rasher would have been . . . "

"Don't . . . don't, Dammo. Rasher was dead the minute he hit the ground."

"But I still *killed* him, Simmo."

There was nothing that could be said. He was right and there was no point in saying any different. I changed the subject.

"So tell me about this job?"

He looked back at me –

"You mean?"

"Yeah, why not?"

I should have known that anything that Dammo was involved with wouldn't be exactly legitimate. He was running bouncers on club doors, Irish club doors, making sure that no "Paddy Bashing" was taking place.

"Christ, I don't know, Dammo, I've never done that kind of thing before."

He laughed –

"For fuck sake, Simmo, would yeh listen to yerself? This is the same Simmo who was the best goer I ever saw, isn't it?"

"That's different."

"How?"

"We were only kids back then."

"Yeah, *exactly,* and look at yeh now, yer a fucking killing machine. Those arms will be enough to put anyone off trying to fuck with yeh."

He took my hesitation as a *yes*.

"Great, here's the address, get there at nine and I'll get you fixed up with a monkey-suit."

"Jasus, Dammo, you never said anything about a monkey-suit, I'm not wearing a fucking monkey-suit."

"Not even for a hundred pound a night, for four hours' work?"

Nancy was against the idea –

"Paul, we don't need the money that badly."

"I need it. I need to be bringing in a wage, Nancy. It matters to me."

Reluctantly she agreed.

It wasn't as bad as I thought it would be. There were six of us, three on the door and three on the dance floor. The lads were all Irish and although they were as thick as shite, they covered each other. There was the odd scuffle but nothing that we couldn't handle. Dammo didn't work the door himself, he'd show up at some stage in the night, handing us our wages and every now and again offering the lads work at another club after closing time at the one we manned. He always asked me but I was always in too much of a hurry to get back to Nancy. The extra money came in handy and Nancy even took to working nights so we could spend more time together during the day.

One night a gang of English football fans came down to the club. There were about twenty in all. As usual they didn't all come together but in twos, hoping to get in, but we were wise to them and refused them all. They left, shouting the usual insults about us being *murderers* and *thicko Paddies* but that was that.

We quickly forgot about them. Frogman (because instead of saying "I told you so," he always pronounced it, "toad yeh so") was telling us about a film he'd seen called *Last Tango In Paris*.

"I swear teh Jasus, lads, the amount of tit in that film is unbelievable."

In the background they were playing a slow set with Donny Osmond's "Puppy Love" being followed by Roberta Flack's "The First Time Ever I Saw Your Face" and Harry Nilsson's "Without You". Big Mac and me were arguing over who Roberta's song was about. I was adamant it was Bob Dylan but he was saying Don McLean and even though I was arguing the toss, inside I had a niggling suspicion that he was right. Suddenly around the bend a car came skidding. The driver didn't seem to be in full control because it was swerving from one side to the other but we all knew where it was heading. Big Mac was the first to react, he slammed the doors closed and called for the iron bar that we used for securing it at closing. While I went to fetch it he leaned his weight against the door –

"Big Mac, get away from the fuckin' . . . "

As I tried to finish my sentence the door came crashing in with the impact of the car. Big Mac lay motionless underneath. They were out of the car and running –

"Paddy Bastards Go Home."

As the words landed so did the petrol bomb, smashing on impact with Frogman's face and exploding into an inferno.

Frogman screamed in agony, a scream I'd never heard the like of before. His pain catapulted him out into the street, where he fell on the ground. I ran out pulling off my jacket but the gang stopped me getting to him.

Eventually the revellers came out. The gang, seeing the onflux ran off chanting "Rule Brittania".

We managed to put the flames out before the ambulance came and they brought him to the hospital, even though we all knew it was a hopeless case. Big Mac lasted eight days but never regained consciousness.

It made the news, not headlines. It seemed that quite a few people agreed with the mentality of revenge.

Dammo was mad. I'd known him to go out on a limb before but this time he was really mad.

"We can't let them away with this. If we do they'll walk all over us."

Sammy L agreed, but Sammy L would do anything for a fight.

"Look," I reasoned, "we're all angry at the moment . . . "

"Angry," shouted Dammo. "I'd say that's the understatement of the fuckin' year."

I continued –

"Well, OK, call it what you like but we're better off leaving it in the hands of the police."

"I don't believe I'm hearing this." He was walking up and down in the warehouse we had met at. "They kill two of us and you say let the police handle it." He kicked a large cardboard box marked television and you could hear the screen break. "The police don't give a fuck about Paddies. They all say the only good Paddy is a dead one."

In my heart I knew he was right –

"Well, what do you think we should do?"

"I think we should retaliate. They hit our club so let's hit one of theirs."

"But we could hurt innocent people, let's wait 'til we can find out who done it and get them."

Sammy L spoke –

"The lads were innocent and they killed them. Frogman had a wife and five daughters . . . his wife had just told him she was pregnant again but no one cared about that."

He was right, in a strange kind of way he was right, or at least I had no good argument to give against it.

So Sammy L, Dammo, Johnny, Muscles and me got in Dammo's car and drove around for an hour or two. Eventually we spotted a fella and girl walking down a street with not a car or person in sight.

Dammo sped up and we bundled the two of them into the car.

He was struggling under the weight of Johnny and she was whimpering like a doll –

"Shut her fucking up!"

Sammy L smacked her open-handed across the face – she simmered down but still sobbed –

"What's going on? What did we do? Is it money? Here . . . " She held out her bag "Take it . . . go on, please, take it."

No one answered and that seemed to make her worse.

"Please . . . please don't hurt us . . . please . . . "

Dammo turned away from the wheel –

"Will you PLEASE shut the fuck up!"

We reached the warehouse. We bundled them both inside, he tried to struggle against it, burying his feet into the ground but Muscles and Sammy L just took one arm each and lifted him in.

Dammo paced up and down in front of them –

"You're not so fucking brave now are yeh?"

The lad looked confused –

"What are you on about?"

Without warning Dammo punched him in the stomach, it was only Sammy L and Muscles' hold on him that kept him from falling.

"Don't get fucking smart with me, right?"

He moaned –

"I . . . I . . . I don't know what you're on about."

Dammo punched him three more times, each time harder than the last, like a punch-bag. She started crying, Dammo pointed at her, shouting –

"And you, you can shut up or you'll get some of this too."

She shrieked back, I stepped between them –

"Take it easy, Dammo."

He was out of control, just like that night in Dublin –

"Take it easy? Did they take it easy on Frogman? Did they take it easy on Big Mac?"

"You don't know that this lad had anything to do with it."

"Of course he did, they all did. The police, the scum who did it, the press, they were all in on it." He turned back to the lad and punched him again and again and then in the face. It was only then that I realised there was blood everywhere. It wasn't just digs, he had a blade. Sammy L and Muscles seemed to notice at the same time because they let him fall. As he hit the ground Dammo was on top of him, stabbing him again and again. I went to stop him, the girl was screaming, Johnny was standing mumbling –

"Fuck, fuck, fuck . . . " over and over again.

As I got to him, he turned knife in hand and held it at me –

"Come on, fuckface, fancy yourself do you? Remember Rasher, he fancied himself too and look what happened to him."

I held my hands out to the sides.

He smirked –

"That's it, Simmo, back off."

I took one step backward but, just as he thought he was in control, I propelled myself at him kicking the knife out of his hand. It flew up into the air and across the floor. He reacted quickly, grabbing my leg and pulling me to the floor. I hit my head hard on the ground, it cracked but this wasn't the time to worry about such things. The minute I hit the ground I spun, like a child down a hill, avoiding the boot that was aimed at my head.

He ran for the knife, I crawled after him, pulling him to the ground but he reached it and taking a firm grip of it swung round connecting with my arm. He pulled it out and made for a second lunge. My body wanted to faint with the pain but my brain pushed me into overdrive. I grabbed his hand and stopped him, then slowly I turned the knife at him. He bit into the open cut on my arm. The pain was unbearable, I knew if I didn't react now it was going to be curtains for me. With every ounce of strength that was left in me I pushed, driving the knife straight into his chest, he gasped, his eyes opened wide and then nothing.

I struggled to my feet, all the men were standing there speechless –

"Where's the girl?"

They all looked at each other guiltily –

"She was here a minute ago."

It was then that we heard the siren and the white car speeding into the warehouse. Sammy L took to running. So did Johnny. Muscles hit the ground, hands behind his head. I reached the car, turned the key and she started first time. I hit reverse and careered the car through a pallet of boxes, past the squad car and through the open gateway. They didn't give chase but I knew it would only be a matter of time before back-up would have the number plates. Three turns later I abandoned the car, broke the back side window of an Alfa Romeo and seconds later after hot-wiring it I was away. As I drove off I spotted five police cars zooming around in all directions.

Nancy nearly fainted when she saw me, I collapsed onto the sofa. She wanted to call an ambulance –

"No."

"Paul I have to, you've lost too much blood."

"Nancy, I can't go to the hospital. If I do I'll be arrested."

I ended up having to tell her the truth and as I did I could see a blank look come over her face as if to say, she didn't know me anymore.

She patched me up as best she could and after sleeping for the best part of two days I packed when she was gone to work. By the time she would have got home after her shift I was back in Dublin, staring down at the Liffey's murky water from O'Connell Street Bridge.

Chapter Twenty-One

Dublin had changed. I had changed.

I wasn't the bony-arsed kid who was shocked when he saw the sight of blood. I wasn't the lad who got his hair ruffled by his Da's clients. I was someone who had seen people getting killed and who *had* killed. Once you've been through *that*, things change. Life becomes cheap, it becomes dispensable and more than anything you no longer respect it. I knew now that if needs be I could kill again. I also knew that if needs must, I could walk away from anyone, no matter how I felt about them.

Ma was delighted to have me home again. She cleaned the bandage on my arm every day. Da never said anything, but I knew he too was happy to have me home. It wasn't until I was fit and well again that he told me why.

We went to the pub and after the third or fourth drink Da opened up to me –

"I've got the big C."

He said it in the same way he may have said –

"I've got a tip for the three thirty at Haydock."

Right between his supping of a new pint and lighting a fag. If there had been football on the box I might have missed his telling me at all.

"You've got what?"

"The big C."

I couldn't believe what was unfolding in front of me. On one hand he was telling me that he was dying. Then on the other hand he was lighting up another ciggie, the very thing that had him in the state he was in. He must have read my mind, 'cause he looked at me, then the cigarette, then smiled –

"Bit late teh change old habits now. Besides, the damage is done, so I may as well enjoy me last few days."

"How long have they given yeh?"

"If I don't have the op, three months."

"And if you do have the op?"

"It's not an option."

"What do yeh mean it's not an option? Yeh have teh have it."

"There's more chance of the Pope being a Rangers fan. Naw, son, if I've teh go, it'll be all in one piece, not little bits of me scattered across an operating table."

"And what about Ma, doesn't she get a say in this?"

"No, she doesn't. And I don't want you goin' and upsetting her either, do you hear me?"

I didn't answer.

"I mean it, Paul. It's my decision, I don't want them doctors opening me up and experimenting on me, when I go I want to go as I am, OK?"

Reluctantly I agreed.

Maybe it was my imagination but from that day on he got steadily worse. You could see it in his face that the pain was draining every last bit of fight he had left. He'd let the business slip too. Ma was on his back about money all the time. At first I thought it was just her. After all, the woman could spend for the nation, but it wasn't that. When I broached the subject he just passed it off, saying it was something of nothing and he had it under control.

Two nights later I happened to be sitting in the same pub when I overheard a conversation a stool away from me. I was reading me paper, minding me own business, when suddenly I could swear I heard me Da's name being mentioned.

"You don't worry about Simpson, you leave Simpson to me."

Naturally my curiosity got the better of me as he continued –

"Simpson is a has-been, no one listens to him any more, he's not a threat. If you take a loan off me I guarantee that you don't have to worry about paying back Simpson a penny of what you owe him."

The other man was sold, but still a little anxious –

"What do I do when Simpson calls at me door?"

"Tell him teh fuck off!"

"Yeah righ'."

"OK, when is he due again?"

"Thursday morning."

"Right, I'll be there and I'll deal with him. I've done it before, it's no big deal."

Thursday morning Da pulled up outside the flats. His movement was slower than I'd ever remembered it. He called to two flats without answer, a third that handed him his few bob and then to one answered by the nervous man from the pub. The man looked ashen with worry –

"Ah the hard man, come in outta the cold for a minute."

Da entered, taking his hat off as he did.

I walked to the door and listened. At first the voices were muffled; slowly they became raised –

"I'm telling you, Simpson, from now on you don't knock on this door, comprehend?"

Da obviously answered but I couldn't hear what he was saying, then Mouth Almighty was back in again –

"I couldn't give two fucks how much you're owed, it's old news, forget it, old man, if you know what's good for you. Yer man here is getting his loans from me from now on and all previous monies owed are null and void."

I stood back from the door and gave it one good kick. It snapped open. Before anyone could react I hit Mouth Almighty with a baseball bat across the shins, there was a loud crushing noise and he fell to the ground holding his shins in agony. I grabbed his throat and lifted him by the neck onto the settee.

"Now what's going on here?" I asked.

"Man," he said rubbing his shin, "you've just made the biggest mistake of your life."

"Really?"

"You've just signed your own death cert."

I laughed and turned to Da –

"Jasus Da, you didn't tell me you were visitin' a comic."

I swung the bat and connected on the shins again; he doubled up in pain.

"Now you listen to me, this is Simpson territory and a little punk like you ain't gonna change that. You understand?"

He looked straight at me –

"Fuck you!"

Without hesitating I hit his legs again.

"No please *don't, don't* . . . "

But it was too late. I had the bat raised and it crushed down on the exact same spot again.

"Now I want you out of here NOW."

"I can't WALK."

"I don't remember asking you could you walk."

I grabbed him –

"Da, open that window, Fuck-Face here is leaving."

Da opened the window, I pulled Fuck-Face to it.

"Jesus Christ, we're on the fifth floor . . . "

I lifted him to the window sill, and held him over it.

He looked over his shoulder to the ground below –

"Please don't do what you're thinking of doing."

"I'm not thinkin' of anything. I just want you out of here and you won't walk."

"I will . . . I will . . . "

I pulled him back in and pushed him toward the door. He tried to get up but couldn't. Still he kept moving, Da opened the door and watched him struggle down the hallway.

When he was gone I stared at the man left in the flat. He was visibly sweating –

"It wasn't my idea." He looked to my Da, "Honest, Mr Simpson, that's the first time I ever set eyes on him."

I walked close to him, slapping the baseball bat into my open hand –

"So that wasn't you I seen with him in the pub the other night?"

He started to cry –

"Oh Jesus . . . " he ran to Da's side, fell on his knees and held Da's leg. " . . . Please, Mr Simpson, I'm sorry. I had no choice . . . he said it'd be OK, he said you'd understand. Mr Simpson, I never wanted to go along with this."

Da pushed him away –

"But you did Terry, you did go along with it."

He buried his head in the lino on the floor.

"What do you want me to do with him, Da, break his legs? Fuck him out the window?"

He cowered along the ground to Da's leg again. Da kicked him off –

"Have you got my money, Terry?"

He sat up, pulling at his pockets –

"*Yesss* . . . here . . . *look!*"

Da took the crumpled twenty-pound note –

"OK Terry I'll tell you what. I'm gonna call Simmo here off you but, from next week on, you're gonna pay twenty-five pound a week. We'll call the extra fiver a fine, a fine for not being loyal."

Of course he agreed.

And that's how it went. We went around all the non-payers and sorted the situation out. Word had got around to most of them but those who hadn't taken notice were soon brought back into line.

For once in their lives the doctors had got it right. Two months later Da died, and I took over the business. Time flew and before I knew it I was twenty-five years at the same game. It takes over your life, you don't meet people in the usual way. You're suspicious of everyone who tries to get close to you. But it does have its bonuses.

Chapter Twenty-Two

I had a nice apartment in Dublin. None of your shitty little one-bedroom efforts; this one was three-bedroom and overlooked Howth Harbour. I drove a BMW when making me rounds and I also owned a Porsche for when I wanted to impress people. Everything I owned I paid for by cash. I'd a telly in every room. I'd two video players, the latest camera, a computer with the Internet, two CD players, you name it and I had it, and none of that "fell off the back of the bus" shit. No, the police could call all they liked 'cause I had receipts for everything.

So life was good. I ate in fancy restaurants, I went to premiers, had life membership in the K Club and Portmarnock golf courses and when I wanted female company there was always someone who had run up debts and needed to keep me happy.

I'll cut to the chase. A woman in need with loose morals can be a great ride. They'll do anything they think you might like in order to pay off the debt. The trick was never to act interested. I mean if you seem too eager they'd take you for every penny you had, you'd end up owing them. And there were the right aul toe-rags, the ones that were giving it to the fruit and veg man for two pound of carrots and a bag of spuds. Don't mock it, there were plenty of them, plenty of them who never paid a taxi fare, never paid for an ice cream for their kids and literally got their bag of coal off the coal man. I had no time for them. No, the ones I liked were the ones who you'd never think in a million years would ride. The ones who turned their noses up at you, the ones who never let the shop deliver, because they didn't want people knowing they were from the flats.

At first it was a legitimate call, just to collect the money due. A bit of friendly chatter and an offer of extra money around sale time. She couldn't refuse. Just a few quid that the husband didn't know about, enough to buy something in Brown Thomas. Something small so she'd get a Brown Thomas bag and then the rest in Dunnes and Penneys, but stuffed into the Brown Thomas bag. And so it went, the bill owed grew and she began to fall behind.

"I'll pay you the rest next week," she'd say with a smile.

It'd be the first time she had smiled at me and the first time I didn't smile back at her –

"OK, but you know next week you have that, your usual amount and the penalty for late payment."

And the next week she'd come to the door and ask me in –

"About that money, I haven't got it, you see the ki . . . "

But I'd cut in –

"Mrs, I'm not interested in your excuses, I need payment. If you ain't got it maybe I should have a word with your husband?"

She'd panic –

"NO, there's no need for that, I'll get it. I just need some time."

I'd usually give her two to three weeks, until she was in so far she had no way out. Then I'd make my play –

"Listen babe, you still owe four hundred pounds of your

original loan, you owe seventy-five pounds arrears and twenty pounds in penalties. If you don't pay today you're gonna have to come up with one hundred and seventy-five pounds next week just to get back on track." At this point I'd move closer and rub her face. "Now I'd hate to have to tell your husband or ruin that pretty face of yours, but I have a reputation to think of."

She always started crying and I always consoled her.

"Hey come on, come on, it ain't all that bad, I'm sure we can come to some arrangement." I'd lift her face up and smile at her.

She'd have hope in her eyes –

"Do you think so?"

I'd start undoing her buttons –

"How about if I put everything into one big loan." I'd squeeze her tit gently, "And go back to the original payments," I'd kiss her tit, "the ones you could afford," hand up the skirt, "but it has to be our secret," knickers off, "we have our reputations to think of."

And she'd let me do it, there and then, on the settee that I'd probably lent the money for. And afterwards she normally thanked me for being so understanding. I never let it get into a regular occurrence, never an affair. It was a once-off, that made them feel they had got a good deal and meant that I was never out of pocket and a ride better off. The next week it was back to business as usual, me smiling and she paying, with her air of grace.

Peter Collins's wife was one I'd have liked to get, but she was strong and no matter how hard she had to work she always managed it. There'd been a few times when I thought, maybe she would crack, but each time she escaped the net.

PART THREE

DAVEY'S DECISION

Chapter Twenty-Three

I sat supping me pint –

"You've come a long way, Davey my man," I thought. "It's hard to believe that in three months you could fall so in love."

Anyone else, yes, but not *me*. Maybe this was the male menopause. I'd only just read about it in one of the Sunday paper supplements and it certainly had all the trademarks of it. You know, finding a younger girl attractive, starting to gel the hair, wearing younger clothes, and only yesterday I'd found meself tapping me foot to a Fatboy Slim record.

Still, if this is an illness, I'm not going to a doctor. Fuck no, I'm having too much fun.

It all happened three months ago. It started off as a normal enough day. I left Tracy in bed. I never used an alarm, I never needed one; it was just as well, 'cause I liked to get an early start and there was no point in both of us being up. I had my own routine. I got up at six and took a shower. We had one en suite, but I preferred the one in the bathroom. The water pressure was much stronger and I found it easier to regulate. The en suite one was always either too hot or too cold. You either roasted your balls or else you ended up freezing the arse off yourself. The bathroom one was just right, never too hot

147

but never freezing. I remember reading one time that Paul Newman jumps into an ice-cold river outside his home every morning, just to invigorate himself. Well, fair dues, I mean he's a class actor, but there's no way I was ever going to freeze the balls off meself just to feel invigorated. No, whenever freezing cold water hit my privates, they shrivelled up like a fucking tapeworm, and it was next to impossible to have a decent piss. If you didn't pull back all the skin off it, your pee could go anywhere, and if you gave it a good shake to get it back to normal size, people could think you were having a wank. After all, we always said three shakes is a wank and it'd take a good dozen shakes before you'd coax the little fucker out.

Once I'd done the three S's – shit, shave, shower – I lashed on the Sure deodorant, (so it was really four S's) got dressed and headed down the stairs.

I always put the kettle on first, then the radio and then I'd get me cup ready. I drank out of a mug with the caption "I wish I was down the pub". Kettle boiled, I made a good strong cup of Lyons tea. I'd tried all the other brands, the herbals, tea leaves, but in the end the cheapo Lyons tea bag gave me as good a cup as any.

Tea made, I sat down and then, and only then, did I have a cigarette. People wrecked my head with cigarettes, this thing of every time you looked at someone and they with a fag stuck out of their gob. After the first cigarette, there was no enjoyment. That first cigarette was what smoking was all about and so I never let anything get in its way. OK, I'll admit that during the rest of the day I smoked maybe fifteen, maybe twenty, depending on what I was doing. But it was the first ciggie, the first few drags, that you spent the rest of the time trying to get back.

I was always on site well before eight. In the first few

hours I got most of my work done. After eleven, you had every Tom, Dick and Harry coming and asking you questions. All the suits would show their faces, all buzzing around as though the world would stop if their busy little body wasn't fucking running it. Jasus they pissed me off! What did they think we were doing for the three hours before they came along and for the seven or eight hours after they left? Scratching our arses?

I swear to God, they brought the whole place to a halt. We'd be working away. There was a plan, there were tools and material, and we had all done our apprenticeships, so we knew what to do. Then in would walk the suit, with his twenty-five different plans, his filofax and his mobile phone. He'd have his hard hat on in the same way a kid who was just about to play with his new construction set would. And he'd get you to stop what you were doing to discuss what you were doing. As if by him saying "continue", it made the job better.

So I'd get down off the ladder and as soon as I had, his phone would ring and he'd stand there talking shite at the top of his voice, while making faces to me, as though I was supposed to feel some sympathy for him.

I'd use the opportunity to have a cigarette break, but as soon as I'd lit up, he'd point to the *"No Smoking"* sign.

I was on a site with no windows and concrete floors and they still said no smoking. Eventually he'd finish his phone call by looking at the phone and saying –

"These things, Christ, I swear, sometimes they're more a nuisance than they are good."

Well, if he really felt that way he should switch the fucking thing off. But no, he didn't and no sooner had we the plans on the table than the bloody thing rang again. I could always tell the difference between a work call and a private one. The business call would be announced to the whole world. The private one would be taken to an isolated corner and mumbled down the phone, with his back to you just in case anyone could lip read.

And after all this, after explaining to him how to read a fucking plan, after pointing out to him that he was looking at the wrong wall on the drawing, this jumped-up nobody, this fucker who was still in nappies when I started on sites, he tries to tell me (in the nicest possible way) to get my finger out. And without further ado he'd be off, talking into his phone as he gets into his company car and drives off to another site, to wreck some other poor fucker's head.

Sometimes I don't know why I gave a fuck, why I didn't just do as everyone else did, stroll in whenever I liked, and take long breaks . . . but I couldn't. I'd left all that behind me in London. Now I didn't feel right unless I had got me hands dirtied. I set me eye on something at the start of a day and I had to get it done. That way I could feel good about me two pints on the way home.

I loved those two pints, they were like that cup of tea and the fag in the morning time. I could sit on a high-stool and feel justified that two pints of Arthur Guinness's finest were going down my sawdust-dry throat. It was the best time of the evening to drink, you felt a certain comradeship with the others at the bar. There was no real need for conversation, not heavy stuff anyway, just a moan about fuck-all on the telly, or the fact that Sky had ruined sport by making it "pay to view".

"I'm telling you," Paddy Mac said from behind his counter, "there hasn't been a decent fight since them whores took over."

And we all agreed. You had Nassim all gob and puffy shorts. OK, he could throw a punch and he was a good little dancer, but this was boxing, not fucking *Riverdance*. Nassim wouldn't have lasted pissing time against the likes of Sugar

Ray Leonard or Hitman Hearns and I'd say there'd have been a severe smell of shite in his little leopardskin shorts if Marvellous Marvin Hagler had stepped into the ring with him. And as for the heavyweights – Jesus Christ, imagine Lennox Lewis meeting Ali or Frazier. For fuck sake, he could hardly beat Foreman and Foreman about sixty years old and as fat as a fool! I couldn't imagine Tyson biting Ali's ear – for fuck sake he wouldn't have even got near him. And they wanted us to pay nearly twenty pounds to watch the ear-eater and the big girl's blouse? They had their shite in large doses.

There was always great comments. And even though I say it meself I think I came out with the best. Like the time they were talking about Andy Grey on Sky showing us on his board where the ball should go and I shouts –

"Shurrup Grey, sure you couldn't tell where the ball was coming from when you were on the fucking pitch!"

I enjoyed a bit of slagging, although I have to admit that they didn't always have a great sense of humour in Mackies.

Joe Dolan couldn't take a slagging about his name. I mean to say you had to laugh if you have a name of a famous person. Another time an aul one tried to get me sacked just 'cause when she was pushing by me she said –

"Excuse me."

And I said –

"Why, did you fart?"

Still, you could have your moans but at the end of the day it had the best pint in Dublin bar none.

So there I was this night having me pint and the door opens behind me. Of course human nature made me look around and in walks three fine-looking things. I let out a low whistle, they looked at me, one with a real bra-burner gaze, one expressionless and the third with a little smile. It was her who came up to the bar –

"Excuse me, is this where the talent competition is on?"

"It is love, but you're a bit early. Things won't get going 'til about nine."

She looked at the clock behind the bar, which was showing seven-thirty –

"Ah, that's OK, sure we've loads of gossip to catch up on. Can I have a G&T, a vodka and white and a bottle of Heineken?"

Paddy Mac looked over at the other two who had sat in one of the partitioned seating areas –

"How old is the little one?"

I looked over –

"Jasus Paddy, your eyesight must be going, there's nothin' small about that girl. Sure, she'd make Dolly Parton look anorexic."

The girl at the bar laughed –

"Who, Mary? Jasus don't let her hear yeh saying that, she's nearly twenty-five."

Paddy made a noise that meant he wasn't actually convinced but he'd give them a drink anyway.

I took another good look at the girl at the bar and commented –

"So are yeh a singer?"

She had a lovely laugh, it was kind of dirty –

"Me? Are yeh mad or what?"

"I'd say you have a lovely voice."

"Go way, would yeh! I haven't a note in me head."

"Ah sure you can't have *everything*, isn't it enough to have good looks?"

She laughed again as she paid Paddy and turned with the three drinks balanced between her hands –

"Flattery will get you everywhere."

I watched as she walked back to the table –

"I sincerely hope so, love."

I turned to Paul Simpson who was sitting two barstools away –

"Would yeh?"

Simpson looked at her through the mirror on the wall behind the counter –

"She's nice all righ'."

"NICE! She's fucking gorgeous."

"Now, now," says Paddy Mac. "Remember, you're supposed to be a happily married man."

"Yeah and I'd be a whole lot happier if I got a hold of her for half an hour."

Simpson laughed –

"A young one like that'd fucking kill yeh."

"I know," I says, finishing the last dregs of me pint, and straightening me jacket for the crisp breeze outside, "but what a fucking way teh go."

I walked for the door, as I reached her seat I stopped –

"I'll see *you* later."

She winked –

"See ya."

That evening I wolfed me dinner down. Tracy was all chat about her day, Christ Almighty, how much can you say about working a cash register? I jumped up from the table –

"Right, I'm gonna get ready and go down for a pint."

"What's the rush?"

"What?"

"What's the rush? You nearly burnt the throat off yourself eating that dinner."

"Little fucking hope of doing that with one of your dinners, it was nearly cold."

"I keep telling yeh, either start coming home when you say you'll be here, or else get me a microwave."

I kissed her –

"Well, you never know, if you're very good I'll get you one for your birthday."

"You can fuck off with that idea. I don't want a microwave, the kitchen needs one, not me. No, a nice bottle of expensive perfume, or a load of Clarins make-up will do nicely."

I got away from answering her question and had a quick shower and shave.

She was watching *Crimeline* when I walked in –

"Where's me green shirt?"

"I only washed it today. Wear the grey one."

"Is it ironed?"

"Well, I didn't iron it."

"Would yeh give it a quick rub?"

"Ah, Davey, I'm only after sitting down."

"Ah go on, it'll take me ages to iron it. I'll bring the iron and the ironing board in here and all."

"And make me a cup of tea?"

"Righ'."

I had the iron and the board in and a cup of tea made in double-quick time.

"Jasus," She says, ironing and watching the telly at the same time. "You're getting very spruced up for just a trip to the local?"

"No, I'm not."

"Yes you are, they're your good trousers and shoes."

I changed the subject –

"Your woman Marian Finucane is very good, isn't she?"

"I prefer her on the radio meself, she never gives the guards a chance to talk."

She'd finished ironing. I grabbed me shirt and started buttoning it up –

"She's fucking righ' too. Let them get a word in and they'll start asking awkward questions. Her and yer man Harvey will end up doing time."

Tracy laughed –

"Shurrup, yeh gobshite."

I kissed her –

"Righ' I'm gone."

"Are yeh not putting away the iron board?"

"I wasn't the one using it."

I laughed. She made a face –

"Righ', just you wait 'til the next time you want a shirt ironed."

"I'll do it when I get back. I gotta go."

"You haven't told me, why the big rush?"

"Ah there's a stupid talent competition on and the place is gonna be packed."

"Davey! Why didn't yeh tell me, you know I love them."

"I never thought of it."

"I would have gone."

"I'd say it's gonna be crap. You're better off staying put."

I found meself rushing along the street, with a little anticipation in me stomach. That sank when I got in and found that there was two old couples sitting where they had been.

I strolled to the bar, pushing through the crowds that stood three deep –

"Paddy, whenever you're ready."

Paddy Mac was under pressure –

"I've only one pair of hands, Davey."

"I've only one mouth," says I.

"That's a matter of opinion," mumbled Paddy.

I got a dig in the back –

"Hey, are yeh buying me one?"

It was the girl from earlier. I felt my heart jump –

"Yeah sure, what're yeh havin'?"

"A glass of Heineken, thanks."

I turned back to the bar –

"And a pint of Heineken."

"No, a half," she shouts.

Paddy looks up –

"Make your mind up, will yeh?"

I was insistent –

"Give 'er a pint."

She shook her head –

"I won't drink it."

"Course you will."

We pushed our way from the bar and found two tall stools against the side wall. Every once in a while, she'd go over to her friends. The small one with the big tits seemed to be giving her a hard time about me. When she came back I asked –

"Well, does Dolly not like me?"

She laughed her dirty laugh. She'd lovely teeth. I liked teeth. I liked someone with straight white teeth and she had lovely ones.

"Don't let her hear you calling her that. She has this thing about her boobs, she's always talking about getting them reduced."

"There's a fair bit of reducing to be done on them."

She laughed –

"I know, lucky bitch."

I let her see I was looking at her –

"Jasus, you're not too badly off yourself."

"Would you stop!"

"I'm telling you, more than a handful's a waste."

She giggled and leaned into me, I put my arm around her and gave her a hug.

156

The night flew on, the acts were crap. Well I thought they were. I only sang along to some of them because she did. As Paddy Mac called time her friends came over –

"Are you right? We're going."

She got up to leave.

"You're not going, are yeh?"

"I have teh."

"Have one more . . . for the road."

She looked at the girls. Dolly spoke –

"We're going."

She looked at me –

"Sorry, another time, yeah?"

"When?"

She bent down and kissed me on the cheek –

"See yeh the weekend, in here."

I smiled –

"Is that a date?"

She smiled back –

"What do you think?"

Chapter Twenty-Four

I couldn't get Amanda off my mind. I walked home that night like a love-struck teenager. I kicked a can down the road ahead of me, following it out onto the road when it went scurrying out there. If I was asleep the kicking of a can would really annoy me. You'd be woken by its tinny sound banging off the concrete pavement. And then just when it had stopped, when someone had left it because they'd got bored kicking it, someone else would come along and start kicking it the other way. Regardless of how much you tried to block it out, you couldn't.

But tonight I didn't care, I kicked and chased the can like someone coming home from getting his hole for the first time ever.

Even when I got in I was still singing. Tracy had the light on upstairs –

"Is that you, Davey?"

"Why, who are you expecting?"

"Oh, just a young hunk, who comes around every now and again."

"Well, sorry, it's only your husband."

I went in and popped on the kettle, I sat down and found myself humming Elvis's "Wooden Heart". I hated the song, I hated Elvis, but I found myself humming away as though I was his number one fan. As though I was one of those sad whores who go to his anniversary every year dressed up in suits to make them look as fat and ugly as he did, just before he died. Did none of them realise that the reason Elvis was swallowing so many tablets was 'cause he was depressed at how fat he'd got? He wanted to look like he had when he was a sex symbol. And here were all these eejits dressing up as him and not one dressed the way Elvis would like to be remembered.

Tracy walked in and her voice caught me by surprise –

"Are yeh making a cuppa?"

I made us both a cup and told her all about the crap acts and how she hadn't missed anything. And as I talked I thought about Amanda. I grabbed Tracy as she walked to the sink to wash her cup –

"Give us a gooser."

"Go way, yeh eejit."

But when I kissed her she didn't refuse my tongue. I brought my hand up under her pygama top and squeezed her tit. She was still in great shape. OK, she went on about cellulite and she did have a bit, even though I told her she didn't but I'd seen girls ten years younger who were worse with it. Her body pressed into my touch and her tongue got harder and more forceful. I pulled her nightdress up and she helped it off.

"What brought this on?" She whispered, as I sank my head onto her nipple. I didn't answer, I was thinking of Amanda. I caressed her thinking of Amanda's youthful breasts and as she moaned with delight, I pictured it being Amanda who was delighting in my touch. My hand reached into her knickers and though the words out of her mouth were –

"The curtains aren't pulled, anyone could be looking in."

Her legs still parted so she could feel the full pleasure of my bulky fingers. She moaned loudly and her body gyrated in time to my probing. I lifted her onto the table.

I looked at her and her eyes were shining in anticipation. I pulled hard on her undies, driving them past her knees, and she kicked them off the rest of the way and wrapped her feet around me. I was in, my stiffness parting her soft warm flesh and I pushed hard until there was nowhere further to go –

"Oh, Davey."

I said nothing, I couldn't, to call her name would be to ruin my fantasy. I pulled back, almost out, then hard back in, my balls pounding hard on her. She pulled my shirt up at the back and her fingers clawed as I made love to her. Our cries were both of blissful pain. Her face cringed in pain yet she begged for me to go faster and I moaned knowing welts were forming on my back.

When we finished I lay on top of her, softly kissing her tits, as she ran her fingers through my hair –

"I must let you out more often."

Chapter Twenty-Five

Friday was a long time coming. I thought about her a lot. Not purposely; she'd just come into my mind and I couldn't get her out of it.

On Friday I was edgy all day. I wanted to go out and buy some new gear, but how was I going to explain that to Tracy. Tracy had long given up on me going shopping. I'd hand her the money, give her a lift to the shops and when she was finished she just had to ring me. I never said I wouldn't wear that. She had great taste. I always trusted her choice and I knew that when I was cleaned up I actually cut a fine figure.

There was something about Amanda that was different, that had me acting the way I was. I mean, I hadn't been the most faithful husband in the world. I'd had a few little flings and the odd one-night stand, but they never even came into my mind until they were standing in the same room as me. Amanda didn't even have to be anywhere near and yet she was on my mind. It was stupid, she wasn't even twenty-two. Christ, I was nearly eighteen years her senior. When I was eighteen she wasn't even born. She was only one when I got married, it made no sense. I'd been with better-looking girls too, like the married one from Tralee. Jasus, now she was a *cracker*. She'd come up to Dublin to look after her sister's house, while she was away in America. Her husband had a good job with an oil company that kept him away for a month or so. I tried every chat-up line I had and ended up with her in the scratcher on the first day I met her. Still the minute I had had her, as she lay naked on the bed, with a figure that was straight from *Playboy*, all I could think of was getting away, in such a way that she wouldn't take the hump and not give it to me again.

I knew nothing about Amanda. I didn't even know her second name. She could have been Jack the Ripper's daughter for all I knew. I didn't know had she got a boyfriend, had she got a job, nothing. But we'd clicked, she'd laughed every time I cracked a joke, she'd rubbed against me. I hated girls who were all maully, but she touched nice and casual, letting her hand lie on my thigh long enough for it to be deliberate but not so long as anyone else would notice.

Once again I said I was only dropping down to the pub for a quick pint and maybe it was guilt but I saw Tracy look at me kinda curious.

"Wha'? What's wrong with yeh now?" I said.

She smiled to herself but said nothing. That really annoyed me, it was bad enough having to ask what was wrong without having to drag the fucking words out –

"Come on, what's wrong with you?"

"Nothin'," she was still smiling, that *I know something you don't* smile.

"Is there a law against smiling nowadays?"

"Yeah, there is when it's you."

"Well, then yeh can go fuck yerself, I'm not telling yeh now."

She settled herself down on the settee with her bag of Malteasers and her bottle of Diet Coke. She was looking a bit hurt and although I was thinking –

"You can go and shit, I'm not that interested."

I knew that if I didn't make the effort, by the time I came

back from the pub, she'd have a right face on her and that could last for the guts of a week.

I looked at my watch, a quarter to eight. I still had plenty of time. I walked around and sat beside her. I put me arm around her –

"Ah, is my little love upset?"

She pulled away from me, her eyes never leaving the telly –

"Fuck off."

I moved closer again, but she moved right to the edge. I followed and put my arm around her again –

"You're gonna fall off the end if yeh keep on going."

She didn't smile, but the frostiness of her look was dwindling. I continued –

"Come on, tell me what you were smiling about?" I nudged her, "Ah go on," I nudged her again, "Ah go on," I started tickling her, "Ah go on, go on, go on, go on."

Tracy hated tickles, she was wriggling uncontrollably, trying in vain to escape my hands –

"Gerrrooffff . . . OK . . . OK . . . I'll tell you."

I stopped tickling her.

She jumped up and ran for the door laughing –

"Fuck off, I'm not telling you."

I caught her before she reached the door and started tickling her again.

"OK, OK! I swear I'll tell you."

She was breathless and I stood over her, ready to resume the torture.

"I was smiling 'cause I thought it's nice the way you tell me you're going down the pub, it's nice."

I was puzzled –

"I always said when I was going out."

"Yeah, but now it's as though you're asking me if it's OK. It's like as if I don't like it, you won't go."

I could feel the relief in me –

"Of course I'd stay if you wanted me to."

"Good. I'll put on the kettle for us."

I was just about to say something, I had to get out, but she laughed –

"I knew that would shock you. Imagine you missing a Friday night?"

"I wouldn't mind."

"*Would yeh go way outta that!* If you stayed away on a Friday they'd have a search party out for you."

She wrapped her arms around me and we kissed –

"But just in case I'm asleep by the time you get home," she kissed me again, "wake me."

I sat in Paddy Mac's with me pint. My hands were clammy and I couldn't stop my foot from tapping. Paul Simpson was seated with a short in front of him. I'm sure I could have struck up a conversation with him, but I was too nervous. Every time the door opened I found myself looking in its direction. Paddy Mac noticed –

"Jasus Davey, you're very nervous tonight, have yeh not paid the telly licence or what?"

"How could yeh afford anything and the price you charge for a pint?"

He laughed and walked away.

I watched the door for a good two hours and seven pints, then I gave up on her and went home. I wished I had seen a cat on the way home 'cause I wanted to kick something. The little bitch was trying to make an eejit out of me, well she could go and take a run and jump.

As I put my key in the door it opened. Tracy was standing there in a little nightie. She'd bought it at a knicker party her friend had thrown. Knicker party! From what Tracy had told me about it, it was more like a fucking porn party. They had dildos and vibrators the size of a donkey, in every fucking colour too. She said the biggest was a black one and it had veins sticking out of it and when you switched it on it spun round. They'd had dirty mags and massage creams, thongs, leather gear, rubber gear and every type of outfit you could want. Tracy had bought this little frilly nightie, it was black and seethrough and I always knew when she had it on she was in the humour for a ride.

"I heard you coming," she says opening the door.

I pushed in and slammed it shut –

"What the fuck are you doing opening the door in that? I could have been anyone."

She rubbed up against me –

"Ohhh yeah, a complete stranger."

I walked into the kitchen and to the press with the whiskey in it.

I poured meself a double and swallowed it in one. She was sitting across from me, her legs open and still living out her little fantasy –

"So big boy, how about it? My husband will be home in a few minutes."

I stood pouring a drink, looking at her, but still in a rage at Amanda –

"Do you do this much when your husband is out?"

She ran her hand on the inside of her thigh –

"All the time . . . come on, take me."

My voice was flat –

"Have you any idea how fucking stupid you look?"

Her eyes, which had been closed as her hand touched herself, now sprang open. I was on a roll –

"Look at yeh, with your hand up your fanny like some aul slut."

Her hand fell from the top of her leg.

"Is this what you get up to when I'm not here? Feeling yourself, pretending it's some young stud? Who in their right mind would touch you, eh?"

I walked over to her, touching the nightie –

"And who in their right mind would find this attractive? It looks like the wrapping off a Quality Street sweet."

Her hands wrapped around herself as though she was trying to hide her body.

"You're fucking pathetic. And you expect me to get a horn looking at yeh? You're having a fucking wank at the thought of kids riding you and yeh expect me to get off on that? You're fucking sick! It's no wonder I fuck off to the pub. I'll tell yeh, thanks be to God we don't have kids, 'cause I'd hate to have a daughter in case she ended up looking like yeh."

She got up and walked out of the room.

"That's righ', fuck off. Go on teh bed and finish what yeh started."

I drank a half bottle before I went to bed. She was on her side, wrapped up in her dressing-gown and her long cotton nightdress. She lay at the furthest point on her side of the bed, like a frigid pole. I didn't care.

Next morning I tried to apologise; she ignored me. I could tell by her face she'd been crying and when I went to throw my tea bag in the rubbish bin I saw the torn remains of her nightie.

Chapter Twenty-Six

It was a miserable Saturday. We sat in total silence. I went to the bookies and laid on a bet; the racing was going to be on the telly. When I came home Tracy was watching ice-skating on Eurosport. As I was in the bad books, I couldn't turn it off. She knew, she knew exactly what she was at. She knew I always watched the racing and she knew I hated ice-skating. I don't care what they say, but it's not a sport. It's dancing on ice. Like fair dues, they're very fucking *good* at it but it's not a sport. Anything with music, pirouettes and marks out of ten is not a sport. I mean to say, you don't get extra points for the way you look or the state of your clothes in any other sport. You never hear that United have won a match because one of their forty-two kits is nicer then the opposition's, or because Gigsy smiled when he was scoring.

Tracy always did things like this when we weren't talking. If it wasn't this, it'd be an old film, and not just any old film, it'd be *The Sound of Music* or *The Wizard of Oz* or worst of all some chic flick like *Little Women* or *An Officer and a Gentleman*.

If I had to watch that fucker Gere in his white uniform one more time I swear I'd kill her.

So I endured the Eurosport coverage of ice-skating followed by a 1956 film about five student nurses and all the capers they got up to. I wouldn't say it had been funny first time round.

Around seven I asked her did she fancy going for a drink. She ignored me.

"Is that a yes or a no?"

"It's a yes."

Great I thought, that's a breakthrough.

"Well, come on, get yourself moving."

"After this."

"This" was Cilla Black. Jesus Christ! How could anyone in their right mind watch *Blind Date*? They were all gobshites with their stupid fucking answers that led yeh to believe they were all gorgeous nymphomaniacs who would be bonking the arse off yeh as soon as the wall went back.

And there ye'd stand watching the two good-looking ones go by and when you finally saw her, yeh had to give her credit for a good imagination. Because there was no way she was the curvaceous blonde she had described. So it was off to Barbados and when you got back the fat little bitch, who had promised to gobble you night and day, suddenly turns into Miss Prim and Proper. Jesus, it made me skin crawl. But we sat through it and then she took an eternity to get ready and came down in a dress that made the local nuns look racy.

We sat in Mac's, her with her half of Bud and me with me pint, not talking and looking in opposite directions. I looked up at the bar and wished I was with the lads.

"Go on if you want," she says, reading me mind.

"Wha'?"

"I know ye'd rather be up there talking a load of shite to them than sitting here with me."

I turned to her and put my hand on hers. She was freezing and the look she gave me was colder. I removed me hand, supped me pint and answered –

"How long is this going to go on for?"

"How long is what going to go on for?"

I looked away –

"You know wha' I mean."

She got all sarcastic –

"Oh you mean how long will I dress like a fucking packet of Quality Street and feel meself thinking of other men? God, I don't know."

"You know I didn't mean tha'."

"Well, you said it."

This was annoying me –

"I know I fucking said it, but I didn't fucking mean it."

She clenched her teeth and leaned toward me –

"Don't you dare use that kind of language at me. You hurt me, you can't just say those things and then expect everything to be OK. It takes time."

We fell back into silence, I reached for her hand and she didn't pull away. As the music played her foot tapped along with the sound and after an hour or so she sang along with "Lady in Red".

I got up and ordered another round. As I stood at the bar I chatted about the racing, trying to find out had me horses won. I looked down at her and she smiled back. My eye caught the door opening and in walked Amanda and her friends. I could feel the colour leave me face and I grabbed my drinks and got away from the bar before she saw me.

Tracy moved close as the latest act slaughtered "You to me are everything", her hand grabbed mine and she squeezed, I looked round at her and smiled.

"Go on, give us a kiss," she laughed.

I looked around me –

"Ah Tracy, yeh know I hate that kind of thing."

She laughed out loud and looked at me as though I had two heads –

"Since when?"

"I always have, yeh know, in public. There's a time and a place for that kind of thing."

She went to kiss me –

"Would yeh ever stop outta tha', you sound like an aul fella."

I avoided her advances and made my way to the toilets. As I passed Amanda I called –

"Thanks for last night!"

She spun round but I kept walking.

When I came out of the toilet she was waiting –

"I'm really sorry about last night, something came up at the last minute and I couldn't make it."

"A better offer, righ'? Don't worry about it, it doesn't matter."

"No really, it wasn't anything like that. I had to do a double shift and I'd no number for you. I tried ringing here but the phone was out of order."

I looked over at the phone and there was a sticker on it.

"I got here for last orders but you were gone."

She stood waiting for my response.

"Another time then?"

She smiled –

"How about now?"

My heart skipped a beat, I had to think fast –

"Sorry, no can do. Prior engagement."

She looked disappointed –

"Oh I see, pay-back time."

"No, nothing like that." I looked around and grabbed her close. "It's the ex, she's been stalking me."

She laughed out loud, I laughed too.

"Only messing, but it is the ex, I arranged to meet her to iron out a few things."

"I didn't know you were married?"

I winked at her –

"There's a lot you have to learn about me."

"Is it over long?"

"Years."

"Then why are you meeting her again?"

"'Cause divorce is finally in. We've just to go over a few points, nothing too much, but I better get back, don't want her stalking you too."

She smiled. I moved on a step, then turned and kissed her –

"How about in here tomorrow night?"

She nodded, we kissed again and I went back to Tracy.

"Who were you talking to?"

I gulped down the dreg ends of my pint and placed the new pint on the mat.

"No one."

"Yes, you were."

"Oh the girl, ah that's just the daughter of a fella I'm doing the extension for."

"You seemed very friendly."

I kissed her –

"You know how it is, you have to get on the good side of the customer. Come on, let's drink up and have an early night."

Chapter Twenty-Seven

Things were back to normal with Tracy. When I came down the stairs on Sunday morning, *The News of the World* was waiting beside the biggest fry you could imagine. I called Tracy's breakfast Noah's Ark 'cause it had two of everything. Two eggs, two sausages, two rashers, two bits of white and black pudding, two tomatoes, two waffles, two slices of fried bread and a load of toast. All washed down with a pot of tea. It was pure heaven, fuck the cholesterol. I hated all that shite about healthy eating. There was nothing like a good fry-up, especially when you had had a bellyful of drink the night before. I'd no time for all that shite about bowls of soup before you went out, or buckets of water when you came in. The only cure for a hangover was a fry-up first thing in the morning, followed by two pints at leisure, when the pub opened up at half twelve.

Tracy sat across from me, watching me gorge on her meal. She said she loved to cook for me because I really did it justice. She had that look of pure love in her eyes. She always had it after we made love. I hated that, it made me feel guilty. To Tracy it was lovemaking. An extension of what went on, on a day-to-day basis. For me, it was a ride. A straight leg-over job. I had a horn, she had no knickers and I was in and out as quick as possible. The last two times had been different, more like when we had started, with lots of kissing, kissing of lips, kissing of body and touching and she came in a way that made her seem youthful again and as I entered she held on as though this was our first meeting, or our last. But again I felt guilty. After all, it wasn't her I was making love to, it was Amanda.

I wiped the plate with a slice of white pan bread. And she smiled, then took the plate off me and hummed along with Doctor Hook's "A Little Bit More". Tracy always played Doctor Hook when she was in good form –

"You go in and relax, there's a Grand Prix on."

"I was thinking of going down the pub." I said, kind of guiltily. I held her from behind, my hands cupping her breasts and my head buried in her neck. She moved back against me –

"Well, don't be long. Dinner will be around half two."

I kissed her neck and had my jacket half on as I spoke –

"No worries, sure yeh know Paddy, he'd never let you stay behind on a Sunday."

The bar had the usual suspects. I strolled in, ordered me pint and looked down the line –

"Jasus, you're a sorry-looking bunch."

I seen Joe at the end of the bar –

"I'm telling yeh, Joe, if you lower yer head any further your nose'll end up in your pint."

I laughed, they didn't.

The door swung open with a load of giggling and it was the girls. Amanda saw me and waved over, I waved back and made a sign asking did she want a drink. She shook her head and nodded in the direction of her two friends.

Paul Simpson's head rose to have a look at what was going on –

"You're a jammy sod, Davey."

I ran me hand through my hair –

"You either have it or you haven't." I looked at my reflection in the mirror, "Fortunately for me . . ."

He cut in, sounding pissed off –

"Don't tell me, I know you have it, righ'?"

I laughed –

"Well, you said it, Simmo, not me."

She kept on looking over and me, I kept a banter going with the lads. Girls like the most popular fella, the joker in the pack. Paddy Mac flashed the lights –

"Right, drink up lads, time for the Sunday roast."

I held me glass up –

"Give us another in here and one for Simmo too."

Paddy Mac looked up to heaven –

"Have ye no homes to go to?"

I'd only just paid for the pints when Amanda was over –

"Howya?"

"Howya yourself?"

"What are ye doing afterwards?"

"Now? Nothin'."

"Wanna come back to the flat for a bite to eat?"

I looked over at her mates –

"Wouldn't Pinky and Perky mind?"

She laughed –

"Pinky and Perky are going home for dinner, I've got the place all to myself and I've a large Goodfellas pizza ready for the oven."

"What topping?"

"Pepperoni and peppers."

"How could a man resist?"

She looked nervously at her friends, who were starting to look at their watches –

"OK, meet me at the Church in ten minutes . . . and bring some beer."

I looked after her and Simmo watched her too, I called Paddy, he shook his head –

"Christ Davey, would ye look at the time. I couldn't risk giving ye another pint, I'm sorry. It's more than me licence is worth."

"I only want a take-out. Give us a half dozen Guinness and a half dozen Heineken?"

Ten minutes later I was stepping off me barstool. Simmo sat looking straight ahead of him –

"I hope you were in the boy scouts?"

"What?"

"The boy scouts, you know, always prepared."

"Fuck yeah, will the chemist be open?"

He searched his pocket and threw two red-foiled condom packets on the counter. I snatched them up before anyone saw them –

"That should keep you going."

She was waiting, moving from one foot to the next as if dancing. She saw me and came toward me smiling. She grabbed my arm and we went to her place. The pizza was put into the oven and the cans opened, I was only two mouthfuls into mine when we kissed. She was eager, her hands pulling at my shirt. Within a few seconds we were naked on the floor, her on top of me, holding me down as I pretended to struggle. She teased me with her nipples, putting them close to my mouth and pulling them away whenever I tried to kiss them. Each time she did her tits bounced playfully and I wanted her more.

She reached down and took my prick in her hand and from under the cushion of the settee took out a condom and expertly slipped it on.

"You must have been in the girl guides, always prepared," I laughed.

"You men can't be relied on to think of safety."

I was in her as she spoke and she slowly lowered herself on me with a sigh. She wriggled her bum down and arched her back, to make sure she had all of me inside. Then she dictated the pace, moving from slow long strokes, to short violent ones that made her moan with delight.

I counted potatoes. One potato . . . two potato . . . three potato . . .

It was the only thing that meant I wouldn't come too soon.

She wriggled . . .

Six potato . . . seven potato . . .

She spun round, her back facing me.

Sixteen potato . . . seventeen potato . . .

It slipped out and she came down on it . . . ooch . . .

Then it was back in and she was rubbing my legs as she pounded down on me.

Thirty potato . . . thirty-one potato . . .

She was back facing me, looking down with the look of a rodeo girl riding the prize bull, her body was covered in beads of sweat and I was hanging on trying to get to fifty potato, when her back arched again and she screamed out loud, animal-like and suddenly my body stiffened too and my moans excited her more and she swore –

"Oh *yes*, fucking *yes*!"

And her thighs tightened around me and drained me of anything that might have been in reserve.

She collapsed on top of me, pushing her sweaty nipple into my mouth. I was used to a break at this stage, a roll on my side, a fag and a little snooze but she was ready for action, pulling at me, as I sucked like a baby being breastfed for the first time. I could feel a tinkle down below and pretty soon he was up again, not letting the side down.

We must have fallen asleep after that, for I awoke to a shout –

"Oh fuck, the *pizza*."

She jumped from the bed and ran in the direction of a mass of smoke. The room was full of smoke and the smoke alarm was screeching at the top of its voice.

"Open the fucking window," she screamed.

I looked around and could barely make it out. I crossed and had to struggle with it. The smoke raced out. Her door was being pounded down –

"Hello? Is anyone in there?"

She was putting on kitchen gloves, trying to get the cremated remains of the pizza out –

"Will you get that?"

I looked over to her –

"Me?"

"Well I can hardly go, can I?"

Outside the caller was getting ready to knock the door down, his shoulder had already hit the door without success but his female accomplice was telling him to try again.

"Quick, Davey, he'll be in on top of us."

I ran to the door –

"It's all righ', we're grand," I coughed.

There was silence outside, then the girl spoke –

"Who's that?"

"I'm a friend of Amanda's."

"What happened."

"We forgot about a pizza in the oven but, it's OK now."

"Are you sure?"

"Yes really, we're fine. Thanks for the concern."

They walked back to their flat, sounding disappointed at not getting in. It took a good twenty minutes before the smoke left the room. We had to make do with a few cans and two batch cheese and onion sambos but we had some laugh about it.

Suddenly I noticed the clock, quarter past one. Jesus Christ, where had the night gone. I jumped up –

"I better go."

She grabbed me –

"Oh come on, you don't have to go, do you?"

She kissed my back and her arms held on to me.

I tried to prise myself away from her, without offending.

Each time I opened one hand the other closed tighter. We giggled but I needed to get away –

"Come on, Davey, stay the night, the girls aren't coming home and . . . " she tried to sound like a child, "I'll be home all alone."

I got away, stood up and moved quickly from the bed. She crawled after me.

"I gotta go, I've an early start in the morning."

I had my boxer shorts and was pulling them up, she grabbed my trousers and hid them under the covers –

"You could easily leave from here."

I moved to her, my hand out –

"I can't, I've got to put on me working clothes and get me tools. Come on, give us the trousers."

She giggled as I lunged for them –

"Ring in sick."

"I can't do that, I'm the boss."

"Well, bosses are allowed to go in whatever time they like."

I grabbed the trousers and started putting them on –

"You're joking, if I didn't show, them useless whores I have working for me wouldn't lift a finger."

I zipped up.

"You're mean." She jumped on my back and sank her fingers in.

I bent down and let her flip off my back –

"You fucking bitch."

She laughed, I looked in the mirror, there were eight long claw marks down my back and in parts they bled.

"What the fuck did you do that for?"

She rolled around with laughter –

"You won't leave me again in a hurry."

I felt along the welts –

"Christ Almighty, that fucking hurt."

She came to me –

"Aw, is my little baby sore?"

I pulled away –

"Keep away from me."

She laughed –

"Don't be such a cry-baby," she reached out and kissed along the scrapes. "There . . . Amanda made you all better."

I got out, agreeing to call around the next night, and raced home.

I could see the light on upstairs and knew she was still up. As my key turned in the door she was on the stairway –

"Davey?"

I came in without a word and headed for the kitchen. She followed –

"Davey, what happened? Where were you? I was so worried, you said you'd be home for dinner, I . . . "

I opened the fridge, took out a bottle of milk and swigged it.

"Something came up."

She looked stunned –

"What? What came up?"

I wiped my mouth –

"What is this? The Spanish Inquisition?"

179

"I was worried!"

"Yeah, well don't be, I can look after myself."

"Where were you, Davey?"

"Jesus Christ, Tracy, what is all this? I was in the pub."

"All day? All night?"

"I went for a game of cards at one of the lad's houses."

I couldn't look at her as I said this.

"No one else knew about it?"

I turned –

"Wha'? What did you say?"

She looked sick with herself, as though that had slipped out by mistake –

"I . . . I went down the pub . . . "

"You what?"

She got defensive –

"I was worried."

"So you decided to make a fucking show of me."

"You were due home for . . . "

"I know, I know. So because I didn't make it for your poxy roast, you decide to send out an all points bulletin for me. Thanks a lot, Tracy. You've just made me the laughing stock of the pub. I hope you're fucking proud of yourself."

"But I was . . . "

"Worried, I heard you. I heard you the first time and the second and the third."

I walked out of the room and up to the spare bedroom.

Minutes later I heard her lock up everything and climb the stairs too. She stopped outside the door –

"Goodnight."

I ignored her. That hadn't worked out too bad at all.

Chapter Twenty-Eight

Tracy was putty in my hands for weeks after that. She never mentioned that night again and even a couple of nights later when I came out of the bathroom without a top on, she never said a thing, even though it was clear to anyone what the marks on my back were from.

If anything, she seemed to be more satisfied than she had been in ages. We were back to our once a week quickie, in between *Father Ted* on Channel 4 and the late film on BBC 1 on Tuesday nights.

Tuesday was the only night I didn't see Amanda. I spent most of my weekends round at hers. Her flatmates weren't too impressed but we didn't care. Besides, we spent most of the time in her bedroom, thinking of new positions. Every once in a while we'd get a bang on the wall from Holy Mary, but that only made Amanda more determined to moan louder and I got great satisfaction in rattling the bed's headboard off the wall.

We couldn't keep our hands off each other, the minute I met her we'd be in each other's arms. We didn't even talk that much, it was physical and fun, no big commitments, no pressure. What made it better was that she started working nights, so there wasn't even any pressure on me to stay over. She started work at ten, so I was home and all by twenty past and Tracy would have a big feed for me and be all concerned that I was working too hard.

Amanda and me had an understanding. OK, there were things I didn't tell her . . . like I wasn't actually separated . . . not quite, but fuck it, that would only complicate the whole situation. There was no way she was going to understand that. No way that a young thing like her could understand that despite the fact that I no longer "loved" Tracy, I still *"loved"* Tracy. I mean, you can't spend fifteen years of your life with a woman and not still have feelings for her . . . but Amanda didn't need to know that. All she needed to know was that I loved her too. That every time I saw her, I got a hard-on that a man half my age would be proud of. All she needed to know was that any time she wanted a meal out, she got it. There was nothing I wouldn't do for her and now three months down the road I wanted her to know it.

PART FOUR

AMANDA'S ADVENTURE

Chapter Twenty-Nine

I had fancied Davey from the first moment he'd opened his mouth. Granted he was old enough to be my father, but I liked older men. I always *had* ever since my babysitter had let me stay up and watch *Magnum* on the telly. My mother would have gone mad if she knew that the babysitter had let me stay up that late. But it was great, we used to have a big bowl of homemade popcorn between us and Carmel, the babysitter, would say the weirdest words ever –

"He's a ride . . . I wouldn't throw him out for eating chips in bed . . . you could crack nuts in the cheeks of his arse."

And of course I was sworn to secrecy. Well, I was hardly likely to rat her up and ruin our special nights, so from that moment on I loved older men. Especially ones who looked like Tom Selleck, and Davey Brady was the nearest thing you were going to get to Tom Selleck in a pub like Paddy Mac's.

We'd only just moved into the new apartment. Mary said technically it wasn't an apartment, because it was an old building renovated to specifications, where an apartment was a purpose-built building. I told her that she could shove her technicality up her hole because, if we were paying one hundred and sixty pound each a month for it, it was an apartment. Anyway it was huge in comparison to the last place we'd had. Now *that* was a flat. Two little box bedrooms and a sitting-room-cum-kitchen-cum-my bedroom, *cum fucking everything*. At least this one had separate bedrooms and I made it number one rule that beyond our bedroom doors, what we did was our own business.

After getting the bags in, our first stop was to suss out the local. I'd been to Paddy Mac's once before. It wasn't a million miles from our old flat but that had been on a girls' night out and it was just one of about a dozen pubs we'd been to. When we'd been passing in Celine's brother's van I'd seen a notice for a talent night so I'd convinced the girls to give it a go.

They could really get on my tits at times.

Celine was so prim and proper, I'd say no fella had got his hand above her knee, never mind any further. She was a culchie, from some bog in the arse-hole of Cavan. She was easily twenty-six, although she said she was only twenty-three and no matter what, she went home every second weekend. She hated Dublin but, as I said, if she didn't stay here on the weekend how in the name of Jasus was she ever going to get to like it? I mean Dublin is *really* happening, I read in *U Magazine* that it is THE happening place in the whole of Europe. Imagine living in THE happening place of Europe and going home for the weekend to milk cows and walk hand-in-hand with Padraig O'Malley who she'd been walking hand-in-hand with since she was twelve. For fuck sake, Dublin was nursing a hangover from weekend to weekend, it was just recovering on Friday evening and there was Celine queuing up with all the other "Oh, I don't like Dublin, it's too big" bogheads.

She knew every saint's day that was ever made, not just St Patrick's Day and Easter – she knew Corpus Christi, Assumption, Ascension. I'm convinced she knew ones that the priests didn't and she was always going to confession, but what she had to be asking forgiveness for, I never knew. She hated bad language, even my favourite saying –

"Really gets on my tits" she frowned on. I used to argue –

"But *tits* isn't a curse."

And she'd look at me with that *holier than thou* look and say –

"Well I couldn't imagine the Pope saying it, now could you?"

"No, but then again he hasn't got tits has he. But Mother Teresa probably did."

I'd laugh but she'd start blessing herself, go all red and flutter –

"Well, may God forgive you talking like that about the dead."

Mary came from Dublin, somewhere over the south side and if you let her she could be a right prude. She worked in accounts and was always going to different places to do the books. I told her she must be crap at her job because everywhere she went the place closed down. But it was true, in the ten years I'd known her she'd had four different jobs. She never left, it was always because the places closed down. She was tiny, fellas were always mistaking her for years younger than she was and it was an easy mistake to make, if you didn't look at her chest. Once you did, there was no mistake. There's no way she could have grown them in eighteen years or anything like it. They were huge. Celine used to say we weren't to mention them, but how could you not? I mean to say we lived together. I saw them swell as her periods approached and you couldn't help but make a comment. I pitied her, no fella ever went with her for her looks or her brain, it was always for her tits. She'd walk in and you could see them pass her over and then second-taking, when they noticed her tits. Then they'd turn to their mates, they'd all look and some smart ass would say something and they'd all laugh. Then sure enough one of them would be over and asking her tits up to dance. They never asked her face, it was always her tits, and as soon as they were on the dance floor the first thing they'd go for was *them*.

Then she'd slap their face and that would be the end of the romance.

So it was down to me to bring the fellas back, and I had to say I had a fair record in that department. Celine thought I was a bit of a tart. I'd argue the point –

"If I were a fella and I was bringing all these partners home, you'd all slap me on the back and call me stud. But, because I'm a girl, you all call me a tart."

Mary used to say no one ever said life was fair and maybe she was right.

Anyway we were in Paddy Mac's and I'd ordered the drinks and had a laugh at Davey's comment about Mary. But as soon as I got back to the table I knew they weren't impressed.

I was putting the drinks in front of us all and I had to ask even though I knew what was wrong –

"What's up?"

Celine was holding Mary's hand, in a comforting way –

"You, Amanda, flirting with him."

As she said it her eyes narrowed and she hissed the word *"him"* out while looking at Davey at the bar. Anyone would swear he was Lucifer himself the way she said it.

"I wasn't flirting."

"You fucking were," whispered Mary.

On hearing the curse, Celine blessed herself and then patted Mary's arm some more.

I took a couple of mouthfuls of my drink in silence and we all looked down at the table –

"Oh, this is gonna be a great night," I looked at Celine. "You're jealous because I'm chatting to a fella and she's sulking 'cause they thought she was underage."

"It's nothing to do with that, she's upset because he said those things about her and you . . . you laughed."

"And who died and made you the spokesperson for the department of large breasts?"

Mary started crying again –

"Oh, stop it the two of you. Just drop it, OK?"

For a few seconds we fell into silence but I thought of what Davey said and spluttered into my drink –

"But you have to admit, it was funny."

Davey swung round and said his goodbyes but promised he'd be back later. It seemed to calm the situation when he'd gone and when the talent show started some of the acts were really quite good. We all agreed that the lad the compere said worked in the bar was best.

I had almost given up on Davey when he came in. I watched as his eyes shot around the room looking for me and with a few drinks in me I was brave enough to let him know I was happy he'd made the effort.

Of course at the end of the night the ugly sisters were over, and seeing how it was our first night in the new apartment I reluctantly agreed that we'd better go home together. I ran back, got a quick goodnight kiss from lover boy and arranged to meet him at the weekend.

I was happy and drunk as we walked home. I started singing, I always sang when I was happy. I linked the two of them and sang "Uptown Girl". I loved Billy Joel, I knew all the words, though when I got drunk I had a tendency to mix them up.

Celine broke away from my linking –

"Amanda please, you'll wake the neighbours."

"I don't care, I'm happy."

We were at our apartment.

Mary agreed with Celine as we walked up the stairs –

"Happy is fine, but just not so loud, OK?"

"But I'm happy and I want the whole world to know . . . "

I broke into song again, this time it was Captain Sensible's "Happy Talk" –

"Happy happy *(hic)* talking Happy *(hic)* talk, Talk about *(hic)* things *(hic)* you'd like *(hic)* to do . . . "

Celine was full of venom as Mary opened the door –

"You're not happy, you're drunk."

"Oooh," I let on to be scared. "The scary witch says I'm *(hic)* drunk." I put on my best Groucho Marx voice and pretended to smoke a cigar –

"Well honey *(hic)* I may be drunk *(hic hic hic)* and you my dear are ugly *(hic hic)* but in the morning I'll *(hic hic)* be sober."

Mary was by my side –

"Come on, Mandz, let's get you to bed."

She looked at Celine for help –

"Don't look at me, not after what she just said."

But Mary did look and reluctantly Celine helped –

"Well, OK, but I'm doing this for you, not her."

I tried to break loose –

"Well her has a name. And her didn't fucking ask you anyway *(hic)*."

They dragged me to my bed and dumped me unceremoniously on my unmade bed. Mary started taking off my boots. Celine looked horrified –

"I'm not undressing her."

"Just her boots, if we don't her feet will be destroyed."

I fell asleep with thoughts of Magnum, flying down the road in his little red Ferrari and me with sunglasses and a bikini sitting in the passenger seat. Except Magnum wasn't Tom Selleck, he was Davey Brady.

Chapter Thirty

By the weekend it was Davey Who? That's the way it always was for me. Well not always, there had been Billy. Billy Kennedy had been the love of my life. I was sixteen and he was the bouncer at the local disco. He was gorgeous, with his perfect physique, his thick moustache and his dickie bow. A cross between 007 and Selleck. I use to stand at the stairs looking up at him throwing out the troublemakers. It was effortless, poetry in motion. He never lost his cool, he always gave them the option of walking out the door, but sure those lads had shite for brains. They always thought they were able for anyone and everyone. They'd make a swing for Billy and he'd be as swift as a lion, pouncing on them, neatly folding their arm behind their back and frog-marching them out the door. I loved the way he always brushed himself off afterwards, like they had been a bit of dirt that had got on him. All the other bouncers thought Billy was the best too. You could see them stand back in awe.

But he wasn't just all muscle. He had a gorgeous smile and he never lost an opportunity to show it off, he was a charmer. He had a word for every girl that walked into the place –

"Howya babe? That's a new dress. New hair style? Very nice."

Or –

"The colour of you, you must have been away."

Everyone got a compliment. It didn't have to be a new dress, the hair mightn't have changed since birth and they could have been milk bottle white and not been any further than Mullingar in their whole life but Billy the Bouncer always said something.

I'd stand at the bottom of the stairs looking up at him and the other four bouncers, and every once in a while he'd look down, chew his chewing gum, straighten his jacket, roll his shoulders and wink. That made it worth the entrance fee alone. And he always had a comment, every time he passed me –

"All righ'?"

"Jasus, you're looking sweet tonight."

"Are you not dancing?" Even when he was going to the toilets he'd say something –

"Just nipping to the jacks, catch you later, yeh?" and I'd nod as my heart raced and I'd watch him all the way until the door closed behind him. Then I'd watch the door until he re-emerged and walked back toward me, zipping his fly, blowing out his cheeks and saying –

"God, I needed tha'?"

I bought him a card for Valentine's Day and handed it to him on the way in. All the lads laughed but he smiled and said –

"Thanks, luv." Then he kissed me, on the cheek, but it sent shivers through my whole body.

The disco was great, it was a proper one with signs for *"Neat dress essential"* and *"Over 21s only"* and even when a new bouncer tried to stop us going in one night, Billy was there smiling, telling him we were regulars.

Regulars no less. We'd only been there four times, I'd only stood looking up the stairs four times, but I couldn't remember a time when I hadn't been in love with Billy the Bouncer.

I went with my two best friends, they were both eighteen, but as we linked arms and walked up to the disco I still looked older than them.

Ma and Da didn't care what I did, not that they didn't *care*, but because I was their only daughter, they never stood in my way. I suppose they were afraid that being an only child I might be missing out on things, things that a child in a big family would have. There were curfews but when they were broken nothing happened. Oh a bit of a lecture, the old line about –

"We didn't know where you were, if only you'd phoned."

I'd say sorry about a hundred times, eat whatever was put in front of me, let Da kiss me on the cheek and say –

"Well, at least you're OK."

– smile and say "Yes, Dad, I'm fine." And that would be that.

On his way back from the toilet Billy stopped –

"The card was really nice . . . here, I got you this." He held out a rose, a single rose that a girl had been selling earlier.

I could have cried, he'd got me a rose.

I took it –

"It's beautiful, thanks."

I kissed him on the lips.

"No problem, someone left it in the jacks. Still, it's the thought that counts."

And he was right, he'd seen this rose in the toilets and thought of me. He'd probably been bursting to go to the toilet but he'd still thought of me.

"Listen . . . "

"Amanda, my name's Amanda."

"Yeh, course it is. I knew that."

He smiled. God, Billy the Bouncer knew my name. Billy the bouncer had gone to the bother of finding out my name.

"Listen Mandy, why don't you stay behind afterwards for a drink and a chat?"

I smiled –

"Great."

"OK, just hang back when the others are going."

He was gone, back to the door, whispering to the other bouncers, who turned around and had a look at me. He was probably telling them he'd asked me out and they were probably all green with envy.

I begged Trisha to say I was staying at hers if anyone asked, then I rang Ma and told her. She was going to start moaning but I cut in –

"Ma, you always say to let you know, so I'm letting you know."

Reluctantly she agreed.

When the place emptied out there were only the staff, the bouncers, the DJ and a handful of us girls. Billy sat talking to his mates, boasting about the thumping they'd given some fella earlier.

"Why? Had he been making trouble?"

I asked wanting to be part of the conversation.

"No, I just fancied the bird he was with."

They all laughed and I made a noise too.

The drinks flowed fast and my head was spinning, one by one everyone left, until there were only six of us left.

"I'd better have one last look around for any bodies," Billy said rising from his chair. He looked at me. "Are yeh coming?"

I jumped down, too fast, the place was moving.

He grabbed me –

"Hey, steady."

We walked around the club. It was a lot smaller now that the lights were up. He walked me into the office and as soon as we were in he was kissing me and pulling up my skirt.

I was dizzy, feeling sick and his tongue wasn't helping matters –

"Please, Billy, hold on."

He was pulling at my tights, not caring if they ripped and now that they were around my knees, his hand groped at my undies –

"Come on, you know you love it, you got me that card, didn't you?"

His tongue was back in my mouth –

"Billy, please don't, I don't feel well, I think I'm going to be sick."

My undies were down now and he was rummaging at his trousers –

"You'll be grand."

But I wasn't grand, I tried to put my hand over my mouth but it was useless, I puked up my night's drink, all that day's food, and half the lining of my stomach.

Billy was standing over me cursing –

"You stupid bitch, do you realise the trouble I'll be in if the boss finds out about this. Jesus Christ, look at the fucking mess you've made."

As if I didn't know, as if it hadn't all come up my throat. As if I wasn't the one bent over, with stomach heaving and me knickers round me knees. The door opened and two of the bouncers stood there –

"For fuck sake Billy, you'd want to get that cleaned up and fast. Hendry just rang to say he was on his way."

Billy cursed again and the next thing I knew I was outside in the alleyway, with me bag, me jacket and nowhere to go. I tried to tell Billy but he wasn't interested. I couldn't go home, Da would have the place locked up. Trisha would kill me if I knocked on hers. It was three in the morning and I was freezing. A car went by, then slowed down and an old man leered out –

"Doing biz?"

I ran and the car sped off in the opposite direction. I spent the night walking around. When I came upon people I'd quicken my step. Eventually an early morning shop that did coffees and teas opened and I went in. When the shops opened I walked around for an hour or two, before heading home and going to bed.

The next night I went to apologise to Billy but the bouncers wouldn't let me in –

"Sorry love, you're too young."

I'd learned a valuable lesson, never trust a man, and never depend on them for a place to stay.

So as soon as I'd woken up the next morning, I'd forgotten about Davey. I'd found it the best way to deal with fellas. I'd gone to a different pub every night in between and completely forgotten about him until he came up to me in the pub. By the time he came back out of the toilets I had it all worked out. How I'd tried to contact him, but I couldn't. He seemed to swallow it, especially when I acted all hurt that he was with someone else. We kissed and I thought, fucking idiot, who do you think you're fooling?

Chapter Thirty-One

The girls were going to be away and I was bored. Suddenly there was Davey, paper under arm, fag in mouth and getting ready for a pint. The answer to all my problems. I mooched over and told him I had the place to myself; he didn't need to be asked a second time.

There's something special about going with a married man, especially one who was old enough to be your father, and especially one who thought he could pull the wool over your eyes.

You'd want to see the face on him as he walked up to meet me. He was trying to look cool, swaggering along, pretending not to rush, when all the time his legs wanted to break into a sprint. He was like the cat that was about to get the cream.

I wanted a fuck, pure and simple. I wanted to be in control of my own destiny, I didn't fancy being alone and I wanted to teach him a lesson. A very expensive lesson.

He surprised me in bed. He was better than I'd imagined and quite caring. He seemed to be enjoying the fact that I did all the work. He was looking at me as though he hadn't seen a naked body in years. The truth of the matter was, he probably hadn't. She probably kept herself well wrapped up in cotton, to the ankles, nightdress.

His face was a picture when he saw the time. For a man who had no one waiting for him, he was in one hell of a rush. I left my calling card, down his back, sure I'd never see him again. But the next night he was back for more. I don't know why, but it became a habit, I still got out on my own, telling him I was working shifts, but most nights I was happy to be Davey's bit on the side.

Like when all was said and done, Davey was OK. He was good-looking and available whenever I wanted him. He wasn't jealous and every time I asked for a few bob, or a meal, there was never a problem. On top of all that he was capable of making me laugh and pretty good in bed.

I hadn't noticed the weeks roll into months. It's funny how you get into a bit of a rut, and because it was a happy rut, I didn't notice. I was doing the one thing I swore I'd never do, the one thing that I hated most about my parents, I was getting into a routine. A convenient little arrangement, just like they had.

Ma and Da weren't in love, they were just too scared to do anything about it. Da had had an affair, oh years ago when I was in my early teens but I remember it like it was only yesterday. I remember the rows, the denials and then the tearful confession.

The "I'll never do it again" the "It was a once-off, a silly one-night thing, it meant nothing".

Like that was supposed to make Ma feel better. As if knowing that it was some scrubber who he had picked up and used for his own pleasure, someone he knew nothing about, someone he used just to empty his sack, as if this was to make her feel better. I wanted her to throw him out, I wanted her to punch and scream and tear at him. I wanted her to throw all his clothes out the window, to shred all his suits, but no. Ma just sat there and listened to his whimpers, made him promise not to do anything like it again and never to mention her name in the house again.

In a way, she blamed herself, for not always being available when he needed her.

They had never been the same after that. Something died within their relationship. That bitch had taken it, had torn the walls of trust down. The scrubber who meant nothing had robbed my mother of her dignity, had made her acccept a man that wasn't perfect, and she had robbed Da of his respect for Ma. For although he was glad to be taken back, in truth he had never left. A fifteen-minute tears and confession session later he was back in the marriage bed. And a spark was gone from them.

That bitch had taken that from them, from us all. Things were talked about in a whisper, things were done now "for the sake of the family". And because they were done for a reason they lost something because of it. She'd taken that in one *one-night stand*. Taken it all with her, all our happiness, all our trust, all our respect, all our familiness. And she probably didn't even know she had. She probably never realised that she had such strength between her legs.

I spent the next ten years trying to get that back. I slept with men to feel the strength. I made them fall in love with me, got them to tell me how much they loved me, got them to confess to their wives and let their kids feel the loss and then, when there was nothing left to take, I walked away.

And I swore that I would never be with someone when it had become a routine. When it had come to the stage that you knew what was going to happen tonight and tomorrow and tomorrow week.

Davey had been a novelty at first. Then he had been a good lover. Then something to annoy the girls with. I knew his wife had to know, if she had as much as half a brain in her head. Now he was becoming what I was going to be doing tomorrow and tomorrow week. A routine.

Monday – my place at seven, take away-pizza, cans, bed and he was gone by ten.

Tuesday – we didn't see each other.

Wednesday – pictures, pub, quickie in his car and home.

Thursday – pub and bed.

Friday – pub, a disco and bed.

Saturday – cans at my place, take-away, video (and a blue) then as I sleep, he heads.

Sunday – early session in the pub, afternoon session in the scratcher.

And so it went. It was fun, my life was packed, I hadn't enough hours in the day. I was running from my bed to my job, from my job home, quick wash and hey presto he was there. When he'd gone, I was either out the door to a disco or straight asleep, waiting for the alarm to start it all again.

My life was passing me by.

I had a good Leaving Cert. Good enough to go to University but I took a year out and got myself a job to make a few bob. Of course, Uni went on the long finger. I'd got used to the money, I couldn't imagine trying to study, do a part time job and socialise. I wanted to travel the world. I wanted to see the Seven Wonders of the World. I wanted to sail down the Suez, to bungie-jump in Australia, to cross the Golden Gate Bridge. So I saved. Trouble was, just as the money was building, a nice dress appeared in the boutique window. Paddy's Day or a birthday or Christmas arrived and the money was gone again. The result was I was here, twenty-three years of age, never out of the country without my parents, no University degree, a dead-end job and a married boyfriend.

It was getting time to move on. I'd just got notice that the factory was closing down, that meant redundancies. Most people would be shitting a brick but me, I'd be there top of the queue, waiting for my big pay-off. If they needed voluntary redundancies to keep the place afloat, Saint Amanda wanted her name in there.

And if the layoffs happened there was no way I was going to stay around here. There was no need for Celine or Mary to know yet. After all, they'd just signed a contract for the new place but as soon as that cheque was in my hand, it'd be straight to the bank and changed into traveller's cheques.

Davey would have to be told too but first I had to find out what his surprise was. He said he'd be waiting. Well I'd let him sweat a bit.

PART FIVE

JOE'S JOURNEY

Chapter Thirty-Two

If I had been told a year ago that I'd be sitting in my local with a bag, full of my life's possessions by my feet, I'd have laughed. If someone had told me three months ago that I'd be making plans to spend the rest of my life with the girl who had bumped into me, spilling my pint, I'd have said they were mad.

Three months. Three glorious months. I'd spent the first twenty-nine years of my life in turmoil and now, three months later I had made a decision, for the benefit of myself.

And it all could have gone so different. In a weird way I had Davey Brady to thank for it. I hated Davey, I cringed every time the gobshite opened his mouth. Davey never missed an opportunity to slag me. Why I had ever told him my name, I'd never know. The minute Davey spotted me coming in he'd start –

"How are the Drifters these days?"

Davey was the only one who laughed now but it didn't stop him. And when he found out that I was a bachelor as well he never shut up –

"Take my advice, amigo, stay that fucking way. Once they get that ring on your finger, yer fucked. Yeh won't get a fucking ride unless it's yer birthday or she wants a kid."

I had tried to defuse the situation –

"It's not just about that, Davey."

"Oh, I agree, there's more to life then riding. There's hand shandies, blow-jobs and if you're really lucky the odd diddy fuck."

There was a woman sitting behind him, when he said that –

"Do you mind?"

Davey answered as quick as a light –

"Not at all, but is it OK if I finish me pint first."

He'd got barred for that, but he wormed his way back in, and now he was as bad as ever.

I tried to sneak off without him noticing but he always made a comment –

"Heavy date?"

I had to answer –

"No, early start in the morning."

And he'd look around for support. I always imagined him in one of those old Hammer horror movies. You know, when Doctor Frankenstein had just quietened the mob, with their torches and batons, telling them it wasn't his little monster who had killed half the neighbourhood. And they were all believing the doc and ready to go off home, when one little fucker would notice the monster and shout –

"There he is, let's kill him."

And they'd all go whoring after the monster and burn him to death. Well Davey Brady was like your man. Always wanting support, always wanting to have a mob behind him and he'd wait till they were all listening before he went on –

"Would you ever fuck off, you've got a bit of skirt waiting, haven't yeh?"

I'd smile and he'd take it as agreement.

"What is she like? No let me guess. I'd say she's a nice leggy blonde, no no, I'd say you're more the small dark-haired kind, am I righ' or what?"

I just kept on fixing myself for the walk home. There was no point in telling him the truth. Besides, in a strange way Davey had done me a favour. As far as the lads were concerned I was a bit of a stud. Davey had built this image that all the other lads looked up to. In their eyes I was hung like a donkey. Always sneaking off to meet some new bird, while they sat on their arses lashing back pints and watching their beer bellies grow. I got a wink from the lads on my way out and when I rushed through the door at the end of the night, to catch the last orders, someone always called –

"Fair dues, Joe, you've got your priorities right."

There was no point in bursting their bubble. No point in telling them that there was no blonde with long legs, no dark-haired bird with big tits. No brunette with a size eight waist, or a size ten waist or any size. There was no bombshell, no red-head, no skinny girls, no frustrated wives, nothing.

Imagine if they found out that the real reason for my early departure from the pub, and for my late entrance for the last pint, was nothing other than Mother.

That evening, I walked outside, turned my collar up against the westerly wind, and walked briskly down the road. As I turned the corner of Mother's cul-de-sac I could see the net curtain rustle in the downstairs sitting-room. I cursed under my breath and quickened my step, almost running to the gate, up the path and through the front door. I could see her shadow making its way into the kitchen –

"Joseph, is that you?"

I hung my coat up on the banister and walked into the kitchen –

"You know it's me, Mum."

She was busying herself at the oven –

"How would I know it was you?"

"Because you were spying at me coming up the road."

She held a Pyrex dish between her oven gloves and walked to the table, which was set for the two of us –

"Don't be talking such drivel. Now wash your hands in the sink and get this into you. It's your favourite, Irish stew."

I walked to the sink, sprayed some Fairy Liquid on my hands and scrubbed them with the nailbrush –

"I'm not talking drivel." I dried my hands in the tea towel, "I seen the curtain move."

She spooned a large ladle of stew onto my bowl and a smaller amount on hers –

"That'll be the breeze, there's an awful draught in that room."

There was no point in arguing. If I persisted she'd go quiet, start crying, telling me about her poor health and how hard it was being stuck indoors, by herself, all day. More to the point, she wouldn't go to bed. She'd sit sniffling into her hanky, poking the fire and watching the Oireachtas report, and if she did that there was no way I'd get out for last orders.

If that happened I'd have to content myself with listening to one or more of my three hundred and sixty LPs, my four hundred and two seven-inch singles, fifty (collector's items) twelve-inch singles, my two hundred and three tapes, and as of today, with the latest edition to my collection, one hundred and forty CDs. She'd made me a prisoner in my own home, and while there, music had become my only escape.

And there was no point in telling her that I hated stew either. Well, not that I hated it more like I hated having it every Wednesday. Mother liked routine. Every morning I came down to a fry, never scrambled eggs or cornflakes or even porridge, always a fry. My lunch was cheese sandwiches wrapped in tinfoil, with a packet of King cheese and onion crisps. Dinner was stew Monday and Wednesday, and cabbage and bacon on Tuesday and Thursday. Saturday was chicken and Sunday was chicken and cold meats. All dinners came with boiled potatoes and two veg, followed by either rhubarb and custard or jelly and ice cream. Friday I escaped dinner on the pretence of working late. And that was it, seven days a week, fifty-two weeks of the year, except at Christmas, when we went with Auntie Angela to my sister Sissy's house.

I hated Sissy. I hated them all. Sissy, Chris and Ann. They were my brother and sisters. They'd all gone, flown the nest, as Mother would put it. Like they were some kind of mythical birds, some rare species that everyone loved and adored. We'd be out in the front garden, Mother and me, picking up papers that had blown in and got caught in the chicken wire that divided us from our neighbours. And Mother would dictate the paper-gathering and as people passed she'd stop and talk to them. They'd ask about the others and Mother would always give the same answer –

"Oh sure, all the others have flown the nest."

I could feel the sympathetic look of the passer-by on me.

"But Joseph is still with me. Ah sure, there's no moving him."

They'd all smile and go on their way and I'd be left with a handful of waste paper. Left to eat the cabbage and bacon on me own. To listen to Radio One, to bow my head and beat my chest for the Angelus and to watch the Nine O'Clock News, no matter what else was on.

I hated them all. If I heard Mother saying how great Chris was, just once more, I'd go mad.

Good old Chris. Chris who had the great job and the lovely wife. Chris with the fancy job. Chris who had kept the Dolan name alive with his beautiful twins, Mark and Simon. And wasn't he great to have named the boys after their grandfather? Chris who sent the beautiful bouquets, specially delivered by InterFlora on Mother's Day. Wasn't Chris great?

Well no, actually, he wasn't. Those flowers that took pride of place on the windowsill, so all the neighbours would see them, were impersonal. He didn't even bother to sign them himself; the message was always written in the florist's scrawl. And sure we'd need to have a picture of him to remind us what he looked like, it had been that long since he was home. Every once in a while he'd send a video tape of the family and get the boys to say "Hello, Gran." It'd be played over and over again, and every time it was, she'd laugh and say –

"Aren't they beautiful?"

There was always an excuse as to why he couldn't visit, or why Mother couldn't visit him and although Mother swallowed every line he spun, I knew there were times he'd had to come to Ireland on business and not bothered his barny to drop in.

But it wasn't just him. Sissy was every bit as bad. She lived in her big fancy semi-detached in Templeogue, with her husband and three kids. Her husband had a big job with some insurance company and they were always entertaining. Still, despite all the parties she threw, despite all the rooms she had, the only time we were invited over was for Christmas Day. And it was just the day, not the night-time too. Oh no, the night they were going to a party. We were picked up after ten o'clock mass, driven out, given a few glasses of wine, the usual pressies and a meal wearing stupid party hats. We were home and all by seven just in time to watch the reruns of *Morecambe and Wise*.

It was as obvious as hell that she was ashamed of where she came from.

The only one who helped out was Ann. She called in on Mother twice a week and once a month she took Mother overnight.

I hated my life, but there was no way out. I had no social life, no friends other then the other lads who stood and sat around the bar at Paddy Mac's. Even then, it wasn't as though you'd call them friends. They were more like people who shared the same space. We all talked about things but at the same time, talked about nothing. There were those there who I'd see outside the walls of Paddy Mac's and they wouldn't even recognise you.

Most of my old "friends" had all either moved on or got married. Lads that I had hung around with, played my guts out with on the football pitch, were now fathers themselves. They came back to the area but only to visit their parents. As they drove by they'd beep their horns and wave. The odd time we met in person the conversation was always stilted. Trying to remember old friends who had moved on too.

Now, my only real friends were the voices on my records. I had evenings in with Bob Dylan, Jim Croche, David Bowie to name but a few. I'd give myself theme nights, nights where all the artists had something in common. Like all Motown singers, or Rock 'n' Roll, or Ska. But Mother would start banging the floor shouting –

"Joseph, I can't hear myself think."

And so, my *friends* would have to be packed up for the evening.

I'd tried to break away myself but each time something happened.

Everything had been OK while Dad was alive. We'd been a normal everyday family. I was fifteen at the time, playing for the under-sixteen team and when the older teams were a player short, playing for them too. Dad came to all the matches. He was so enthusiastic. The manager would give his team talk and then Dad would always say a few words.

It was funny, 'cause for all his enthusiasm, he hadn't got a clue.

Dad had been a boxer, nothing to write home about by all accounts, but that was his sport. So he used boxing terms to describe what he wanted us to do –

"Johnny, you're a southpaw right?"

Johnny would look at him like he had two heads. I'd have to explain –

"You're left-handed."

"Yes, yes, that's what I said, you're a southpaw, so I want you to come to your marker, slide under, bring your shoulder down like you're going to go right, then shimmy and go left and swing an up and under across. Got it?"

All the lads loved Dad. Especially when there was trouble on the pitch. He was the only adult shouting –

"Hit him!"

It was a shot out of the blue when he died. We were all fussing around packing for a weekend in Donegal. We were in and out packing the car and getting things ready.

"I bags my tapes for the first hour," called Chris.

Sissy started to whinge –

"No, I'm not listening to Frankie Goes to Hollywood."

"Well tough shit, 'cause I bagsed it."

"Mam, Dad, Chris said a curse."

He went to pinch her –

"No, I didn't."

"And he tried to pinch me."

Dad came around the door –

"Righ', neither of you are getting a choice." He shouted to me, "Joe what do you want on?"

I was delighted. Dad was the only one who ever took my choice into consideration. I grabbed my Bruce Springsteen "Born in the USA" and the other two moaned. Dad had a look and smiled –

"That looks good." He caught Ann on the stairs, "And what would you like to hear?"

But before she got to answer we all shouted together –

"Prince, 'Purple Rain'."

Dad laughed –

"OK, so it's Springsteen and Prince, that's settled."

Mother made tea and a salad and told us we wouldn't be going anywhere until it was all eaten. Dad said he was going to take a nap, because he had a long drive ahead.

We savaged every scallion and leaf of lettuce and Mother made a batch of sandwiches and filled the two flasks with tea before going to call Dad.

He never woke.

The doctor said it was a massive heart attack. The priest said we should be thankful he didn't suffer and happy in the knowledge that he was going to a better place.

The accountant at the factory said that Dad hadn't signed up to any insurance policies and as such Mother wasn't entitled to anything from them. Still, as a token gesture they paid for the funeral and the managing director, who Dad used to curse from a height, said some very nice things about him.

Mother changed.

She was never one for going out, but now she didn't go further than the garden gate. She became mean, resenting us having lives. Ann was seventeen and going with her boyfriend for two years. Suddenly he wasn't good enough for our Ann, suddenly Mother didn't want her staying over in his house, or him staying here. It put a strain on them. She never let them be alone like before and eventually they broke up. He had a girl from around the corner pregnant within three months. Mother threw this in Ann's face –

"See, that's all he wanted, that's what they all want. They use you and then, when you come to depend on them, they leave you in the lurch."

Ann met Paul on the rebound and married before the year was out.

Sissy moved out almost immediately on the pretence that

she needed to be nearer her work. I knew she was living with her boyfriend and didn't want what had happened to Ann happening to her. I stayed on in school and did my Leaving Cert. Then I took a job in the local Quinnsworth, as a trainee manager. Chris went to England for a summer break with an uncle over there and never came back. That's when things went really bad. I should have noticed, I should have acted on it there and then and if I had, I'd probably have stubbed it out.

But I liked living at home. I had friends, I had my music, I had my football and I was good at that. Quinnsworth were great about it, they sponsored the team and when we were in an important match they let me have time off. I never had to work overtime on training nights and the manager said they had plans for me, if I kept my bib clean and kept showing the enthusiasm I was showing.

A week later I was brought into the office. There was a course in wine being held. This was when wine wasn't big in Ireland. It was when fellas drank pints, got pissed and still drove home. Wine was for woofters and down and outs. But, the manager said, wine was the way forward. I was one of only three trainees picked for the course. It would be hard work but there were trips to France, Germany, Spain and Italy as part of it.

"A chance in a lifetime."

That's how the manager described it.

I couldn't wait for the shop to close so I could get home and tell Mother. She'd be so proud. She was always talking about how well Chris was doing and now, she'd be able to say the same about me.

I could get a bus that would leave me at the end of our road but I'd just missed one and I didn't fancy having to wait another fifteen minutes for the next one. I ran all the way home and burst through the door, out of breath.

Mother was laughing with excitement at the state of me –

"What is it Joseph, what has you so hyper?"

I spoke at a mile a minute –

"Big opportunity . . . the boss said . . . a course . . . France, Germany . . . only one of three . . . chance of a lifetime . . . "

I hadn't noticed Mother taking a seat, she was gasping for her breath –

"Mother, what is it?"

She grimaced –

"Oh nothing, just a twinge, it'll go."

She grimaced again, I ran to her side –

"Will I get the doctor?"

She held my hand –

"Sure there's no point. Just sit down and tell your Mother about the trip."

I was panicking –

"What do you mean, no point?"

In pain, she pulled herself upright in her chair –

"I had the doctor already."

"How come you never said?"

"I didn't want to be upsetting you, you have enough on your plate."

"What did he say?"

Her face curled up in agony.

"Mam! That's it, I'm getting the doctor again."

"No son, there's nothing the doctor can do, there's nothing anyone can do," she blessed herself, "except the good Lord."

She told me about the lump, about the X-rays, about cancer running in the family. She made me promise not to say anything to the others. That together we'd get through it.

The next day I went into the manager and explained the situation. He was disappointed, not just because they'd have to find someone else but for me as well. He told me if I needed time off just to ask.

That was the first in a long line of illnesses. I found it strange that I never saw the doctor, stranger still that she never needed to be hospitalised and strangest of all that the illness always got worse when there was a chance that I could be going off somewhere.

The management had been sympathetic, at first. Terry Cash, a trainee who was only in the place a wet day, got to go on the course instead. Then I had to make excuses when I'd been offered a transfer to Galway as an assistant manager. There were another three courses and two assistant manager positions that I had to refuse, before I was brought into the head office.

The area manager had a file and he flicked through it, without once looking up –

"We've put a lot of time and energy into you, Joe."

"I know, Mr Williams."

"Your staff reports are among the finest that I've ever seen, but you can't stay a trainee manager forever. There's a course starting in Cork on Monday. It's three weeks and I want you there. All expenses will be paid and you'll have to stay down there on the weekends."

"Thank you, Mr Williams, I really appreciate this."

Mr Williams looked up from the file –

"Don't let me down, Joe."

"I won't, Mr Williams."

I went home and explained the situation to Mother.

"Well, naturally you'll have to go on the course. Sure you can't be letting that fine education go to waste."

"Now, Mother, you know this is down in Cork?"

"Of course I do, I'm not stupid. No, you go, I'll manage, sure I'll have to."

That night I heard a thud in Mother's room, she called out and I ran in to find her sprawled on the floor, writhing in agony.

I rang Ann and explained the situation.

"Joe, I can't help you. The kids have the measles, I'm up to my eyes in it."

I rang Sissy.

"Joe, I'm sorry, but Mother staying here is out of the question. We're leaving for our holidays in Florida the week after next . . . "

I cut in –

"That's not a problem. Just take her this week. Ann can take her the next week."

"No, I'm sorry. You know I'd help if I could, but I've just so much to organise this week I can't."

I tried to reason with her but, realising it was useless, I cursed her from a height and hung up.

I left three messages for Chris. He never returned them.

I was told I couldn't remain a trainee manager all my life. They were sorry but it was probably best for all concerned if I handed in my notice.

I came home to the sound of mother singing –

"The tablets worked then?"

"The tablets? Oh yes, they worked, but look. Look what my darling sent me."

Standing pride of place on the mantelpiece was the ugliest bouquet of flowers I'd ever seen and a card, written by the florist –

"Get well soon, Chris."

That was eight years ago. I'd picked up a job on the factory floor. With the references Quinnsworth had given me, they offered me a job as part of management. It would have involved going away on courses. I said I'd be happier just doing manual labour. I swept floors, packed cases onto trucks and watched people who had started years after me move on, while I stayed exactly where I'd started.

Chapter Thirty-Three

So that night, three months ago, I backed down again. I let her have her way, just as I always did and after moaning about all the drivel on the telly (mother never cursed) she went to bed. I was out the door as if I was on fire. I knew she'd be looking out her window, watching me go.

I made Paddy Mac's just as he started shouting –

"Come on now folks, have ye no homes to go to?"

Paddy caught me in the corner of his eye and handed me two pints –

"Don't be letting anyone see you getting them."

"Cheers, Paddy."

I had few pleasures in life, fuck it, I had *no* pleasures in life, bar my pint and my music. The football had been lost to Mother's illness after we'd been due to play in a tournament in France. I could have gone back the next season, but what was the point?

I was just on my second mouthful when it was knocked from my hand. It fell in slow motion, I grabbed at it but only managed to topple it on its side. The glass splattered as though it had been hit with a hammer and suddenly the bar counter was awash with glass, my beautiful black Guinness and its creamy head. It looked like a dirty sea running across the counter and mixed in was my blood as though there had been a shark kill in the sea of Guinness.

She was by my side, apologising and trying to mop it up with a paper tissue, Paddy Mac looked over and cursed –

"Leave it, fucking leave it. I don't need a goddamn claim for injuries too."

She was red in the face and repeating the same word over and over again –

"Sorry, sorry, sorry . . . "

I smiled, wiping myself off –

"It's OK, honestly, don't worry about it."

She noticed the blood –

"Oh God, you're bleeding!"

"It's nothing really."

She had my hand and was rubbing furiously with her paper tissue at the wound –

"I think you need stitches."

Paddy Mac was wiping the counter down with a cloth –

"Give us a look." He grabbed my hand and pressed down hard around the wound. Then he threw my hand away.

"It's only a scratch."

I pulled my hand down by my side. Paddy Mac said he'd get me another pint, she started searching her bag –

"I'll pay for that."

"No need," said Paddy Mac. "It's on the house."

She looked at my jacket –

"Well, at least let me pay for the dry cleaning of your jacket."

I laughed –

"If this was dry-cleaned it would fall to pieces. Honestly, you're fine. There's no need to do anything. Accidents happen."

I could tell she was still very embarrassed and couldn't wait to get away.

She faded into the crowd and that was that, or so I thought.

But as she left with her friends at the end of the night, she waved.

Saturday night I got in at my usual time and Paddy set my two pints up with his usual refrain –

"Don't let anyone else see ye with them."

Then he turned to the rest of the shop and shouted, *"Have ye no homes to go to?"*

I was standing there, enjoying the bit of freedom I had earned. It had been a hard day, what with the garden to be done and a picture to be hung in the hall. Anyone else and a picture would be a five-minute job, but not Mother.

"Left a bit, a bit more, no, no, no! That's too far . . . yes that's better . . . now up a bit, higher, a bit higher . . . yes, now straighten it, up, up, no the right hand . . . " and so it would go for the afternoon. Then when all that was done, she insisted on watching Pat Kenny. Mother hated Pat Kenny, he'd spoken bad about Gay Byrne, or at least that's what one of the papers said he'd done and, since then, Pat couldn't do a thing right. She even switched off Radio One when he was on. Yet tonight she wanted to watch him and so we'd to sit through people flogging their books, to the latest model to break into the big time. God, they all looked the same to me, big toothy smiles, tits that some photographer was going to tell them would have to be enlarged if they wanted to succeed and that gaunt look that told you that they honestly thought that good looks meant you didn't need a brain. The music was good, I'll give him that. Pat always had great music but I had to admit that the thought of a pint was more appealing. Mother watched everything, moaning as she did. I watched the clock and it seemed not to be moving at all.

Eventually she decided to go to bed and I got out. Sometimes I wondered would I actually like a pint as much if I could pick and choose when I could have one. Like if there was no Mother, would I enjoy every pint as much as I enjoyed these ones. I suppose it's like with the Lotto. There's them that say you couldn't be happy with that much money. Still, if I wasn't happy couldn't I just give it away? The same with the drink. I'd like to try a spell when I could come in whenever I wanted and drink 'til I fell on my face. If I didn't enjoy it, couldn't I always revert to this way of a pint at the death?

"Hi."

The voice came from nowhere. I spun around and didn't see anyone who fitted it. Then I looked down and saw her, the girl who had spilled my drink the other night –

"Ah howya?"

"See there's no disasters tonight."

I smiled –

"No."

We stood in silence. I wished I could say something, but nothing came out. She seemed as embarrassed as me.

"Sorry for disturbing you, I'll go."

She went to walk away, I grabbed her arm. Too hard –

"Oh sorry, I didn't mean to grab you, it's just . . . I . . . I . . . I'd like you to stay . . . that is if you want . . . like if you have somewhere else to go . . . your friends . . . " I could feel my face start to go red. "They'll be wondering where you are."

She smiled and touched my arm –

"No, they won't."

I was still nervous –

"Yeah, but you're probably going on somewhere."

"No, I'm not. Let me get my drink and I'll be back to ye."

While she was gone I cursed myself in my brain. *Come on Joe, relax, get your act together, just talk to her.*

She was back. She sat up on the stool beside me. We smiled at each other –

"You're back."

God what a stupid thing to say, of course she's back.

"Yes, I'm back."

We sat in silence, then both of us talked at the same time.

"So where do you work?" "So what do you do?"

We laughed, I recovered first –

"Sorry, you first?"

She looked like she was going to say, "No, you," but she didn't.

"I'm in O'Brien's factory."

I frowned, puzzled, I was sure I'd have noticed her –

"Me too, what department?"

"I'm in the office."

"Oh."

She smiled –

"Is that a good *Oh* or a bad *Oh*?"

I got flustered. *You stupid idiot, she thinks you're anti-office.*

"No, no, it's good. It's just I thought I knew everyone on the floor."

"So what department are you?"

I was embarrassed. I swept floors and loaded vans. It had never bothered me before but now it did –

"Loading bay."

Her face looked puzzled as if she was thinking that O'Brien's didn't have a loading bay, but she just said –

"Ah, that's good."

Her friend came over –

"Are you right, we're heading?"

She looked at me –

"Do you mind?"

"No, not at all, you go on."

Her friend cut in –

"You can come with us, we're heading to the Kitchen."

Her eyes were on me, but I couldn't make out if the look was one of wanting me to go, or wanting to kill her friend for asking me.

"Naw, you're all right. I don't think the Kitchen is quite my style."

Never a truer word said. Sure wasn't I the gobshite who had the chance to see the first ever U2 concert in the Dandelion Market and I wouldn't go. I could hardly go to the Kitchen now, could I?

She was off her seat quickly, too quickly, knocking back the last of her drink. Her friend walked off –

"I'll get the coats."

She stood in silence for a moment, then spoke –

"Are you sure you won't come?"

"No, thanks all the same, it's not really me."

"Is it anyone? Come on, it'll be a bit of craic and if you don't like it we'll leave."

"Another time, yeah?"

She looked hurt. She went to walk away –

"Fine, see you again."

I panicked –

"NO, WAIT!" I shouted.

She stopped.

"Sorry, I didn't mean to shout. I didn't mean to sound uninterested either. It's just I really don't want to go to that Kitchen place. But . . . "

She cut in –

"Yes?"

"But, I would like to meet you again."

She smiled.

"That's if you would like to."

"Well, under one condition." She looked very serious. "That you tell me your name."

I laughed –

"It's Joe, Joe Dolan."

She stretched out her hand and shook mine –

"Mary Moore, glad to meet you."

As we shook, her friend came back. Mary looked at me –

"I'd better go."

She stood looking at me and me at her –

"Joe?"

"Yes." I answered excitedly.

"Can I have my hand back?"

She laughed, I looked down and realised that I still had hold of her. I let go as if it was on fire –

"Sorry."

She laughed.

"So, Joe Dolan, when are we meeting again?"

My mind went blank, she answered her own question –

"Tuesday?"

"Yeah, Tuesday."

"See you here about seven?"

"Great."

She smiled again, leaned over, kissed my cheek and walked away –

"See you then, Joe Dolan."

Chapter Thirty-Four

It wasn't until she had gone when, I'd finished my pints and was walking down the road toward our turn that I thought of Mother. Usually it would send a panic through my body, thinking of how I was going to get around her, but for some strange reason it never happened.

Mother had ruined so much of my life, so many opportunities, so many romances. Well, that was a lie. There hadn't been that many romances,only the one.

I'd known Peggy Cosgrove since I'd started in school. We were friends, best of friends. I'd thrown worms down her back, put spiders in her pencil case and thrown snowballs every winter at her. I'd been her patient in Doctors and Nurses, she'd been my wife in Mammies and Daddies. We'd swum in the Liffey together and when her foot had got caught in the spokes of an old bike someone had thrown in, I was the one who dived in to release her. Peggy could climb a tree as good as anyone, she was great at the three-legged race and no bad footballer either. Well she was never picked last. We spent every moment together. I couldn't imagine a time without her. I missed her when her family went on holidays. When we went on holidays I begged for her to come and when she wasn't allowed, I wrote a postcard a day, and brought her the biggest stick of rock home.

Peggy was the first girl I loved. I was six and everyone was writing initials on their desks, I wrote JD loves PC.

All the rest of the class laughed but she kissed me, my first kiss, and said she loved me too. For a whole week we held hands and sat beside each other, then I wouldn't give her my poster of Abba so we stopped holding hands and I scrubbed her initials off my desk.

She was my first Valentine, proper Valentine. I sent her one of those huge cards, with the message *"I love you this much"* on it. We were fourteen and thirteen respectively and I didn't even write one dirty verse. She sent a small card with nothing but dirty verses. I had to hide it from my parents, who were very surprised that she hadn't sent one. She was the first girl I kissed properly, on the lips, tongues and all. Later she was the first girl I touched, the first girl I saw without her top on and later, much later, the first girl that touched me.

Daddy dying changed everything. Mother became rude to Peggy. She'd answer the door and say –

"Oh, you again." Then leave her at the door 'til I came in. She would burst in on us as we listened to records in the front room. Unannounced, she'd just come through the door. Peggy became reluctant to open her blouse, because of the frequent attacks. I tried putting a chair up against the door but, when she saw that, Mother banned us from the room altogether.

Peggy stopped calling. We still dated, but I had to go around to hers or meet her outside the cinema. I started working and we had great plans, plans of running off to Gretna Green, and marrying, but it never materialised. Mother got sick, sometimes just when I was about to walk out the door.

I'd go back, help her to her seat, make her a cup of tea and sit with her. She'd tell me to go, but cough so much, grimace so much that I couldn't. Then she'd say –

"Well, you better ring Peggy and let her know, tell her your mother is sorry for being such a nuisance. Invite her over."

Though I couldn't see it at the time, Mother knew exactly what she was doing. I'd ring Peggy –

"Hi Peggy, how are you?"

She wouldn't answer my question –

"Joe, where are you? You were supposed to be here half an hour ago."

"I know, I'm sorry . . . it's just Mother . . . "

"Don't tell me, she's not well, right? Tell me what is it this time? What new disease has she come up with today?"

It would go on and on, I'd try to explain, Peggy would get more and more frustrated and eventually she'd slam the phone down saying –

"Well, stay with your precious Mammy then."

I'd try ringing back but her phone would be off the hook.

It would take me a week of phone calls, cards with silly verses on them and a big bunch of flowers before she'd see me. We'd be OK for a week or two but, then Mother would act up again and things would be back to square one.

Peggy hated the way everyone else in my family was getting on with their lives and I wasn't. The way I was letting opportunity after opportunity go by. I knew she was right, but I resented her telling me. I'd say stupid things like –

"I don't ask you to choose between me and your mother."

It made no sense, her mother never got between us in the way mine did. But I felt I had to defend Mother in some way. After all, Father was dead.

Peggy always pointed out that my dad had died over five years ago, and everyone else had got on with life without him.

She was right, Peggy was always right, and I knew that regardless of what, I had to make a stand. The next management position that came up in Quinnsworth I was

225

taking and come the countdown of the New Year I was going to get down on my knee and ask Peggy for her hand in marriage.

New Year's Eve came. I'd gone into a fancy jewellers and bought a solitaire diamond ring. I hoped it was the right size. I'd borrowed a ring she always wore on the same finger on the right hand, so the girl said there wouldn't be much difference.

We hadn't seen much of each other over the Christmas, Peggy had been to see her sister who lived in London and was only coming home on New Year's Eve. I was really excited, I'd told no one. I had run over it time and time again. As we stood waiting for the last few seconds of the old year to pass, I'd go down on bended knee, in the middle of the crowd at Christchurch and propose.

I rang her house a few times in the day, only to be answered by her father, telling me she wasn't home yet.

Mother was in good form too. She was all excited about the New Year –

"We'll have a nice tea and watch the festivities on the telly. RTE always do a good show, then when the bells ring we'll go out on the road and greet the neighbours."

I had to be positive –

"Mother, I won't be here for the New Year; I'm going down to Christchurch with Peggy."

She looked shocked –

"But . . . but you always stay in for the New Year."

"Well not this time."

She said nothing. She walked away and a couple of hours passed without her coming back. I put on the kettle after watching a summary of the year that was. It was nearly all about the Gulf War. All Desert Storm and embargos. Everyone was fighting the Iraqis, the Brits, the Americans, the Yugoslavians. The Birmingham Six got out of prison, Winnie

Mandela went in. Terry Waite was released, Freddie Mercury died, so did Robert Maxwell, and Bryan Adams whinged his way through "Everything I do, I do for you".

Kettle boiled, water in teapot and Kimberley Chocolate on the plate, I called Mother.

I carried the tray into the sitting room with all the goodies on it. I placed it on the coffee table and poked down the fire, then threw a few more briquettes on it.

I shouted from my seat –

"Mother! Tea!"

I poured the tea and ate a Kimberley, then another. We'd only opened the box on Christmas night after coming back from Sissy's and already they were nearly all gone. I rose and walked out to the hallway –

"Mother, your tea is getting cold."

I listened for a response but there was none. I walked up the first six steps of the stairs –

"Mother?"

I ran up the rest of the stairs. I knocked on her door, but still no answer –

"Mother? Are you all right?"

I pushed the door but it was jammed. There were no locks or bolts on any of our doors, not even the toilet, which often caused embarrassment. I pushed harder, still no budge.

I put my shoulder to the door and, keeping my body low, pushed hard. It opened enough for me to look around it. She was lying in a bundle behind it.

"Mother!" I screamed.

I pushed hard, using every bit of strength I had and opened enough to get through. Then I picked her up and put her on the bed. I rubbed her hand –

"Mother . . . Mother."

Nothing. I tried to get a pulse, but I was panicking so much

I couldn't find one. I placed one hand open-palmed on her chest and thumped with the other . . .

One . . . twice . . . three times.

She coughed, I sighed.

For a moment she looked around as though not able to work out where she was.

"Mother, are you OK?"

She seemed confused –

"Yes . . . how did I get here?"

I tried to explain –

"You went upstairs, you'd been gone a long time . . . so I came up to find you."

"Yes, I remember. You upset me, I came up to get away from you, I fell and called out to you, but you had the telly on."

"Mother, I'm sorry."

"Oh it's OK, I know I can't expect you to put me first."

"It's not like that."

"Whatever, you go and do your own thing."

"I can't leave you alone."

"'Course you can, you were all set to."

"That was before I knew you were sick."

"I could fall at any time, my legs aren't what they used to be."

I felt guilty –

"I'll make you a fresh tea."

"Only if you have the time."

I went down to the kitchen and put the kettle on again. The phone rang. I picked it up on the fourth ring. The line was bad –

"Hello, hello?"

There was a crackle and a hiss and it went dead.

I had only gotten back into the kitchen and the phone rang again. I cursed under my breath and walked back out –

"Hello."

My voice was cross.

"God! That doesn't sound the voice of someone who's had a great Christmas."

"Peggy! Howya? Where are you?"

"I'm still in London . . . "

I was so excited to hear her voice I cut in –

"Did you have a good time?"

"Yes, but . . . "

"Never mind, you can tell me all when you get here. What time does your plane get in?"

"That's just it, I can't make it?"

"Aah no, what is it? Fog?"

"No, nothing like that."

"Decided to stay on a while, enjoying the lights of the big city, who could blame you, you . . . "

"Joe, shut up, will yeh?"

I stopped and she let the silence linger down the phone for a minute –

"I met someone."

Silence on her end again. I coughed –

"Who?"

"It doesn't matter who, you don't know them."

"But us, what about us?"

"There is no us, Joe. There hasn't been an us since your father died. You can't pee without your mother . . . "

"But that's all going to change, I'm gonna . . . "

"Don't Joe, please don't. It'll never change, you'll never change, she'll never change, we'll never be anything."

"We will, Peggy, we will. The next promotion that comes along I'll go for it, we'll move, we'll marry."

"NO, JOE! It's all talk. You say all this, then she puts her spoke in and you can't stand up to her. It's over."

I went to argue, to tell her about the ring but, on the other end of the phone a beeping noise cut across her –

"Joe, I'm going to get cut off. I'm sorry, Joe, really I'm sorry. Have a good New Year."

The line went dead. I held the phone, shouting down it. I stood staring at the dead phone.

Mother's voice broke the silence –

"Who was that?"

I didn't answer. I walked back into the kitchen and made the tea.

When I got back to her room she looked pale and old –

"I thought I heard the phone."

"You did, it was Peggy."

"Oh," she said, "what time are you meeting her?"

"I'm not. We're over."

She said nothing. No *why*, no *sorry*, no *do you want to talk about it*.

An hour later, she got up and we watched RTE together. Every half hour on the button, she said –

"Isn't this nice?"

I drank so much tea I thought I'd burst. We ate the mince pies Mother had made and ate cheese sandwiches. As the clock struck twelve we hugged and went out to meet the others on the street.

Mother came in and rang all the family. No one was home.

Well, it was eight years on now. Peggy had married and divorced the fella from London. She never came back, except on holidays and even when she was home she ignored me. I could see even now, she had no respect for me.

Well, once bitten twice shy. I'd lost Peggy, never did get the promotion and spent my days loading vans and sweeping floors, all thanks to Mother.

Well, this time Mother would know nothing about Mary at all. Maybe something would happen, maybe nothing would. Either way it was going to be my fault, no one else's, if it failed.

Chapter Thirty-Five

I told Mother I was working late and wouldn't be home until later. She asked how late and I said I didn't know. She asked me to ring her as soon as I did know but I didn't bother.

She made me extra sandwiches, so I wouldn't be hungry.

I had to sneak my clothes out in a bag; luckily she didn't notice.

I was in good humour all day and when the buzzer went I went into the men's toilets and washed under my arms in the sink. I had a shave and changed. It was still only quarter to six,.I walked out the factory gates, the smell of Blue Stratus strong in the air. A car pulled up –

"Someone looks smart?"

"Sissy!"

She smiled –

"Don't look so surprised. Jump in, I'll give you a lift home."

"No."

It sounded very abrupt.

"I mean I'm not going home, not directly."

She looked vexed –

"Is that fair on Mother? After all, she is old. She needs proper looking after."

"Well if you're that worried you can always take her for a while."

"That's not an option. All I'm saying is that she's been alone all day, the least you could do is go home for a couple of hours before you go out."

I was going to have a go at her, but I knew if I did, she'd tell Mother and she'd know I wasn't working late.

"Are you going to the house?"

"Yes, I think it's time Mother made a will."

"But she has nothing to leave."

Sissy looked at me like I was some kind of imbecile –

"It shows you what you know about property. That house is worth a bob or two."

"But that's my home. I live there, I pay the bills."

"When Mother dies that house will have to be split four ways. It's only fair, everyone agrees."

"Who's everyone?"

"Chris, Ann and me."

"And when did you all have this out?"

"Last week when Chris . . . " her voice faded.

"Chris was home and he didn't visit Mother?"

She was red in the face –

"He was very busy, he had . . . "

"He had time to visit you . . . and for you and him and Ann to have a little chin wag."

She looked embarrassed –

"I must rush. I have a game of bridge at eight-thirty."

I leaned into the car –

"Don't tell Mother you saw me."

She shook her head –

"She deserves to know where you are."

"Fine, but remember, she deserves to know when Chris is over too."

She tore off, not looking in her mirrors and almost

colliding with an on coming car whose driver slammed on his brakes, hit his horn and shouted after her –

"Fucking women drivers!"

I entered Paddy Mac's to a low whistle from Davey Brady –

"Very snazzy, who's the lucky girl tonight?"

I smiled, walked to the other side of the bar and ordered a pint.

Five minutes to seven the door opened and in walked Mary. She looked beautiful. Her skirt was just above the knee and her jumper was tight on her top. I hadn't realised how big she was. She smiled and walked toward me. As she did Davey shouted –

"Howya, Dolly?"

She glared at him, so did I; he seemed oblivious to both our looks.

I walked and met her five paces from where I was drinking, she held her cheek up and I kissed it.

"Oh, very continental," called Davey.

"Ignore him," I said to her.

"I intend to."

We planned to go and get something to eat, after a drink or two, but the conversation flowed so well that it was ten thirty before we realised it. We went to the chipper, with full intentions of going back to her apartment to eat them. As we reached her road, she cursed –

"Ah fuck!" She looked so annoyed, "I'm sorry Joe, that wasn't meant to come out."

"What is it?"

She was looking at a car up ahead –

"That's Davey Brady's car. That means he's in there. I don't think I could face him."

"Davey is in there, why? I don't understand. Davey's married isn't he?"

"He's supposed to be separated. It doesn't matter, I just don't think I could stomach him."

We walked along the canal, eating our chips and burgers and onion rings, chatting about everything and oblivious to everything and everyone. I found myself telling her about everything. About Father, the family, my jobs, my friends or lack of them and most of all my mother.

She never spoke, not once as I explained. I'd look at her and she'd smile, nod, look sad and squeeze my hand but she never voiced an opinion one way or the other.

When I'd finished I turned to her –

"Sad, amn't I?"

"I don't think so."

I looked at her suspiciously –

"No? Well, I think I am. I think I'm pathetic."

She held my hand tighter –

"Don't be so hard on yourself. All you're guilty of is loving your mother, that's not a crime."

"Maybe not, but I shouldn't have let her monopolise my life the way she did."

"That wasn't all your fault."

I looked away –

"I know."

She cut in –

"But it wasn't all your mother's fault either."

I was curious –

"You don't blame Mother?"

She held both my hands –

"She lost her husband, you lost your father. There was bound to be a void, a huge void for both of you. This isn't about apportioning blame."

"No?"

"It's about forgetting the past, forgetting who's to blame

and getting on with the rest of your life. This is the first day of the rest of your life."

I smiled –

"You reckon?"

She was smiling too –

"Yes, why not? You can spend the rest of your life blaming your mother, blaming yourself, blaming your father. Making the same mistakes day in, day out. Or you can take your own destiny in your own hands and start again."

Suddenly it was as though she had come out of a trance and realised that she had said too much –

"God listen to me, spouting off, telling you how to run your life. We don't even know one another and I'm telling you what to do."

I held her –

"I did ask."

For the first time, I realised the difference in height. I bent down and kissed her –

"Thanks."

She looked straight at my eyes –

"For what?"

"For being honest."

We held each other close, across the road a milk float clattered by –

"What time is it?" she asked, watching it pass.

I looked at my watch, then looked a second time –

"Twenty-five past three."

Her face looked as shocked as mine.

We grabbed a taxi, she jumped out at her place, we kissed and said our goodbyes, then I continued home. As I paid the taxi man I could see a light on in the hallway and a curtain flicker in the sitting room. As I walked up the front garden the door opened. She was standing there crying –

"Where have you been? I've been worried sick."

I found myself making up an excuse about working late and then a union meeting and then going back to a workmate's house.

We drank a cup of tea together.

She was very upset –

"You should have rung."

I agreed.

"I was five minutes away from ringing the guards."

"Mother!"

She was adamant –

"Well, I was. I had all manner of visions of you. Slumped in a gutter, with a knife in you."

I got up and kissed her head –

"Well I'm sorry, but I'm grand. Now come on, let's get off to our beds or there won't be any point in us going."

Chapter Thirty-Six

The next day my eyes were in the back of my head but I was the happiest I'd ever been in my life. I was sweeping the floor, whistling to myself, oblivious of what was going on around me.

The voice from behind me brought me out of my daydreaming –

"You look as bad as I feel."

I swung around to find Mary there, a folder in her hand. At first I felt those butterflies that they say you get with your first crush but they quickly vanished as I remembered the brush in my hand and the pile of dirt at my feet.

My voice was harsh –

"What are you doing here?"

She smiled –

"I work here, remember?"

"No, I mean what are you doing here, in Departures?"

"There were some papers needed initialling by the Area Manager, so I thought I might as well get a breath of fresh air."

I couldn't relax, I kept looking up and down the corridor, as if we were doing something illegal. She copped that there was something wrong –

"I'd better get going."

I let her get a few paces away.

Inside a voice was screaming at me to say something –

"Can I see you again?"

It blurted out, sounding all wrong. She stopped, I continued –

"I mean, can we go out again? I really enjoyed last night."

She smiled –

"Me too, but not tonight, I'm knackered . . . and I think you could do with an early night too."

The voice in my head called to me again, don't let the opportunity go –

"How about Thursday then?"

"Same time? Same place?"

I nodded.

She started to walk off –

"See you there then."

I watched her go and once she'd disappeared from sight I continued my work, whistling as I went.

Every time that we met, nothing else mattered. She asked about my mother, she understood the difficult situation I was in, she didn't pressurise me, or condemn me, or ask for anything and because she didn't, I felt more like giving everything I had.

Mother knew there was something up but, because I was giving nothing away, she could do nothing about it. I was getting down to the pub at my usual time and Mary would be there with a pint ready for me. All the lads were surprised to see me with the same girl, surprised to see me bringing one of my floozies back to my local. One of them whispered as much to me as we shared the urinal.

"I'm surprised at you!" He said looking straight at the tiled wall in front of us. For a split second I didn't realise he was talking to me. Lads usually say some throw-away comment when they're standing in front of a urinal, something that could be picked up on, or let flow down the gutter along with all the piss. Usually it was something like –

"An awful waste of beer, all this piss."

"Pity you can't recycle this stuff."

"I'd say that Paddy Mac has a pipe running straight back into the kegs from here."

So when it was a personal comment I was lost for a moment –

"Sorry?"

I looked over, a thing men never do. We can stand together, willies out not two foot from each other but God help the man that looks at another man with his willy hanging out. I quickly looked back at the wall.

"I said I'm surprised at you, above all. Bringing a bit of fluff to your local. Jasus, when you dump her you'll never have a moment's peace."

I couldn't quite take it in that this man who, judging by the pot belly on him, hadn't seen his own willy, never mind anyone else seeing it, was telling me how to dump a girl. But as always I didn't argue –

"Suppose so."

He shook his willy a couple of times, then zipped up –

"Still, a standing prick and all tha', wha'?"

Without washing his hands he walked out.

Well, they could think what they liked, I was happy. No, fuck it! I wasn't happy, I was delirious, I was over the moon, a new man. And if I was a new man it was time I acted like one. It was time I carved out a life for myself.

I came back to Mary, nodding to the fat man who winked a wink that meant – "don't thank me for that piece of information."

"Who's he?" asked Mary.

"The brains of the urinals."

"Do I want to know more?"

I laughed –

"No, I don't think you do."

I took a few sips of my drink –

"Mary?"

"Yes."

"I've been thinking . . . ."

"Now, that could be dangerous."

"No seriously, I have. I've been thinking about going for promotion."

She was quiet. I continued –

"You know, the next time it comes up."

She still said nothing.

"You don't think it's a good idea?"

"It's not that . . . "

"What then?" I was getting a bit nervy, like I was about to hear something I wouldn't like. "Do you not think I'm up to it?"

"No, nothing like that, it's just . . . I'm not supposed to say anything."

"Tell me."

"OK, but you've got to promise that you won't tell anyone else. If this got out there'd be murder."

"God, this sounds very ominous."

She looked around, moved closer and almost whispered –

"The factory is in trouble."

"Trouble? What kind of trouble?"

"Financial, it hasn't been making money now for years, that's why I wouldn't go looking for a promotion. You'll be lucky, we'll all be lucky to have jobs at all. They're going to start offering voluntary redundancy in the next few months."

I went quiet.

"I'm sorry," she said, touching my hand.

"Why? It's not your fault." I looked up and smiled. "Is it?"

"No! of course not. But I'm sorry to dampen your hopes."

"Well, don't be. You're the reason why I'm thinking of doing this anyway. And besides, there's plenty of places I can look for a job, a decent job, with decent money, so I can ask you something and know you'll have no reason to knock me back."

"Do you mean what I think you mean?"

I returned to my drink –

"You'll have to wait and see."

Chapter Thirty-Seven

The news of redundancy hit the shop floor about a week later. There was panic all round and a lot of hostility to the office. At lunch one day Mary and another one of the girls from the office were surrounded by four of the biggest mouths on the factory floor.

"Here they are now, the bitches responsible for us losing our jobs."

The girls ignored them.

One of the men grabbed Mary's arm –

"Hey you, I'm talking to you."

She looked scared, he kept hold of her.

"Please let go of my arm."

"Not until you hear a few home truths."

I grabbed his shoulder –

"Let the lady go, Peter."

He swung round, still holding her arm –

"Lady? I don't see any ladies here, all I see are two little tramps responsible for me losing my job."

"They're only doing their job, Peter. Only totting up figures. If the figures don't add up that's not their fault."

"Whose fault is it then, Mr Know-it-all?"

He let go of Mary, but she stood looking on –

"Leave it, Joe, it's not worth it."

But I couldn't leave it. I couldn't leave another bully getting his way –

"I'd say if productivity is down, it's the likes of lazy fuckers like you who are as much to blame as anyone."

He looked back at his cronies –

"Would you look who's calling me lazy? The fucking sweep."

They laughed.

"Yeah, I'm the sweep, but at least I'm not letting on I'm anything other than that. I'm not the one running his machine at half speed, or getting things caught in it, so he doesn't have to do anything. I'm not the one with a boot full of merchandise."

"That's slander, Joe, I'd watch me mouth if I was you."

"Yeah, well, you're not me. And it's only slander when it's not right. Why don't we get security to have a look in your boot?"

"Nobody's going next or near my car."

"Fine, just keep your hands to yourself and we'll forget this ever happened."

That night Mary was all over me, telling me I shouldn't have said what I said but she was glad that I had. She told me that according to figures the factory needed to get at least a quarter of the staff to take voluntary or it would have to close down completely –

"But the likes of your job, I reckon, is safe."

"I don't care, Mary, I'd be glad to get out of the place."

"I'm not being smart, Joe, but what would you do? I know they're always going on about the Celtic Tiger but, believe me, if you haven't got qualifications the length of your arm, or years of experience in some field, forget it."

I sat feeling hurt.

She reached over –

"Joe, I'm not being hurtful for the sake of it. The redundancy package is good but it won't last forever and you don't want to spend your days looking at your mother across the table."

Of course she was right.

What did I know about? What field was I an expert in? I had a huge collection of music and books and that was it. I could tell you, without a shadow of doubt, what was number one in the charts at any time in any year. I could tell you the day Glen Miller died in a plane crash, or Louis Armstrong's first UK gig. I could quote from every song in every musical from *Cats* to *Fiddler on the Roof*, but what good was that?

Chapter Thirty-Eight

Over the next few weeks we had lots of conversations just like that. Each one just went to prove to me, more and more that my life was a mess. I needed to be brave, to take a chance, to do something for *me*.

Then one evening I came in and Mother was sitting crying –

"Mother, what's wrong?"

"You're late."

I was, but not *that* late. I'd met Mary after work and we'd talked about the latest offer from management. She said it was definitely the last they'd be putting forward and that anyone who wanted it had to have their name in by twelve the next day.

"Sorry, I got a bit held up . . . "

"With what? Your fancy woman?"

She took me by surprise. She smirked –

"Thought you could keep your little affair secret from your mother, did you?"

"It's not an affair."

"Well, you don't seem proud of her, sneaking around like you do. Is she married?"

"NO!"

"Well, what then? You definitely don't show her off. You haven't once brought her around here."

"I didn't want to, OK?"

"Why? Is she so ugly you'd be afraid of scaring your poor mother to death?"

"Mother, don't be so rude. You don't even know her."

"And whose fault is that then?"

I couldn't answer, of course it was mine, but what good would it do to tell her the reasons I'd kept Mary at bay.

"How did you find out?"

She laughed –

"Oh, your mother still has a trick or two left in her, despite what you may think. There's still a few people who talk to me as a human being, not as a hindrance."

"I don't treat you badly."

"Of course not. My son has a girlfriend, but rather than tell me, he sneaks around having a sordid little affair. He heads out leaving me alone and me not well."

"Mother, there's nothing wrong with you. There never has and God knows, there never will be."

She nodded –

"And you'd know? You've suddenly become an expert on my health?"

"I'm not saying *that* but you know as well as me that you never get a doctor."

"You ungrateful little cur! All that I've done for you . . . "

I cut in –

"Done for me? What have you ever done for me, other than ruin every chance I ever had!"

Her face was red with fury –

"Stop it, stop it. I forbid you to talk to me this way! You'll apologise to me now, do you hear me?"

"No, Mother, I won't apologise. I've said nothing that I shouldn't have said years ago."

"So this is what your fancy woman has taught you. How to be cruel to your mother!"

"I didn't need anyone to tell me what to do or what to say."

She started to cry.

I was so angry. She was pulling out all the stops but this time I could see them for what they were –

"You can give that up for a start. There's no tears falling, Mother."

She picked up the poker that was lying on the fire hearth beside her and threw it at me.

"You ungrateful little bastard! Sissy was right about you."

Her face changed, realising she had said something she shouldn't have.

"What was that? What was that about Sissy?"

She cowered, pretending to be crying.

I walked over to her –

"Mother, what did Sissy say?"

She wiped her face –

"Nothing, son, your mother is just a bit upset. We're all tired. Let's get some tea. How about if I made us both a big fry up? Wouldn't that be nice?"

I grabbed her arm and stopped her from moving out of her chair –

"MOTHER, WHAT DID SISSY SAY?"

She pulled away –

"Stop, Joseph, you're hurting me."

But I didn't stop and eventually she spoke again –

"She said I should change my will. She said they all deserved their cut too."

"But this is my home."

She said nothing.

"Mother, what did you do? You know we've always said this was my home. What did you do, mother?"

Still she said nothing. I pulled away –

"You did it, didn't you? You fucking changed the will."

I banged my hands on the table.

"Why, Mother, why?"

"It seemed fair. An even break between all four children. They've been good to me and you . . . you were going behind my back meeting this fancy woman, planning, plotting."

"Sissy told you, the bitch." I stormed back to her. "Did she tell you that Chris had been home but hadn't bothered to see you? Did she tell you that they all met up?"

She was holding her hands over her ears –

"Stop it. Stop it. Stop telling your lies!"

I stormed out of the room and up to my bedroom. I looked around at everything I owned all neatly stacked in place. I pulled my bed across and, jumping on it, reached above the wardrobe and grabbed down a suitcase. I started packing things in it, not caring whether they matched or what they were.

She arrived at the door –

"Here, Joseph, I brought you a nice cup of tea. We're all hot and bothered, sure it must be the weather . . . "

Her voice trailed off as she saw the suitcase –

"Joseph, what are you doing?"

I kept packing –

"What does it look like I'm doing?"

"But . . . why? There's no need. We'll all sit down and talk this over. We'll . . . "

"It's too late, Mother. I'm doing what I should have done years ago."

"But . . . what about me?"

I stopped and looked straight at her –

"Get one of the others to look after you. After all, they should do something for their quarter share in this place."

I pulled the case shut, leaning my knee on it so it would shut.

I pushed by her, taking my leather jacket from the wardrobe –

"I'll call back for the rest of my stuff in a day or two when I get sorted."

She followed me down the stairs, stopping half way –

"Where are you going?"

I pulled my jacket on –

"I haven't a clue, but anywhere is better than here."

"You're going to *her*, aren't you?"

I looked straight at Mother, my eyes showing the honesty of my answer –

"If she'll have me, yes."

She was screaming as I opened the front door –

"I'm not well . . . the doctor said . . . "

I grabbed the door knocker and as I left I swung it hard –

"Tell Sissy, I'm not interested."

I could hear her shouts as I walked down the garden. The door opened –

"I'm cutting you out of the will, do you hear me?"

She could do what the hell she liked, cut me out of her will, cut me out of her fucking life for all I cared. I just kept walking and at that moment I felt freer than I'd felt in years.

PART SIX

MARY'S MOMENT

Chapter Thirty-Nine

It was great being one of the girls. Not having to live at home, listening to Mum and Dad's endless arguing. Or worse still, the deadly silence that came after it. The hours of sitting in atmosphere that you could cut with a knife. With Mum and Dad using you as a mediator –

"Will you tell your father that his dinner is ready?"

And she nearer to him than me.

"Will you tell your mother that I'm not hungry, and that if I was hungry I wouldn't be eating that rabbit-food she's calling dinner?"

He never looked up from the paper.

And then she'd about turn with a –

"Would you tell that father of yours, that it's not my fault that all *his* mother could cook was a cremated rasher?"

And it went on and on until I screamed –

"Oh shut up the two of you!"

And then they'd forget their argument and join forces against their evil spawn.

No, I was better out of it. Even if Amanda and Celine got on my nerves every now and again.

I'd known Celine from secondary. Dad's job meant that we were always moving home. That meant I went to countless schools and never really had time to get friendly with anyone. My secondary years were spent in Cavan, that's where I met Celine. I never really got on with her, she was a bit of a know-it-all. In sport she was tall so she always made all the teams, but me, I was small and I was always last to be picked. I hated sport. It was stupid, running around after pieces of leather or rubber, carrying sticks and skelping the legs off each other. Jumping up and down on the spot. I mean to say, what good was that going to do you unless you were getting a job in an orchard? I hated every sport but I hated basketball most. It was the big game in the school. Each class had a team and if the class was big enough some classes had two teams. It wasn't an option to say you didn't want to play. I was on Celine's team, she was the captain and she never played me. I sat on the bench having to get excited every time Celine went running toward the basket and sailed through the air to give us another two points. I found the ball too hard, too heavy and too bouncy. The board was miles away, even when I was right under it I found it so hard to score. On top of all this I hadn't grown an inch in height for the last three years and instead, I was growing out. I was four foot five inches. That's fifty-three inches high and my bust was thirty-six inches. That was only a difference of seventeen inches, it was nothing. I was nearly as wide as I was long. And it was all out front, DD the woman in the shop said, as if I was supposed to be happy about it.

Every time I got on I was conscious of the sniggers from the boys who always came to watch. The thought of them making comments put me right off, and so every time the ball came near me I panicked and either dropped it, threw it out of play or foot faulted. I'd look at Celine and she'd throw her eyes up to the sky. Two minutes later I'd be back on the bench, cheering, while Celine scored another beauty.

I did get my chance one day. It was the semi-finals and Celine had brought us through almost single-handed. We were up against the best side in the competition, and Celine was scoring like there was no tomorrow. The trouble was that every time she did, they went up the other end and scored. There'd been a bad dose of the flu in our class and our team was down to seven fit players, including me. They played with the same five until Jenny slipped and twisted her knee. Patsy went on and I was the only fit player on the bench. I prayed that no one needed a breather or got hurt. There was thirty seconds left and we were ahead by three points when Margie Rice fouled one of their players, gave away a free throw and reached five fouls which meant she had to go off.

Celine ran over, as lean as a greyhound, and beads of sweat falling from every part of her. I thought sweat was disgusting. She looked at Jenny who was sitting with her ankle in a bucket of ice –

"Any chance of you coming back on?"

Jenny shook her head, Celine looked at me –

"Right, Mary, come on. All I want you to do is to go down the other end of the court and bring one of their players with you."

So I was a bloody decoy, they didn't want me touching the ball.

I ran on and the boys, who were a bigger than usual crowd, all cheered as my bra strained to keep my tits in place. I ran past the centre circle and stood. One of their players came to mark me, but someone shouted –

"Move up, don't bother with that one."

Their first shot went straight into the basket. The referee indicated they'd another two shots. Their second went the same way. Still thirty seconds left and they were only a point behind. Their player shot the last shot, the clock started again.

Twenty-nine . . . the ball was in mid-air . . . twenty-eight . . . all the players were moving under the basket . . . twenty-seven . . . it hit the back board . . . twenty-six . . . it ran once around the ring . . . twenty-five . . . it ran twice around the ring . . . twenty-four . . . it fell out . . . twenty-three . . . hands clammered for it, touching it but not grabbing hold of it . . . twenty-two, twenty-one, twenty . . . Celine's hand reaches out and pushes it over everybody . . . nineteen, eighteen . . . it comes toward me . . . seventeen . . . I grab it and pull it into my chest . . . sixteen, fifteen, fourteen . . . I freeze as everyone heads in my direction. . . . twelve, eleven . . . there are screams from everywhere –

"Get her . . . throw the ball . . . tackle back . . . run Mary run . . ."

Ten, nine, eight . . . They were on me . . . "Get her . . . Mary, throw it!"

I was facing my own basket watching them come. I closed my eyes and as hard as I could, I threw the ball over my shoulders . . . seven . . . six . . . five . . . the ball bounced ten yards away from me and careered high into the air . . . four, three . . . girls from both sides chased after it . . . Celine was like a gazelle as it bounced for a second time, she snatched it in midflight and shot . . . two . . . one . . . the ball sank into the basket as the buzzer rang out.

We all hugged and kissed, and in that second I realised about the beauty of sport. No one slagged me, no one said it was a fluke, they all just joined in the celebration and even though I didn't get to play in the final, it didn't matter.

After that Celine chatted to me, on and off.

The next year Dad's work moved him again and I never saw Celine again until she moved to Dublin.

Celine was very trendy, what with her long lean body, everything she bought she got off the peg. No turning up trousers, no letting out jackets, no measuring for bras. I dressed to try to hide my shape. God, men never seemed able to talk to my face. We started going to discos, but the only fellas interested in me were fellas interested in diddies. And they made no bones about it, they'd come over and say –

"Did you grow them yourself?"

Break their heart laughing and expect me to dance with them. Then the ones who said nothing, just thought you knew what they wanted. They'd go to kiss me, but their hands would be on my boobs already. It was a nightmare. I hated discos. I loved the music and the chance to dance, but the continual battle with men was just too much. Sometimes I wouldn't bother going out at all, but the alternative was to stay in and listen to Mum and Dad.

I got a job in an accountancy firm. I loved the work and the opportunity it gave me to leave home. I couldn't believe my luck when Celine said she needed to move out of her digs. We got a flat. It wasn't great but at least it was cheap and it was ours. We advertised for someone to share and that's when I first met Amanda. Amanda was mad, she was so bubbly and outgoing, that she was like a breath of fresh air. Celine wasn't too happy about Amanda moving in, but we needed her input to the rent so she had no choice.

The first night Amanda moved in we all went out on the town. She was known everywhere we went. Fellas were buying her drink and if they weren't, she was robbing drinks off the tables.

She danced to every fast number, asked fellas up for slow songs and decided to throw a party back in the flat. Celine nearly went mad when she found out. The next day the flat was like a bomb had hit it, but all Amanda wanted to do was to go out drinking again.

Whatever, we all got on, most of the time anyway.

Chapter Forty

I hadn't got a lot of luck with fellas. I suppose I wasn't what you'd call a classic-looking person. I wouldn't turn heads, I wouldn't make them look twice. If it wasn't for my boobs, I don't think anyone would ever have noticed me.

I wasn't like Celine. I wasn't sporty and elegant, and I definitely wasn't like Amanda. She could go into a room and light it up, but me, I preferred to sneak in and get into a corner where I wouldn't be seen. The girls would try to encourage me to come out of my shell but I'd always been like this.

I suppose it was because I was part of such a big family. I was slap bang in the middle of a family of seven. Mum never had time to blink, never mind cater for everyone individually. Our table was like a war-zone. The food was brought out in large bowls and it was up to everyone to get what they needed. You'd be elbowed, scratched and prodded with a fork as you tried to get your fill. The result was that the more aggressive members of our family got the best of the food and the rest of us had to make do with the scraps. I loved desserts. Every night mum would make a huge jelly, or a rhubarb pie with custard and there'd be lots to go around. It resulted in me never fighting my corner and taking solace in sweets and other fattening things. I became described as having puppy fat. Like it was something cuddly, like a labrador pup. All I was short of was a toilet roll. Mum would say it at least twice a week, especially when talking to the neighbours.

She'd look at me after someone had said I looked lovely in my dress and say –

"Sure she's grand, and that bit of fat is only puppy fat. It'll be gone in a year or two."

Except it didn't go after a year or two, or three for that matter.

I became a teenager and the puppy fat was still there. The rest of my family were like whippets but me, I got bigger and bigger, I grew a chest and started wearing glasses. I was prone to acne and my teeth were in a brace. I never got a Valentine. No, that's a lie, I got one, which was from my father. He'd been doing it for years. I recognised his writing. It was so embarrassing. My sisters all had three or four, even my brothers managed to get some really dirty ones, but me, I had one, with flowers on the front, written in my father's handwriting and marked "guess who?"

I let on I didn't like that kind of thing but really I wanted to be the same as anyone else, with the same amount of cards as everyone else, with the excitement of trying to work out who had sent what. But I had the one. I often thought I'd have been very wary of someone who found me attractive anyway.

By my Leaving Certificate I'd lost most of the spots, my teeth were out of the brace and my puppy fat hadn't gone completely but it wasn't the problem it had been. I still wore glasses but for my Debs Dad bought me contact lenses. It was the nicest thing he'd ever done for me in his life. My brother Colin had a friend who was two years older then me. I had a crush on Michael since I first saw him. Back then he didn't even look in my direction but lately I'd caught him looking over at me when we were in the same room. Michael had a lot of girl admirers. Whenever I passed him in the street he always had a girl on his arm, and some nights I'd hear him and Colin talking about girls and what they did and didn't do with them.

Most of my friends had been with a fella. they'd all French-kissed and let fellas take them to the back row of the cinema or into the cemetery on their way home. They all talked about heavy petting and wearing and being felt up. Some of them even talked about going all the way. Me, I hadn't even successfully passed the French-kissing stage.

Rupert Henry was the first boy to take an interest in me. I hated him. We were both fourteen, I was puppy-fat with glasses and acne, he was just plain fat and ugly. He had horrible long greasy hair, which he scratched all the time. His shoulders were a mass of dandruff. In class he'd use his Parker pen to scratch big lumps of the stuff out of his head, then he'd rub it off onto his trousers.

He had the personality of a snail, and anytime he wasn't scratching, he'd be eating a Curly Wurly or some such thing. But despite all that, I still went out with him. The reason was simple: he was the first boy ever to ask.

We went to the pictures (not the back row). He bought enough food that you'd think we were going into hibernation, not the cinema. There were three large bags of sweets, two Cokes (large) and a bucket of popcorn. He bought two Snickers and a Twix and as he paid he turned to me and said –

"Do you want anything?"

Reluctantly he shared some of his popcorn, I got three bon bons, a bite of his Snickers and after much sulking a sip of his Coke, which he accused me of drinking half of.

I fell in love that day, right there in the cinema. No, not with Rupert, with Tom Cruise. He was just the most gorgeous thing I'd ever seen on two legs. And he was so cool in his uniform. *Top Gun* was just the best film I'd ever seen. I told myself that I was going to buy the soundtrack the minute I got out.

Halfway through the film, Rupert put his arm around the back of my chair. Two minutes later, as he munched through a packet of Scotsclan, his hand landed on my shoulder and rubbed as though he was trying to rub something out. He pulled me close to him and pushed his face toward me. I could get the smell of popcorn off him. Our lips smacked, loudly, together. The minute they did, his fat little tongue was trying to force its way into my mouth. I pulled away, Jesus Christ, it was as though he was trying to get his food back. His hand stayed perched on my shoulder and he went back to munching. He didn't try again until the guy out of *ER* died. This time I let his tongue in. It was sprinting around from top to bottom and across from side to side like a squash ball against the walls of a court. Suddenly he stopped and yelled out. His tongue was caught in my brace. He was yelling at the top of his voice and talking in indecipherable words –

"Moh tong', moh tong' eh caugh'!"

People were turning and laughing at the sight of him standing over me, talking like the Hunchback of Notre Dame.

Eventually I had to put my hands onto his tongue and jerk it out. It was horrible, like a little fat worm. He sank back into his seat feeling his tongue and crying –

"It's cut, me tongue is cut."

I sat stone-faced. I went so low into my seat that I couldn't even see the film. I wanted to die. I wanted to be back home in my room, listening to Mum and Dad fighting, I wanted to be anywhere other than in the cinema.

Then, to make matters worse, he tried to kiss me again. I pushed him away –

"Gerroff!"

I grabbed my coat and ran crying from the cinema.

I feigned sickness for the next week so I wouldn't have to see Rupert. When I did have to go back to school, I cornered him and told him if he ever told anyone about that day, I'd cut him into little pieces and feed him to the mice in the science lab.

After much coaxing Michael agreed to take me to the Debs dance. I heard him tell my Dad that finances were tight at the minute and I know Dad gave him money because he told him that for that kind of bread he'd better show up in a tux, with chocolates and an orchid.

I was in a state, Michael was meant to be at our house at seven o'clock and it was already twenty-five past. Dad was giving Colin daggers looks.

"What? It's not my fault."

"Well, I hope to Jasus he shows up, or you'll be going."

I started crying –

"I can't go to my Debs with my brother. I'd never live it down."

Mum was dabbing at my cheeks –

"Don't cry love, you'll ruin your make-up."

"You'll go with whoever I say you'll go with. I'm not forking out that kind of money for a dress and tickets for them not to be used. So if I say you'll go with your brother, you'll go with him."

Colin threw his hands into the air –

"Don't I get a say in all of this?"

In unison we all shouted –

"NO!"

Just then the door bell rang.

Colin made it first –

"Thanks be to Jasus. I was nearly having to take me Da's suit out of the mothballs."

Michael laughed and sauntered in, without a care in the world.

Dad attacked him –

"Where the fuck were you?"

His eyes were in the back of his head, but he still looked gorgeous –

"Yo, chill man. I'm here, ain't I?"

Dad walked up to him and sniffed his breath –

"Have you been drinking?"

It was obvious by his eyes that he was high as a kite –

"Never touch the stuff man, honest."

Dad grabbed his car keys –

"Come on, let's get going."

Mum picked up the camera –

"A few pictures first."

I saw Colin whisper to Michael but I couldn't make out what he said, Michael nodded –

"Right on, man, sure I got them here."

He produced a Quinnsworth bag and took out a box of Quality Street and a bunch of roses. The price tag was still on the sweets and most of the roses were broken –

"Here you are, Colin's sister."

He always called me Colin's sister.

"What in the name of God is that?" Dad asked as I took hold of them.

Michael looked stunned, as if he couldn't believe that Dad didn't know.

"It's like, flowers and sweeties, man. You know, just like you ordered."

"I meant a fucking orchid and a proper box of Milk Tray."

Michael laughed, he was the only one who got the joke –

"Oops! Guess I boo-booed. But you know, Horticulture was never my best subject at school."

Mum glared at them all –

"Forget it, Mary has an orchid anyway. I was afraid you wouldn't pick the right colour, so I got one today."

"Yo, Mrs M, lifesaver."

"Can I have a picture?"

Michael seemed to notice me for the first time –

"Wow, Colin's sister, major transformation."

I laughed. Mum backed us up against the drawn blinds.

"What in the name of fuck is that?" Dad screamed, pointing at Michael.

Michael looked down at himself, then noticing what Dad was pointing at, smiled and replied –

"Oh the T-shirt, yeah man, ain't it radical?"

Dad was speechless as Michael continued –

"I just seen it in a shop and thought I gotta have it. Who needs a shirt and dickie bow, when you can have them all in one on a T-shirt?"

We got the photographs taken and drove to the Debs in total silence. Dad told us that we were to get a taxi home. Then as we got out, I saw him give Michael more money.

I enjoyed the night. All the girls were jealous that I was with Michael. Well, not exactly with him. He stood at the bar with his friends and us girls danced to everything from Jive Bunny to LuLu. The only time that he got up was when they played a Guns and Roses song, and that was just to stand in the lead guitar position and shake his head like all heavy-metal heads did.

The night ended in the hotel and started on the streets. We were free of prying teachers' eyes and as we walked the streets we sang at the height of our voices –

"Take me dancing naked in the rain."

We reached the Burlington, had breakfast and back out onto the streets to sing and dance some more.

"Been around the world and I . . . I . . . I can't find my baby . . . "

We reached Stephen's Green and the boys decided we'd go in and feed the ducks. It never occured to us that we'd nothing to feed them with. With much hardship, a lot of strain and a fit of giggles, we all got over the fence. I'm sure we didn't look too lady-like and one or two of us must have torn our dresses, though we didn't notice at the time.

As we walked through the park we sang more songs and the gap between couples widened. It was as though without speaking, the boys knew what each one was thinking. They put their jackets around our shoulders and walked hand in hand. The songs grew slower –

"And when you rise in the morning sun."

We got to the ducks and held our hands down as if going to feed them. They weren't interested. It seemed like they weren't quite awake, or perhaps it was 'cause they'd never seen people at this hour of the day. Couples disappeared. Onto benches, some on the grass, some behind bushes until there was just Michael and me. We stopped by the bandstand. He ran on the stage and got down on his knee –

"Mammy, I walked a million miles for one of your smiles . . . "

I giggled at his mimicking.

He came to me –

"Come on, let's dance." He pulled me to the stage and started singing –

"Tonight, won't be like any night . . . "

He was right: as we danced, it was like nothing else mattered. I wanted to bottle it, to put it in a time capsule and hold it for the rest of my life.

He twirled me round and round until we both fell with dizziness, laughing, into each other's arms. He held me close and we stared at each other, without words, for what seemed ages.

"Do you fancy a toke?"

I stared at him, puzzled –

"What?"

"A bit of draw."

From his pocket he pulled a homemade cigarette. I knew it was cannabis or some such shit.

"NO!"

He smiled, sat up and lit it. He pulled in the biggest breath I'd ever seen anyone take, the top of the cigarette shone like a nightfly, then he exhaled and it was as though he had just found the answer to all the world's problems –

"You've never tried this, have you?"

"NO, and I've no intentions of either."

"Why?" He took another toke. "It's great shit."

"It's illegal."

"Most of the good things in life are. But it's harmless, all the coolest people take it." He drew on it again. "But hey, if you don't want to enjoy yourself, well, don't let me stop you."

I hesitated for a second, he watched me, then held it out in my direction. I took it.

He sat upright, an excited look on his face –

"OK, now just barely touch your lips with it. Don't wet the top of it."

I did as he said and waited for my next instruction –

"Yeah, that's it. Now suck in until your lungs are full and hold it for as long as you can."

I sucked. It felt hot as it moved into my lungs, my eyes felt as though I was after peeling an onion. I could feel the smoke come back up my throat and banging on the palate of my mouth, wanting to get out. I held on, like I used to when holding my breath under water in the bath. He was smiling. I could feel my head go light and my face go purple. Eventually I couldn't hold it anymore and I spluttered out. He took the cigarette off me and inhaled as he watched me. At first I just lay there looking up at the top of the band-stand, thinking to myself that it could do with a lick of paint. It wasn't having any effect on me.

Then suddenly someone switched on the lights, they must have, because where the paint was crumbling was now a mass of beautiful coloured rabbits. They bounced up and down to the music, a carousel, and Michael was singing along with it. He had a beautiful voice and the words were the most beautiful words I'd ever heard in my life –

"Colin's Little Sister, are you OK? Mary baby, you OK? Here, have some more . . . " The rabbits were changing into little pink and yellow elephants all in a row, tied together by the most beautiful bow I'd ever seen. "You know you sure are beautiful. I never really noticed before, like not with all that fat and your specs but you are, you are beautiful."

One of the elephants had tiny golden slippers on and was dancing up my leg.

"You like that, don't you?"

I smiled, took another lung full of bliss and felt the little elephant tickle where no one had ever tickled before. He was pulling my new undies down.

I tried to say –

"Dirty little elephant."

But nothing came out.

Michael was on top of me. Still his voice sounded so beautiful –

"You know I really like you, don't you?"

And at that moment, as the elephants danced across the sky, I knew he loved me, and that I loved him. I loved him and the elephants and the rosebuds, the bees that had started to buzz, the birds that sang along with him, I loved them all, I loved everybody and everything.

Michael was grunting and groaning, something wasn't quite right, I felt sore down below and something was inside me that didn't belong inside me. Michael was telling me Colin needn't know about this, that it was our little secret and as he said that he stiffened and the thing in me spat something out and then got smaller. He lay on top of me for a minute, saying that was fucking great. He rolled off and lit another of his "cigarettes".

I felt funny. My head was spinning, the elephants were gone, his voice had gone into a muffled sound and from my stomach I felt a sudden retch.

I pulled myself to a sitting position.

Michael looked at me –

"You OK, babe?"

I couldn't answer. The retching had moved from my stomach to my throat and into my mouth. I tried to move but I couldn't. Without further warning I puked. I put my hand to my mouth but it was no good. My dress took the brunt of it.

Michael jumped to his feet –

"Shit."

I unloaded my stomach of everything I'd had over the last twenty-four hours and even when there was nothing left my stomach still retched. My head was pounding with the biggest headache in the history of mankind, and those elephants were on a stampede inside it. I held my head between my two hands, afraid to let go in case it exploded. I looked down at myself. I was a mess, but I couldn't understand how my knickers were on the ground, away from me.

Michael looked across the park –

"Come on, we better get you fixed up. The others are coming."

Sara was the only one who seemed to be talking sense –

"What the fuck has been going on here?"

Michael looked embarrassed –

"She got sick, probably too much to drink."

"Bullshit. Did you give her that shit you smoke?"

"She wanted some."

"BULLSHIT. You bastard." She looked at my undies, picking them up before anyone else saw them. "I suppose she wanted that as well."

Sara draped her coat around me and we got a taxi back to her place. She let me sleep, rang Mum to tell her where I was and when I came round, she had some clothes out for me.

My head felt like it was never going to be the same again.

She gave me a cup of tea and two Anadin –

"Mary what do you remember about Stephen's Green?"

I wasn't in the humour for a *Questions and Answers* time.

"Mary, it's really important, what do you remember?"

"Not a lot. Feeding the ducks, well trying to feed them . . . The band-stand. Lying down with Michael . . . feeling sick, very sick and then you coming over."

"Mary, did you and Michael smoke a joint?"

"No! Of course not."

"Mary, I'm not your mother, tell me the truth."

I hated getting caught out. I nodded.

"OK. Did you do anything else?"

"What do you mean?"

"I mean did you go all the way with him?"

"NO! What kind of girl do you take me for?"

"Think Mary. Think hard."

"I don't have to think, I can't believe you're saying that."

"Your dress was ruined."

"I got sick, remember?"

"At the back, with blood."

That silenced me.

267

"And your undies were on the ground."

I got a flashback, I remembered the knickers on the ground, and there was all that grunting and that thing, inside me, spitting.

"Oh God." I put my hand to my face, covering my shame. Sara was beside me –

"It's OK, it's OK. At least we know what happened, now we can do something about it."

I peeped through my hand at her –

"What do you mean?"

"We can go to a doctor and get the morning-after pill."

"I can't do that, I can't go to a doctor."

"Why? Do you want to have a little sprog hanging out of you and you barely finished school?"

"No, but . . . "

"But what? But, it was your first time? How many times do you think you have to do it before you get pregnant?"

"Maybe I should wait, see if I get my period, it's due in a few days."

"And what then? What if you're pregnant? What do you do? It's too late then for the morning-after pill. You leave it that long and you're on the next boat to England for an abortion."

The doctor I went to was female, which was a relief. She didn't ask any awkward questions and told me I might feel very sick after taking it. I knew I couldn't feel any sicker than I did at this moment in time. I swore to Jesus and Mary and Joseph that I'd never take another drink, another joint, or have sex again, if they just helped me this once. The doctor told me that if I got sick within three hours of taking it, I'd have to take another, but fortunately I didn't. It was six weeks before I got a period, she'd told me it might be, but it was the longest wait of my life.

Chapter Forty-One

We outgrew the flat. It was time to move on. The new place was really spacious and we each had our own room. I was glad of that. Amanda had a habit of taking one-night stands home, and they had a tendency to be very loud while making love. We had a rule that if you brought a fella home you slept on the sofa bed, but still, the next morning you'd go into the sitting-room-cum-kitchen and God knows what you'd see. Their clothes would be scattered across the place. Her bra on the lampshade, his shirt on the chair, his trousers in the middle of the floor and her undies beside them. Worse still was the fact that the cover could be off them and they'd be there naked or as near to naked as didn't matter. And these fellas didn't believe in covering up the minute you came in, not at all. There *it* would be, just lying there in its bed of pubic hair, relaxing after a hard night's riding.

And no matter where you were in the room, you were drawn to it, and its one eye seemed to follow you everywhere you went.

They were horrible-looking things. At least us women had nice neat little bodies, everything tucked away nice and neat. Men had this *thing* dangling, covered in wrinkly skin that made it look at least thirty years older then the rest of their body.

The lovers would wake. She'd scurry away from him and he'd sit there scratching his thing, then his head and then a big stretch before another scratch at the lower region. This time he'd give it a wiggle, as if trying to wake it and it would get a little bigger. Then he'd pick up his clothes and head for the toilet. They all did it. They all stood there, naked, asking –

"Where's the jacks?"

Then they'd come back and, leaving the toilet seat up and the toilet door open, ask –

"Any chance of a cuppa?"

It was as though they thought we were all their maids. I'd point to the kettle and say –

"It's just boiled and there's tea bags in the press."

They never made their own tea. They'd rather do without it. Amanda would hide in another room, not wanting to see them –

"God, he was a lot better-looking when I saw him in the night club."

Eventually they'd get the hint and go, leaving us to clean up the stains on the floor around the toilet. Amanda would sit on the sofa, coffee in hand, going through everything that had happened –

"He was so funny, did you hear the noise of him. He wanted me to pretend he was a bad schoolboy, I told him he could fuck off. I wasn't into that kinky stuff. He wanted me to smack him and all. Smack him, I said I'd fucking kill him if he didn't shut up."

Celine hated Amanda's post mortems –

"Amanda, the next time you bring a stray home, will you make sure he can aim right. I'd say he missed the toilet bowl completely, the amount of pee on the floor."

Amanda would giggle –

"I know he had a crap aim, sure I had to help him put it in last night. He kept missing and letting it fall out."

"God, spare me the details, just get the floor cleaned in there."

And Amanda would swear she'd get it cleaned, but we'd end up doing it ourselves.

So with the new apartment we gave her the en suite room. It meant that she could do what she liked, they could miss the bowl every time, it wouldn't bother us.

Besides, my room was nice too. It was the smallest in the apartment but still, it was twice the size of the one I'd shared in the flat, I had loads of room for all my bits and pieces. For all my books I had two long shelves over the bed and there was a double wardrobe, which was more than enough for my clothes. The bed had drawers under it. I used one of them for my undies, another for my shoes and yet another for my jumpers. In the last drawer I just dumped all the junk that I kept convincing myself meant something to me.

I had Nik Kershaw's autograph. I'd gone to see him in concert at the Stadium. He was brilliant and afterwards I'd waited in the freezing cold for him to come out. He was really nice. He signed a photo I'd bought at the back of the Stadium. I couldn't make it out as his name but I still kept it safe. God, it must have been fifteen years ago now. I had all his records; "Wouldn't it be Good" was my favourite but I loved "Dancing Girls" and "The Riddle" too. I'd had his posters plastered on every wall of my bedroom at the time, now I only kept his autograph and I wouldn't even let anyone know I had that.

Typically, Amanda wanted to go and suss out the local pubs. More likely she wanted to suss out the local talent.

Paddy Mac's was a bit tatty. The seats were all in need of a cleaning and the few stragglers at the bar looked like they had come with the place. Amanda joked with an aul fella who made a remark about my boobs. The others watched us like we were all meat at a market. All except one. He seemed a bit shy, as everyone else watched Amanda's return from the bar, and then mumbled to each other, he finished his drink and was gone.

Despite everything, the night turned out OK. In fact, better than OK. Amanda went missing and we found her sitting all cosy with the fella from earlier. But the music was good. It was a talent competition. Some brewer's promotional thing. Each pub had heats and semi-finals then a final. The winner of each pub's competition went on to a regional final. Then eventually it came down to a finale and the winner walked away with a holiday in Barbados and a recording contract worth ten grand.

I thought that was great, but Celine put the dampeners on it by saying that it was cheap advertising for the brewer. Still, the standard was very high, better than the ones on telly. Some of them took it really serious, they had backing tapes and their make-up done, others got up in a drunken stupor and made the electric organ player's life a misery. We all agreed on the winner. He was tall, blonde and very good-looking, but on top of all that he could sing too.

It was great fun, listening to everything from Elvis's "Wooden Heart" sung by someone in a glitter suit, sideburns and no teeth, to Patsy Cline's "Crazy" being sung three times. There was a lot of the *Titanic* song too, but in the end the tall blonde got up, sang Berni Flint's "I Don't Want to Put no Hold on You" and everyone loved him.

At the end of the night I wanted to get a packet of peanuts. The bar man was busy shouting at everyone to drink up and get out. The place was crowded, people laughing about the acts –

"Did you ever see anything like yer woman singing 'The Power of Love'?"

"I know. I thought she was going in for a wet T-shirt competition – the cut of her!"

"She'd 've had a better chance of winning it if she had."

I pushed through them, my "Excuse me," being lost beneath the noise of the place.

I kept pushing, until I reached the bar. I was still hidden from his view and despite my calling he didn't see me. I gave one last push, just to clear a space for myself, when suddenly a pint hit the counter and smashed into smithereens. I was so embarrassed. It was my fault, all my pushing and shoving. I apologised profusely, offering to buy another pint, but he wouldn't hear of it. He was so nice, and the nicer he was the worse I got. He cut his finger wiping up, I acted like it needed major surgery. I didn't know what was wrong with me and then it suddenly hit me. I fancied this guy like mad. And the more the thought hit home, the more I apologised. I made my excuses, never expecting to see him again.

I'd blown it, the first really nice guy in the history of my life and I'd acted like a complete imbecile.

Chapter Forty-Two

Wonders would never cease. Far from blowing it, we actually started going out together. Joe was great, a real gent, and the only person I'd ever met, more messed up than me. But he was honest and he didn't rush things. In fact it was me that had to make the first moves. Joe would gladly stand and talk for hours. That was fine by me, but every once in a while you wanted to stop talking and kiss.

Joe's mother was a right old cow, she had a stranglehold on him that was hard to believe. Still, there was no point in saying anything against her. Sometimes that was really hard, I mean to say, when you looked at the shitty job he was doing and how intelligent he was, it made you want to scream at him –

"Stand up for yourself."

But I also knew that if I ever as much as said that, that he'd clamp up and that would be the end of him talking about his mother, or anything for that matter. So I'd let him rant on hour after hour about her and his family and his ex. In fact I enjoyed it, most of the time. I liked the idea that someone trusted me so much, that they could open their heart to me. It was a big compliment really. And I didn't mind all the sneaking around that we had to do. The late dates, when most people were just thinking of going home and our date was just starting. I kind of began to understand what Amanda found so appealing about her married man.

There was something really sexy about not doing things other people did. About secret meetings and grabbed moments. Something about walking the streets 'til four in the morning, while most of the city was tucked up in bed. I liked getting ready so late at night, and arriving into the pub at such a late hour.

And I liked being one of Joe's girls. He'd told me that the lads in the pub had thought he was a right Casanova. It was nice to be thought to be going out with Casanova. I had been the girl who couldn't get a fella in a fit and suddenly I was the girl who had captured Casanova's heart.

We never ran out of things to talk about. There was work. I hated the fact that I knew the place was closing and couldn't warn everyone. I wanted to shout it from the highest high. After all, there were people getting mortgages on the strength of their jobs. And I knew there was no job. I knew that in six months, a year if they were lucky, most of them were all going to be out on their ears. And it didn't matter if they had a mortgage, a new car, or a gansy-load of kids to support, they'd be gone.

I had to talk to someone about it, and it was nice to have Joe for that. But it wasn't just our worries that we could discuss. He'd come flying in of a night, knocking back his drink and wanting to know who had won the latest heat of the talent competition.

Joe was a wealth of knowledge. He'd say, "Who won?" and I'd say a girl singing "I Only Want To Be With You" and he'd say, "Dusty Springfield, 1963, Phillips."

Joe knew them all. Some nights the lads at the bar would use him to settle arguments.

"Joe, what year did Pink Floyd have their first single chart success – '68 or '69, there's a fiver on it."

And he wouldn't even have to think about it –

"Neither, it was '67, the same year as Cream, the Monkees and Jimi Hendrix . . . "

"And what was the song?"

"See Emily Play."

"And they never argued the facts with him. No one ever said –

"I don't think so."

Or –

"Are you sure about that?"

If Joe said it, it was right.

It was hard to believe that the same person, the one thought of as a stud with a knowledge in music, the lad who had been on the last team out of the area to win the Leinster Senior Cup, could spend his days sweeping dust from one place to the next.

Still, sometimes when he spoke about the future, you could see the sparkle in his eyes. You could see the ambition and the want that was lacking in quite a lot of people his age who had tried and failed. At least Joe still had that hope.

At moments like that I wanted it to be more like the movies. For him to suddenly become the big executive in the thriving company. For the wicked witch (his mother) to be banished forever and for him to marry the ugly duckling, now a beautiful swan (me). But it never happened. He dreamed of opening a second-hand record shop, selling memorabilia, and ordering in records for collectors of vinyl. I didn't like bursting his bubble, but I thought it was better than him getting his hopes built up.

Everything between us was perfect, except for two things. One was that I wanted him to stand on his own two feet before we stood together. There was no point in me telling him what to do about his mother. If he did anything and it went wrong, he'd blame me for the rest of his life; he had to sort that situation out for himself. He had to do it soon. I needed, no, *wanted* a man to be a *man*. I wasn't a bra-burning feminist. I wanted to be at home and minding the children, in our little semi-detached, while the man of the house had a career that gave us a good standard of living, a nice car and a holiday every year. A job that meant you didn't have to worry where the Christmas presents were coming from.

At the moment, that wasn't Joe. Oh, I didn't want it to happen overnight, I had no intentions of settling down to the role of motherhood just at the moment, but he had to be working towards it.

Secondly, we had to make love. At times that seemed further away than the first. We talked until there was nothing left to say and then one of us would notice the time and there'd be a –

"God, is that the time, I never noticed, last time I looked at my watch it was quarter to twelve."

"Doesn't time fly when you're enjoying yourself?"

Then there'd be a bit of a joke about no sleep, and eyes in the back of the head. A quick peck on the cheek and a taxi home.

Now I know I'm not a sex machine and on a scale of one to ten, I'd be at the lower end, but I still needed the odd cuddle. I needed a kiss and a hug, and the nibbling of ears and the touching of bodies and . . . and to make love. I wanted to see what all the fuss was about. I wanted to lie beside someone I loved afterwards, just holding each other. I used to picture it at night, as I lay listening to Amanda and Davey.

Her bed was right up against the wall that separated us. All night you were able to hear them, her groaning, her calling him to talk dirty and he only too willing to oblige. And as he talked his talk, she moaned in delight and the head of the bed banged in rhythm with their performance. And though I didn't want to have my headboard bang against a wall, or to be called –

"A mickey-mad cock-sucker."

I did want to have Joe in bed with me.

I wanted us to be the naked ones, us to be the ones calling to each other in ecstasy, and afterwards I wanted us to be the ones holding each other. I pictured how nice it would be to be tucked in under Joe's arm, my head on his chest and him stroking my hair, telling me how much he loved me.

But even getting a kiss was a big deal.

I know it was as much my fault as his. I encouraged him to take his time over his mother. I agreed when he said it wouldn't be a good idea if we went to his house. I even agreed to our late night meetings. And I didn't want to go home to the apartment because Amanda and Davey were there. I didn't want it to seem like a knocking shop. For us to be sitting watching telly and them to start howling in unison about what good fucks they both were.

And I most certainly didn't want to be in bed and making love, listening to them. God forbid that it would get into a race, or a competition to see who could last longest or who was loudest! NO! So when I saw his car at the driveway I insisted that we walk on, eat our chips in the open and TALK.

We had arranged to meet at our usual time.

I was quite looking forward to the night. It was the final of the talent show. Blondie had made it the whole way through but so had some other really good acts. It was going to be very close. I prided myself on being able to pick the winner. I'd only missed out once in all the rounds and even then I thought the singer I picked was ten times better than the oldest Spice Girl in town.

I was getting ready, Celine was throwing a wobbly with Amanda over the noise of her stereo. Amanda couldn't care less, she was on cloud nine after receiving a call from lover boy.

The phone rang again and Celine called me, "Mary, phone."

I panicked for a minute, who was ringing me? I thought of my father, he hadn't been the best lately and I hadn't visited in the last couple of weeks. I felt nervous and guilty. If something had happened I'd never forgive myself.

I walked to the phone, Celine passed me, mumbling something about being like a switchboard.

I picked it up hesitantly –

"Hello?"

It was Joe, he sounded funny, different than I'd ever heard him before. I asked if everything was OK and he said he'd explain all when we met. He asked if I could get to Paddy Mac's as soon as possible.

It all sounded very mysterious.

PART SEVEN

TRACY'S TALE

Chapter Forty-Three

What was I like, talking to myself. Cursing Davey from a height out loud, and he not here, and no one here. But he really annoyed me. I had to talk out loud. I know they said it was a sign of madness but it was madder to sit in a house all day and say nothing, just because you saw no one.

And it could easily happen. There were days when, after Davey had walked out the door, I didn't see another soul, until he walked back in the door, at God knows what time.

Despite living in a place with people everywhere you looked, I could go the whole day without saying one single word to another person. I didn't want to become one of those sad ones who went shopping every day, just to have a chat. Christ no, the very thought of having to doll yourself up to go and chat to Barry the Butcher, and he with a fucking toupee that had more life in it than him. I always said if I got to that stage, I'd sign myself into a mental institution.

But fuck Davey, he didn't care about me anymore, it was plain as day to see. The way he'd been blowing hot and cold and treating me like one of those moany wives. There were a lot of things I *was* but I wasn't moany. Christ, I wish he could be like he'd been the first time I saw him.

I remembered it as though it was only yesterday. The weatherman had forecast a beautiful day and, for once, he had got it right. Usually I'd be decked out in a skimpy little number waiting for the sun's rays to bronze me, only for it to bucket down with rain and me end up looking like a cross between a drowned rat and a very flat-chested entrant in a Miss Wet T-shirt competition. But they'd got it right. In fact we were in the middle of a heat wave, the sixth day in a row that the temperature had reached the high eighties. Normally that would have been enough to have me in great humour. Normally I'd have woken early, blast out the Beach Boys tape I'd bought for days just like this and nothing, but nothing would get me down. Today, however, was different.

Today was my birthday.

I was twenty-two years on this planet, living in a shitty little bedsit that you wouldn't swing a rat in, never mind a cat, in Kilburn, an ocean away from my family, and not one of them had sent a card that got here on time. Christ, you'd think they'd have made an effort, considering the day. They knew fucking well enough what the post was like, so they could have sent them early. There was no harm in being early, I would have kept them on the mantelpiece unopened 'til today. But there was no point in coming late. They knew I made a big thing out of birthdays and the like. No one ever got a card from me late, or a present that wasn't wrapped and with a bow on the top. And I didn't get cheap paper either, none of your "ten for fifty" paper, or your "three cards for a pound". No, I chose every card as though it was special. I thought about who I was sending it too. None of your –

"Ah that'll do, it says birthday, doesn't it?"

I chose with the person in mind, I wrapped the present with the minimum of sellotape, so they could keep the paper as a memento. I hated it when they shook the card for money and tore the paper off, it was so disrespectful of the time and effort I'd put in. But regardless, I still did it.

And they all knew how I was, they all knew that I wanted a present, not a gift-token or money. God, the whole idea of giving was to put some thought into it.

So to me, it was useless giving me a card a day late. I was celebrating my twenty-second birthday, not my twenty-second and a day birthday.

I could imagine the face on my mother if I did this on her. If I said I was arriving home on Stephen's Day rather than Christmas Day. If I forgot Mother's Day or one of their birthdays, I'd never hear the end of it, but when the roles reversed there was no fuse.

It was a crap, crap day.

I'd woken expecting to hear the phone ringing off the hook, but not a sound. I'd moaned that much that Jenny, the girl who shared this shoe box with me, decided to give me a handmade card. It was a plain A4 sheet folded in half and then in half again. On the front she'd drawn a flower (Art wasn't her strong subject) and written Happy Birthday. Inside it read –

"Happy 22nd Birthday Tracy, sorry about the card. Love Jenny."

Then on the bottom was –

"P.S.I.O.U. a pressie."

That was it. That was the sum of my birthday greetings. That was it, one plain white page, folded, no envelope, left on the kitchen table in the middle of the half-used cornflake box and the milk carton. I went to the press and found that there was no bowl for my cornflakes. Jenny hadn't bothered cleaning hers from her ice cream last night and had used my one. I turned on the hot tap and it ran cold. The bitch had used up the last of the hot water. I rinsed the bowl under the tap and dried it on the tea towel.

I sat, poured myself a large bowl of cornflakes, then went to pour the milk. It was empty.

"Fuck you JENNY."

I heard the postman, he must've been late. I rushed to our door and down the stairs. I was only in my nightdress and no slippers. My mother would have had a seizure if she'd seen me. Bare feet on someone else's carpet. I'd be getting bunions and verrucas and God knows what.

But there was never anyone about at this time.

I reached the hallway taking steps three at a time. There was a postcard from Germany for the fella in number four. Three letters and a parcel for the other flats, and even Jenny had got a bank statement, but me, *I got fuck all.*

I couldn't believe I'd taken a day off for this.

On my way back up the stairs I caught my foot on something sharp –

"Ah fuck."

I sat on the stairs cursing –

"Fuck, fuck, fuck."

A head popped out from behind a door –

"Do you mind, pleeze, it is very early."

I held my toe and stared at him. He closed the door quickly.

"Shurrup you little Paki bastard," I moaned quietly.

"Ah now, that's not very charitable of yeh."

I looked around to see Philly walking up the hallway.

"Yeah. Well I'm not in a very charitable humour today."

He smiled, pretending to be afraid of me –

"Sorry I spoke."

I smiled to myself –

"So you should be."

He looked me up and down –

"Nice outfit."

"Well I didn't expect to be spied on."

He held out his hand –

"Come on, I'll give you a hand."

I limped with him down the landing, and to my door. It had locked. I pushed against it, but there was no go.

Philly asked did I want him to break down the door.

"*No,* Jesus Philly. Do you want me thrown out?"

"Well it's that or through the window."

I could have done with a bunt up, but I knew I hadn't any underwear on. I told him to go ahead and I'd talk to him later.

He looked puzzled but went on his way. Once he'd gone I climbed unceremoniously out the window, onto the fire escape and through our window.

God if someone had seen me, I never would have lived it down.

Just as I got in, the radio went dead. I knew straight away what was wrong. We'd run out of money in the meter. Well I was fed up being the one to fill the meter and get the milk. Jenny paid her way, but she never did any of the things herself.

I got dressed, grabbed a towel and exited. Let Jenny come home and find the place in darkness, no milk and the dishes not done.

I was going to go to Kilburn Park but there was a bunch of winos at the entrance and I saw a bus coming so I jumped on that and ended up in the centre of London.

The English don't give a damn what they look like on a sunny day. You have women who have gone off the Richter Scale for Obesity, walking down the road with flannel shorts and Majorca T-shirts, ice cream in hand and the layers of fat wobbling with every step. Yet they didn't care. Then on the same street at the same time, you had a black man, built like a chiselled statue from Rome, wearing the tightest vest and a pair of Lycra shorts that not only showed his lunch box, but his breakfast, dinner and tea too.

They had the right idea.

I nipped into a chemist, bought a high-factor sunblock and headed for Hyde Park. Hyde Park was like the Phoenix Park in Dublin. A huge public park that people didn't use half enough. Still, on this summer day it was packed. Just as I got there a couple, who were in danger of getting arrested for indecent behaviour, decided to find a quieter spot to finish what they'd started in public.

The girl was bleached blonde, a Londoner who you expected to talk with terms like "Tin of fruit, apples and pears and 'er indoors." She pulled her shorts over her bikini bottoms, draped a cardigan over her shoulders and ran barefoot, giggling as she headed to a shaded tree.

He was gorgeous. An Italian, with a great physique and bronzed from head to toe. His shorts couldn't hide his excitement and as he gathered all their belongings, I couldn't help but stare at him. Aware of my gaze he looked up, smiled, and then ran after Blondie.

God, I was pathetic. Not only was I the only girl I knew who had postcards of foreign hunks on her wall, now I was actually gawking at fellas in the open and imagining being with them.

I needed a man, and quick.

I threw my towel on the grass, put some cream on myself and lay back. My mind was racing. I was beginning to feel guilty. Guilty about cursing my family from a height. Maybe there was something after happening and they didn't want to upset me. And that was the reason they'd not sent my cards. Guilty about giving out about Jenny. If it wasn't for her I'd have no one in London. And she had made a card, it wasn't up to Blue Peter standard but at least she'd done it, and wasn't I always the one saying it's the thought that counts. I felt guilty about the way I'd cursed the little Paki and about work. Poor Carol would be snowed under now with the breakfast crowd. Especially now that they were renovating the offices across the way. All the lads would be in for their full breakfast. Trouble was each one wanted something different.

"Full Irish" the Irish would shout.

That had two eggs, two slices of rasher, two sausages, some tomatoes and black and white pudding.

"Full English" the Londoners would call.

That had the same except no white pudding and beans instead of tomato.

Then you'd have every combination –

"English, skip the beans, give us chips."

"Irish, no tomato, have you any mushroom?"

"English without the eggs, extra sausages."

"Irish without the pudding, extra toast."

"BLT without the lettuce."

And they all wanted to be served at the same time.

She'd only have cleaned up and got a quick cuppa, before they'd be back in for lunch.

All of the lads on the building sites lived in flats and most of them didn't know how to boil an egg, never mind cook a decent dinner. So the Café was where they ate all their meals and poor Carol would be run off her feet. Still she'd done the same to me on more than one occasion. Besides all the tips would be hers.

The sun had a way of making your mind drift from subject to subject. I thought of the family again, this time I was back blaming them, The Italian caught my eye. God, had it really been six months since I was with a man. And even at that it had only been Adrian.

Adrian Robson, what a plonker, with his high-flying job on High Street. Into "stocks and shares", always dribbling on about "bulls and bears" – it was stupid. He tried to explain it to me, tried to make it exciting, sitting there in his pin-striped suit, but no matter what, it always sounded stupid to me. I'd met him in the restaurant. He used to come in because on High Street you couldn't get a decent chip. You could get hot dogs and kebabs and decent dinners, but not a decent chip.

I knew we'd never stick together. I think he always considered me his bit of rough. He'd love me, but marry someone else. But the truth was, I was only going with him because I had no one or nothing else. Jenny was going with someone, Carol lived miles away and none of my relatives visited. So it was either him or sit in on my own. Eventually I decided that sitting in would be better than hearing about a stupid "bear".

He couldn't come to terms with being dumped. But I knew it wasn't the dumping but the fact that a chippy waitress had dumped him that really got his goat up. He started hanging around, sending me flowers and ringing the phone in the hall of the flat at all hours of the night. Eventually he stopped. We'd got Philly to answer and let on he was from British Telecom investigating nuisance phone calls.

Myself and Jenny had gone mad after that. It turned out she too had been going with her fella so she wouldn't be stuck in on her own, so once I was free, she dumped him and we hit every club in London.

Jenny used to bring fellas home with her, I couldn't.

I really wanted to, wanted to use someone purely for sex. There were times over the last six months when I needed a good shag, not the timid lovey-dovey stuff, not the flowers, chocolates and dinner of a lover – but a good hard fuck. I wanted to just DO IT. Someone to come in, do the biz and go. A one night stand, on my terms, but I couldn't.

I'd be riddled with doubt and guilt.

I could hear my mother –

"Tracy Connors, how could you?"

My father –

"You let the whole family down, madam."

And as the guy, who had just bought me drink after drink, left me home and said –

"Can I come in for a coffee?"

I found one side of my brain scream –

"Oh yes big boy, you can have a coffee and anything else you want."

While my mouth said –

"No thanks, I really can't. Another time, yeah?"

As I pecked him on the cheek and ran for the front door.

And no sooner would I be in bed than the door would burst open and in would fall Jenny, all giggles and sloppy kisses with her latest one night stand. They'd be oblivious of me as they crashed onto her single bed, he ripping at her blouse as she clawed at his back. Then they'd be at it like wild animals, not caring that I was there, not caring that the lamp was on or that the curtains weren't pulled.

And I'd lie there, twisting and turning, pulling the pillow over my head to drown out her groans as he entered. But as his movements increased and her pleasure reached new heights, I couldn't help but listen. Sometimes on nights when I was really frustrated, I'd reach beneath the sheets but, just before my hand reached my undies, before I'd get a chance to pleasure myself, my mother's voice would break the mood –

"Tracy Connors, how could you?"

And I'd stop, pull my hand away and close my legs.

I was brought out of my daydream by a touch on the shoulder.

"Hummmm?" I muttered, not knowing what was going on.

He was leaning on one knee beside me, his chest hairy and bare –

"You were snoring."

I was suddenly aware of having drifted off, I jumped up afraid that my hand had been between my legs –

"I don't snore."

I was adamant, and angry through my embarrassment.

"I've news for you, *you do*."

The sun was directly behind him, I put a hand over my eyes so I could look at him –

"What the hell do you think you're doing coming over to me like that? Is that your idea of a pick-up?"

He put his hands up as though surrendering –

"Hey listen, I thought I was doing you a favour, my mistake."

He rose and walked slowly back to his T-shirt and runners that lay not five feet away from me. He turned his tape recorder up, put his sunglasses on and lying on one elbow, with his back to me, began reading his sports section.

After a few minutes, I realised he *had* done me a favour. God knows what I would have done, and Jenny had always told me I snored, and on top of all that, if I hadn't put some more sun cream on just then, I'd have burnt to a cinder.

I looked around me and coming down the pathway was a man with a soft drink stand. I bought two Cokes and walked over to him. He never turned, so I put a can against his back.

He jumped –

"Ahhh."

He turned to face me as he screamed –

"You wagon, I didn't know what was happening."

I held the can out to him –

"Truce?"

He took it from me, and I sat down opening mine as I did.

He shook his violently and opened it, spraying me –

"Truce."

I wiped myself off –

"I guess I deserved that?"

"Yes. You did."

I smiled and reached out my hand –

"Can we start again? I'm Tracy."

He took my hand and shook (great grip), he smiled (great teeth) –

"Davey Brady, glad to meet you." We shook and he wouldn't let go, "But . . . you do snore."

He laughed, I went to pull away to hit him but he held me –

"No listen, that's a good thing . . . "

I stopped struggling –

"Go on?"

"You know usually, I'd have had to sleep with you to find out something like that . . . but with you, I know it already, so you won't have to be embarrassed when we end up in the sack together."

God, he was so confident, he was forward and brash and I knew that that night I wouldn't be listening to my parents' voices – or caring if the light was on or the curtains were open.

Chapter Forty-Four

That day we talked and laughed and ate and drank and when the evening turned cool he put his jacket around my shoulders and we walked, still laughing, still talking, back to his place. It was small and messy but he made no excuses for it. He pushed a pizza box and a bag of laundry to the floor, threw me to the bed and had sex with me. It wasn't love, it was lust, pure undiluted lust. He was like a wild animal on me and I loved every second of it. And I screamed and sighed just like Jenny as he whispered filth into my ear, while taking me.

That night turned into a morning and another day. We never left the house. He showed me where the toilet was, rang in sick for me, and when we got hungry he ordered in a pizza.

That day we talked 'til there was nothing we didn't know about each other. We made love until I couldn't make love anymore. Even the thought of going to the toilet ached my legs.

I said I must go home, he said yes you must, but I didn't. I stayed the evening. I stayed until I had to go and even then he walked with me. We held on to each other as if to let go would mean to let go forever.

My mind was spinning. For the first time in my life I was truly happy. If a plane crashed straight in front of me at that moment, I don't think it would have changed a single thing.

As I opened the door to my flat, Jenny jumped off her bed –

"Jesus Christ, Tracy, where the hell were you?"

I started to smile, but noticed she was crying –

"I was . . . out. Why? What happened?"

"Nothing fucking happened, except I didn't know where the hell you were."

I put my arm around her shoulder, but she threw it off –

"Fuck off Tracy."

I laughed –

"Jenny? Hello? What the fuck is going on here? This *is* Jenny 'the stop out' I'm talking to, isn't it?"

She was sobbing uncontrollably. I put my arm back around her, this time she left it there –

"Hey, come on Jenny, what's up? This isn't like you."

I handed her one of the Kleenex hankies from the table that doubled as our dresser.

"It's just . . . I was worried . . . you never stay out . . . I know I'm always doing it . . . I know I don't ring or nothing . . . but . . . that's me . . . I got home . . . no lecky . . . no milk . . . no you! . . . I didn't know what to do . . . your mum rang, I'm sure she thinks I'm mad . . . "

I panicked –

"You didn't say anything to her did you?"

"No, I said you were gone to the shops . . . I didn't know where you were . . . " She buried her head in my shoulder, "I had you in some laneway with your tights around your neck."

I laughed –

"You've been watching too many of those thrillers."

She laughed too, blew her nose again, then wiped each eye –

"So where were you anyway?"

I didn't have to answer; at that very moment she looked up, saw Davey and knew.

Chapter Forty-Five

Davey and me were inseparable. I went to work and he'd come and sit watching me from one of the booths, then he'd walk me home and if Jenny wasn't there we'd make love on my bed. Other than that we'd go to his flat and make love there. We were always making love. Always spending our time in some sort of undress. I couldn't say no. I'd be walking around work in a trance, exhausted and promising myself an early night, by myself. Then he'd walk in, I'd see the glint in his eye and it took me all my time not to drag him there and then into the café's toilets and fuck him.

Mother was giving out, asking where I was when she rang, but I didn't care. I didn't care that the cards had been late, didn't care that they all had gift tokens. All I cared about was being with Davey. It never occurred to me to probe into Davey's background.

Jenny would ask me all kinds of questions about him –

"Where's he from?"

"Where does he work?"

"What age is he?"

"Is he married?"

And I couldn't answer one of them. Davey and I talked non-stop and yet at the end of it all, I knew nothing about him . . . and what's more I didn't care. He made me happy, he made me feel happy and whenever I did bring the subjects up, he always somehow avoided the answers. Not in a way that was obvious, but in a way that made me feel I couldn't care less.

Two weeks and three days after we met, Davey asked me to marry him.

We were in bed, just having made love. It was a Sunday and his radio played in the background. He'd just jumped out of bed and made us both a cup of tea. We sat up, both our tops exposed. He was the first person I ever felt confident enough with to actually be naked around. Even with Jenny I had to have clothes on. She could float around topless and even if I came in and she was naked, she wouldn't hurry to get dressed. *I would,* I'd grab the first thing that came to hand and cover myself. But with Davey it was different. Davey had kissed every part of me, complimented every part of me, and often sat just looking at me. I loved it. I loved his comments, his touch, his everything.

So we sat there, in silence. I lay into him and he held me close with one hand and held his cigarette in the other.

We often sat like this, lost in thought, half listening to the radio, half drifting to another world.

Tina Turner's "What's Love Got To Do With It?" was followed by Bronski Beat's "Smalltown Boy". As The Bluebells' "Young At Heart" came on, I nudged him –

"Hey Davey Brady, what are you thinking of?"

He held his gaze for a minute, then as I sat up and looked him straight in the eye, he answered –

"Well Tracy Connors, I'm thinking of asking you to be my wife."

A month later I was at my mother's house introducing Davey to them for the first time –

"Mum, Dad, this is . . . . Davey Brady . . . my husband."

Davey and I moved into his flat, always on the basis that we'd get a better place, soon. Davey had big plans, the building trade was great in England, he was a fully-fledged carpenter and was able to earn eight hundred pound a week, no problem. All we had to do was live on my wages, save his and in next to no time he'd have enough to start his own firm.

But there was a problem, a major problem. Davey didn't like work. Oh he spoke about a good day's labour, but actually getting down to doing it was a totally different thing.

I didn't notice it at first. I was so full of our plans that I worked every hour God and Mr Poppalucas gave me, and I did it with a smile. I earned more tips than anyone else and I served more tables than two of the other girls put together. Mr Poppalucas was happy, I was happy and so was Davey –

"That's great Tracy, the way you're earning we'll be able to save some of your money too."

But Davey wasn't finding work easy to come by. I'd point out sites as we passed, sites with signs begging for workers. Davey always had a reason not to work –

"They're looking for labourers and brickies, I'm a carpenter."

"The wages aren't right, I'm not working for that."

"They don't do good work, I don't want to get a bad reputation."

And he was always meeting people –

"Important people" he'd say, "People in the know."

Of course he'd have to have some money to splash around, "couldn't have these fellas thinking they were mixing with someone out of work."

"Work breeds work," he'd say, taking another twenty from our kitty.

Then he'd show up at the café, looking for free grub, half cut and telling me –

"Any day now, any day."

But *any day* never came. The odd time he did work, he spent the money in the pub –

"You got to speculate to accumulate."

Except he never accumulated and the only thing those acquaintances of his ever seemed to accumulate was beer bellies.

We struggled on my wages, the building next to the café was finished and the builders had left, which meant half our regular trade was gone out the window. Our tips nosedived. Mr Poppalucas had to cut our hours and Davey was still all talk, no action.

Our sex life nosedived too. The glint had gone off our marriage, the honeymoon period was over. I began covering myself up, aware of my nudity. Most nights I was too tired to want sex, but even if I did, he was either out "networking" or flaked out on the bed drunk from his lunchtime "meeting".

The bubble burst. Even the hard workers were finding it hard to get work, the likes of Davey hadn't a chance. I was seriously contemplating getting a second job, just to make ends meet.

We were still in the dingy flat.

I'd given up trying to clean it, it was a waste of time. I'd have it spick and span, but when I came home Davey had it like a bomb had hit.

I'd just got in from work one evening when Davey came in. I hadn't seen him look so excited in months.

He picked me up and swung me around. I wasn't in the humour for his messing.

"Put me down," I snapped.

But he kept swinging me around and around.

"Have I told you lately that I think you're the most beautiful woman in the world?"

I frowned, tried to release myself from his grip, but couldn't –

"Put me down, you big idiot. You're drunk."

He breathed into my face –

"Haven't had a drop."

He was lying, I could smell the faint aroma of stale beer, but he wasn't drunk. I didn't call him a liar 'cause to be quite honest I was happy just to see him in such good form.

Eventually he let me down but proceeded to dance around the room (what space there was) with me.

"Davey! Whatever is the matter with you?"

He smiled, a smile I hadn't seen in so long, held my head between his hands and spoke –

"We're going home, baby, we're going home."

Maybe I had underestimated the amount of drink consumed –

"Davey, you're home already."

He shook his head as if trying to get rid of a dirty taste from his mouth –

"No, not here. Not this dingy kip. I'm talking about Ireland, I'm talking about Dublin, our *real* home."

It had never been something that we talked about. Usually we just referred to here as home. I never thought about going back. I'd no real love of Dublin, and from what Davey had ever led me to believe, neither had he. Yet here he was jumping around the room, as though he'd just found the promised land.

We talked into the early morning about how the arse had gone out of the British market and how Dublin was hopping. His eyes sparkled with delight as he told me about Temple Bar –

"I swear, according to Ronnie, they're building apartments and hotels to beat the band. There's so much work that carpenters can name their price. He says they're earning a hundred and eighty into the hand a day, seven days a week."

I wanted to say about Ronnie, he was a nice bloke but we all knew he had a tendency to exaggerate. Still, I said nothing, this bubble would burst of its own accord, like all the rest had. I bit my lip and thought of the few hours that were left 'til I had to get up. That night we made love like we hadn't done in ages. I had forgotten what a lover he was and that night I came louder than I ever had before.

Next morning, he was up before me, with a cup of tea ready for me. I hadn't seen Davey up before me in . . . I couldn't ever remember him being up before me.

He said he had so much to organise, so many people to see, so much to do. He kissed me and was gone out the door. I called after him –

"Davey, money, do you need money?"

But he just shouted –

"Later love, later."

I went to work and forgot about the plan. Mr Poppalucas was saying if business didn't pick up soon, he'd have to close altogether.

Around midday Davey darkened the door. That was about par for the course. He'd sit down, bum a coffee and tell me the sob, sob story of how the deal had fallen through.

He went to one of the many vacant booths and shouted to Louis to put on a full Irish, with chips, loads of bread and the largest pot of tea in the house.

I slid over to him, glaring at him and shaking my head in the direction of Mr Poppalucas, who of late was even begrudging us giving Davey a cup of coffee for free –

"Davey! For fuck sake, you can't expect to get all that on a slate."

His voice was loud and from his pocket he produced a wad of tenners –

"I don't. I'm going to pay for it. And anything anyone else wants too."

He looked around at the empty restaurant.

"Davey, where in the love of God did you get that?"

He laughed and tapped his nose.

I hissed –

"Davey!"

"God almighty, you're a right little nosey thing." He leaned toward me, "I sold the telly and the stereo and pawned me mother's wedding-ring."

"Christ Davey, what are we going to do now without a telly or radio? We can't afford to go out. What are we going to do, stare at the four walls?"

"Tracy, love, it won't be for long."

"That's what you said when we moved into the flat together, it won't be long. But look at us, how long is it now?"

He reached into his pocket and took out two tickets –

"Can you live without the telly for three days?"

I couldn't believe my eyes –

"You . . . "

"That's right, I bought the tickets and what's more, I want you to hold onto this money. Just so I'm not tempted to spend it on a bon voyage party."

"But . . . what about my job, I have to give notice. I can't just jack it in."

He called Mr Poppalucas, who came over, expecting Davey to be looking for something –

"I sorry Davey, you nice man, but you gotta pay. Like everyone else."

Davey laughed –

"It's nothing like that, Spiros. Tracy has something to tell you." Davey prompted me to continue.

"Mr Poppalucas, Davey and I are thinking of going back to Ireland . . ."

Davey cut in –

"Not thinking, going."

Mr Poppalucas looked nonplussed –

"That's OK, Tracy, you're a good worker, you deserve a holiday. You tell me when and how long and I'll have your money ready."

"It's not a holiday, Mr Poppalucas . . . "

His face changed –

"Nothing bad, no bad news I hope?"

I stuttered on –

"Nnnooo . . . nothing like . . . tha' . . . "

Davey was irritated by my stumbling –

"For fuck sake Tracy, tell the man."

Mr Poppalucas looked puzzled, worried –

"Yes please Tracy, you must tell me."

"We're going back to Dublin . . . to live."

We all went silent, Davey smiling, me trying to figure out the look in Mr Poppalucas's eyes.

They seemed to fill up –

"When? When will you go?"

"Friday."

"So soon." He hesitated. "I have often thought of going back home, to Paros and my home town of Lefkes. Back to my people."

Davey was blunt –

"Well why don't you? There's fuck all keeping you here now. Britain is a spent force. This time next year, there won't be a shop in this area still open. It'll be a fucking ghost town."

Mr Poppalucas nodded in agreement –

"You know, you're probably right, Davey."

"I know I am."

Mr Poppalucas looked at me, the way a father looks when he knows his daughter is all grown up and leaving home –

"Tracy, I will miss you. You are a good worker . . . and a friend. Come Friday I will have all your money ready."

He walked away, I thanked him but . . . I don't think he heard me.

Saturday morning we were back in Dublin. It was drizzling rain and I was tired from the coach and boat journey. Davey had made contacts on the boat. Come Monday he'd be starting his new life. He turned to me and hugged me –

"This is it, darling, I know *this* time, *this* is it."

Chapter Forty-Six

For the first few years Dublin was great. Everything had changed. Every shop was looking for staff and on the building sites Davey was in huge demand. His attitude to work changed – he enjoyed earning good money. We stayed with my mum for a few days, but it was never a long-term solution.

Mum and Dad asked questions of Davey that I still didn't know the answer to. Davey would either say nothing or grab his coat and say he was off to the boozer.

Eventually we moved into our own apartment and then we actually got a house. Everything was coming true, just as Davey had said it would.

A nice three-bedroomed house that needed very little done with it, other than the odd lick of paint. A new car every year, always one that caught your eye as Davey drove by. We had the money for a sun holiday every August and we always got away, just down the country mind, every bank holiday. Davey had enough money to go for a drink every night. We had the money for both of us to go, but I knew that during the week it was mainly the local men that went to Paddy Mac's. The wives weren't brought out until the weekend. So there wasn't a lot of point in me sitting in a booth with a vodka and tonic, while Davey stood at the bar, talking to the lads about whatever sport was showing on Sky that night.

It made me laugh, most of them had Sky at home, but they still preferred to go to the pub to watch it.

There was only one problem.

We had been trying for a baby on and off for about four years. Even when we weren't trying, I wasn't taking any precautions.

I tried everything. The sexy music, the kinky gear, the missionary position, doggy style. I stuck thermometers under my arm, in my mouth and up my arse with no results. I used the Billings method, I used no method – but nothing.

We read every book, we got out videos, I lay upside down, had baths, tried special foods but to no avail. The only two things that we didn't try were counsellors and tests. Those were the two things Davey wouldn't have anything to do with –

"You go if you want. I'm not having some quack telling me that my childhood was shite. And I'm definitely not having a doctor poking around down there. There's fuck all wrong with me in that department!"

And that was that.

Davey was adamant that if there was a problem, it wasn't with him.

I did everything, I gave up my job, stayed at home and rested when they said *rest*, exercised when they said *exercise*. I went to the Doctor, let him poke and prod and take samples but there was nothing wrong. The doctor could see no reason why I couldn't conceive.

He wanted to see Davey. So that was that. My biological clock was ticking fast toward forty. Davey was losing interest in me. He was spending more time in the pub, less time in the bed.

But at least he always paid me attention. He always joked and kidded with me, he chatted away like a true friend and no matter what, he always came home.

That was until recently.

He had started getting dressed-up going out to the local. That wasn't his style. Not during the week. He always went in after his work, sawdust on his clothes, dirt on his boots. Now it was his best trousers, his newest jeans and always a shower.

Oh, he'd had affairs before, I was sure of that. Davey wouldn't be going without sex and he sure as hell wasn't taking it at home. Still they weren't like this, they never affected our time together but this one, whoever she was, *did*.

He was confusing me. One minute he was affectionate, touching me like a woman and not the barren vessel I had been made feel of late. The next day, he mocked me as I tried to turn him on again. Then the next day it was back to being all over me again. I'd heard someone on about the male menopause, but I don't think that was what was wrong. Davey had another woman and *I* wasn't going to stand for it!

The final straw was the day Davey didn't come home for dinner. It sounds small but he'd got out on the pretence of only a few pints before the pub closed for the holy hour. We'd been messing in that nice sexy way.

He'd gone, I'd the meat on, the vegetables and potatoes cleaned and so I nipped upstairs to have a quick bath and to make myself nice for his return.

I expected him back at around half two. I had candles on the table and I'd chosen a CD of seventies love songs to get us in the mood.

By half three I knew the dinner was ruined, but I was determined it wouldn't spoil my plans.

By seven I was fit to be tied. I'd thrown out both dinners, cleaned the kitchen and got halfway through a bottle of red wine.

By nine thirty I'd called him every name under the sun. I'd cried my way through the remainder of the wine and sobbed along with everything from Art Garfunkel's "I Only Have Eyes For You" to The Manhattans' "Kiss And Say Goodbye."

It was close to closing time when I went down to Paddy Mac's. I was trying to search the crowd for him, but I was too small.

Suddenly by my side was John Michael. I only knew him from the odd time he'd served us, or the odd word he'd passed with Davey as he cleaned the tables.

"Are you looking for Davey?" he asked, picking glasses off a table close to me.

"Yeah," I said, still straining to catch a glimpse of him.

"He hasn't been in this afternoon or night. Paddy said he was in this morning all right."

"Are you sure?"

He smiled –

"You don't forget when he's in, you should know that?"

I smiled back at him, though I didn't feel like it –

"No, it's just I was expecting him home hours ago. Maybe he's gone somewhere else. I'll see yo . . . yo . . . u . . . "

I was just about to finish my sentence when I was grabbed by a drunken stranger –

"Come on gorgeous, let's dance."

I pulled away –

"Fuck off."

He was persistent –

"Ah don't be like that."

He came toward me; before he got any closer, John Michael had him in a half-nelson, frog-marching him out the door.

When John came back in he looked anxious. Paddy Mac was looking over, his hand under the counter, on an old baseball bat he used for such occasions.

"Are you OK, John?" he asked.

John nodded, looked at me and asked the same of me.

"I'm fine, I'd better go."

John grabbed my arm –

"No wait, I'll give you a lift."

"There's no need."

"I'd prefer to, just in case your man is outside."

He OK'd it with Paddy Mac and drove me home, waiting for me to open the door and check the house before he left.

Later, as Davey lied through his teeth, I thought of John.

Chapter Forty-Seven

I was cleaning the next day, trying to keep my mind off what had happened and all that was said, when there was a knock on the door.

For the first time in my life, I was hoping it was them Jehovah's Witnesses. God, they'd know what hit them. I was gumming for a fight and those little fuckers were perfect. Standing there in their shirts, ten times whiter than mine were, no matter what I used. And they never had a hair out of place, not one. And those whiter-than-white smiles – all American homely boys. God, they made me sick. Whatever happened to a six o'clock shadow, hair out of place, clothes crumpled. I'd be afraid of their God, he must be some kind of a cleanliness freak.

I swung the door wide open, ready to let rip –

"If yo ... "

I stopped dead in my tracks,

"John . . . Howya? . . . I . . . I . . . I . . . you were the last person I was thinking of."

He backed off –

"If it's not a good time . . . "

He indicated toward the road.

"No, no," I stepped aside, "come in."

He hesitated –

"Are you sure?"

I smiled –

"Of course. Really, I was expecting the Jehovah's."

He looked puzzled; I continued –

"Don't ask, it's a long story."

We walked into the kitchen –

"You'll have a cuppa?"

"Only if you're making one."

I told him to sit, poured water into the kettle, turned it on and then joined him at the table.

"So, what brings you to this neck of . . . "

Before I finished he had my purse out –

"You dropped this in my car."

I blushed, as though he'd said something he shouldn't –

"Thanks. I hadn't even missed it."

He smiled. I took the purse, stood up and walked to where the kettle had boiled. I made tea without asking whether he'd prefer coffee and poured some biscuits onto a plate.

"I hope you don't take sugar. I gave it up and so I don't keep it in the house."

"No, just milk. Why did you give up sugar? You don't need to lose weight."

Why was he making me blush so much? –

"Would you like a sambo? Sure you must be starving working down in the pub."

I went to get up, to not be facing him with my big red face but he stopped me –

"No, honestly, I'm fine. I haven't even been in yet. I just noticed the purse on my way and I thought I'd bring it around."

"That was nice of you, there was no need to rush."

We sat in a kind of awkward bitty conversation, followed by stupid conversation mode. Then out of the blue he spoke –

"Listen, I've got to come clean. I didn't see your purse today. I seen it last night. And I didn't call round just to give it to you, I wanted to see you, see how you were."

I answered too quickly –

"I'm fine, everything's fine. Stupid me, over-reacting. Davey went mad when he heard I'd gone down the pub. I can't blame him either."

"Well, I can. He's mad to be treating you that way."

I fumbled at the cups –

"I'll make a fresh cup."

I let them slip, spilling onto the table –

"Damn! I'm an awful idiot." I got a cloth and started cleaning. John sat, I could feel his eyes on me –

"I've embarrassed you?"

I kept cleaning, not looking at him.

"No, you didn't."

"Well, I spoke out of turn."

I said nothing. He stood –

"I'll go."

I looked at him –

"You don't have to."

He smiled –

"I think I do."

As he left I asked him not to say anything about giving me a lift or being around. He told me he wouldn't and I believed him. He walked to the gate, and as he closed it he looked back at me –

"Bye."

I walked down to the gate –

"John."

He was at his car –

"Yes?"

"Call again, will yeh?"

He smiled –

"Try keeping me away."

And that was how it began. Simple, isn't it? And now, three short months later, I was in this mess.

PART EIGHT

JOHN MICHAEL'S ONE MAN BAND

Chapter Forty-Eight

I was nervous. There was so much talent here. So many good acts, but I needed this. I needed to win, no matter what.

I'd been trying to achieve something worthwhile all my life. People always said –

"Ah you're young,"

– but it didn't make any difference. In this business, twenty-five was over the hill. I needed to make it now.

I looked around. I needed a cigarette and I needed to see Tracy. She promised she'd be here.

OK, so you could argue that Paddy Mac's wasn't exactly the Palladium, but everyone had to start somewhere. I mean to say Rod Stewart didn't start off playing Wembley, Oasis had to do a lot of small venues before Glastonbury and even the Beatles started in the Cavern – and that was a right kip.

I'd gone out of my way to visit it when we'd gone to see the play-off for a place in the Euro Championship against Holland. The match was in Anfield. But what a waste! Saving for months, begging for time off and we end up getting slaughtered. Ireland had to admit, we had a second-rate international team now.

We'd have to wait a few years for the under-eighteens to come of age, or for Brian Kerr to take charge.

Anyway, we all headed over on the boat. Everyone was skulled by the time we landed. Everyone bar me. I was on a mission. I wanted to see all the streets I saw at the start of *Brookside* and most important, I wanted to see the Cavern.

I strolled around the streets meeting endless Dutch supporters in their orange boiler-suits and searching every street for the Cavern. I was expecting a huge place, with loads of memorabilia and a certain air about it. An air that you could say –

"Yeah, you can see why it's so famous."

But it was a kip. I nearly missed it. I was walking around, looking everywhere but in front of me and I bumped into this mountain of a man.

"Watch your fucking step mate."

I said –

"Jasus sorry, I didn't see you there."

His mate, equally big and ugly, laughed –

"What? You blind or something?"

I wasn't even minding him. The bar they were standing at, the dark kippy little door with the steps down to the entrance, was the Cavern. I couldn't believe it. I knew the old place was well gone, but I was expecting something better than this.

Jasus, this was the kippiest pub, in the kippiest street, in one of the kippiest towns I was ever in, and yet, the Beatles had started from here.

And so if the Beatles could start from that dump and go on to the dizzy heights they'd reached, surely to Jasus I could do half as good from a local in Dublin.

I knew I couldn't expect any favours, just 'cause I was the local boy. Most of the acts were local; besides, tonight was the final and that was being judged by a panel. I knew one of the judges was from a big record company. Another was from a teen magazine, and the third, a man in his fifties was from the brewery. I spotted a man that fitted his description with his hand on the arse of the girl who won the heats two weeks ago.

"Well that's that vote gone," I thought.

Suddenly I was trapped by Mrs Crosby and Mrs Phelan. They were regulars in the bar. Most nights I served them their glass of Guinness. I knew they loved Sonny Knowles and hated all that loud modern music. They were decent aul widows.

"Com' 'ere you."

I smiled and walked over to them –

"Hello Ladies, how are you tonight?"

Mrs Phelan put her arms under her ample street trader's breasts, lifted them up and said –

"Never mind us. I hope you're not going to be playing any of that modern stuff tonight."

Mrs Crosby added –

"None of that O-AS-IS crowd or them Firelighters!"

I laughed –

"It's *Firestarter,* Mrs Crosby."

She got impatient –

"Firelighter, Firestarter, it's all the same. Noise, that's all it is."

"Oh you're right, Peggy, noise. And not even decent noise. Com' 'ere." She leaned into me. "Will yeh sing an oldie? "Pennies from Heaven", will yeh sing tha' for us?"

"Tell you what Mrs Phelan, Mrs Crosby. I want to sing my own song tonight." They looked disappointed. "but that's only for them judges. Afterwards I'll come over, we'll have a sing-song and I'll sing anything you want."

They smiled –

"You're a good boy, John Michael."

I saw Tracy come in, but she didn't notice me. We'd talk later. Right now I had to get ready.

Some thought this was only a little local talent show, but you had to win this to be in with a chance of getting to the final and getting that recording contract.

I'd dreamt of a recording contract ever since my first breath. I had to win! I couldn't stand another night of being a barman!

Chapter Forty-Nine

Life in the bar trade could be fierce boring. The smell of stale beer was on everything you wore and hard as you tried it was impossible to keep a shirt clean for a full shift. There was always some gobshite of a drunk who spilled a drink, or a leaky tap. Just as you thought you'd kept a clean shirt, you could guarantee that you'd lean into a little pool of Arthur's finest that hadn't been wiped up.

And there was no point in getting angry, sure Paddy Mac would just smile and say –

"Sure it goes with the territory."

Anyway, what with the smell of smoke off you, you couldn't wear one twice. Still, I wouldn't have it any other way. The smell was chronic, but smoke added to the atmosphere. Besides, if they hadn't got the pub, where in the name of fuck were smokers gonna smoke? They were treated as lepers as it was. They're run out of restaurants, movies, shops, even hairdressers. There's hardly a place left now that's smoker-friendly.

I was in McDonald's and one of those Ronnie Girls with the "Have a nice day" smiles says –

"Sorry, no smoking area."

Now maybe her batting eyelashes would work on some horny pre-pube teenager. Maybe it would work on your man with the dodgy afro who sang "I'm In Love With My McDonald's Girl". But not *me*.

I was interested in my Big Mac, my fries and a fag –

"So where is the smoking area?"

She smiled again –

"Sorry sir, we're a no-smoking restaurant."

My burger was getting cold. The ash on my cigarette was getting long and I wasn't in the humour for the hassle. I mean to say, she was pointing to a sign that you wouldn't see unless you were looking for it and secondly she had an over-active mind if she thought you could classify McDonald's as a restaurant.

"Listen love, why don't you go and tell Ronnie that if he doesn't want to serve me that's fine but he has served me and the fact that he *has* means I'm gonna finish the meal I paid for before I go."

She smiled and scuttled away.

I was just about finished when two security men (no smiles) came over to me. They just stood there, with their walkie-talkies, bubble jackets, shaved heads and "don't fuck with me" looks.

Bambi, the McDonald's girl, is in between them.

"I hear you're giving this girl hassle," says Number One.

"No," I replied.

"Well, she said you did," says Number Two.

I took another bite out of my Big Mac. Third bite and it was gone; I'd hate to see the small Mac.

"She asked me to stop smoking, I said *no*, no hassle, no nothing, just a plain NO."

"Well she says . . . "

I cut in –

"Listen mate. I couldn't give a fuck what Bambi said, all I want is to have a fag, OK?"

Number Two looks at Number One, then to me –

"But you're not allowed to have a fag in here."

I stubbed my cigarette, half-smoked, into the Big Mac box –

"I know that now."

I got up and walked out, One and Two followed. I reached the door, walked out and as I did, a squad car screeched to a halt. The guard calls to the two security men as he exits from the passenger door, fixing his cap –

"Everything all right?"

Number One says nothing but, nods in my direction.

The guard calls to me –

"Stop right there."

I stop.

He walks up to me, taking out his notebook as he approaches –

"What's your game?"

"Nothing."

"That's what they all say."

So I go through the whole story again, along with my name and address.

I felt guilty, even though I'd done nothing. I could see my family having to get a campaign to free me. They'd have to get your woman that got the Birmingham Six off, to defend me. I'd have to go on a hunger strike and Daniel Day Lewis would play me in the film and he'd have to hunger strike too, just to get into the role.

But in the end, sense prevailed. The garda put his notebook back into his pocket and said –

"Don't be smoking in there anymore. Now off with ye."

Another good thing, for me, about working behind the bar was the unsocial hours. I hadn't got friends, not that I could go out with. While they were at play, I was at work and vice versa. It left me with endless hours to practise guitar. I loved my guitar. I'd always played guitar, ever since I could remember.

I'd played in the school choir and at the folk mass on Sundays. I'd even had a band.

Getting a band together wasn't as easy as I thought it would be. I had these grand illusions of putting an advert on the school notice-board, getting the best four musicians who would all have the same ideas, the same input and after our first gig, we'd have the record companies queuing up offering us contracts.

But of course that was how a film might have it. I put the note up and for two weeks I had every weird fucker come up and want to be in the band. I could see them coming, from the long-haired rocker wanting to be in the next Iron Maiden, to the girls with the pink eye shadow wanting the next Bananarama.

I wanted to go back to punk rock, you know, like the Boomtown Rats. After all, it was over ten years since they'd had a hit and I felt the world was ready for a reincarnation of Punk. We'd had revamps of the sixties and seventies, we'd heard re-releases of everything from "Always On My Mind" to "Tears On My Pillow". Stock, Aiken, Waterman were doing everything in the charts. You couldn't put the telly on without seeing Kylie Minogue. Babies were getting christened Kylie and Jason. Something had to give. We couldn't keep going with this nice nice music and I felt that, when the bubble burst, punk would be back with a vengeance.

Punk was cool. I'd seen the videos of the Sex Pistols spitting at the crowd and dressing to shock in all their ripped gear and pins through their noses . . . I loved the lyrics and the way the crowds just jumped around like lunatics and all those crazy Mohican hairstyles.

After watching disaster after disaster, I finally got the band together. There was Tony from the Glen, who was always banging things, so he got to be the drummer. There was a better drummer in the school, but his father hadn't got a van, so he didn't get in. I played lead and Smokey was lead vocals. Smokey was an evil-looking bastard and had a voice that sounded like a black man. No, not quite Otis Redding . . . He had yellow hair, matching teeth and wore a T-shirt with "The Pope is the antichrist" across it.

We'd two girls who wore black, painted their faces white and sang . . . no, *screeched* backing vocals. The final member was Snake. He could play bass and play it well.

We didn't make it; there were a lot of reasons, but the bottom line was, we didn't make it.

We couldn't get a place to practise because our music was so loud. Being punk wasn't the same as acoustic. We couldn't agree on a name either. We were fixated with the nose – torn between "The Snotrags" and "The Bogies", we ended up with "The Golliers".

Smokey thought it was great. He said every concert we could golly the audience. The girls said *no way,* and Snake said he didn't fancy it either, because someone would get up and kick the fuck out of us. I tried to explain about punk but they weren't convinced.

On top of that, I had a problem with writing the lyrics. I liked writing love songs, nice lyrics like –

"It's Monday morning
And I'm so blue
Because I'm missing, missing
I'm missing you . . . u . . . u . . . u."

But the punk lyrics were more –

"It's fucking Monday bitch
And my balls itch
It's all 'cause of you . . . u . . . u . . . u."

We got one gig. It was a disaster. There was a cancellation in the local hall and we got the gig. The lighting wouldn't work. The girls refused to wear the short skirts we'd picked for them and ended up standing at the back in coats. The drummer started spitting at the audience but his spits landed on Smokey and they had a row on stage. Afterwards Snake said he was leaving us and joining a band that did weddings; one of the girls said her father didn't like what he was after seeing and that she wouldn't be back and the drummer said he wouldn't play with Smokey again.

I disbanded the band. I think we wouldn't have gotten another gig anyway.

It put me off music for a while.

That's when I got my apprenticeship with Paddy Mac's. I cut my hair and took the rings out of my nose and ear.

Paddy took a shine to me. Some bars take the piss out of apprentices, making them do all kinds of dirty jobs, keeping them behind to do all the cleaning, without any overtime pay.

But not Paddy. If you did have to stay, he'd pay you time and a half.

Despite his kindness, I often threatened to leave, thinking there was something better out there. The other man's grass always being greener and all that. But Paddy always talked me around to staying.

"Finish out your apprenticeship, then by all means travel the world. The bar trade is universal, believe me, they're crying out for good bar workers from here to Las Vegas and back."

I'd say I didn't want to spend the rest of my life pulling pints, that I wanted to make records and he'd smile. He never ran me down, he'd just smile and say –

"And I'm sure you'll do it, but isn't it nice to have a trade to fall back on, just in case."

And he was right.

I loved to spend the whole day tuning my guitar and writing, then rewriting my songs. But it didn't pay the bills and so I needed some other way of making money. Right now, the bar trade was as good as any. It gave me my own free time, quality writing time. And when Davey Brady was sat at the bar, I knew Tracy was sitting at home, waiting for me.

Chapter Fifty

I remember the first time I saw Tracy Brady. When I say the first time, I mean the first time I ever took any notice of her. I'm sure she'd been in a few times with Davey but I'd be cleaning the ashtrays and the likes and Davey always came to the bar and got the drink himself.

It was a few weeks away from Christmas. The parties had started. Jesus, they started earlier every year. It was a great time to be a customer, but a crap time to be working in a pub. Fellas would drink themselves sick and yet yeh couldn't bar them because *it's Christmas*.

They could drink all day . . . *it's Christmas*.

Bring kids into the bar . . . *it's Christmas*.

Sing stupid songs . . . *it's Christmas*.

I hated "White Christmas".

But when the locals tried to uptempo it, I hated it even more. Flying through it like there was no tomorrow, then making it a part of a medley that included "Mary's Boy Child Jesus Christ" and "Rudolph The Fucking Red Nosed Reindeer."

Whoever invented Christmas hated two things. Music and barmen.

And no sooner had they finished singing then they'd try to grab a girl and have a dance or a quick kiss.

It was one of those kinds of nights.

I'd never stopped going the whole time. The one chance I got for a quick fag, the toilets blocked. Not the "lads" of course, the "girls". If it was the fellas, you could just close the cubicle, 'cause we'd three cubicles and loads of urinals, but the girls only had the two toilets so I had to do my impersonation of a plumber. I knew before I got in what it was.

The girls are dirtier than the fellas. At least with the lads, it's just a case of a bad aim, but the girls throw whole toilet rolls down the toilets and as for them bloody pads . . . every night you could be guaranteed that the toilet would be blocked.

At last the serving was finished. I was just clearing up bottles and she came in. I knew by the way she was looking around she was looking for someone and don't ask me how, but I just copped who she was.

After I'd left her home, I couldn't get her off my mind. There was something about her. I stayed awake most of the night and most of the night I spent thinking about her.

Then the next day I nearly ruined it all, embarrassing her with my stupid words.

Still, the way that she came to the gate and asked me to call again gave me hope.

I called during the day, always on the pretence of being around the area, and we'd sit and chat for hours.

She asked about my music and said she'd always wanted to learn to play the guitar and I said I'd teach her.

The first few times that's what I did. I tuned the guitar and got her to hold her fingers to make C, G and F chords. We'd fall about the place laughing because of the sad attempt she'd make of them. In the end I'd sit and play song after song for her. As the weeks rolled on, the songs moved from the first song that came into my head to love songs, songs that I knew meant something to her. Karyn White's "Superwoman" always brought a tear to her eye and so did a very slow version of "I Will Survive".

Every time I played a song, we'd sit and talk about it or how it made us feel and suddenly from a silly song we'd go off on a tangent and end up talking about ourselves. She loved to hear me talk about my ambition and she encouraged me. She asked me to sing some of the songs I'd written myself, but I never did. I'd sing old Harry Chapin songs about life on the road and the hardships of it; she loved the sentiments. I sang Joni Mitchell's "Coyote". She'd never heard it before but loved the line –

"Problem is, Coyote, we just come from such different sets of circumstance."

Every time I arrived she'd beg me to sing it, and though she never learned any melodies, she loved the guitar.

Then one evening I watched Davey with Amanda, cuddling up to each other, laughing and joking as though they hadn't a problem in the world, as though they were lovers and no one else mattered. I cleaned the ashtray off their table, finding it hard to even make small talk. He turned to her, kissed her and whispered that they should drink up and go. She asked was he not expected home and he laughed and told her the usual excuses he'd used.

I went back to the bar and asked Paddy could I go.

He looked at the clock –

"Bit early, isn't it?"

"I know, but I have a little business I have to take care of."

Paddy looked around the bar –

"Go on, it's not as though I'll be run off me feet."

I grabbed my jacket –

"Thanks Paddy, I'll make it up to you."

I was gone out the door and running down the road. I knew my car would be safe parked beside Paddy's. I ran the back alley and jumped the wall to Tracy's back garden. Then I sneaked up in the shadows to her gate and opened it. I tapped on her front door. I stood at the side. She came to the door and called –

"Who's there?"

"It's me, John."

I could hear her hurry to unchain the door –

"John? Is everything OK?"

I assured her it was, apologised for the late hour and accepted her offer of tea.

We talked and I sang until I couldn't sing no more. I stared at her and she at me, our hands touched, then I kissed her. Her lips hesitated, not parting, not encouraging. I went to pull away, but they sprang into action, afraid that the opportunity would be missed. They were nervous, quivering, ready to please but afraid that they wouldn't.

We kissed until my jaws felt sore. I pulled away and held her face close to mine. The parting of the lips seemed to lead to rationality on her part –

"Davey could come home, he said he had a job out of town, but if he finished early he'd make the effort to get back."

I held her, kissed her eyes –

"Tracy, Davey was in the pub tonight with . . . "

She pulled away, held her hands over her ears –

"Please, I don't want to hear this, I don't want to know."

Carefully I pulled her hands down. She was crying. I wiped away the tears –

"OK, I'm sorry. It was spiteful of me, forgive me?"

She nodded. I continued –

"It's just that . . . I'm jealous."

She looked surprised, her voice was still weak with the tears –

"Jealous? You, jealous? Of what?"

"Of him having you."

She smiled –

"That's so sweet."

She kissed me again and the kiss led to our hands moving to each other's clothes. Our lips never left each other as we stripped, sometimes clumsily, sometimes giggling, until we were naked in each other's arms. Our bodies seemed to know each other's needs. I entered her and we fitted perfectly together, like a beautiful jigsaw.

We made love, not sex. It was done with the minimum of

movement, as if the holding and the kissing was more important than the penetration. Her body was in perfect rhythm with mine and as I came she squeezed me close, and kissed as though she never wanted me to go.

Afterwards we still held each other tight. I went to tell her that I loved her, that I never felt like this with anyone else in my life, but she put a finger across my mouth and said –

"Ssssh, don't say a thing. Let's just hold each other."

And so we did. Not just that night but every day and night that we met after that.

I wanted her to know how much I loved her, but every time I went to tell her she'd stop me –

"John, you're twenty-five, I'm thirty-five."

"Age doesn't matter."

"Not now, but in ten years, twenty years, thirty years time? You're single, you've the whole of your life ahead of you, I'm a married woman, for God sake."

"So?"

"So, it'll never work. Let's just enjoy the *now*."

"But I don't want you thinking I'm using you. I want you to know that I love you."

"I know you do."

She always said that, never "and I love you".

She came to every round of the talent competition. She'd sit, chatting to some of the other women or on occasion with Davey and when I'd come out, I'd feel her eyes on me. It didn't matter what part of the room she was in, I'd spot her and when I got up on stage I'd sing to her. That made the songs sound more meaningful.

I sang –

"I Don't Want To Put No Hold On You", "Without You" and even "Superwoman". And every time I did I won.

Now tonight I was standing here ready to go on, I looked for her again. Where the hell was she?

THE BIG DAY

Chapter Fifty-One

– Simmo –

"Peter, Peter, Peter."

I was standing back at his door and he was standing gawking as though Jesus Christ had just risen and appeared to him. I pushed by him –

"I'll invite myself in."

He recomposed himself a bit –

"Yeah sure, to what do I owe this pleasure?"

I walked around, as though I was walking around an art gallery with Picassos and Rembrandts on the walls. I spoke casually, studying the photograph of his wedding day on the wall –

"I've come for my money."

I didn't look at him, but his voice sounded nervous –

"But we have an agreement."

I turned, stared at him, looking puzzled –

"Have we?"

"Yeah, yeah." He was relieved, he lit a cigarette. "You're coming back in a few days for your money."

I still played dumb –

"But today was collection day, why would I make another arrangement?"

"'member? I hadn't got the dosh."

I pretended I'd just clicked it, snapping my fingers –

"That's right, that stupid cunt of a wife of yours didn't leave you the money, wasn't that it?"

He laughed –

"That's it, the stupid cunt."

I took three steps closer, we were no more than four foot apart –

"Then how come I saw you in the local down the road today?"

His face went white, he took a drag on his cigarette, then he went a bright red –

"Me? *Naw,* must 'ave been a mistake."

"No mistake."

He laughed again –

"Honestly Simmo . . . "

"DON'T. Don't do it. Don't make matters worse by lying."

"I wouldn't. I mean I'm not. There's another fella looks . . . "

I grabbed him by the arm and swung him into the wall. The door was still open, I slammed it shut on his arm. He cried out, I opened and closed it on his arm, five, six times. He sank to the floor, crying like a baby –

"Please no, no more. I'm sorry, I'm really sorry."

I dragged him by the arm to the settee and left him lying against it, sobbing his apologies.

"Where's my money?"

"I'll get it. Give me a few days."

"You got a hearing problem? I said where's my money?"

He was uncontrollable. I grabbed his arm, he cried out –

"Oh God pleeaazze Simmo, a few days, you have the telly. I won't let you down."

"But you already have." I let go of his hand. "Now that telly, that's mine 'cause you lied to me. All deals are now null and void and I want payment. Hard cash or payment in kind. What's it to be?"

"But I haven't got it."

I walked over to him, made a grab for his arm –

"Sorry? I think my hearing is playing up, I could have sworn you told me you haven't got it."

He sobbed –

"I'm sorry, I'm so . . . "

"Yes I know, you're so sorry. No good. Sorry was this morning's answer. Answer now is, money or in kind."

I walked around the room again. Stopped once more at the photo –

"This? This could do?"

His sobbing stopped for a minute –

"What, the photo?"

"No, not the fucking photo. The missus. Let me have your missus and we'll call the debt quits."

"You're fucking mad?"

I turned –

"You're in no position to call anyone mad, least of all me. The way I look at it, you don't have any other choices. The only thing worth more than her in here was the telly and that's mine now, or had you forgotten?"

"I couldn't . . . "

"Or wouldn't." I held my hands up, "But that's fine. I respect the marriage vows. I was just looking to help you out. You fucked with my reputation, made me look bad. I can't afford to lose face."

From my jacket I took out a hammer.

"Oh, sweet Jesus, Simmo, *don't*."

"Peter, Peter, Peter. What option do I have? I gave you the choice, you chose . . . "

"No wait, wait . . . You want Debbie to . . . "

"Fuck me. I want your wife to fuck me."

His eyes closed –

"And that'd make us quits?"

"Clean slate. I'd even give you back the telly and twenty quid for you to have a drink, while we do the dirty."

He sat thinking about it. I looked up and smiled –

"Hey Peter, look, now you can ask the woman herself."

Chapter Fifty-Two

– Debbie –

Peter struggled to get up but fell –

"Love, I can explain. You see . . . "

I was looking toward Simmo as I answered –

"Don't bother."

Simmo didn't even have the good grace to look embarrassed by the whole thing. He just stood there with that smirk, the smirk people who think they're better than us have.

I directed my questions to him –

"What's going on here?"

"Why don't you ask your husband."

"'Cause I'm asking you."

He smiled –

"I'd rather not get involved in a domestic matter."

I didn't answer, I just stared at him. He tried to outstare me, but no one ever did that, he continued –

"I came to collect, Peter hadn't got the money and so we're trying to see can we come to some other arrangement."

I didn't bother saying I'd left the money, it didn't matter what I'd left or hadn't left, all that mattered was what was going on here now –

"And part of this arrangement was me sleeping with you?"

He smirked –

"It was an option."

I glared at Peter, he reacted as though I'd hit him –

"Love, there's no way I was gonna go along with that."

I spat the words out –

"You fucking liar, I heard you."

He was grimacing, crawling away from me –

"I had to, you seen him, he's a fucking madman, there's no reasoning with him. He was gonna kill me, honest teh fuck he was."

I moved toward him, he kept crawling, like the snake he was –

"So, you were prepared to let him fuck me instead?"

He crawled, I walked after him. He got to a corner and his body kept moving until he was a distorted ball in the corner –

"It wouldn't have happened. We were messing, weren't we Simmo?"

Simmo looked at him –

"No."

I lashed out my boot and kicked and kicked until I couldn't kick anymore. Until I couldn't lift my foot. He cried like a baby, never once avoiding the blows, as they rained down on him.

I turned and faced Simmo again –

"Twenty-five pounds will keep you happy 'til next week?"

"Perfectly. But like I said, we can wipe this slate clean in one fell swoop."

I rummaged in my pockets and found the twenty-five. It left us with nothing. The children were staying at my sister's for a few days and I'd given her a few bob towards their cost. She loved having them, especially knowing the life, or lack of life, they had here. They loved it at hers too, a phone call every once in a while was all they wanted from us. It was sad to think that that's how they felt about their parents, but it was true.

I'd paid the rent and a few bob off the bills as well and that twenty-five was what was going to get me out to see the final of the talent show. I handed it to Simmo. I could feel Peter's eyes looking at it pass. Even in his present state I knew he wanted it for himself, for the bookies, one last try at his system. I knew that in a few weeks from now, if everything was OK, he'd smack me around because I'd handed it over. But things were never going to be OK again.

I looked Simmo straight in the face –

"You can go and fuck yourself."

He smirked again, kissed the notes and walked out the door –

"See you all next week."

I walked after him and slammed the door. I turned to Peter; he was getting up –

"The fucking bastard, I'm telling yeh love, he's cruising for a bruising any day now."

I walked over to him and slapped him hard across the face.

"Wha'? Wha' was that for?"

I walked past him, took the whiskey bottle from the table and went into the bathroom. I locked the door.

He banged on it –

"Ah come on love, please. For fuck sake, you know I'd never have let him lay a hand on yeh. I just got carried away, I got a tip and I thought I could make a few extra bob."

I said nothing. Usually, I'd cut across him, tell him to fuck off, tell him to get out. But this time I said nothing and that scared him. He was desperate for me to give him some response but none came.

He banged on the door again –

"That bastard broke my fucking arm . . . Do you hear me?"

335

He cried out, "Ah, the fucking pain. I need to go to the hospital."

I ran the bath, poured some Radox that the children had bought me for Christmas into the water and stripped off. He kept banging, cursing me from a height.

I lay into the bubbles, the water was hot, hotter than I'd usually have it. It went silent outside, I lowered myself right under, until my head was covered.

Down the end of the bath was Peter's razor. I leaned up and took it. I opened the whiskey and took a large swig. I opened the razor, took the blade out and ran it across, first one, then the other wrist. I cut in deep, under the water and the water turned shark-attack red. It stung but only for a second. The blood mixed with the Radox-soaked water and they made me drift.

I was away from here, in another time and place, with no Peter, no Simmo and no hassle. I was free and nothing mattered.

Chapter Fifty-Three

Debbie's Flat

Peter gave the door one last kick, then shouting –

"Fuck yeh, fuck yez all,"

– staggered to the couch and lay down.

He reached over to his cigarette packet, opened it up, then finding no cigarette, crunched it up and threw it across the room.

He looked around, saw Debbie's bag, then with his face crinkled in pain strained to pick it up. She'd three cigarettes left, he took one out, put the packet in his pocket and lit up. As he smoked, he searched the bag – nothing, not even a fiver.

A knock on the door startled him –

"Who is it?"

He didn't curse, just in case it was Simmo.

"It's Conor."

He sat puzzled for a minute –

"Conor who?"

The person on the other side of the door laughed –

"How many Conors do you know? It's Debbie's brother, for fuck sake. Now are yeh going to let me in or not?"

Peter struggled to his feet and, barely opening the door, made his way back to the settee.

Conor stood with a bag over his shoulder, looking around –

"Where's Sis?"

Peter indicated with his head –

"Didn't know you were out?"

"I've been out for three years."

"Wonder you're not back in then, isn't it?"

"Very fucking funny. I see you haven't changed."

Peter lit a second cigarette –

"I'd offer you one but . . . you know yourself, only a few left."

Conor threw a duty-free bag at him –

"Here, thought you might like them."

Peter looked in the bag at the four hundred cigarettes –

"Good man. Hit the kettle on, make yourself at home."

Conor filled the kettle –

"What's taking Debbie?"

"She's having a bath." He struggled to sit up, stubbing out the cigarette and opening up the new box of stronger ones –

"You here for long?"

"Couple of days."

"You working?"

"I've got a job as an IT technician."

"A wha?"

"Computers."

"A few bob in tha' I'd say?"

"Can't complain."

"So the prison's done yeh some good then?"

Conor didn't answer. He walked over to the door of the toilet and banged –

"Hey Sis, come on out, see your little brother."

"She'll be out in a minute. So are we going for a celebratory drink or what?"

"Yeah, later, why not."

Peter coughed –

"You couldn't see your way to lending us a few bob?"

Conor sighed –

"I see some things never change."

He pulled a wad of notes from his wallet, Peter's eyes lit up –

"Fifty should cover it."

Conor handed the money to him but, as he did, noticed how poor his movement was –

"What's up with you?"

"Nothing, just hurt me arm, that's all."

For the first time Conor looked closely at him –

"Those marks, you've been fighting again, haven't you?"

"It's no sweat, don't worry."

Conor looked to the bathroom door –

"Did you hit Debbie?"

Before Peter could answer, Conor was at the door, thumping it.

"Debbie, Debbie! It's Conor. Do you hear me? Conor. Open up Sis!"

He turned to Peter –

"If you've hurt her, so help me God, I'll . . ."

Peter was defensive –

"Honest to God, I haven't touched her."

"You'd better not have." He turned back to the door. "Come on Debbie, stop fooling around."

Still no answer.

He looked at Peter –

"What the fuck is going on?"

Peter shrugged his shoulders. Conor called again –

"Debbie? Right Debs, if you're not out when I count to three, I'm gonna break the door down."

He stood back from the door –

"ONE . . . TWO . . . THREE"

On the third he ran with his shoulder against the door; it crashed open. He landed in the middle of the tiny bathroom –

"Jesus Christ, Debbie!"

He was at her side, the bath was red, he rubbed her hand –

"Debbie, DEBBIE! Can you hear me?"

Peter appeared –

"Oh fuck!"

Conor shouted at him –

"Get an ambulance!"

He stood there, muttering, *"Oh fuck"*, over and over again.

Conor stood, grabbed him by the shoulders and shook him –

"GO. Get an ambulance. NOW!"

He staggered out the bathroom and headed for the front door, Conor shouted –

"Where the *fuck* are you going?"

"To phone an ambulance."

"Use my mobile."

After ringing he stood watching Conor rubbing her arm and talking to her –

"It's OK Sis, everything's OK. Hang on . . . the ambulance is coming, it's on its way."

She wasn't responding. He turned to Peter and said –

"I'm giving you one chance to tell me what happened here. One chance . . . and you better tell the truth."

Peter told him all, more or less. He told him about Simmo, hassling them for money owed. Told him how Simmo propositioned Debbie and how it was the mercy of God that he'd walked in when he had, with the twenty-five pounds, or Simmo would have raped her.

The ambulance men worked hard and quickly. Conor and Peter travelled with them in the ambulance to the hospital. While they waited Peter was seen to. As he came back with his arm in a cast, the doctor appeared. There was nothing anyone could do. She'd lost too much blood, he was sorry but . . . .

Conor grabbed the weeping Peter against the wall –

"Shut the fuck up, do you hear me? Where does this fucker Simmo hang out?"

Peter shook –

"Whhyyy?"

"Never mind fucking why, *where does he hang out*?"

"Tonight? A pub called Paddy Mac's. Drinks there all the time."

"Right, you and me are gonna pay him a little visit."

THE BIG NIGHT

Chapter Fifty-Four

– Davey –

"Where the fuck is Amanda?"

I looked at me watch for the hundredth time. I swear, by the time women shifted their arses into gear, the mood was gone off men.

This ring was burning a hole in me pocket. This wasn't me, not the me I had become anyway. Time was, moons ago, when I did spontaneous things like this, but that hadn't happened in a while. Tracy couldn't have kids. We never discussed it but she couldn't. We'd tried everything and it hadn't worked. I'd no hard feelings. After all, these things happen. But every man wants an heir, every man wants to go and watch his lad play his first match, every man needs to sit and watch Formula One with his own son. Every man needs to show his next generation how to shave, how to handle his pint, how to place a bet.

Tracy was a great girl but she couldn't give me that. If she could, things would have been different. It's the need to procreate that makes men shag everything in sight. I heard some biddy say *that* on the Pat Kenny Show and it was true. I was coming to the age where I needed that. If Tracy had arrived with a bump, it'd solve everything. After all, we had more in common. All this riding had been great to begin with but, after a while, it took it out of you. There were nights when a game on the box was a better option. And Tracy knew my habits. She always had the dinner on, always knew what kinda clothes I liked, even enjoyed the same music as me. We were compatible.

Amanda, she was a live wire. No sooner had I the business done than she was there, dragging and pulling at it, poking her tongue in my ear, shoving her tits into me mouth, giving me a handful of pussy. She never stopped. And sooner or later, *he'd* react. He'd get hard and she'd be on him, like a bronco rider in a rodeo. I swear to God, it was raw red from all the use. But she was of an age that could give me a kid and that was suddenly mattering more than anything else in the world. Besides, it was nice to have a younger woman on your arm. OK, it was a bit of a trophy and all that. But trophies were nice things to have every once in a while.

– Amanda –

He had my curiosity up, I'll give him that. Still, there was no rush, whatever Davey had would wait.

I decided to hit a few pubs on the way. The girls were acting up, Mary was after getting a phone call and was flapping around the place. Celine was in one of her humours, I think she was due or something. Either way, neither of them wanted to come with me, so I headed off by myself.

I sat in the first pub and looked around at the talent. What talent? Whoever said Irish men were the most attractive in the world was either an awful messer or blind. I sussed them out. Every one of them winking at me in that "single woman sitting in a bar on her own, she's a good thing" way. And the state of them, with pot-bellies and their pints. Christ! Give me Italians any day. They always dressed so well, with designer gear and beautifully polished shoes. The Irish in their runners and Wrangler jeans that only came halfway up their arses just hadn't got the same appeal.

I had the best of a bad bunch, and I had *him*. Poor old Davey would jump through hoops if I asked him. He always dressed reasonable too. That was the nice thing about having a married man. His wife dressed him, so you always knew he'd be decked out properly.

Still, what with the factory laying off, our days were numbered. I was going to get a few pound redundancy and I sure as hell wasn't going to spend it in this shithole of a country. No, I was off to work on the Continent. In one of those fancy bars, amid the throngs of tourists out for a good time. I'd seen the girls doing it when I was on holliers meself and sure they had the best of both worlds. They had the sun in the day, they could drink and have the craic while they worked at night . . . and they got paid for it.

I'd put my name forward for redundancy and as soon as I got the money, I was gone. There'd be other Davey Bradys, richer ones with more to offer.

I was just getting ready to leave this kip when in waltzed three foreigners. I sat back down. Davey and his surprise could wait.

– Tracy –

I knew he'd forgotten all about our shopping. I knew he'd be sitting in the pub now, getting nicely merry. I'd have to tell him there. I had a shower and changed into my best, sexiest clothes. I wanted him to remember how good I could look, what exactly he was missing, when I told Davey our marriage was over.

I walked down the road there was so much to do tonight. I had to end my marriage and start the rest of my life. And most importantly, I had to tell John Michael that he wasn't just getting a partner, he was getting a family too. I couldn't believe it. At first I thought it was just everything that was going on that had my period overdue. I mean to say, the last thing I thought of was that I'd be pregnant, but I was.

The pregnancy had me acting funny, eating at weird times. I got a longing for a burger and chips, no, more than a longing, I had to have them. I crossed the road and went into the chipper. I ordered and took a seat. As I sat I earwigged on a conversation behind me. It was two suits. They looked out of place but they were oblivious of anything or anyone.

The fat one was very enthusiastic –

"I'm telling you, Steve, this guy is shit hot. He's got the voice of Garth Brooks, the looks of a pop star and he can write. He's a winner."

The skinny man was hesitant –

"I dunno, Marty. If he's so good, how come he's never been noticed before?"

"I don't know. Maybe 'cause he's been working in a dump like this all his life, maybe 'cause he doesn't play in public. I dunno, all I know is *he's great*. He's what we've been hoping for. If he goes to the Grand Final, he'll be snapped up. We can get him now. He's raw, but he's unattached and eager. I'm telling you, this guy can go all the way, and we can be along for the ride."

"What did you say his name was again?"

Fat man laughed –

"John Michael . . . but who cares, we can change that."

They drank up their coffees and walked across the road to Paddy Mac's.

– John Michael –

I'd spent my whole life waiting. Waiting for my first guitar, waiting for fame and fortune to come knocking, waiting for the love of my life, and now, they all seemed to be arriving at the same time. I know people were saying it was only a silly pub competition, but to me it was the break I'd always dreamt about.

People from here don't get opportunities, they don't have connections, no friend who has a friend. Here you had to work your arse off ten times harder to achieve half as much. It was true what they said, we were all in the gutter but, I was one of those looking at the stars. I was the one who would spend every day, do anything that I had to – to get out of here and make something of my life.

The first few rounds of this competition were a piece of cake. Singing seventies songs like "I Don't Want To Put No Hold On You", smiling like Berni Flint had on *Opportunity Knocks* and getting the vote of every little granny in the place because of it and every little grandad 'cause I'd pulled them a pint only hours before.

But now, tonight, it was serious. Four people stood between me and the next round. Four people had the power, in their vote, to stop me from moving onwards and upwards.

Tonight I had to do my best, tonight I had to sing like I'd never sung before. I'd decided to sing a song I'd written myself. I always knew that panellists preferred new material, they gave you credit for being original. Chances are if I sang a Berni Flint or a Nilson number I'd get a juror who'd hate it.

Whereas even if they hated my own song, they had to give me credit for writing it.

I'd written it about Tracy. Life had never felt so together until I'd met her and as I played the guitar, the words were just there.

There had been two acts already; one had been a fairly pathetic magician but the other was a girl who was always winning Karaoke in the local pubs and she'd decked herself out to look just like Cher and her "Shoop Shoop Song" was a great one to get the crowd going. I was the next act but one. As Tom Kearns got up with his Elvis cape blowing in the fan's breeze, two suits came up to me –

"John Michael? I'm Marty Burns of Elastic Records and this here is our International Producer Steve Lomas."

I was stunned –

"THE Steve Lomas?"

They both smiled. Marty went on –

"I've heard you sing and I like what I hear."

Steve Lomas cut across –

"Like! This guy got me to fly in tonight just to hear you."

"Hey, don't tell him too much. I haven't signed him yet."

"Signed me? Is this a wind-up? Who put you up to this?"

Marty must have seen how annoyed I was. He pulled a card from his pocket and quickly handed it to me. It was very professional, laminated and finished in gold writing, with the emblem I recognised from records I had of Elastic Records.

"I'd really like you to come on board."

The last bars of "Now or Never" finished and the MC was asking the audience to give him a big hand. After the lukewarm applause, he introduced me.

"And now, ladies and gentlemen, we have a face I'm sure you're all familiar with . . . it's John Michael with an original composition called 'You're My Sunshine In The Morning'."

Marty turned to me –

"Go on son, knock 'em dead, then afterwards we'll go somewhere else and talk."

I walked on stage still looking back at them and almost walking into the microphone stand as I did. There was muted laughter from the crowd. I fixed myself on my chair, tuned my guitar, found Tracy's face in the crowd and began –

I smiled down at her as I strummed the intro, but her eyes looked as though she'd been crying.

"Been a lot of times without you
When I told myself I didn't care
We might have fought
Didn't talk
Was kinda glad to get you out of my hair
But lately it's been different
And I love you more and more
And the only time I'm truly satisfied
Is when you're at my door

You're the sunshine in the morning
You're the snow on a Christmas Eve
You're the flower that lights my springtime up
So promise me you'll never leave

Could have done things
If I'd never met you
Could've sailed the world alone
Could've eaten in fancy restaurants
Where I lay my hat
Call my home
But you're here now
And it's different
Everything has its place

349

And the only time I'm truly satisfied
Is when I see your face

You're the sunshine in the morning
You're the snow on a Christmas Eve
You're the flower that lights the springtime up
So promise me you'll never leave
Yes you're the sunshine in the morning
You're the snow on a Christmas Eve
You're the flower that lights my springtime up
Soo prommise meee
You'll never lee . . . ea . . . ve . . . "

As I finished, Paddy Mac's went wild. People were standing applauding, stamping their feet on the ground and banging the tables with their hands.

Marty Burns and Steve Lomas were applauding too.

I looked at Tracy, she was smiling, clapping and crying. I indicated for her to come to me, but she shook her head. Suddenly the MC was egging on the crowd for more applause and Steve and Marty were helping me from the stage –

"See, Steve, didn't I tell you he was great?"

"You sure did, but I didn't believe he was *this* good."

Marty slapped my back –

"Johnny boy, we gonna make you a star. Come on, let's go celebrate."

I looked at him –

"But what about the competition?"

"Forget the competition. You already got your recording contract," he said, pointing to the piece of paper sticking out of his pocket.

"And," said Steve Lomas, "If you got more songs like that in you, you got a hit album just around the corner, too."

I saw Tracy again, trying to push her way through –

"John, John."

Her voice was drowned in the cries of congratulations.

"Come on, John, let's get you out of here," said Marty.

"Just a minute, there's someone I gotta talk to."

"OK, but make it snappy. Steve is on the midnight flight out of here and I want you two to have studio dates arranged before he goes."

I grabbed Tracy and pulled her through the back exit door and out into the laneway.

"What did you think?"

She smiled –

"You were great."

"And the song, did you like the song?"

"I loved it."

"I wrote it about you."

She didn't look me in the eyes. I continued –

"But guess what, the best thing of it all, I got a contract, with Elastic Records and you won't believe it but STEVE LOMAS is going to be my producer . . . can you believe it? STEVE FUCKING LOMAS."

I noticed she was crying –

"Hey?" I pulled her face up, "don't cry, this is good. This is you and me out of here. Next stop a big penthouse wherever you want." She was still crying. "Come on Trace, what's wrong?"

She bit her top lip to stop crying, then spoke –

"We can't go on."

"What do you mean *can't*? Of course we can."

"NO, we *can't*."

"What is this? Is this that bastard Davey? Are you afraid to tell him," I went to walk back in. "'cause I'll do that. In fact I'll take pleasure in telling him."

She stopped me, put a hand on my mouth to stop me saying anything else, and spoke again –

"Sssh, it's not like that. It's us, I don't love you . . . "

I pushed her hand away –

"Yes you do, of course you do, we love each other."

"No, no, I don't. It was fun, it was flattering. You so young, so popular and me . . . me just a housewife. I was bored, I was looking for excitement . . . and you just came along."

"But . . . you said . . . "

"Just words. They meant nothing, they were for the moment, I knew they were what you wanted to hear."

"You don't mean that? You can't."

"I'm sorry, John. Really I am. I never wanted to hurt you, I never thought it would go this far."

Marty Burns and Steve Lomas were in the laneway now –

"Hey, John, it's time we weren't here."

A taxi pulled in at the top of the lane, they packed my guitar into it, then got in themselves.

I looked at her. I was crying –

"So what now? What do I do without you?"

She rubbed her hand softly against my face –

"You'll find someone else."

She tried to brush my tears away, but they flowed faster than her hand –

"But I don't want anyone else, I want you."

"I'm married, John."

I fell to my knees and pushed my head into her stomach –

"Please, don't leave me, please . . . "

Her hands ran through my hair –

"Don't do this, don't make it any harder than it is."

From the taxi, Marty roared –

"John, come on, we gotta hit the road."

She helped me up, I cried, she cried, we held each other close and kissed. She pulled away –

"Go, John. Go."

She turned and ran through the exit. The taxi beeped its horn, Marty called again. And I went.

– Tracy –

I ran back inside, straight into the ladies. There was a queue for the cubicles but, as a door opened on one of them, I ran into it and locked the door behind me. The girl who was next in line banged the door and cursed me from a height but I didn't care. I sat on the toilet and cried like a little baby.

I couldn't believe I'd done what I'd done, but I *had*. I had no choice. Not since I'd overheard the two men talking. I couldn't do that to him. I couldn't hold him back and, regardless of what he thought, I *would* hold him back. He always talked about how hard a slog it was to make it in the music business. How you needed to be able to devote every waking moment to it. How nothing else could come before it, and I knew he firmly believed this. So how could I tell him he now had a partner and a baby to support? Every move that he made he had to consider not one, not two, but three people. And most of all I knew that he'd make sacrifices for us. He'd spend time with us, time that should be spent on music, he'd spend money, money needed for sessions and guitars and the like. He'd start working part-time and that would make him a part-time everything. A part-time musician, part-time partner, part-time worker and a part-time father. Or worst of all, he might give up music completely, to concentrate on family life. And one day, maybe not for years and years, but one day, he'd resent us for holding him back, for ruining the dream, the dream that made him special. The dream that made him John Michael.

I'd stood at the back of Paddy Mac's listening to him sing to me, and me alone, knowing I was going to break both our hearts but also knowing there was nothing I could do about it.

And all the while, as I told him I didn't love him, as I saw him fall to the ground, I wanted to just pick him up, tell him I loved him and get into the taxi with him. But because I loved him, I let him go.

The banging persisted on the cubicle door –

"Come on you, you're not the only one who needs the loo."

– Amanda –

After one or two carefully flirtatious glances in the direction of the foreigners, one of them came over –

"Signorina, may we buy you a drink?"

I smiled, hesitated, but said, "yes".

As soon as the drink arrived he was telling me his life story.

Tito was from Rome, his family owned a whole chain of bars across mainland Italy and its islands. He was in Ireland looking for staff. I let it be known that I might be leaving my job very soon, and if the offer was right, I might, just *might* consider a move abroad. He spoke a very attractive deal. A bar in Sicily – I'd be the manager and I'd have my own apartment, with a car, as perks of the job. The wages were working out at about three hundred pounds basic and on top of that I could earn the same again on bonuses. It would cost me next to nothing to live there, as his family owned the restaurant next door and I would be able to eat there for free.

We were getting on favourably and I could tell by Tito that it wasn't just my skills as a worker he was interested in. His hands drifted to my legs and I didn't exactly beat them off. There was an endless supply of drink coming from the other end of the bar from his friends. When Tito had gone to the toilet, his friends spoke to me –

"You like Tito, yes?"

I smiled –

"I think we can work well together, yes."

"Work well together?" His friend seemed puzzled.

"Yes, Tito has offered me a job in his family's bar in Sicily."

They both laughed.

"What?" I asked, slightly annoyed at their babbling in their own tongue.

They continued laughing and speaking to each other.

"Oh, fuck off. Did no one ever tell you it's bad manners to do that?"

One of them approached –

"I am sorry. Really. It's just, Tito has . . . how would you say – a vivid imagination."

He must have noticed my mystified look.

"Tito works in a chipper up the road. He hasn't seen Italy for twenty years and I don't think he has ever even seen Sicily, not to mention owning a chain of bars there."

Tito came back, and they took to talking in Italian again. I took my bag off the counter and walked out. He tried to grab my arm but I avoided it.

Maybe I'd make Paddy Mac's before closing.

– Mary –

Joe had sounded funny. Not funny "ha-ha" but funny in a weird kind of way. I was worried. He wouldn't explain, just wanted me to get down to Paddy Mac's as soon as I could.

I rushed around the apartment like a woman possessed. Originally, I had planned to go with Amanda. After all I wasn't expecting Joe to be there until the very last drink. I had to make my apologies to Amanda and yet not tell her anything, 'cause if she knew something was wrong she'd be sitting in the middle of us, all ears, for juicy gossip.

By the time I reached the pub, it was packed out to the door. There was a space beside Davey Brady, but I knew he was keeping that for Amanda. Besides, I knew Joe would rather do without a pint than have to spend the night with him.

Joe was seated at the bar, beside a rather shady-looking character called Simmo. Joe said Simmo was all right, but I didn't like the look of him.

As soon as I got to Joe he stood up and let me have his stool –

"No, Joe, you keep that, I'm sure there's another one somewhere."

But he insisted and so I sat down. I noticed a large bag on the ground –

"What's that, your washing?"

He didn't smile back –

"Can I stay at yours tonight?"

I was puzzled –

"Of course, but . . . what's wrong?"

Over the night he told me all that had happened. All about coming home and his mother having a go at him and finding out about the house and how he'd just had enough. I sat, listened and felt so sorry for him. When he'd finished he asked me again –

"So, is it all right to stay at yours tonight?"

"Joe, you can stay as long as you like, but this will all blow over."

He cut in –

"No it won't. I won't let it. I'm sick of people telling me how to think, what to do. I'm sick of people always assuming that I'll go back to Mother, like we're joined at the hip or something. Well we're not. I'm sick of being boring old Joe. Who never takes a risk. Sensible, reliable Joe . . . " He looked for my reaction. "I'm going to take a chance. I'm leaving home, I'm taking redundancy and I'm going to try and start up my record shop. I know you have doubts about it, maybe it's a mad idea, but I'm determined to make it work. And if it fails, well at least I'll know that I've tried. That I've lived. I'm going to make it work because I want you to marry me, Mary."

I sat stunned.

"I want you to be my wife."

I couldn't say anything. I just jumped off my seat and wrapped my arms around him.

– Tracy –

I came out of the toilet and walked, in a daze, through the crowds. Some girl was on stage with a bouquet of flowers singing the "Shoop Shoop Song" and Paddy Mac was starting to flash the lights for last orders.

I heard my name being called. I looked around; it was Davey.

"Tracy." He had a few beers, a few too many. "Com' 'ere."

I walked over.

"Sirrown, have a drink."

"No thanks Davey, I'm going home."

He was insistent –

"Ah, have a drink outta tha'."

I sat and he called an order.

"Tracy, what's wrong with us?"

I looked away, and went to get up –

"I'm not discussing this, not here, not with the state you're in."

He grabbed my arm –

"Please Tracy, listen to me, please."

I sat again, he continued –

"I love you."

"Well, you've a funny way of showing it."

"I know, I know all dat, but I love you, no matter what. You and me, you see, you and me, we go back, righ' back, back before any of this shit, back to when babies and things didn't matter . . . "

I looked at him –

"What are you on about? Babies and things, what's that supposed to mean?"

"You know I . . . I . . . I always wanted a baby, but . . . it wasn't to be . . . nobody's fault . . . not blaming anyone . . . "

"And I didn't?"

"You see, there you go. I didn't say that . . . All I'm saying is I wanna baby and . . . if you . . . I mean . . . if we can't . . . you know together . . . then I have teh . . . "

"I'm pregnant."

"Like I say . . . " It seemed to take a moment to register what I'd said. "You wha'? What did yeh say?"

"I said I'm pregnant."

"You mean . . . *a baby* . . . "

"That's what it usually means, yes."

He hugged me, then jumped up, knocking over the table. The man at the other end shouted –

"Yeh stupid fuck."

– as he was drowned.

"Oops sorry. Sorry, let me buy you another drink, let me buy the whole table a drink. Hey Paddy, drinks all fucking round . . . "

Paddy Mac looked over –

"I'll stand the drinks you knocked down, but the bar's closed for anything else."

"Ah Paddy, for fuck sake . . . "

"Davey, you're skating on very thin ice as it is, now don't push it."

"But I'm celebrating," he looked at me, "we're celebrating . . . she's preggers, my Tracy's *preggers*."

"Well I'm very glad for you, really I am. But I've stopped serving five minutes ago."

I pulled Davey down –

"Davey, stop, you're making a show of us."

He turned to me, put his hand on my belly and said –

"I tell yeh, I know I'm drunk and all . . . but I swear, on me mother's grave . . . I'll be the best fucking father in the world."

I laughed –

"OK, OK, I believe you, now stay quiet."

But he kept going –

"And I swear on me own life, I'll never play away from home again. I've been a fool Tracy but . . . no more." He stood up, pulled a ring from his pocket and shouted.

– Amanda –

I jumped out of the taxi and from the door I could here Paddy Mac shouting –

"Have ye no homes to go to?"

Fuck it, I thought, too late for a drink, but Davey should

359

still be in here. He'll be a little peeved, but I'd soon work that out of him.

I burst through the door, the place was packed but I could see him, he was standing with a small jewellery box in his hand.

I waved and he shouted.

– Davey –

Amanda had stood me up. The ring was burning a hole in my pocket. I saw Tracy, I was drunk. I called her and she sat down. God, she looked great tonight, like she had all those years ago in the park. I told her so, not in so many words. And as I spoke I realised that I loved her and if it wasn't for the fact of wanting kids, we'd never part.

Then she dropped the bombshell and it was as though all my birthdays had come at once.

I stood, not steady, pulled the ring from my pocket, as I stood the door opened, I shouted as Tracy laughed and Amanda waved –

"I want the world to know . . . *I love my missus.*"

– Simmo –

I couldn't believe it. The place was like some kind of a madhouse. On stage was this apparition singing a Cher number, thanking everyone from her mother to the sponsors and it only a fucking local talent show. She must have been shagging one of the judges to have won tonight. I'd stayed longer than I'd banked on, but I was enjoying the buzz of the place.

Have Ye No Homes To Go To?

Joe Dolan was sitting beside me and he hadn't said a word all night. Then that little one he was shagging had come in and he never shut up. Over at his table, Davey had a face as long as a love-starved puppy, then his missus was over and suddenly he was jumping up and down declaring his undying love. Beside me Joe and his mot were swinging out of one another.

The only one acting normal was Paddy. He was belting out at the top of his voice –

"Have ye no homes to go to?"

HAVE YE STILL NO HOMES TO GO TO?

Chapter Fifty-Five

Mrs Dolan struggled in from the door. Her breathing was hard and her tongue lewd –

"You're no fucking son of mine, Joe Dolan. You're like that father of yours, a useless waste of space."

Suddenly, she clasped her chest and fell to the floor. Her chest felt like it was exploding. She struggled, unable to walk, along the floor to the telephone in the kitchen. She tried to climb to it, but had to pull it down on her. Slowly, in pain, she rang her daughters; the phones rang out without answer.

Paddy Mac's, she thought. She dialled the number and on the third ring it answered.

"Can I speak to Joseph Dolan?"

The voice on the other end asked –

"Can you speak up, I can't hear you?"

She tried again and again, but each time the voice on the other end couldn't hear. Eventually they apologised and hung up.

Her chest burned and suddenly she felt a sharp pain once, then twice, then nothing.

She lay silent, unmoving, beside the phone.

* * *

"I'm not going in," said Peter Collins nervously, "I can't."

"You have to," replied Conor.

"He'll kill me if he sees me, I can't do it."

"And I'll fucking kill you if you don't."

Peter knew Conor was mad enough to mean what he said.

"Look, Peter. This fucker killed your fucking wife, my sister. Now, I'm not letting him get away with it."

"I'm scared."

"I know. I know you are. All I'm asking is that you point him out. Peep in, tell me where he is and I'll do the rest."

Peter was still hesitating as a taxi pulled up and a girl got out.

"Just go in behind her. No one will see you."

As Amanda opened the door, he followed, not letting the door close and peeping out from behind it.

He was back out in a flash.

"He's in there, on a stool."

"For fuck sake, where? What stool?"

"The minute you walk in, at the end of the bar, there's two stools. There's a bird sitting on one, he's on the other."

"You're sure?"

"'Course I'm fucking sure."

Conor went to walk in –

"You'd better get offside, Peter. You can't be seen to have anything to do with this."

Peter didn't need a second asking.

Simmo tapped Joe on the shoulder –

"Sorry to break you up, but I'm off to the jacks and then I'm gone. So, if you want the stool, feel free."

He got up and went to the toilet.

Joe sat down, kissed Mary again –

"So you never answered me, will you be my . . . "

Conor stuck the knife into Joe's stomach, twisted it, then pulled it towards his chest, he pulled it out, waved it at everyone, then ran out the door.

Joe fell to the floor, clutching his belly.

Mary screamed –

"Joe!"

She looked up at the crowd –

"Someone call an ambulance."

Simmo walked out of the toilets, saw the commotion and exited out the back way.

Joe lay bleeding. Paddy Mac had put a towel on his wound but he knew it wasn't enough. Mary held Joe's head in her lap, caressed his hair and said over and over –

"Yes, Joe, I will marry you."

The ambulance arrived, followed by the police. The ambulance men exchanged glances and each one knew it wasn't good.

It was late, the police had the names and addresses of everyone who had been there. The senior garda spoke –

"OK, we have your details, it's late, I know you're all tired, so why don't you all just go home. We'll be in touch."

But still the crowd stood.

Paddy Mac took a deep breath and shouted –

"Come on Ladies and Gentlemen . . . You heard the garda . . . *Have ye no homes to go to?*"